KATHLEEN EAGLE

MYSTIC HORSEMAN

Withdrawn

MIRA®

If you purchased this book without a cover you should be aware that this book is stolen property. It was reported as "unsold and destroyed" to the publisher, and neither the author nor the publisher has received any payment for this "stripped book."

ISBN-13: 978-0-7783-2514-7
ISBN-10:   0-7783-2514-8

MYSTIC HORSEMAN

Copyright © 2008 by Kathleen Eagle.

All rights reserved. Except for use in any review, the reproduction or utilization of this work in whole or in part in any form by any electronic, mechanical or other means, now known or hereafter invented, including xerography, photocopying and recording, or in any information storage or retrieval system, is forbidden without the written permission of the publisher, MIRA Books, 225 Duncan Mill Road, Don Mills, Ontario, Canada M3B 3K9.

This is a work of fiction. Names, characters, places and incidents are either the product of the author's imagination or are used fictitiously, and any resemblance to actual persons, living or dead, business establishments, events or locales is entirely coincidental.

MIRA and the Star Colophon are trademarks used under license and registered in Australia, New Zealand, Philippines, United States Patent and Trademark Office and in other countries.

www.MIRABooks.com

Printed in U.S.A.

For Abby on her high school graduation.
Walk in beauty.

Chapter One

Dillon Black slept with the horses.

Not the best bedfellows he'd ever had, but far from the worst. Most of them were heavy with foal, and there wasn't a nag in the herd. Having slept with his own kind of over-due female, Dillon would know. But some studs just naturally had it made. Others were only human.

South Dakota sod was not the most comfortable bed he'd ever had, either, but the view was incomparable. His blanket was made of stars. From where he lay on the rise above the Grand River, he could see every square foot of ground he truly cared about, even on the darkest night. The prairie was never fully dark or completely quiet. Something was always happening.

Lovemaking, for instance. The flat at the foot of his sleeping hill rolled all the way to the place where Earth spread her grassy hair about her shoulders, made her knees into two hills, opened her legs and let the night sky prevail. She took her voice from the coyote and her breath from the night breeze. She was enjoying herself. Dillon could feel it in her rocky bones, and it was all to the good, as long as the coyotes and the cats kept their distance from his mares. He kept his hunting rifle in plain view, hoping any preda-

tors who might be sitting on the fence would take it as
reason enough to hang back. That and the fact that Dillon
was actually wearing his glasses. He never missed when
he remembered to wear his glasses.

And he was about to see a miracle happen not fifty yards
away. Closer, if need be. Sugar, the baldface dun he'd been
watching over, had already blown her water. She'd been up
and down a few times, and she'd extruded two twiggy legs.
She was down for the count now. Fifteen minutes, tops. But
she was nervous, and it wasn't about the foal. It wasn't
about Dillon, who knew better than to crowd a foaling
mustang. There was something out there, something that
was all teeth and claws. And for the next fifteen minutes
there would be nothing the mare could do about it. Every
part of her was committed now to giving birth.

Rifle in hand, Dillon eased his way down the slope. The
mare had picked herself an open spot where she couldn't
easily be trapped. All she needed was a little time, and she
would have her baby on its feet and running with the herd,
probably by sunup. She lifted her head and eyeballed her
guardian, letting him know he was too close. He took her
cue, squatted on his heels and laid the rifle on the ground.

From this angle, the mare seemed to float on the moonlit
river, adrift in a spillway of stars. It was the perfect vision
for a moment like this. Dillon and his partner called their
ranch The Wolf Trail, after the Lakota name for the Milky
Way. It was a grand gesture on the part of two Indian
cowboys who'd hit the ground hard and earned their re-ride.

But what the hell? Wasn't this the *Grand* River? It
flowed from past to present, gathering strength from
winter's sleep and power from the spring equinox. The
great Sitting Bull had lived and died on its banks only a

few miles upstream. And tonight Dillon imagined the old man kicking some of those stars loose and sending them tumbling home to brighten the night for the granddaughter of one of his favorite horses, for such was the heritage of Wolf Trail Mustangs.

Sugar grunted. Scoffing at him, was she? Dillon shook his head. The mare had about as much time for a man as a mite right about now. Female heritage, the instinct to survive and produce another survivor, that was her be-all and end-all at the moment. *In the moment*, if horses had moments. If horses had wishes—if they *were* wishes… How did that go?

How about, *If wishes were horses, Sitting Bull's people would ride?* The descendants of Sitting Bull's people would ride the descendants of Sitting Bull's horses if Dillon's horse would get her wish and produce another survivor. That was the way it should go, *would* go, as long as Dillon kept the teeth and claws at bay.

"Easy, girl. I know there's something out there. It won't get past me, I swear."

Stop trying to get all philosophical and just listen to the night, Black Bear, he told himself. This night. It's all that counts right now.

Black Bear was an ancestral name, or part of one. His great-grandfather was Black Bear Runs Him, but the name had been shortened twice—first cut in half by some agency record keeper, and then halved again by Dillon's father, who'd lied about his name, age and anything else that might have kept him from enlisting in the army right around 1943. Surnames weren't part of Lakota tradition, but neither was record-keeping. Dillon would take his beloved grandfather's name one day, when he felt he'd earned it. He would make Dillon Black Bear legal. Like blood and the eternal river, it was a name that connected him to the Lakota circle, and he needed all the connections he could get. They kept his feet on the ground.

But tonight the notion of a river flowing out of the past was distracting. Mixing with an imagination like Dillon's, the current stirred up a fiery vision. Flames danced on the water, taunting him with the river's memory of another grand gesture. His damn fire, his dream afire. Whatever he couldn't remember about that night, the river remembered for him in a single reflection, indelibly etched in his brain. It showed him what was left of Dillon Black when he'd pushed himself up from the mud. A crazy drunk flipping God the flaming bird.

Remember when Dillon Black torched his house?

He'd had…what? Seven years to live it down? He had to be pretty close. Lucky seven. He still got razzed about it once in a while—first rule of Indian humor being you were allowed to give only as good as you were willing to take—but he would hate like hell for anybody to mention it in front of Emily.

His daughter was coming home for the summer. His home, his stomping grounds. The place where she was born. She'd lived with her mother for what was undoubtedly the better part of her life, but she was coming home because she believed in the horses and the sacred circle. And, wonder of wonders, she loved her dad. Whenever Monica had told the girl that she was just like her father, it generally meant she'd fucked something up. Some small thing, but the kind that could lead to a big thing unless Monica nipped it in the bud.

No way was Emily just like her father. The part of her

life after they'd left him might have been—okay, *was*—
better than the first part. But lately Dillon had begun to
believe she took after the better part of him. Her horse
sense, for one thing. Her interest in her father's people.
Little things, maybe, but enough to convince him that he
still had a better part, even though he'd split the sheets with
his better half.

The mare's big body shuddered with the proof of her
pain. Dillon felt it, just as he had the three times Monica
had gone into labor, giving him two living children and one
dead one. He couldn't share the intensity of the mare's
pain, but he felt its depth and heat. She was doing fine. It
wouldn't be long now.

It was good to have this birthing to occupy his mind,
good to feel useful after the bad news he'd gotten earlier
in the day. Nothing tragic—nobody had died or moved to
Texas—but news of the kind of personal defeat that made
him see the fire in the river. His grant proposal had been
turned down, the one Emily had worked on with him when
she'd stopped over at Christmastime. He should have been
able to make it happen. He could have talked to a few people on the Tribal Council about the idea to expand the
horse camp he'd put together with Emily last summer with
a little help from one of the local churches. He thought he'd
made a good presentation to the selection committee, and
people had been shaking his hand over it ever since. It was
all his daughter's doing, he'd told them. She was studying
horses at Montana Western University. She was already ten
times smarter about horses than her ol' man, and he'd been
around them all his life. The grant money was in the bag,
they'd said.

What bag? Emmie would be out of school for the summer soon, coming home to an empty bag and an empty promise. He hadn't asked for much—just enough to finish the kitchen and bathrooms in the old church building he'd been fixing up over the years, and a little more for supplies and camping equipment. Kids had been hounding him all winter about getting in on his next horse camp, but without financial backing, it would be hard to accommodate them all the way he wanted to, which would put a crimp in his daughter's plans for her big honors project for school.

Crimp. Not the complete kibosh. He had a little cash put away. He could round up a couple of tipis this year and add an overnight trail ride to the program. They'd had bigger ideas, though, the beginnings of an ongoing program. Flushed with last summer's success, Dillon had developed a sense of mission. He didn't want his generation to be the last to keep and know horses in some small but blessed semblance of the old Lakota way.

The foal's head appeared, slick and slender, glistening wet. Dillon's stomach quivered as the mare's muscles undulated with the final push. In a stunning split second, the slippery foal slid free of its frantic host. Mother and baby were especially vulnerable now. All they needed was a few minutes for the mare to catch her breath, transfer a last shot of her life's blood to her baby before it hauled itself up on wobbly legs and broke the cord and finally begin expelling the placenta, which could take a bit of time. The mare lifted her head and nosed her new baby.

But the coyotes smelled it, too. They were close. Dillon sensed the heat of their bloodlust and their stealthy advance before he could detect any movement. Then shadow slid past shadow. They were downwind, but the succulent smell of a fresh birth overpowered the scent of a mere man.

Dillon remained perfectly still while he rehearsed the shot in his mind's eye. When he moved, he was quick, sure and deadly accurate.

Chapter Two

Monica Wilson-Black slept with a window open. Time, place or season made no difference. Her former husband had introduced her to the wonders of the night sky—available for a limited time only in the world she had, in the end, happily left to him—and clean air. He'd been a fresh-air freak, and the open-window habit had stayed with her, along with the children and half the family pictures, which she'd transferred from albums to indexed file boxes.

He'd burned his half.

Monica had been sleeping single for more than ten years. Or not sleeping, as had lately been the case. Her routine—working until bedtime, reading until sleep time, and then putting a down comforter between her tired body and the Minnesota spring chill—just wasn't doing it for her anymore. For some reason her brain had become a nightly spawning ground for worries.

Menopause, maybe. Nice, normal menopause with its limitless symptoms.

Menopause, she wished.

On the whole, her life had never been better. The kids were doing well. Her knack for decorating on a shoestring had turned into a business, two books, guest spots and finally a regular television show. It had been seven years since the divorce had actually been final. A few technicalities had dragged the process out—the fact that her children were enrolled members of their father's tribe, that he never wore a watch, seldom had phone service and only looked at his mail about once a week—but she'd needed the actual divorce less than she'd needed a new address.

Lucky seven, except for one little bump in the road.

It had been eighteen months since she'd sacrificed a piece of a lung. A small piece, really, and she'd managed to keep it a secret from nearly everyone. The kids knew, of course. Not every friggin' detail, but they knew they'd been right about her smoking. It could kill her. But it hadn't, and on the whole, life was good. It was only that one small piece that had been contaminated. Her doctors had been clear on that point. They'd gotten it all. Contamination contained, cut out and cast away. Worrying was simply part of her nature—one of the few parts she could do without. Otherwise, she liked herself better than just about anyone she knew.

Except for her children. Emily and Dylan had gone her two better. Emily was truly good, and Dylan was a seriously talented musician. They were her legacy. If anything happened to her, they had her genes, and goodness and talent would prevail. They had their father's genes, too, but Monica's were surely dominant, at least in the important areas. It was fine with her that they had their father's looks. Dillon was one hell of a looker.

Fortunately, they'd never had to rely on his bread-winning capacity. Monica had always made a decent living, but making do with *decent* had gone out the window the day she'd discovered her television persona. What self-respecting celebrity, however minor, could or should live by bread alone? She and her children lived well, as well they should. Emily would get her undergraduate degree in another year, and Dylan was so talented that colleges would be throwing money at him when the time came. There was little to worry about, really.

Other than the fact that Emily could not be dissuaded from wasting another summer on an Indian reservation involved with another one of her father's doomed projects. And the fact that Dylan, soon to be sixteen, could not be persuaded to venture beyond the self-imposed limits of his secure triangle—home, private school and McPhail Music Academy. He hardly knew his father.

Worse—and this was her own fault—his father didn't know Dylan.

Dillon and Dylan. Her son was only a few letters away from being a Jr. A few letters and a million light-years. But Monica had been the one to fill out the birth-certificate application, and maybe she'd been a bit pompous in those days. For conversational purposes, she had been mentally well rehearsed on the subject of naming her children after her favorite poets. It had turned out to be one of the many topics she'd prepared that only came up in conversation when she brought them up herself, which was why she was so well suited to her current occupation. Teaching had stunted her growth. High-school kids were like husbands, their attention rarely encompassing the answers to their own questions, assuming they cared enough to ask you anything.

Monica remembered the look in Dillon's eyes when he'd signed his son's birth-certificate form. Not cold, but certainly cool. She'd been ready for him to say something, ready to remind him that they'd talked about this—or she had, anyway. But he'd signed without challenging her spelling. By that time, he'd known better. Like everything else, she and Dillon had seen eye to eye on names. One of her eyes to one of his. They'd agreed that names meant something, but they couldn't agree on what that something was.

Truth be told, by the time Dylan was born, Monica had known the marriage was headed south. It had taken her a few more years to get out of Dillon's house, off his land and head east, but the handwriting—scrambled by her libido, but undoubtedly scrawled across the wall all along—had been coming into focus when she'd christened the child with the name they'd first chosen for the second baby, the stillborn boy whose grave had been marked by his father: *Little Black Bear Runs Him.* They had been living in Montana at the time, but Dillon had taken the body back to South Dakota and placed it in a desolate prairie graveyard near his relatives. Monica had refused the dead child a given name, had visited the tiny plot only once, and only for a moment. It was enough. No point in dwelling in territory where she had no control.

To her mind, rather than being a point well taken, it was the absence of point well proven. And well worth the cost if somehow the kids' dues were paid in the bargain. But Emily was her father's daughter, determined to pay her own dues, and she was old enough to decide how she would go about it.

Still, having little say about Emily's crazy plans didn't mean Monica couldn't get involved. With her connections, she could see their plan for a one-shot summer camp and raise the stakes to a whole new level. She could give them an hour of fame and a future in the summer-camp business. The way things seemed to be shaping up for her health-wise, and the more she thought about it…

But in the end, what would other people think? How would it look if she got involved? Her concern was for more than appearances, even though the appearance of grandstanding on her part would never do. She really wasn't like that. Monica Wilson-Black was Every Woman. In the end, she truly didn't want anyone—not even, in her heart of hearts, Dillon—to think badly of her.

A sporadic cough turned serial, forcing her to sit up, throw her legs over the side of the bed and hack to the point of pain before she gave in and reached for a cigarette. Too early for coffee. She got up, pushed the window open a few more inches and blew a killer stream of smoke. Budding trees cast sketchy shadows across the moonlit backyard. In the flowerbed directly below her bedroom window a swath of Emperor tulips had closed up for the night. Drifts of daffodils had already bloomed and faded with little notice this year. The earliest days of spring had galloped past.

The pool stood empty. She would have it filled and tended for show, but after Emily left for the summer, it would get little use. Her television show was called *It Only Looks Expensive*, but Monica had spared no expense in creating the showplace where she and her children could, in theory, spend quality time making Kodak moments and entertaining their friends. The pool had gone in just in time for Emily's high-school graduation party. Two more years and Monica would have the place all to herself when she wasn't broadcasting her show from her own kitchen or workroom. If she hung on to the house for two more years.

If she *had* two more years.

But of course she would. Why wouldn't she? Things had a way of working out, because she wouldn't have it any other way.

She'd built the show herself from weekly ten-minute spots on a local morning show to half-hour syndication for cable. She'd built a lot of things from the ground up— contacts into networks, opportunities into accomplishments, children into young adults. Monica was a go-getter, and given more time, she would go get a good deal more.

Two was the magic number. In six months she would be two years beyond her surgery. Not that she was thinking about it, talking about it, marking off the days or anything. That kind of behavior would be counterproductive, and Monica was nothing if not productive. Two was only a number. When she reached it, *then* she'd call it magic. Meanwhile, there would be no sidelining Monica Wilson-Black. She was a major player.

She crushed the last half of the cigarette in a small plastic ashtray. The one vice she'd permitted herself seemed to be making up for all the vices she'd avoided. Proof that all it took was one. In her next life she would opt for total perfection. She'd gotten off the smokes for a good six months but started in again last summer. Now she was taking a different approach, allowing herself half a cigarette at a time. Since she hated waste, she would soon be obliged to quit. She'd been down to four halves a day until she'd smoked a whole one last night when she was on the phone with Emily.

"You just don't want me to spend another summer with Dad," Emily had claimed. "It has nothing to do with what's going on with you or D.J. or any internship you want to arrange for me, and you know it. You want me to be like you, and I'm not. It's as simple as that." She paused long enough to dramatize, and then lowered her voice to a tender timbre. "I love my father. I know you don't, but I do."

"You *should* love your father. I have no problem with that, Emily. It's just that you have so many opportunities right here, and this might be the last—"

"It's not going to be the last anything, Mother." Emily sounded half disgusted, as though Monica had been piling on guilt, which she surely had not.

"The last summer you spend at home." Monica had scowled as she pulled the carafe from the coffeepot and touched the glass. Cold. It was either nuke it or miss out on her fourth cup. "All right, yes, I have a problem with you choosing his home instead of mine. *Again.*"

"It's not about you or him. It's about the horses. It's about—"

"It's about your father." Monica took a turn at the dramatic pause. "I know him."

"What's that supposed to mean? *You know him.*"

"I know all about his quixotic schemes and how seductive they can be."

"The Mystic Warrior Horse Camp is a good idea, Mom. We proved it last summer. It brought the horses back into those kids' lives, as Dad would say, *in a good way.*"

"And you're not sure what that means, but it's so simple, it must be profound."

"I have no idea what *you* mean."

"But since it's something I said, whatever the meaning, it has to be mean-spirited."

"Oh, get over yourself, Mother."

"All right, I will." Monica had smiled, enjoying the notion that her comeback bore gifts. "Remember how you said that your project would be perfect for Ella Champion's makeover show?" Monica had landed a spot in the rotation of guest decorators on the network reality show, *Who's Our*

Neighbor? thanks in part to her friendship with the production manager who scoped out projects for the show, which focused on small communities and common people in need of an uncommon infusion of television fairy dust.

"And how you laughed and said *get real*? Like you thought I was serious."

"You sounded serious."

"Yeah, right. Like I don't know what Dad would think of having a TV crew come in and mess with his property."

"His *property?* A trailer house and an old church?" Had she been talking to anyone else, she might have laughed again. But she caught herself and changed her tune. "No, really, honey, I think you might have hit on something. Your father and I get along well now, and, frankly, quixotic schemes make for good TV. He's got the Indian mystique going for him, plus the reservation with all its problems. And can you imagine what we could do with that place? I can. You planted the damned seed in my head, and it won't stop growing. It could be—"

"Now *you* sound halfway serious."

"I'm never halfway anything, Emily, you know that." She'd dragged on her cigarette. "I'm fully over myself at the moment, thinking completely outside the box. It could be…quite a project. Quite a story. We wouldn't get into unpleasant details, but we could show a family—"

"We wrote an excellent grant proposal, Mother. I know it's going to come through. That's part of my honors project—the grant proposal," Emily enthused. Clearly, she really didn't think her mother was serious. "Nobody else's honors project even comes close. It has everything. It's more than just a dream. We're going to make it happen."

There was no changing Emily's mind, and, ultimately,

that was probably not a bad thing. She wanted to do something worthwhile. In this post-Age of Aquarius world, what kind of a mother would discourage such instincts?

Which was why she had already approached her good friend Ella with the idea. Not a word to anyone but Ella—unlike her former husband, Monica never made promises she had no chance of keeping—but she knew her friend. She'd mapped out Ella's buttons. Had to. Her friend was also a business associate, and buttons, like contacts and bottom lines, were part of the business of living and earning a living.

And Monica no longer had time for a simple friendship.

Chapter Three

Ella Champion was a night owl.

The deck of her unique Minneapolis condo didn't come with the night sky she remembered from some of the more rural bits and pieces of her gypsy childhood, but the view of city lights and the Mississippi River made the place worth keeping no matter how little time she was able to spend there. She'd bought the condo years ago for her ailing mother, who had stayed there as long as Ella stayed with her. As soon as Ella had gone back to work in L.A., Mama had returned to her "retirement" cabin in the north woods once and for all. After all that was said about the little that could be done, Ella had decided to keep the place for herself. It was a far cry from Southern California, where her rent was high and her digs were modest. Not many people could say they owned the top floor of a repurposed Midwestern grain elevator.

Ella adjusted the fringed stadium blanket over her shoulders, braced her feet on the deck railing and tipped the chair back on two legs, the better to view the white-horned moon. Up north and out west, people were looking at the stars and thinking about infinite possibilities. Ella had a finite schedule and a moon in the fourth house, which was supposed to signify an abiding connection with the past, interest in her heritage and attachment to her mother. Ella had a healthy respect for abiding belief systems, but her astrological chart clearly was way off the money. She was no mama's girl.

Mama's heritage was another matter. Ella had inherited her mother's face in a lighter shade of brown. Dark eyes closely underscored by angular cheekbones gave her an exotic look that mainstream Americans who'd never been to an Indian reservation couldn't quite place. The bolder their attempts, the more Ella enjoyed playing with them, especially in myopic Hollywoodland.

You look like J.Lo without the booty.

You're looking south of the wrong border, buddy.

Spanish? Italian? Black Irish?

Try a pigeonhole closer to home.

So maybe she'd inherited a touch of Mama's attitude along with the face. But unlike her mother, she was not about wasting energy, time or talent on hopeless causes. Which was why she was bemused by her new plan. She blamed the champagne. She rarely drank the stuff, but it had been included in the package, and she'd figured, what the hell? She'd agreed to Monica Wilson-Black's gift of a day at the spa without considering what it meant to spend a whole day with the woman. In for a pedicure, in for a pounding. Once she'd secured an ear, Monica was relentless, and it was amazing the way a few bubbles softened the edges of a hard sell. There was something compelling about the way the woman raised the curtain on an idea that would mix her signature shabby-to-chic decorating with Indian heritage, history, a mother's love and a *Who's Our Neighbor?* makeover. Monica was the queen of persistence and sow's ear magic.

They'd hooked up on the local scene a few years back. Ella had been on her way out of Twin Cities television just as Monica was breaking in, but they had kept in touch. Which mostly meant that Monica had kept in touch. In their business, West Coast connections were never relegated to the inactive file. And it had paid off in both directions. With Monica's star on the rise in the Midwest and a good word from Ella, she had been tapped for national exposure as an occasional guest decorator on *Who's Our Neighbor?* Viewers' favorable response to Monica earned kudos for Ella, so she made a point of calling whenever she was in town. And Monica always had a surprise up her sleeve, like a day at her latest spa discovery. Perfect for brainstorming, she'd said.

"What your show needs is a killer project, Ella," Monica pitched across the divide between massage tables after Ella acknowledged a slip in the ratings. Eyes closed, cheek pressed and puddling against the white tablecloth, Monica looked like a woman whose happy pill was just beginning to take effect. A slip in the viewer share was the scent of heaven to Monica's nose. "I have a suggestion."

"For me? Or for us?" Ella was open to suggestions. And as driven as the woman was, Monica had a Midwestern sensibility about her that gave Ella some welcome breathing space in the rotation of quirky TV designers she used on the show. Monica's on-camera personality was plainspoken, practical and neighborly. A suggestion from her was well worth listening to.

"I don't know. I should probably lay it out and then just back— Mmm, that's good," Monica cooed over whatever was being done to her below Ella's line of vision. Her face scrunched into a sightless frown. "But, no, I won't back off.

I want this. It would be like coming full circle for me, and that's part of the appeal. This is a back-to-the-future kind of project. Going back so that people can move ahead."

"Mmm-hmm. Meaning?"

Monica opened her eyes, zeroing in, relegating the soft lights and New Age music to mere undertone. "I'm talking about boosting your show's ratings by getting down to the emotional nitty-gritty."

"That show's already being done on another network. One of the ubiquitous 'Extremes.'"

"And its share is off the charts. You've got the community-building theme going, but you need the three P's. You need plight, pathos and personality, and I can deliver it all in one project."

"Namely?"

"You've met Dillon."

Ella arched an eyebrow.

Monica met the arch with a knowing smile. "Yes, *that* Dillon. Dillon with an *I*. As in very easy on the eye. Not the best husband material, mind you, but he'd make good TV."

"You want to do a makeover project for your *ex-husband?*"

"It's perfect, isn't it? Marvelously gut-wrenching on so many levels. You've got your underdog, your downtrodden, your community spirit, your family reunion. Best of all, he's cleaned up his act. Reformed and ripe for some dramatic reward, delivered to a cheering American public subconsciously longing to expiate the sins of the fathers without giving up any real estate."

Manipulative on so many levels, Ella thought, and started with, "Are you trying to get back with him?"

"Noooo, God, no. We're fire and water, pure and simple. What I want is a great project for my good friend Ella."

Monica closed her eyes again and smiled with the half of her face not pressed against the table. "And a great project for Emily. And another collaboration for me, but admittedly on a bigger scale than I've had before. I'll be part of the pathos."

"You're willing to sell a piece of your personal life?" So much for Midwestern sensibilities.

"Just enough for a hook."

"It wouldn't be fair, Monica. I can't choose a project out of personal interest."

"Of course you can. You're a producer. You're the person in charge of doing just that. Oh! Yes, right there." With a freshly French-manicured fingernail Monica—who must have laid claim to the special-treatment table—signaled the masseuse. "Keep doing that. Mmm, there. More of that. Mmm. Like I said, Ella, whatever this game of ours is about, it certainly isn't fair play. You want entertainment in all its shabby glory, and entertainment you shall have. Once you get these people to let their guard down…"

"*These* people?"

"Dillon's people. Your people. Ella, they're your people, too. That's what makes this idea so—"

"If you're talking Indians, my mother was from a different tribe. A different kind of Sioux."

"Lakota," Monica amended, as though being somebody's ex-wife made her an expert on beinganything but full-blooded white.

"That's what I mean. She was Sioux, but not Lakota. *Sioux* is the term most people recognize. And I don't trade on my Native ancestry. You know that." Feeling gypped on the massage front—or, rather, the back—Ella strained to lift her head, look back and link a face to the timid hands at work on her shoulders. "Don't be afraid to put some muscle into it, Cindy. I'm a pretty tough... I've got pretty tough skin." It had been ages since she'd thought of herself as—in Mama's term—a "skin."

"Dillon likes to say that he was Indian when Indian wasn't cool. Hard to imagine him being anything but cool. Hard to imagine, hard to predict, damn hard to live with." Monica pushed herself up and flipped over, shielding her chest with the sheet without missing a beat and then fluffing her hair with slender, elegant fingers. She had the kind of style that gave other women pause for self-inventory. *Her hair gets shorter every time I see her. Must be in now. Wonder if I could do that?* "He was too young for me, to start with, and that never changed. God knows I tried. 'Marry 'em young and raise 'em the way you want 'em' doesn't work with males."

"But you got two great kids out of the deal," Ella said airily as the masseuse began covering her face with pale green paste that smelled of cucumber.

"We lost one," came the soft reply. "I did. Between Emily and Dylan, I lost a little boy. Stillborn."

Synthesized music seeped over them like a cold front.

"Strange term, isn't it? *Stillborn?*" Monica drew a deep, audible breath. "When I was a little girl, I overheard my mother tell someone that she hadn't planned to have a baby, but I was *still* born. She was probably making a point about the will of God or some such thing." Her voice dropped dramatically. "I couldn't believe I'd lost him. They didn't say, 'The baby's dead.' They launched into some medical mumbo jumbo, and all I could think or say was, 'But he was *still* born, right?' Just like his mother. It didn't matter what anyone planned or didn't plan. Right?" She gave a little *tsk*. "Stillborn."

After a moment Ella said, "But you do have two great kids."

"And I have plans for them. You have children, you make plans. You lay out the plans, and you let them choose. But Plan A is always the most attractive." Monica gave a dry chuckle. "*I'm* a producer, too."

A director, maybe, Ella thought. The star of her own reality show, definitely. But Monica Wilson-Black would never make it as a producer, nor would she want to. Producing wasn't all it was cracked up to be, particularly when you were an associate. It was damn hard work, and now that she'd moved up to line producer, the choices Ella made could make or break the show.

But Monica was right about one thing: she needed a killer project, one with all the elements Monica had named. And like Ella, Monica would never have gotten this far without very good instincts.

Chapter Four

Ella Champion had never gambled at an Indian casino.

She'd been to Vegas twice, and she'd done well at the blackjack tables, but she had been trying to impress a man the first time and ducking the lame crowd she was with the second. Story of her life. Forever either seeking attention or trying to escape it.

Her father had taught her to play cards. According to Ella's mother, Tucker Champion was a good player. Whist, hearts, five-card stud, blackjack, even solitaire. Ella hardly remembered the man, but she knew the fine points of his games, and the need to prove herself with a hand of cards ran deeper than memory. But in the end, the cards held about as much appeal for Ella as Vegas itself. Good venue for studying people up and down the winner-loser spectrum. Otherwise, the place was a lot of hot, dry air and a huge waste of electricity.

But the Indian casino perched on a windswept bluff just north of the South Dakota state line was different. Daunting. Breathtaking. Even guilt-making. Ella had the right skin, but she wouldn't fit in. Didn't want to, really. Didn't care much for fry bread and beaded doodads. Didn't identify with the statuary in front of the portico. Noble savages on horseback. It was the kind of film role she'd repeatedly been offered and turned down. She looked the part—the female version, anyway—but she was no actor, and even if she were, the part didn't fit.

And if it doesn't fit, you won't be a hit.

Her life had little to do with who she was and everything to do with what she did. Ella always played to her strengths, none of which would ever land her in front of a camera. But if it wasn't for her, there would be nothing to film. She gave the director something to direct, the actors something to act. Reality television was about as real as rain in Southern California. People like Ella set it up to *look* real.

But unlike most of the players in her business, Ella truly believed in the premise of the show she'd helped to create two years ago, after coming up through the ranks on several other productions. *Who's Our Neighbor?* was more than her own personal big break. It was a reality show that really was about something. It was transformative—even though, yes, the transformation often turned out to be mostly cosmetic—but ideally the makeover project was more about community than singling out an individual or a family and calling them the lucky winner. And when it worked, Ella quietly added a notch to her belt.

And now she was bringing it full circle. Indian country.

It was early evening. Pink and lavender dressed the distant horizon, and spotlights illuminated the statues. They gave her pause, these silent, beautifully-sculpted representations of her mother's ancestors. Or cousins of the ancestors of Thelma's ancestors. Early on—she could almost name the day and time—Ella had chosen her father's world. Not that he had been anywhere to be seen by that time, but she knew who he was, and that knowledge gave her half an identity. It was the half she understood, the half that gravitated to big plans, big ideas and big cities. She understood her father's games, but the rhymes and reasons for her mother's bag of tricks had simply eluded her.

Not that Thelma Bear Dancer had kept her tricks to herself—she was a tricky one, that Thelma—but she hadn't been one for explaining them. *Watch and learn* was the unspoken motto of the Indian activist, the charismatic rabble-rouser. Ella had heard the speeches, watched the news clips and seen the scars. As a child she had quietly followed Thelma from Minneapolis to Seattle to L.A. and back again, and she had heard the woman proclaimed a hero and a martyr to a faded movement. The politics, the protests, the power to the people. Thelma Bear Dancer's people. Ella had her mother's face and form, but had never been privy to what went on in the woman's head as times changed and causes were all but forgotten.

Ella had watched, and what she had learned was that whatever the game, when it's over, you cut your losses and move on. Come up with a new reason, a new rhyme, and you make it big.

Big wins came in all kinds of packaging. Education was big for Ella. Art was big. Self-expression was big, and the medium she'd chosen was very big. But the message? It was there. She always managed to work it in, and if no one else saw it, well…it was there.

Right, boys? We know what we're doing.

The bronze warrior who was posed to pitch a spear through her heart kept his counsel.

She checked in at the desk, then took the elevator to the third floor and what passed for a suite. It had a separate sitting room and a Whirlpool tub—which she put to immediate use—but other than the Native art, it was a standard highway overnight. She'd made reservations for three nights. She would probably be canceling the last two when she came to her senses about turning Monica's ex-husband into a makeover story. She hadn't been able to reach him by phone, but she'd spoken with his daughter, soon to be on her way back from school. He would be around, Emily had said, either out at the ranch or at the casino, where he worked as a dealer. Ella was getting closer. She'd only met him once, and she was looking forward to seeing him again.

Yes, *that* Dillon, Monica had said. Between females, that had been enough to say everything. He was one of those uncut gems that flashed a few tempting facets and dared some woman to try to make something of it. A reformer like Monica couldn't help but take him on. Ella was a different story. She was no gem cutter, no designer or *re*-designer. But she was pretty good at cards, and because she had a particularly vivid memory of meeting the man, she was curious to discover whether there were any fine points to Dillon Black's game.

She dressed simply, as was her custom, but her jeans were impeccably cut, and her white silk man-tailored blouse called for a camisole. With her hair pulled back, she started out with a favorite pair of inlaid lapis and silver earrings, signed by a well-known Zuni jewelry designer, then switched to generic gold hoops. No Native trappings, no invoking tribal ties. Indian people could pretty much pick each other out in a crowd, even when the blood was diluted by half and the visitor had gone mainstream. At least Ella was only marginally Hollywood. But damned if she would try to be anything but the self she'd finally come to terms with, looking good without trying too hard. She didn't mind turning heads, but let them keep their distance. All she wanted to do was float an idea. She wasn't there to get involved.

The brightly-lit corridor, with its offshoot gift shop, arcade and restaurants, served as a buffer between the hotel lobby and the casino, where blinking lights and low-key electronic four-note tunes lured slot players like carnival barkers for the new millennium. Ella crossed the threshold. It was like walking into a theater in the middle of a movie. Suddenly you didn't matter. You were surrounded by people who weren't really there. Eyes on the big picture, you, too, were quickly mesmerized as you groped in search of a niche for your nearly superfluous body. No one was turning any heads here. They were all too busy spinning their wheels.

Ella headed into the thick of things, keeping her eye on the ball—a Customer Service sign posted high and outside. But she ran into a row of blackjack tables well short of the sign, and the man she was looking for was standing behind the first one. The dealer's uniform suited him. Crisp white shirt, black vest, bolo tie. A full, lush head of black hair softened the angles of his handsome face. Nice presentation, she thought. Crazy Horse Monument dressed in Deadwood clothing.

He welcomed her to the table, but gave nothing away— no sign that he recognized her or that they had any interests in common other than blackjack. The three young white women at his table—tight in more ways than one— must have been having themselves a girls' night out. They were more interested in teasing the dealer than in playing their cards.

"Mr. Maverick, you're killing me."

"Where are you hiding all those aces, hmm?"

"Show us where you've got those suckers all zipped up."

They tried to include Ella in the banter, but she only smiled and played her cards right. She avoided all eye contact until she was up eighty dollars, and then she lifted her gaze and caught the smile in his eyes. Risky, she thought. But the exchange was not lost on the three cuties, who decided to give the slots a try before their purses got any lighter.

Ella nodded for a game of one-on-one. "You probably don't remember, but—"

"You're Monica's friend," he said quietly as he dealt cards from the shoe. "You're the Minnesota apple who fell off the tree, rolled around the country and landed in Television City." He glanced up. "Ella. I remember."

"Apple, huh? That's pretty cold."

"You said it, not me."

"I called myself an apple?" The old term for red on the outside, white on the inside. *You don't want to be one or be taken for one.* Ella chuckled. *Yes, Mama.* "What were we drinking?"

"Stiff shots of straight talk." His laughter was easy, unaffected, infectious. "I was visiting Emily and D.J. at Monica's. I was lucky to get a glass of water."

"From what I saw, you two get along quite well."

"What? That's not the way it's done in Hollywood?" he asked as a woman quietly joined him on his side of the table and started cashing him out.

"Are you taking a break?" Ella asked, noticing a young blonde at the cashier's elbow, apparently waiting to replace him.

"I'm being relieved. You're winnin' too much off me."

"Seriously? They're bringing in a new dealer because of me?"

"We replace him when we notice he's getting too friendly," the cashier said with a smile.

"He wasn't being friendly. I'm a card sharp, what can I say?" She slid several five-dollar chips across the table as he stepped past the new dealer. He questioned Ella with a look, and she shrugged. "It's customary to tip the dealer when you're winning, isn't it?"

"If you're a sharp, you would know." With a subtle wave of the hand, he rebuffed her offer. "I was just filling in. Katie, you have a generous tipper here. Deal her some good cards."

"Thanks, Katie, but I'm ready to cash out," Ella said as she quickly gathered her little stacks of color-coded chips. The new dealer gave her a knowing look, as though women cashing out when Dillon left the floor was common practice. Ella let it go. She had a purpose. "Let me buy dinner." She extended her fistful of winnings. "Please. Otherwise I'll be dining alone in a strange place."

"Can't have that." He gave an after-you gesture. "Buffet or menu?"

"What do you recommend?"

"For my money, the buffet. For yours?" With a hand on her arm he guided her past the buffet sign and on to *The Hunter's Club.*

"The menu," they said in unison, and she laughed.

"Hey, what do you mean, strange place?" he asked as they followed a shiny-faced, long-legged waitress to a table on the far side of what felt like a clearing in a pine forest. "This is Indian Country. When you're here, you're family." He took·the chair across from her and tipped his head so he could see past the waitress lighting the table candles. The flame danced in his eyes. "So, what, your plane ran out of gas?"

"I was home for a week. Minneapolis. I have a little condo there." She practically snatched the proffered menu out of the waitress's hand. "What's good here? I'm guessing steak and probably— Oh, they have buffalo."

"Savory buffalo with new potatoes with wild turnip and onions is the chef's selection tonight," the waitress said. "They marinate the buffalo for twelve hours, and then it's slow roasted. It's really tender."

"Mmm. I'll have the Crab Louis with…" She glanced across the table in time to catch him smirking. "Why not?"

"Around here we try to avoid crabs." He gave a lopsided grin. "You don't know where they've been or how long they took gettin' here."

"Why put it on the menu, then?"

"Why ask what's good here? Right, Doris?" Dillon glanced at the waitress. "How fresh are Louis's crabs tonight?"

"Same as any other night," Doris allowed after due consideration. "They're real pink, nice and straight, all the same size and everything."

Dillon nodded. "No shell?"

"It's the legs that come in the shell," Doris said, nearly deadpan. "We've got those on the buffet. These are more like fingers."

"And who knows—"

"—where they've been," Ella recited in unison with Dillon. "Savory buffalo sounds perfect."

"And for you, sir?"

"Where did they get wild turnips and onions?" Dillon wanted to know.

Doris shrugged. "I just read it the way it's written."

"Wild turnips and onions," he echoed, considering, then shook his head. "Nah. Buffalo on a bun, hold the savory."

"You sure?" Doris collected their menus.

"Unless you dug 'em up yourself."

"Not likely," the waitress scoffed as she backpedaled from the table. "They're in season. I know that much."

"Kids nowadays, huh?" He braced an arm on the edge of the table and leaned in. "They're liable to lose us our status as living history, and then where will we be?"

"Eating off the FDA menu, just like everybody else. Time to get with the twenty-first-century program."

"Fine by me. Number twenty wasn't exactly Indian-friendly."

"Maybe you're limiting yourself to a narrow view."

"Maybe," he said with a shrug. "Or maybe narrow is the view for the future." He leaned back. "'Every man for himself' is pretty narrow."

"I agree." She couldn't imagine a better segue into a pitch for *Who's Our Neighbor?*

"I had an interesting visit with Monica this past week. She's doing very well, by the way, considering."

"Whatever considerations we're considering, I'm no longer on the list. But you didn't happen to see my son, did you? How's he doing?"

"He was practicing when I was at the house. Amazing talent."

Dillon's eyes lit up. "He's some fiddler, ain't he?"

"Playing with the city orchestra at his age is quite an accomplishment."

"No doubt," he enthused. "He got his start right here, you know. Took private lessons from the high-school music teacher when he was just a little guy. Music, art, books. Takes after his mom that way. So smart she's smarter than herself sometimes."

"And your daughter gets her passion for horses from her father."

"You could say that. *Passion* is a good word for it. And it burns, burns, burns," he crooned softly, trailing off with an unselfconscious chuckle. "But in Emmie's case, she's really gonna make something out of all that fever."

"Emily says the same of you."

All but ignoring the arrival of the food, he shot her a look that said his interest had just doubled.

"The last time I saw her, all she could talk about was your mustangs." She knew she had him now. She inhaled the pungent steam drifting off her plate. "Mmm, *savory* says it all. I hope it tastes as good as it—"

"What did she say?"

"That you're her hero," she tossed out as she pulled the meat apart with the mere touch of knife and fork. She glanced up, saw him hanging on her easy words, and nodded. "Really. She explained how you persuaded the government to let you adopt mustangs from the herd out in the western North Dakota badlands, because they're descendants of horses that belonged to Chief Sitting Bull, and you're a Sitting Bull descendant yourself. Although, according to what I've read, he didn't leave any direct descendants."

"But his sisters did," he informed her. He lifted his hand, fingers splayed. "The Indian way, relations aren't linear. Bloodlines and pedigrees, that's for breeding horses. Human families are circles connected to circles inside circles surrounding circles."

"So I've heard." She swirled a piece of potato around

in a pool of brown sauce. "You're to be commended for convincing the Interior Department to see it your way."

"More like convincing other interested parties to back off. Some white guys ranching out there near the Montana line started looking into some of the history about how when Sitting Bull and his people came back from Canada and surrendered, the army confiscated their horses and sold them off. These guys are raising Spanish mustangs and what they call American-Indian ponies. They've got a registry and all these charts with neat lines, the whole bit." He illustrated with an air sketch, his supper all but forgotten as he leaned into the telling of his story.

"So they get this story out in a few places—newspapers, horse magazines and like that—tellin' how this French guy, friend of Teddy Roosevelt and married to some rich woman from out East, he starts this ranch near the Badlands. And he's the one who gets hold of Sitting Bull's herd. Like two hundred and fifty mares, because he says these Indian ponies are a superior breed and he's gonna raise them. But the ranch goes bust within a couple years, French guy loses his ruffled shirt, and the horses are gone."

"Stolen?" The story was as rich with local flavor as the food on her plate, and she was happily taking it all in.

"Most likely headed for the hills first chance they got."

"The Badlands," Ella surmised.

"Which is now Theodore Roosevelt National Park, run by the park service and the BLM, who are all set to cull this herd of mustangs, and I'm all set to quietly move in on all the mares they put up for adoption. I mean, we've known about this for a hundred years, right? The government promised to pay for those horses. Pony Claims, they called it. Our great-grandfathers applied for Pony Claims, our grandfathers filled out more papers, and nothin' ever came of it. But this story gets out, all of a sudden people start comin' outta the woodwork. Everybody's all into Indian history, and everybody's brother is raising gen-u-ine Indian ponies."

"Until you convinced them to back off," she supplied, recalling Emily's glowing report.

"Shamed them off, more like. They had it publicly pointed out to them that if what they were sayin' about the horses was true, maybe the guys from Standing Rock should have first claim." A raised palm gave sign of second thoughts. "No, that's not quite fair. You're right, they *backed* off, and we all shook hands and parted friends after me and Nick took our pick of the mares. Maybe they really did see the light." He turned his attention to his burger. "And maybe I should shut up and let you eat."

"You're not slowing me down. This is delicious. Is this really a wild turnip?" She lifted a forkful for her own inspection.

"Looks like the real—"

His eyes widened as her fork passed through his field of vision toward his mouth. Greens, root, sauce and meat hung in the balance, threatening to drip from the tines while he stared, nonplussed. Then out darted the tip of his tongue for a deft catch before his lips closed on her offering.

"Is it?"

He nodded as he reached for a glass of water.

"More?" she asked, oddly eager to please. "This has to be a rare treat. It is for me. Short season, I'll bet, just like any…" She prepared another forkful.

He licked his lip, smiled and forestalled a second bite with a subtle gesture.

"Gen-u-ine wild on-yons." She flashed him a smile as she turned the direction of her fork. His loss, her tasty gain.

Nearly choking on his water, he caught his breath and laughed.

"Get 'em while they last," she chirped. "Before everybody's brother starts raising them."

He chuckled. "Isn't that what they did with wild rice over in your neck o' the woods? I hear they're farming that stuff up north of the Twin Cities. Used to be a rare treat, didn't it? Mostly Indians harvested it."

"They have to label the farmer-grown variety as tame wild rice." She shrugged off the oxymoron. "Yeah, I know. But I think *real* wild rice is still, you know, wild. The Ojibwe still harvest the real wild rice in the traditional way."

"Harvested by gen-u-ine wild In-juns," he teased.

"Well, *you're* raising wild horses."

He lifted an instructive forefinger. "I'm raising gen-u-ine Indian ponies. Ain't no wild In-juns left, honey. We've all been domesticated. You hang around our stomping grounds, you might hear an occasional war whoop, but it's like the lion in the zoo who's gotta roar just because it's in his blood."

"Honey?" She chastened him gently with a look. And herself, inwardly, for not really minding at all.

"Half-assed domesticated?" He lifted one shoulder as he finally picked up his burger. "Enough of my bullshit, huh? What else did my daughter say about the horses?"

"Well, she told me all about the program for kids that you two started together last summer." *Oh, yes, and that's why I'm here.*

"Not what you'd call a *program* really. We got some kids together with some horses. Turned out pretty good all around. We've got horses in the blood, you know." He wagged a cocked thumb between the two of them. "Us Sioux people."

Mouth full, she shook her head. "I missed out on that part," she said when she'd freed her tongue. "I'm only half Sioux. Must be the wrong half. My father was white."

"Our way, we get everything through the mother." He swallowed a bite of what must have been a by now cold burger and gave a perfunctory smile. "But Champion's a great name."

"I don't know much about my father's family. I haven't seen or heard from him since I was quite young. But my mother's people came from southern Minnesota. Not wild-rice country."

"East River Sioux," he acknowledged. "Cousins to us Lakota, the real mystic warriors of the plains. Like they say, it's all about location."

"They're not east of the river—my mother's people— they're west."

"You're thinkin' Mississippi. I'm talkin' Missouri. You're East River Sioux. Dakota dialect, and I'm guessing Santee."

"That's right." She remembered the few words they'd exchanged on the subject when Monica had introduced them. The apple joke, the reference to her urban roots as opposed to him being from the "rez." But that was there. That was Monica's territory. And here was a place she'd read about and thought about but had little to say about. Because who else was interested? "I'm not sure if… I'm not signed up, as far as I know."

"You're not enrolled?" He set the burger down carefully. "That's a surprise, Ella. Your mother was an AIM leader. Real rabble-rouser, big authority on treaty rights and federal government wrongs. I remember her. I mean, she was out there talkin' up the cause, that one."

Ella nodded. "She used to say Indians were the only nationality in this country that has to register with the government. What other people get officially identified according to blood quantum? she'd say. Like your horses' pedigrees."

"Yep. We're Indians only because they say we're Indians. But just between us Indians…" he leaned closer to confide "…I'm Hunkpapa Lakota, and you're Santee."

"Half," she averred.

"They've gotcha goin' or comin', but you haven't figured out which."

"And if I'm not registered, I guess I don't have a pedigree."

"You can fix that if you want to," he suggested. "If you feel like being enrolled would fix anything."

She glanced away. She'd taken care of getting her birth certified herself. She'd had no idea it hadn't been done until she'd needed it for a passport.

"So how's Monica doing?" he asked quietly.

"I think she's amazing, frankly." Upbeat again, she was glad for the change of topic. "Her show just keeps getting better. Some of the celebrity guests she gets to come on in a Midwest market that size? I don't know how she does it."

"Sure, you do."

"Sure I do." She laughed. "She's got brass balls. The part of *no* she understands is the *o. Oh,* all right. *Oh,* sure. *O*kay, Monica."

"*Oh,* yeah. You got the picture." He studied his less-than-half-eaten buffalo burger. "So what part of *okay, Monica* brings you out here?"

"An idea for a show."

He looked up, surprised. "Yours or hers?"

"Her idea. My show. The show I work for." Suddenly unsure of her approach, Ella dabbed at her lips with her napkin. "Monica and I work together sometimes. On our show we use different decorators, pull them in from local TV and cable. That way you get up-and-comers along with the people who have a recognized signature. Monica does the decorating-on-the-cheap shtick to perfection."

"Sounds like a band."

"Funny." She shrugged. "Okay, so you're not into the home-and-garden thing."

"On the contrary, I'm a hell of a handyman. But anything that catches my fancy, I'd rather do it than watch it done."

"You don't watch Monica's show?"

"What does she call it? *It's Cheaper Than It Looks?*"

"*It Only Looks Expensive,*" she supplied with a smile. "Titles are either one word or ten these days."

"I've seen it a few times. That's not her, you know. That's like her telephone voice. And I don't mean that in a bad way. I always admired the way she could turn it on and off when she had to. It's served her well."

"So you've seen the show."

"Once she made a table out of an old door and a bunch of broken dishes. On the show, I mean. I got stuck watching that one at my sister's." He gave a sheepish smile. "And I'm pretty sure I recognized some of those broken dishes. She never throws anything away, you know. She can find a use for any old junk."

"Are you hard on the dinnerware?"

"Used to be. Stuff I use now is unbreakable."

"Have you ever seen my show?" she wondered as she waved at Doris, who had just seated a portly pair of slow-moving seniors. The woman rattled the coins in a tall plastic pail before setting it on the table, bracing her hands on either side and painstakingly lowering herself into the chair as though performing some ritual obeisance. "Coffee," Ella said when she'd caught the waitress's eye, and then to Dillon, "You wouldn't see me, of course, except in the credits. I'm behind the scenes."

"Like a director?"

"Producer," she said with a nod, unsure why she felt compelled to add, "Line producer, which means I do everything except act and direct."

"What else is there?"

"A lot of heavy lifting, but all for a good cause. It's a good show. *Who's Our Neighbor?*" She smiled when he shrugged. "That's the name of the show."

"Sounds religious."

"It's more than just decorating. It's a makeover show. Reality TV?" He turned his mouth down, shook his head. "Very popular these days."

"Like I said, I'd rather do it than watch it. What do you make over?"

"Homes. Businesses. Community facilities. People's lives." She leaned back as the coffee was poured. "I have some CDs in my room if you'd like to see a few clips. Dessert, drinks, my name in the credits."

"For making things happen behind the scenes."

"Out of sight but always within reach—that's Ella Champion."

"My kind of woman." He waved off the coffee. "What are we drinking?"

"I'll have something sent up."

"If you're thinkin' room service, it ain't gonna happen

here." He was already halfway out of his chair. "What's your pleasure, Hollywood? I'll be your room service."

"I think I've got a clip that shows one of Monica's projects, if you're interested in seeing—"

"I'm just dyin' to see."

She didn't like the sound of that. Or did she? He was teasing, and she wasn't ready to shut him down with the power of a glance. It had nothing to do with the prospective project—makeover possibilities could be found anywhere—and everything to do with an uncomplicated smile. Amusement, pure, simple—and free for the taking. Most smiles that came her way were either vacant or dripping with design. But not Dillon Black's.

One thing I know about Indian men, Ella. They can't be made over.

The voice in Ella's head didn't know jack. She'd married a white man.

Because I knew nothing about white men. My mistakes are your legacy, daughter. Take it and run.

Ella laughed when she missed the first green light on the door lock. She swiped the key again and pushed the door open. She rarely made a misstep, and she certainly never ran. She'd found Dillon Black attractive from the get-go. Nothing she couldn't handle. That he was dying to see what she was planning to show him was doubtful. But he was willing. And she was about to turn him into a believer.

Chapter Five

Willing was no problem for Dillon. As long as she had the place, he had the time. What could it cost him to entertain a stopover visitor? Monica's friend, all woman, and part Indian to boot. Hell, she looked Indian, even if she walked and talked Hollywood. Could be an interesting mix. What would it hurt to check out the options?

Since his divorce, the women had been sliding through his life real easy, the way Friday night coasted into Monday morning. He gave at least as good as he got, but he took no risks. He didn't need the grief. He could stand to love a woman only so much. Wouldn't have 'em fucking with his head or his heart, but the rest was up for grabs when she had the place and he had the time.

And unless he had his signals seriously crossed, Hollywood was conjuring up a mental map of his love handles.

He unbuttoned his vest as he took a seat on the sofa. She poured two glasses of wine without asking him whether he drank the stuff. He didn't. Wine was a cheap high followed by a sick low. But he drank enough of what she'd chosen from the limited list to give her hospitality its due respect while he gave her show some fraction of his attention.

He was more interested in the personal details she tried

to spice the program up with. She seemed genuinely proud of turning a run-down bowling alley into a video arcade. From the looks of the teenagers bellying up to the machines, they would have been better off with some bowling. Better yet, some skating. Or, if they were really lucky, some horseback riding. But he complimented her on the flashy arcade and laughed at the story of how one of the regulars on the show had almost gotten arrested for shop-lifting in the local Qwik Stop, and how she'd had to do some "fancy dancing" to keep the incident out of the news.

"I'll bet you'd make a hell of a fancy dancer," he said, taking the opportunity to slide closer and stretch his arm along the back of the couch. "You have beautiful hair. Let it grow a little longer, get yourself a shawl, you could shawl dance. Ever tried it?"

"No, but my mother had a shawl. It was blue with sequined butterflies and a long red fringe all around the edges. It was heavy, and I remember she caught me playing with it once."

"Did you catch hell?"

"She showed me how to fold it properly and hold it around my shoulders. She said she'd give it to me when I got older. I guess we both forgot." She crossed her arms over her full, firm breasts as if to catch the shawl before it slipped away. "I wonder what happened to it."

"I've got a sister who makes them. I could get you a nice one real cheap."

"I'd love— Oh, here's Monica." She pointed at the television screen. "This is the one we did in Oklahoma. She did some amazing window treatments in this one."

It felt weird watching his ex-wife doing her thing on TV while he was trying to put the moves on another woman.

Ex-wife? The term rarely registered. Not that he considered himself married, but the idea of a man X-ing his wife off the books seemed—what was the two-dollar word these days? Inappropriate. Damned disrespectful. Family was family. Monica was the mother of his children. And she'd been a turn-on from the first moment he'd laid eyes on her. The fact that she'd had a little age on her had only added to the attraction. She was smart, classy, beautiful, and she'd had the hots for him like he could hardly believe. "Older Women Make Good Lovers" had become his theme song.

And here she was, twenty years later, with her own TV show, looking smarter and classier than ever, and still pretty damn hot for fifty plus. He wasn't one to count a woman's birthdays. His own, yeah. He was about to hit the top of a hill that had once looked so distant it hadn't even figured into his itinerary. Age was nothing back then. Not his, not Monica's.

How old was Ella? Should he be asking that question before things went any further? Just out of respect, in case she was closer to his daughter's age than his own. Being her friend's former husband was one thing, but Ella knew Emily, too, and it would creep him out if it turned out she was thinking of him as somebody's daddy.

"She has a special appeal," Ella was saying, seemingly mesmerized by the woman on the screen. "She's like a cross between Katharine Hepburn and maybe Meg Ryan."

With a look, he told her that he had no idea what that meant.

"All dressed up and still approachable. You could open the front door and find her standing on your porch. People believe she can bring home the bacon, grow the lettuce and tomatoes in her backyard, make an unforgettable BLT and still have time for a little girl talk. Sort of a post-penitentiary Martha Stewart."

"I guess you could say Monica did her time."

And hadn't he done his?

Damn. Did people really turn on TV to watch Monica hang curtains?

"Now look." She nodded toward the screen. "Here she is with the guy we're doing the makeover for. He was in a terrible accident. Car caught on fire. Wife was killed, and he ended up losing both hands. Four children." Two boys were chasing a third one, who had run off with their basketball. "That's the youngest one—such a little—"

She'd hit the bait that never failed to hook Dillon by the ear. Words like *accident, killed,* and *loss* anywhere near the word *fire,* and he was back in the oil fields choking on smoke. The guy on the screen would know the smell. He wore a baseball cap on his badly scarred head and a sweatshirt with long pants when everyone around him was sleeveless. Burn victims were easily chilled. Nick was sensitive that way, too. To the regular air, the common stare.

Terrible accident. Brother was killed. Oil rig caught fire.

But here was this guy, this walking tragedy, putting himself in front of a television camera. The basketball came flying at him from somewhere off camera, and he made the catch with arms that ended scant inches below his elbows beneath his modified shirtsleeves. The ball thief burst into view on a joyous leap, cheering wildly.

"That required endless takes," Ella said. "Ordinarily we just let the camera roll, but the little boy kept apologizing for not throwing it right and insisted that Daddy could do it. So Daddy kept at it, and we kept at it. He was between prosthetics at the time, but when we did our follow-up interview a month later, he was doing very well with a pair of hooks."

The camera panned to Monica, who was waiting on the sidelines, paintbrush in hand, cheerfully letting Daddy know that she had more stencils ready and he only had two little chairs to go.

"Monica actually had him painting the playhouse furniture with his feet. For his little girl. Can you imagine how she'll cherish that when she—"

"Ssst!" Dillon signaled for silence as he tuned in to Monica's tale of someone else's woe. On camera, she was positioning a loaded paintbrush between Daddy's toes, but she was doing a narrative voiceover that had obviously been recorded later.

"...and my husband's friend was killed. The older brother survived, but he suffered horribly. We were all very close, so I learned firsthand about the particular horrors experienced by burn victims. That's why working on the Murray family project was especially—"

Working hard to contain himself, Dillon turned on Ella. "If Nick ever saw this, he'd string the woman up by her loose lips."

"I forgot about that little anecdote." She lifted one shoulder, as if to say, *No biggie.* "She doesn't mention any names."

He pulled his arm back, retracting, getting a grip on himself along with the top of the sofa cushion. "Has she had any other husbands?"

"She never says *former* or *ex*—that might be off-putting—so anyone who knows you could assume she'd remarried. And she never mentions you by name. I don't usually go for the 'Queen For a Day' angle, but this was a unique segment. It touched us all deeply, but it really hit home with Monica."

"Yeah, I can tell." He gave a wry smile. "Home for Monica is a complete hundred and eighty from *that little anecdote.* Fortunately, this side of the circle, hardly anybody watches that kind of stuff." But some part of him truly wanted some part of Thelma Bear Dancer's daughter to have at least a toehold on the near side.

"Come on, Ella." He nodded toward the screen. "You watch this, you feel embarrassed for him. I mean, it's good you did this for these people, but then you gotta throw it up on a billboard? You're just trading on this guy's troubles."

"Not at all. He's a survivor. He's—"

"No, don't say *it.* Without the dead wife, four kids and look-Ma-no-hands, he's just another working stiff who can't pay his bills. You don't build him a new house unless the TV audience gets to see how bad off he is first."

"They get to see a real-life survivor," she countered. "And we built more than a house. We contributed to the community by building an activity center for children that he—"

"Why'd you pick him?" he challenged.

"Why not?"

"Sure, why not?" He glanced at the screen again. "Not to mention that you caught him between prosthetics."

"That was unintentional. Scheduling can be a bear."

On the television, Monica was pulling stencils off the tabletop so Daddy could admire the flowers he'd painted with his feet. He looked pleased. Even a little teary-eyed, maybe. Dillon willed the camera to give the guy a break, a little privacy, but the shot seemed to go on and on. No tears in Monica's eyes, which was good. Honest. When she was pleased—as he could tell she truly was—she got the grins to beat hell.

Dillon had to smile, too. "She used to make doll furniture for Emily out of egg cartons and shoe boxes. You would've thought they came from a toy store, they were so perfect."

"I know what you mean." Ella turned to him with what he thought was a come-on look. "She told me about the old church building you've been renovating. I'd love to see it, Dillon."

Professional come-on, maybe? "Why?"

"Because I'm all about unusual renovations."

"I thought you were all about making a TV show? The technical stuff? You've got people like Monica to come up with ways to…" He scowled at the screen, where Monica and some young stud wearing a carpenter's tool belt were patting each other on the back over the way his furniture worked with her jungle theme in a kid's room.

"Ways to do what the executive producer wants done," she said, finishing his sentence. "We get recommendations from all over the place, and we look at the potential for an interesting project, consider the people, the community, a whole list of criteria. In fact, that's a big part of my job." She touched the back of his hand. "So I'm dying to see your church."

"I don't think you're *dyin'* quite the same way I'm dyin'. Or was. That being the case, we're at cross purposes here." Hands on his knees, he was about ready to push off. "Whatever you're after ain't for sale, and what I was after…" He glanced back at her, gave her a little smile. "Well, we won't be goin' there. I gotta say, it's been weird."

"What?"

"That," he said, nodding toward the screen.

She aimed the remote in the direction of his gesture and muted Monica. Then she gave him an odd look, like she wanted to take a bite out of him and couldn't decide whether to go for tender or juicy.

"We could help, Dillon."

"Help what?"

"Help you finish your whole project in real style."

Project? He didn't have a project. He had a salvaged building, a herd of adopted mustangs and a few hundred acres of prairie grassland on an Indian reservation.

The image of a man with unmanly tears in his eyes mocked him from a silent TV screen. *Pity* me, *will you?*

"Monica sent you."

"Monica nominated *you*," she said quietly. "Actually, she nominated the Wolf Trail Ranch and its horse program for the local youth."

He stared, incredulous.

"As a project for *Who's Our Neighbor?*" she explained.

Bam. He felt like he'd just knocked back half a pint of hundred-proof hooch. Pure gut-buster. He fell back against the sofa.

And laughed.

"No, I'm seriously considering it."

He straightened up for half a second, and then he nodded, choked out, "I know," and laughed again.

"But don't get too excited yet," she cautioned. "There's a lot to consider."

"Yeah, well, start with this." He was still grinning. He couldn't help it. The woman really thought she was Santa Claus. "The Wolf Trail Ranch is a partnership between me and a guy who would eat nails before he'd get in front of a TV camera. And the horse camp is a dream I cooked up for my kid. She's about to find out—"

"We've got better uses for nails, and we can make your dream camp a reality."

"And that old church building," he went on, shaking his head. "Got it for pretty much nothing but the cost of moving it, and I've been working on the thing in my spare time for years." He raised his eyebrows in mock drama. "They call it Dillon Black's folly, but generally not to my face."

"I'm told it has a history, and we'll work all that in. Dillon, real people's spare time is television people's real time." She leaned closer, hand pressed high over her left breast as she pledged her allegiance. "I'm television people."

"In person, huh? No shit?" He nodded toward the screen. "Is this guy real, or is he television?"

"He's real."

"Maybe in Oklahoma somewhere, but right here he's a shadow you trapped in a box." He winked at her as he stood and leaned toward taking his leave. "That's a little Indian lore for you to take back to Hollywood. They'll believe anything, especially coming from somebody like you."

"But I'd like to…" She followed his lead, scrambling to her feet. "Do you have to go?"

"Yeah." And he felt damn good about quitting while he was ahead. Some feat, considering the way she'd gone from sixty to zero on his straightaway. "Listen, you got any interest in history, we've got history. We've got some sights, some sounds—even some local color, if you like brown. You got some time on your hands, give me a call and I'll show you around. Just ask at the desk. They know how to get hold of me."

He turned at the door, surprised to find her trailing close

behind. On impulse, he touched her earlobe and traced the line of her jaw with his thumb. "But I don't want your makeover, darlin'. I'm fine the way I am."

Chapter Six

Dillon didn't drink much anymore, but the wine he'd sampled wanted a stiff chaser. Or maybe his stiff chaser wanted a dampener. On his way over to the bar he'd heard the craps stickman call a roll of sevens, so he straddled a stool, ordered a Seven and Seven, and raised the glass in silent toast. Then he set it back down and stared at it glumly. He'd never favored either Seven. If he was going to chuck his dignity out the window, he ought to go for the good stuff, at least for the first few rounds. He was toying with the glass on the black granite bar, mentally assembling his short list, when a heavy hand landed on his shoulder.

"What're we celebrating?"

"Vincent." Dillon gave the bar stool a quarter turn and offered husky, moon-faced Vincent Many Wounds a hand-shake. "Just trying to kill a bad taste in my mouth. You ever try that chardonnay wine? Tastes like somebody pissed on the grapes."

"I hear it's been pretty dry out there in California. Farmer's gotta do what a farmer's gotta do." Vincent claimed the next bar stool. "Hey, man, I'm sorry we didn't come through with that grant money you were lookin' for."

Dillon gestured for truce. No apology needed, no sympathy wanted.

No hint taken.

"I was right in there talkin' up your program to the committee," Vincent claimed. "I told how my kid was all high on horses after last summer. That's how it should be for our kids—high on horses instead of that other shit they're gettin' hold of these days—but I couldn't pull in the votes we needed."

We sounded good. Just for that, Dillon was willing to put Vincent's name back on his Christmas-card list.

"You know who talked it down, don't you?"

Dillon shook his head, wishing he could end the conversation.

Vincent signaled the bartender for service. "You gotta know it was Terry Yellow Horn," he confided, head down. Then he stretched his neck and kicked up the volume. "Bud Light." Down again. Strolling chicken, this guy. "His wife's sister did all the talking. She's on the committee. Man, that woman's scary. You know damn well she keeps her ol' man's balls in a jar of pickle juice. Comes time for his funeral, you wanna stay away from the potato salad."

Chuckling, Dillon drew his hand back from the dish of complimentary peanuts.

"It's always the same ol' story. They want everything for the North Dakota side. Nothing for us Hunkpapa living across the state line. Hell, we're the ones that go back to Sitting Bull, and it's his picture all over everything around here."

"Most famous Indian ever lived," Dillon supplied with a nod.

"And it's the seed of his horses you got out to your place," Vincent said. "My boy really liked that all over. Told his sister all them campfire stories from last summer, and now she wants to get in on this year's program. You think you'll be able to do something again? I mean, I'll sure help out, but you gotta let me bring both kids."

"As long as my daughter's still on board after she hears we didn't get the grant. I don't know if, uh…" Confession time. "All right, yeah, I wrote a stipend into the grant for her, but she doesn't even know about that part. I thought it was fair. It wasn't that much. She worked hard, and she wanted to do a lot more with it this year." He sighed. "Bet that's where I blew it, putting that part in."

"It's better you wrote in something for your daughter rather than lookin' after yourself."

"Is that what they thought?" Dillon shook his head and gave a mirthless chuckle. "Last summer, I don't know how much I shelled out. I probably should've kept track, but I wasn't thinkin' about…" He flopped a helpless hand, a dead soldier on the bar. "Hell, I'm no bookkeeper. Only reason we applied for a grant was that we wanted to make room for more kids and do more…more…"

"One guy wants to make another one look bad, all he has to do is break off a piece of the truth and reshape it a little bit," Vincent said, sympathizing. "Like, maybe you were out to get some permanent improvements at your place, and once you got 'er done, who's to say you'd offer the summer camp again? That was the argument. Plus, Terry wants to run a program at the college, and he figures on stealin' yours."

"Let him." Dillon turned his mouth down and reached for the drink he'd yet to taste. "Let him have it."

"I suppose you heard about Jimmy Taylor."

It was a phrase that never prefaced anything but bad

news. Dillon pulled his hand back and shook his head, bracing himself. Jimmy had been so obsessed with the horses last summer, maybe the news was just that he'd grown a tail.

"Tried to hang himself."

Shit.

"Tried?"

"Somebody caught him in time. They got him up in Bismarck."

The two men sat in silence for a time. Vincent sipped his beer. Dillon stared at a muted basketball game on the big screen TV above the bar. All around him, people spoke in hushed tones, as though the *ping, ping, ping* of a machine called "Hot Peppers" and the *ding, ding, dong, dong, dong* of "Lucky Cherries" combined to make a "Hallelujah Chorus."

Vincent finally spoke. "What are they thinking when they do that? It ain't easy, bein' a kid, but that's a helluva way to put an end to it."

"Pretty sure that's not what they're thinkin' about." Dillon drew a deep breath and shook his head. "Not Jimmy. Man, I just can't see him…" But what he was staring at was the cigarette Vincent had started puffing.

Vince took the pack from his breast pocket and made Dillon an offer he didn't even think about refusing. "We see too much of it around here," Vincent said as he flicked his Bic. "One kid does it, pretty soon you've got two or three. That's why we need your horse camp. One of the reasons, anyway."

"Jimmy was in the program last summer. He was a quiet kid, but he was always the first one there in the morning and the last to go home." Dillon squinted through the cloud he'd made. "Your boy got along real good with Jimmy."

"Danny's the one who told me about it. Said the kid was a dumb fuck, but it was more like Danny was mad at him for doing it than anything else." Vincent tapped his cigarette on the lip of a round glass ashtray. "We need more activities around here, D. Especially for the kids. We need more stuff for them to do."

"*We* didn't have anything to do."

"We thought we did. All we needed was transportation, right? Kids in our day were either into cars or horses. With us, it was horses. Fast horses and pretty girls." Vincent smiled absently. "Or was it the other way around?"

"Works for me either way."

"I know it was the horses got me through. Hell, it's hard out here for a kid."

Dillon frowned. "Where have I heard that?"

"Some of that damn rap music. Did they bring that around you last summer?"

"Only once." They'd tried sneaking some of their CDs into the traditional music he'd played when he'd told stories—*you don't listen to the stories, you don't ride my horses*—but he'd jettisoned that crap with a vengeance. Almost felt bad about the one that got cracked. "Even when they turn it down, it's too loud. Must be gettin' old, huh?" Old saying, he thought. *If it's too loud, you're too old.* Could've been a bumper sticker. Or maybe that was some of the ancient Egyptian graffiti he'd read about. Proof that some things never change. "Where are your horses now, Vince?"

"Gave away my saddle when I hung up the spurs. I found a picture of us guys at the Cheyenne River rodeo, back when we were in high school. You, me, Dwaine Halsey, ol' Pogo. Remember Pogo?"

"Pogo the Stick." Never made it past high school, Dillon recalled. Rammed his brother's car into an approach, flew onto the highway and got run over by a semi. "I can still see him scratchin' out that big Brahma with those long, skinny legs of his. Looked like a giant grasshopper."

"Showed my kids that picture," Vincent said. They were both directing their comments toward the mute basketball players. "They didn't believe it was me. Danny recognized *you* right away, though. You haven't changed much, D. Still lean and mean."

Dillon smiled absently as he toyed with his glass, drawing the water ring into an ever-widening circle. "Owe it all to clean country livin'."

"It's been a long time since I lived out in the country. We've got no place to keep a horse."

"There's nothing about this place we call home that ain't country, Vince. We're a horse culture."

"Not since—"

"Since we let somebody else say otherwise? Far as I'm concerned, every Lakota man, woman and child needs a horse." Dillon turned from the untasted drink, the unheard ball game, the unseen peppers and cherries, and offered his full attention to his old friend. "You coming out to Nick's tomorrow?"

"You guys're branding, right? You got a horse for every man, woman and child?"

"Damn straight. Bring the whole crew." He gave a slow grin as he slid down from the bar stool. "Have I got a mount for you, cowboy. We'll show 'em who's in that picture."

"What's your hurry? The next round's on me."

"Thanks, but I just remembered why I quit drinkin'." He reached for the ashtray. "I start lookin' for the cigarettes."

He stubbed out the one he'd just started. "See you to-morrow. Tell Danny Emily'll be there. My daughter. They all think she walks on water." Dillon clapped a hand on Vince's beefy shoulder. "I haven't seen her do it, but it wouldn't surprise *me,* either."

Wineglass in one hand, remote control in the other, Ella polished off the chardonnay while she replayed parts of the show. She took puckish pleasure in playing with Monica's TV image, making her jump around like a puppet, fast-forward, ass-backward. Monica Wilson-Black was a sick woman.

No, she really was. Not too many people knew how sick Monica had been. Ella was one of the chosen few only because they'd been working together when Monica had had her surgery and Ella had been enlisted to help with the cover-up. Why she'd gone along with it was beyond her, if not her inner therapist, who insisted it was all about her inner child's persistent war with its phantom mother. Phantom Mother had yet to weigh in on the matter.

But Monica Wilson-Black was also a *sick* woman. Oth-erwise, how could she go around pimping out her ex-hus-band? He was an attractive man—Ella had made the colossal mistake of saying so the day she'd met him—and it was more than just a physical thing, although there certainly was that. He had a one-of-a-kind air about him. Take him or leave him, he would be who he was. He wasn't bent on impressing any-one, but he could and would if you let him.

Without letting on—not purposely, anyway—she had let him. And she'd let it show. It was nothing big, nothing she could be cited for in a court of public opinion. A giddy laugh, a second glance, a flippant phrase. Nothing he'd chosen to notice, and only later—weeks, maybe months—had Monica flashed an annoying smile when his name had come up somehow. *Didn't I tell you he had some unique assets? I know you tried to ignore them. I also know you failed.*

Annoying as hell.

Ella drained the wine from her glass, muted the TV and started picking up the few stray bits threatening the serenity that came with orderliness—shoes she'd kicked off under the table, pamphlets about the local attractions, an empty bottle, a second glass that wanted draining. She didn't think about it being his until she'd licked the last drop off the rim. Catching herself, feeling gloomy and foolish and half drunk, she stared at it. Then she scowled at it.

And then she laughed so heartily she almost missed the soft tap at the door.

By the time she opened it, he'd almost gotten away, but he turned and gave her a curious look, as though she'd been the one knocking.

"I just wanted to…" He glanced past her. "You got company?"

She felt silly, standing there smiling. "I did, but I bored him with home movies, so he left."

"Heard someone laughing. Must've come from a different room."

"Oh, no, that was us, all right. Me, myself and I. Not everyone gets us, but we love each other's sense of humor." She swung the door wide-open. "Come on in before you catch a chill standing out there with you, yourself and…you."

"Dining alone isn't half as pitiful as drinking alone," he allowed. She backed away, and he followed, closing the door.

"Is that what you've been doing?" Her end of the conversation was an afterthought to reeling in the stupid smile.

"Ain't askin', ain't sayin'. Just talkin' my way back

into your room." He caught her by the elbow before she realized she'd stumbled. "Damn carpet's got some lumps in it. You okay?"

"I finished off the bottle. It's no good the next day. It goes flat."

"It started out flat," he reminded her. "Are you gonna be around tomorrow?"

"Will I have a better chance with you tomorrow than I did tonight?"

He laughed. "Basically, that was my next question, but I was gonna phrase it a little differently."

"That's because you did not finish your wine. *In vino veritas.* Which is—"

"—Hollywood for *drunks never lie.* Only in the movies, darlin'. In real life, you never heard so many lies until the booze starts talkin'."

"I'm not your darling." So what? She wasn't sure when she'd stiffened up, but the easy shrug wasn't happening. "Obviously."

His mouth twitched. "You wanna be? The job's open."

"What I want to be is—" Honest? *Like you?* "—your friend. And as your friend, your new apple friend, I would like to be invited to your home. Because a little bird told me that you have a lovely setting, some wonderful raw material, a fabulous idea that could become, with just a little bit of help—the kind of help a friend like me might be able to—"

"Back up," he warned, signaling stop, drop and roll. "Rewind, back to the invitation part. That's where I was going. If you were gonna be around tomorrow, and if you felt like gettin' down and dirty with me and some of my friends, you'd stand a good chance of seeing how your other half lives."

"What other half?"

"The 'skin half." He chucked her under her chin. "The skin of the apple. You don't mind my sayin' so, you could use a little sun."

"I actually…sometimes I burn." And turned red, for God's sake, but rarely was it because she couldn't stop talking stupid. Had to be those smiling eyes of his that had her chatting him up rather than smacking him down. "My mother never burned. Even when we lived in Minnesota. We'd be inside all winter, but one day in the spring sunshine, and she was as brown as—"

"I've been burned. Plenty of times." He shoved his hands into his pockets and set his gaze on the images she'd left to flicker on the television screen. "We're branding tomorrow. It's a chore, but you invite the neighbors and put on a feed, and it's a good time for everybody but the calves. You'll get to meet my partner and his wife. And Emily should be pullin' in sometime late tonight. Well, early tomorrow. Said she was takin' off today after her last exam and driving through the night. Tried to talk her out of it, but…" He lifted a shoulder and smiled absently at Emily's mother on TV, soundlessly expounding upon the art and craft of Wilson-Blacking the walls of a child's room. "She's not a little girl anymore. Can't tell her what to do, especially when she knows I'll take night driving over a daytime road trip myself."

"She said it was a good ten-hour drive." She shrugged off his knowing glance. "We spoke the other day, so, yes, she knows I'm here. The makeover, you know, it's just an idea," she hastened to add. "Who knows if it's even feasible? I might not even want your old—"

"How old are you?"

None of your damn— "Thirty-four."

"I'd'a never guessed." But he grinned as though he'd achieved something. "Did Monica tell you she robbed the cradle?"

"Cradle*board,* she said, and what? You thought I was her age?"

"I was afraid you were closer to my daughter's age." And he was hanging himself with his silly grin. "So, uh… you might not want my old what?"

"Project. I haven't offered you a damn thing."

"Friendship," he reminded her.

She stabbed a finger in his direction. "*Except* for friendship."

"Didn't your mama teach you not to point like that? You got some catchin' up to do, long as you're here." He used his fingers to enumerate. "We don't point. We don't stare. We don't eyeball a person who's speaking to us."

"We don't ask personal questions, like *How old are you?*" she shot back. "And when did we start calling women *darlin'*?"

He lifted a shoulder. "After you've followed the rules for a few years, you can break one once in a while."

"How many years?"

"Right around forty."

She refused to tell him he didn't look it. She did the math, subtracting his daughter's age. "I guess she did rob the cradle. Not that it matters."

"What matters is whether you have a car or need a ride. If I come to get you, it'll be early. My guess is—"

"Just draw me a map."

He grabbed the hotel notepad, drew a straight line between two X's and added a picture of a mile marker with a number on it. "Here's the church. Here's the steeple."

Box with a caret on top. Box. Rectangle… "Barn. Trailer house. You can see it all from the road, but it's a mile and a quarter in. No gates. We've got a cattle guard." He handed over pad and pen. "I'll be there until I'm not. If nobody's around, you drive another half mile down the highway and look for the Wolf Trail sign and a nice new house. That's where my partner, Nick, lives. He's gonna love you."

"Why?"

"High profile. He loves that shit. Always reads the credits."

"Should I bring the DVD?"

"You wanna make sure Monica never again sets foot on his side of the state line?" he asked, and she shook her head. "Then I wouldn't be showing that around here." He paused, assessing something in her eyes, around her mouth, searching for some kind of sign.

She was no good at this. Never had been. Too much wine, too little resolve, trying too hard not to sway or be swayed. All to his advantage, and it was his move. She had all she could do to hold still.

"You okay?"

She glanced away and lobbed lamely, "What do you mean?"

He lifted his hand as he had before, and she anticipated the same sure, easy, disarming touch from those brown, masculine fingers. Tying one on had nearly untied all her stubborn knots, and his touch was all it would take.

But those fingers made an unexpected landing on her shoulder and gave a little squeeze. Hardly the gesture she'd scripted for them. She looked up to his eyes for justification.

Not there. No rhyme. No reason. Not much interest other than, maybe, a touch of humor.

"Sleep well, Hollywood."

Chapter Seven

Emily smelled the coffee without waking up.

She dreamed of her father tapping on the door, coming in with a big blue mug steaming with new-day aroma, setting it down on the lamp table beside the bed. She knew it was a dream—even as she smiled and he smiled back—because the lime green lamp with the swanlike neck was the one in her room at home, where her mother lived. But the scent was real, and even though the real version of the man she dreamed of would never serve her coffee in bed, she would find him close by if she followed the aroma, now entwining itself with scents that were becoming brown in color—bacon and bread. Homecoming at her mother's would not mean bacon.

But coffee in bed meant time to get up, and that would be Mother. Just coffee. Anything else you wanted, you could get for yourself, but you didn't want grease or cholesterol, because that would be bad for you, and you didn't want anything that had to be cooked unless you had time to clean up. You wanted whole-wheat toast, or whole-grain cereal with skim, or yogurt with granola. Unless you were Mother, who ate cigarette smoke with her coffee. Or unless there were overnight guests, and then the breakfast table looked like a picture in a magazine and the kitchen smelled like a dream. Everything worthy of Monica Wilson-Black.

Under-the-blanket dreams gave way to beyond-the-window din. The cows calling for their calves removed any doubt as to which home she'd landed in. It was the kind of sound she'd missed at her mother's house, the messy kind of memory that married two houses and gave her a sense of purpose. The disconnect was loud and clear, but so was her calling. Her father said she had a gift. Her mother believed everyone had a job to do. Emily lived in two places, but she'd grown up single-minded, strong-minded, so focused that her mind ached with it. *Make the connection, let there be peace.*

She dressed in the jeans and T-shirt she'd tossed over a chair only a couple of hours earlier, pulled her boots on and headed for the kitchen, sneaking up behind the wiry man whose shoulders, once godlike and unreachable, were now eye-level and only human. Intent on running water over a jumble of pots in the sink, he let her do her little sneak-up dance—fake right, go left, surprise him with a big squeeze.

"Hey, Pinky." He made two wet handprints on the back of her shirt. By the time they landed on her shoulders, his hands were warm and barely damp. "I got in pretty late last night, so I guess I was dead to the world by the time you pulled in. What time was it?"

"All I know is it was still dark. I wanted to help with the roundup, but it sounds like I slept through it."

"Nick got everyone bunched up pretty good yesterday. I just ran 'em in a little bit ago. You up for some French toast?"

She wasn't, but he was doing the just-for-you smile, so she came back with her goody-goody nod.

"Your mom's recipe." With a jerk of his chin, he put her to work soaking days-old white bread in spiced egg batter.

"She called," he was saying. "Told her you were here, safe and sound. She sounded real good, wanted to know who was comin' today and who was doing all the cooking. Told her everyone misses her baked beans. She liked that all over." He handed Emily a cup of coffee, fixed the way she'd learned to drink it at her father's house, with the evaporated milk he equated with cream. "I'll bet it's been at least ten years since she's made those beans," he said.

"At least."

"How soon does she expect you out to her place?"

"Whenever." She transferred the first two pieces of bread to the iron skillet he was tending. "How many calves are we looking at?"

"We only lost two. One to coyotes—first-calf heifer must've gotten bred earlier than she was supposed to—and one to scours. But we used that egg recipe you told me about on the rest and nipped that little problem right in the bud. My daughter the veterinarian." He winked at her.

"Your daughter the *pre vet major,* Daddy. So ninety-eight calves?"

"Even hundred. We sold the open cows last fall, but we kept the best heifers, so we're up to a hundred and two head, free and clear."

"Daddy, that's great." They might have been trading report cards, she thought. In the years since her mother had left him, her father had made a new life for himself piece by hard-earned piece. "How many horses?"

"Thirty-six mares. More than we should be carrying on the land we've got, but we talked a guy into selling us eight little beauties he got off Hammarschmidts."

"Weren't they the farmers who were competing for the mustangs originally?"

"Guess they decided the Indian ponies weren't worth putting any of their acreage into alfalfa, which ain't what mustangs want, anyway." The first piece of bread hissed on the flip side. "Prairie grass. The older the better. They thrive on the sod that reaches down to pre-Homestead Act roots. That grass just tastes different."

"You would know," Emily teased.

"Believe it, Pinky, I've got my ways. And that's why I say…" He flipped the second piece of bread. "My daughter the veterinarian. What you're doing is, you're bringing your ancestry along in a good way. You're a descendant of the—"

"—mystic warriors of the Plains. I know. And I do believe you've got your ways. Did I tell you I wrote a whole paper about your invisible twitch?" The painless alternative to the traditional lip-pinching twitch most stockmen used had been in his inventory his whole life.

"A whole damn paper on one little Indian trick?" He gave the achievement an appreciative tongue cluck. "Wait till we show 'em two little, three little, *four* little Indian tricks. Hell, I oughta get myself signed up for the fall term."

"It's never too late."

He slid cinnamon-scented toast onto a plate and ignored her comment. "Nick figured out a way to lease some more land. He goes to talk to a landowner, or he goes into the land office and he gets us whatever we need. People respect him. Always have."

"People love you, Daddy," she said dutifully. "And they always have."

"Man, that stud of Nick's has been pullin' in the breeding fees like you wouldn't believe. He's booked up for the season. That's what you need to get into when you finish school, Pinky." He wagged the spatula between toast turnings. "Nick's got a vet hovering over True Colors practically full-time, seems like. He turned out to be a helluva racehorse. By the time you finish school, your ol' uncle Nick will have a year-round job waitin' for you."

"My dream is to set up a practice out here and work with both of you. You're partners, aren't you?"

"Sure, but the stud belongs to Nick and Lauren." He handed her the plate of hot French toast, but not before taking a slice for himself. "Now, *that's* a partnership," he enthused, loading up on bacon. "Small-time breeder marries big-time jockey. Match made in horseman's heaven. She's been real good for… Hell, they're good for each other. She likes living here. Fits right in."

"Uncle Nick deserves to be happy," she said quietly. She could tell he was meandering toward some unhappy news. Her dad was an easy read. Probably something about the horses.

"Who doesn't?" He offered her a new bottle of Karo syrup, a departure from Mother's recipe, which suggested maple syrup or a touch of orange-blossom honey. "It's just a matter of figuring out the strokes it takes, right?"

"Right." She waved off the syrup and reached for the refrigerator door. "Any jelly?"

He pulled a new jar down from the cabinet above the stove. Grape. Her father's house offered few flavor options, but he'd shopped for her favorites. Ten years ago.

"I can't wait to see what you've done to the church since last fall," Emily said after they'd taken their places at the table and started sweetening up their breakfasts.

"Not much." He chewed. "What happened was…" And chewed. Swallowed. Speared the air with his fork. "It got cold. And then we got snow. And then the waterline…" Sipped his coffee. Shrugged. "I took some stuff out. Changed my mind about…" He went still, staring at his plate. "They turned us down on the grant proposal."

Emily's insides turned to mush, while scenes from the previous summer flashed in her mind. A trio of reluctant thirteen-year-old boys, court-ordered to spend four hours a day for a month helping out at the Wolf Trail, had quickly multiplied into a chorus of kids clamoring to ride horses. She'd stretched her month's stay into three, and her father had accommodated all comers. Pleased with their interest, and just plain tickled when they kept coming back and bringing their friends, Daddy had improvised with what he had on hand, spread the word that he could use a few give-aways and borrowed to fill in the gaps. By August he was making plans for next summer. *This* summer.

But *they* had turned him down.

Those assholes.

For the sake of his disappointment, she hated them in-stantly, whoever they were. For the sake of his feelings, she suppressed her own.

"Why?" she asked.

He shook his head slowly. "I guess they thought I was trying to use the horse camp as a way to get grant money to fix the place up."

"How could anybody think that? That's just wrong."

"Politics is politics, Emmie. Even in Indian country." He looked up, squared his shoulders and slid into his comfort zone. "You can go back a hundred years, even more. Hell, Sitting Bull's assassination was as much about Indian politics as it was U.S. government. You remember how the army settled a bunch of stray Yanktonai people on the

North Dakota side of the reservation and gave them police uniforms? Was it North Dakota then, or Dakota Territory? I know this was Standing Rock Sioux Indian Reservation by then, shrunken way down from what we'd first agreed to, but still, there was a lot more to it than what we've got now. Anyway—"

"Daddy…"

"Listen and learn, Pinky. Us Hunkpapa, we never hardly got along with those East River Sioux. Especially the bunch they moved in on us when they started setting up reservations. Pretty soon they were all signing onto the Allotment Act like good reservation Indians, and Sitting Bull was talkin' against it with every breath down to his last. And that's why we ended up losing so much—"

"How could they turn it down, Daddy?" she persisted.

He glanced away, and she felt guilty for denying him a transparent bit of cover.

"There was nothing in it for us," she said quietly. Not only did she want to know how and why it got turned down, but exactly who made the decision. She wanted their names so she could hate them properly. Her father deserved better. "It was all about the kids. Getting kids together with horses. Now, *that's* a match made in heaven."

"We can still have our—" He laid his fork down and cocked his head like a watchdog. "We got company." He raised a cautionary finger as he slid his chair back. "You should've warned me, Em."

"About…?"

"Your friend. Your mom's friend. Ran into her at the casino last night." He took a quick look out the window. "Taking a little detour on her way to California."

"Ella's here?" She met her father's accusatory glance

with a triumphant smile. "I didn't know for sure, Daddy, and I didn't want to get your hopes up."

"My hopes? Give me a break, Pinky. You know damn well…"

But the dogs were barking, and she began pulling her hair up into a ponytail as she hurried out the front door. Perfect timing! The grant had fallen through, but here was her backup plan. Better than backup, she thought, as she patted one of two suddenly very animated dogs. If Ella recommended Daddy's place for her show, it was a done deal. She couldn't believe how far the scheme had come from its birth as a wild idea that Mother would never go for and Ella would never agree to and Daddy would never…

She paused for a backward glance at her father, who had followed her and now stood on the trailer steps, arms folded, giving her a look that said, *Nice try, Emmie.* A grant from the Tribe was one thing. A hookup with Monica Wilson-Black and company was a horse of a whole different color.

Which put a slight hitch in Emily's giddyup, but not enough that the man behind her or the woman ahead would notice. Besides, this had all started with horses of color.

"You made it!" Emily ducked a low-hanging cottonwood branch and opened her arms to the visitor. "I was afraid you might change your mind."

"You made it," Ella amended. "I was afraid you'd be sensible and take your time. Did your father tell you? He and I had supper together last night at the casino and kind of—" she reined in an effusive gesture, sidestepped a nosy black-and-tan shepherd, and lowered her voice "—shared a few divergent thoughts."

"Hey, we got ourselves another calf wrestler." Dillon hissed at the two dogs as he approached. They slunk a few feet away. "That's what you signed on for, isn't it, Hollywood?"

"If that's the entry-level job," Ella said. "Although, I don't remember signing anything."

"You don't? Don't you remember how we played some cards, and you had a few drinks and started betting more than what you had on you?"

"That isn't exactly the way I remember it."

"Cheap wine'll do that to you, especially when you drink the whole bottle." Emily was relieved when her father hooked an arm around her shoulders and gave her a teasing squeeze. "Don't worry, Em. As always, your ol' man was the perfect gentleman. But whatever you women are trying to finagle, you can be damn sure it won't be at my expense."

"That's the beauty of it, Daddy. It's up to Ella, of course, but if this flies, it won't cost us anything."

"I don't know what kind of flyin' we're talking about, honey, but if you believe that, then we need to plug some holes in your education." He winked at Ella. "Welcome to the Wolf Trail, Miz Champion."

"Thank you." Ella had a perfunctory smile for her host, and an aside for her hostess. "You could have warned me about the attitude."

"Sorry. Guess I've been winging it without the warning system in place." Emily glanced at her father and shrugged. "Who knew you two were so defenseless?"

He stared at her, trying not to laugh. He failed.

"As for you winning the clothes off Ella's back…"

"Now, Pinky, that's not what I said."

"Or did," Ella said. "The truth is, *I* beat the pants off *him*." She eyed the pair of dogs, who hadn't quite given up on getting something out of the proceedings, and then dared a few steps for a clear view of the outbuildings. "I like the church. How old is it?"

"Ninety years, give or take," he said, moving around Emily as Ella's interest focused on the church. *Give or take* was just his way of talking. He could recount the building's years by the paint he'd painstakingly scraped off layer by layer. "Some of the windows are the old wavy glass. The back part with the doors and the plumbing, that section is a little newer. So is the oak paneling, which got painted over somewhere along the way. Getting down to the natural wood was the first challenge. It took me…"

They were several yards away before she was missed.

"You comin', Pinky?"

Grinning, she shook her head.

"Good. Anybody shows up, tell 'em…" He was intercepted by a second thought. "Hey, did you know that Ella's one of our Yanktonai cousins from east of the Missouri River? East River Sioux, we call them."

"I know about the family history, Daddy." Emily laughed and waved them on their way.

"Uncle Nick!" Emily leaped off the trailer steps and into the big man's arms, knocking off his black cowboy hat and nearly bowling him over. Nothing flustered Nick Red Shield like an attack of affection. Like an injection of red dye, the proof of his discomfiture spread through the tentacles of the Rorschach-looking burn scar on the side of his neck.

Emily was one of the few people who could get away with planting a kiss on that very spot. "Where're Auntie Lauren and the babies?"

"Home." Nick swept his hat off the ground and flicked a piece of grass off the crown. "Where chaos reigns. My house is full of women rattling pots and pans and kids rattling the rafters. Had to get out of there before they tied an apron on me." He put on his hat, adjusted the brim. "Where's your dad?"

"Right now he's giving the grand tour." She peered past Nick, surveying the corrals and the adjacent lot, where cows and calves noisily awaited the day's activities. "We have a visitor. There they are." She pointed and waved at the two figures emerging from the side door of the barn. "She's a television producer."

"She almost looks Indian."

"Almost like me? That would be half," Emily reminded him as Ella waved back. "You've heard of Thelma Bear Dancer?"

"The AIM leader? That can't be her. Thelma's older than me."

"She would be if she wasn't dead. That's her daughter. She's interested in Daddy's church."

"Taking it off his hands or joining some…" Nick's smile faded. "Don't tell me, let me guess. He's got this one thinkin' he's a preacher."

Emily burst out laughing.

"The next hot televangelist, right?" The twinkle crept back into Nick's eyes. "What did you say her job is? Producer? Whatever that means." He hooked his thumbs in the pockets of his jeans. "Assuming your ol' man hasn't switched visions on us, how are the plans for this summer's Mystic Warrior Horse Camp coming?"

"Getting turned down for that grant put a major crimp in Plan A."

Nick scowled. "First I've heard about it. Damn." He turned his attention toward the front of the church, where the other two had paused for a close look at the cinder-block foundation her father had built himself. "I offered to help out, but you know how he is sometimes. Just tell me what you need, Em."

"A few more connections and a lot less pride." She touched Nick's long shirtsleeve. "Be nice to our visitor, Uncle Nick. She's my Plan B."

Nick responded to his partner's unintelligible shout with a subtle gesture, equally indecipherable. "Whatever your dad's sellin', she looks ready to buy. If you're the one came up with these plans, I'll assume B ain't for bullshit."

"You know me better than that, Uncle Nick."

"After all, she's…Wasn't her mother from someplace like Wisconsin?"

"Minnesota. Daddy gets his nose in the air and says East River Sioux like he's talking about the Mason-Dixon. We just nod. We have a lot in common, Ella and me." She gave Nick an apologetic glance. "She's a friend of my mother's."

"I've got nothing against your mother." He gave a jerk of his chin in the direction of the old church. "But does she know her friend is your Plan B?"

"Oh, yes," she was happy to report. "Mother's totally down with it. She's the one who pitched Ella the idea."

"Well, Em, there's one thing I know for sure." Eyes on the approaching twosome, Nick leaned closer to Emily's ear. "He can't sell her anything that's got my name on it."

Emily knew next to nothing about the terms of their partnership, but she would have bet her senior year's tuition that they weren't written down anywhere.

"What if she's the one who's trying to sell *him* on something? Like a free renovation. Church, barn, trailer— whatever they decide to make over for our summer camp."

"What's the catch?" Nick Red Shield was one fearsome-looking Indian when he scowled.

"They film it and show it on TV."

"What for?"

"For people to watch, Uncle Nick, but don't say anything yet, okay?" He was staring at her, dumbfounded, and her father was fast approaching earshot range. "You wouldn't object if Ella picked the Mystic Warrior Horse Camp as a makeover project for her TV show, would you? You gotta work with me, Uncle Nick." She glanced in her dad's direction and cut Nick off with a desperate, *"Don't say anything."*

He shot back an incredulous look before turning to her father for rhyme or reason. "Is this the branding crew you said you'd round up, D? I'm already up to my neck in females back at the house."

"Don't judge Wolf Trail hospitality by my partner, Ella. He has his own brand of humor that nobody else gets," her father said. "Ella's Emily's recruit. Started punchin' cows before she lost her milk teeth. She was just telling me her mother named her for Ella Deloria. You know who she was, Em?"

"I know about Vine Deloria, Jr. I did a paper on his book, *Custer Died For Your Sins.* Any relation?"

"Ella was his aunt," Nick supplied as he shook Ella's hand. "She grew up right down the road here in Wakpala."

"But she was 'East River Sioux' as Dillon calls us," Ella said. "I don't know about any particular relation, but my mother was big on Indian heroes and Indian history. Ella Deloria was one of her heroes, because she put herself through college at a time when that just didn't happen for Indians, especially women. And then she did major work with Franz Boaz—big-name linguist studying Native languages back in the day. So I was curious enough to take some anthropology and linguistics courses in college. Boaz was a revolutionary in his field, but my mother was of the opinion that he got all the credit for Ella's work thanks to unimpeachable credentials—white skin and a penis." She paused.

Waiting for a response? Emily wondered. She stole a glance at painfully poker-faced Uncle Nick, whose blush had just gone from up-to-the-neck to over-the-head. She slid Ella a bobbing eyebrow salute.

And then her father laughed. He slapped his partner's back and jarred loose a lopsided smile. "She's kinda shy, but she'll probably loosen up once she gets to know us a little better."

"Actually, that wasn't true," Ella went on without cracking a smile. "About Boaz."

"Credentials came up short," her father supposed, light dancing in his eyes.

"No, he really did have a high regard for..." Ella glanced from face to face, found something lacking and withdrew with a diffident shrug. "Anyway, yes, I was named for Ella Deloria, the anthropologist."

"Then you have roots here," Nick allowed. "We don't ask to see any credentials. We're just glad to have the help." He turned to Emily. "How am I doing?"

She gave a nod of approval.

"So far, so good?" Nick gave her ponytail a playful tug. "I've got the vet supplies in the pickup, college girl. You wanna vaccinate or castrate?"

Emily knew better. No matter what she'd been studying, a woman would never handle the castrating knife at a Wolf Trail branding. She had asked for the job once and been turned down flat, lest her psyche be claimed by some ball-busting spirit, like Calamity Jane or Deer Woman. Branding had its traditions, and in this corner of the world, you had a cowboy-and-Indian blending of ways. Kids wrestled the calves to the ground, stretched them out and held them, while the branding crew organized to minimize the duration of each animal's ordeal.

Emily wielded the vaccination gun, while her aunt Josie ran around stapling numbered tags to fuzzy ears. As the owners of both brand and branded, her father and Uncle Nick shared the chore of applying the scalding end of the iron to the calves' right flanks, the part of the hide specified by their registered brand: a paw enclosing a T.

Vincent Many Wounds had the dubious distinction of being the "cutter." Two young apprentices followed close behind—one with a "ball bucket" and the other with antiseptic spray. Hank Two Dog was in charge of snapping off the bull calves' horns, while his son, Ben, used a thin piece of wire to trim a few older cows' twisted horns. Acrid smoke filled the air as calf shit flew and small hooves got in their licks, and helpers hurried to keep the whole assembly moving toward the final calf and the customary feed.

With the exception of castrating, Ella got to try everything. Emily noticed that she became her father's special project, his personal guest, and he wasn't about to let her hang back and watch. She'd totally given in to taking orders, and finally given up on clean jeans when Emily called time-out for a vaccine reload.

"And a pause for the cause," Vincent declared as he entrusted his tools to the ball-bucket boy.

"How worthy a cause are we talkin'?"

"Worth a smoke?"

"Unless you're ready to cowboy up for a little calf-wrestling challenge," her father called out as he opened the gate between the pen full of waiting calves and the working pen. He wasn't about to lose his crew to any major cause pauses. "First team to flop and stretch wins the go-round. Team with the most go-rounds wins the purse. I'm startin' it out with ten bucks."

"I'll put in ten."

"I've only got five."

"I'll spot you, Ben."

Emily saw her father start to tuck the purse into his jeans when Ella slipped a bill into his shirt pocket and patted his chest. He gave his slow, sweet, that's-my-girl grin. "You never met a bet you didn't like?"

"I'm a calf sharp, what can I say?"

Over Ella's shoulder, he flashed Emily a twinkling glance. "This one's got game."

"So take her on." Emily pointed the injection gun at him and smiled. "Go, Daddy-o."

"You got yourself a dance partner, Hollywood. You wanna lead or follow?"

"If I take the front…"

"You make the catch," he said.

"But the back end…"

"…can be messy."

"I was born to lead," she said as she crouched for takeoff.

At Emily's signal, the race was on. Four four-leggeds dodging four two-person teams of two-leggeds, darting in and out of corners and bouncing off fences like billiard balls after a break shot. Ella's first hit was a miss, leaving her rooting around on hands and knees. She scrambled to her feet with Dillon hard on her heels, but a second tentative try earned her a swift kick from a sharp hoof. She yelped, cursed, snarled, then dove directly for the black-and-white head, and pinned it between her breasts. Her partner secured the hind legs, catching a load of crap in the process. They looked up and grinned at each other across the critter's flank like kids sharing a mud bath.

"Did we win?" Ella asked, body bobbling over the bawling calf.

"You took fourth," Uncle Nick reported over the hot iron as he slid Emily a sly wink. "Unless there's a score for style, and then Ella's got my vote."

"Mine, too." Emily glanced up from her task with a smile for Ella.

Ella, too, was all smiles. All for her calf-wrestling partner.

"You okay?" he asked her as they released the calf, and she checked her arms and hands, finding a couple of superficial scrapes.

He made a fuss over the back of her left hand, which had connected with a cloven hoof, sure to turn purple. No big deal, Ella said. Emily's thoughts exactly. It was the kind of attention he generally reserved for his daughter. Probably good for the cause, this getting his flirt on with Ella, but it was strangely unsettling to watch. Emily had to kick herself mentally. It was jealousy, pure and simple.

Grow up, Pinky.

Which was even more unsettling, not because she didn't want to grow up, but because she believed she already had. Ages ago. She'd been an adult for years, independent and enormously responsible. She wasn't playing around, wasn't looking to entertain herself or anyone else with sports or summer camp or the fantasy world of television. Helping her father turn his life around was serious business, as was helping her father's people. She loved him, and she loved the idea of him as a man who actually *had* a people. It was a big idea, a *huge* idea, and she was whole-heartedly his daughter. She was totally connected—no half-assedness or mixed-messaging about it. She could *totally* contribute.

She was needed.

Ella couldn't say that. Who really needed television? Overcome by a wave of sympathy for her fellow half-breed, Emily noticed that her guest had disappeared when her father offered to put her on a horse. Rather than help push the cattle out to pasture, Emily tracked Ella down, found her sketching in a notebook inside the old church.

"Have you won him over?" Emily asked as she closed the heavy oak door behind her. Her voice echoed in the vestibule, where Ella had found inspiration in the massive rafters he had exposed when he tore out the ceiling.

Ella lowered chin to chest, drew a few lines with her bruised hand and came up smiling. "That'll have to be your job. If I offer the gift horse, you'll have to convince him that it doesn't bite."

"It's not about biting. It's about… Did you show him the kind of stuff you guys do?"

"I did. I think it looks like some sort of…" Ella flexed her hand and grimaced. "It looks like charity to him."

"But he was showing you around. I thought that was a good sign."

"He wanted to show me what he has here. It's very impressive. He's…"

"He's very proud." And deep down Emily was proud of him for being proud, because it was her job to give credit where her mother criticized.

"He's worked hard, knows who he is and what he's about," Ella said. "I envy him that. Wouldn't want to mess with it."

"You couldn't." Emily wasn't sure that was true, but she said it anyway. And she pulled up an example. "When Uncle Nick got married and built his house, he told Daddy he could have the trailer for nothing. But no. Daddy's making payments on it. Uncle Nick told him to put the money toward the camp last summer. But no. Daddy's still making his payments on the trailer."

"And a fine trailer it is." Ella flipped a light switch. When nothing happened, she tried another one. Same result. "But I understand there used to be a house?"

Emily nodded. "Across the highway. I only remember bits and pieces, like the closet my mother turned into a pantry. I could sit in there for hours, especially in the fall, when it smelled like apples. The trees are still there." She shook off the memory. "But that was all pre-Wolf Trail. Uncle Nick says they built this place together. Daddy says it was all Uncle Nick."

"You believe Uncle Nick?"

"After my parents split up, we didn't see much of my father for a while. He'd come to the Cities with Uncle Nick for a day or two for a birthday or something. They'd stay in a hotel, and Mother would drop us off and pick us up. But after a while she softened up and invited him to stay at the house, and he'd come for Christmas, and we'd come out here in the summer. I got old enough, I'd come out on my own for a few weeks or a month. D.J. wasn't interested. He's a homebody. Seriously into music."

"He's good at it," Ella said.

"He really is." Emily smiled. Everyone was proud of D.J. Everyone close to him, anyway—four people—and one closely related but not close, which made five. "Anyway, I don't blame anyone anymore. I don't know how my parents ever ended up together, to tell you the truth. They're so different. You know how much she loves her work, and she could never do that here."

"She was a teacher."

"And he was a rodeo cowboy when they first met." She made a face that said *Imagine!* "The funny thing is, I think they loved each other in their way, and maybe they still do. But that's probably just wishful thinking on my part. Kids want to believe their parents love each other."

"I never held that belief about my parents," Ella tossed off, "but that's a whole different story."

"Your mother was Indian and your father was white."

"And yet different from your parents." She shook her head, gave a little laugh. "You seem to identify equally with both."

"I don't know about equally. I never measured. Like you said, my father knows who he is and where he came from. My mother…" Emily glanced toward one of the original tall windows but not through it. The image of Monica Wilson-Black had imposed itself in the space, palms up, like the supplicant Madonna. "My mother is a self-made woman. Self-conceived and self-made. What family there is on her side is pretty much estranged."

"Maybe that's what she and I have in common."

It struck Emily as a sad commentary, even though Ella sounded upbeat and confident. Like Mother.

"This could be a great project for you, Ella. I guarandamn-tee it wouldn't be like anything you've done before."

"I'm interested, but you need to work on your father."

"If I can get him to agree, can you really make it happen?"

"There are a few things I have to check on to make sure

it's feasible out here in God's country, but I'm pretty good at what I do. And what I do is make shows happen." She slipped her hand into the crook of Emily's elbow. "But this is just between you and me, Emily. I've ridden a horse once, and it ended badly. I admire them. I think they're beautiful animals, but they're scary. Big, bold, beautiful— and scary as hell." She gave Emily's arm a quick squeeze. "I'm a poor excuse for an Indian, no matter which side of the river you're on."

Chapter Eight

When the work was over and the socializing began, Ella sought her natural niche in the woodwork. It wasn't hard to find woodwork on Lauren and Nick Red Shield's backyard deck, but blending in was another matter. The deck seating was apparently male territory. Dillon had given her cursory introductions to the women in the kitchen, filled her request for iced tea from a pitcher in the refrigerator, then hauled her outside and sat her down next to him, where she clearly didn't belong but, deep down, didn't mind being. She wasn't a kitchen person.

She wasn't a party person, either, but between hanging in the kitchen with a bunch of women she didn't know and sticking with Dillon and the guys, well, the choice was a no-brainer. And it wasn't about Dillon. Her choice would be the same on the set of the show. It was carpentry over domesticity, hands down. All she had to do was keep quiet. Once the men got busy one-upping each other, a quiet woman could easily pass for a knot in the wood. The trick—learned during her days as a small fly on the wall in her mother's shadow—was not to laugh out loud.

And, okay, it was a little bit about Dillon. She wasn't

crazy about branding calves, but she would do it again in his company. She'd had a feeling about the man the first time she'd laid eyes on him, when they'd both been in Monica's company. A damper, to be sure, but nothing like Mama and her far-reaching shadow.

Ella welcomed the afternoon shadows lengthening across the deck and, at last, falling across her face like a camouflage net. A refuge, comforting on more levels than she cared to consider. She was too busy considering who among the branding crew might serve on demolition, carpentry or landscaping. Observation was her strong suit. Her eye for character and chemistry made the difference between a memorable episode of *Who's Our Neighbor?* and a dud. And these guys had potential.

"You believe that, Hollywood? Hank's older boy, Sam—he's about so high," Dillon began, his level hand indicating an unlikely four feet above the deck. "What is he, eighteen, Hank? Twenty? You'd take him for a lightweight, but he's like Ben here. Pure muscle. So he's hanging out one night over in Fargo, and some asshole accuses him of being illegal."

"Underage?" Ella asked.

"Under the wrong flag."

"You mean, *undocumented.*"

"Un-white," Hank clarified as he gave a hand-it-over gesture for the can of pop his son, Ben, had just pulled dripping from the ice chest. "The kid's un-verbal, but underdeveloped he sure as hell ain't. Big redneck thinks he's gonna entertain his friends by making the brown kid holler *tio,* so Sam knocks his lights out."

"You believe now they want Sam to pay for the guy's dental work? Where I come from, you pick the wrong fight, you get to lick your own wounds." Dillon turned back to Hank, eyebrow arched.

"Is your son getting sued?" Ella asked Hank.

"He's getting screwed. Charged with aggravated assault. They barely opened those ambulance doors, and that farmer was all lawyered up."

"Some Texas-size jackass comes in begging to get his teeth knocked out, you don't dare oblige him unless your papers are all in order," Vincent Many Wounds put in. "You gotta sympathize with those illegals."

"I think the preferred term is *undocumented*," Ella said, compelled to try again.

"How do they rate a preferred term when they come here illegally?" Vincent wondered.

"They're just looking for honest work," said Ben as he popped the top on a second can of Coke. "I got a friend up in—"

"Il-*le*-gal," Vincent sang out.

"Yeah, but if they start up that guest-worker program like they been talkin' about..."

"Hey, why didn't we think of that?" Dillon said, turning to Nick. "We should have started a guest-worker program." He tapped Ella's thigh with the back of his hand. "About five hundred years ago."

Her Indian half laughed. Her other half cut it short. She wasn't sure which half Dillon had meant to tap.

"I'm thinkin' about it now," Nick said as he glanced toward the sliding patio door. "Thinkin' it's about time we fed our guest workers. Don't know what the holdup is."

"Ain't none of us here goin' hungry, Nick." Vincent slapped his paunch.

"Nobody's going hungry in this country anymore,

Vince," Hank said. "You heard the latest from our old friend, the USDA? They do their reports, hunger is now officially called *food insecurity*."

"Bubbles," Dillon called out to a little girl who'd been lurking near the screen slider. Eagerly she zip-zipped the door and scooted across the deck, flip-flops whapping her heels. "Go tell the cooks that nobody's hungry, but your uncle Nick's showing signs of food insecurity." Dillon took the half-full glass from Ella's hand. "And bring us some more iced tea."

"Just some ice in that would be fine," Ella said. He glanced at her, questioning, and she whispered, "That would actually make it iced tea."

"Sounds like drink insecurity." He patted her knee. "Cold tea is officially listed as iced tea by the USDA. That's with or without ice."

"Right." She'd eaten enough USDA surplus commodities growing up to know that coffee and tea weren't on any list. "Who needs complications?"

"Dillon says you work in TV," said Vincent. "How does a guy get to be on *Survivor?* I could kick ass on that show."

"She-iit, Vince, your tribe voted you off the island a long time ago," Hank said. "We wanna make the Final Four, but we're talkin' the game of life, man. Native survivors. You gotta be hungry. You can't fake that shit." The smaller man gave Vince's round belly a nod. "Your food security is draggin' our side down."

Eyes twinkling, Dillon tag-teamed. "We might survive some of those little eastern tribes, but no chance we're gonna outlive those skinny Crows."

Muttering ensued.

"Crow people are skinny?"

"Not the ones I know."

"Hell, I got a brother-in-law, lives over in Billings…"

"I'm serious. Talkin' to my cousin, here." Vincent leaned toward Ella. "Seriously, can you hook me up for *Survivor?*"

"I wish I could, but that's a different network. I work on a makeover show. I'm here to check out—" she glanced at Dillon, whose eyes said *don't go there* "—some horses I might be interested in."

"Having our mares made over, are we?" Nick turned to Ella. "Watch out for this guy. He'll do anything for a date."

"I was thinkin' surgical enhancement for True Colors," Dillon said. "Add a few inches of stud power. You get in front of the camera, serious as all hell, and you say, 'Yeah, pedigrees don't mean much to our Lakota mares. They expect full service. Size matters.'"

"Damn. Is that what this is about?"

"Hey, TV these days. The nastier things get, the better the ratings." Dillon shook his head. "No shame."

Nick laughed. "Tell you what, Ella, if you can get my little friend to go on TV, *serious as hell*, and say *size matters,* I'll give you just about any horse on the place."

"Whoa." Dillon straightened his right knee and raised his boot heel a few inches off the deck. "This here's a size twelve boot, man. You know what that means."

"Like he said, no shame." But Nick's interest in one-upping his partner slid away with the appearance of his petite blond wife at the patio door. His dark eyes took on a sparkle that brightened his whole face. "Are we on for dinner?" he asked.

"Absolutely," she said, seemingly all for him. "And bring your friends."

The procession filed through the kitchen, past two each

of Nick's sisters and Dillon's, who were tending to food or dishes or toddlers. Emily headed outdoors with a pack of older children, and Lauren Red Shield directed traffic. The long dining room table was set for the branding crew—Nick's and Dillon's "guest workers." Platters piled high with meat, bowls of boiled, baked and fried food, cold, sliced, mixed and melded food—all traveled the length of the table, hand to hand. A basket of Nick's sisters' fresh fry bread was especially well received. Ella couldn't resist. What harm could one piece of deep-fried bread dough every ten years do? The bad news was that it was fried in lard. The good news? No trans fat.

Fry bread would have to be worked into the show. She envisioned a more traditional feed—buffalo, venison, dried roots and berries reconstituted into soup—and, yes, mostly for show. *The* show. Ella was all about the show.

"So, Ella, what kind of makeovers do you do on TV?" came the challenge from the head of the table.

"We do big renovation projects. We build stuff that can change lives. For instance…" She glanced over to find Dillon diligently attending to the food on his plate. "Well, we were talking about immigration a few minutes ago. I'm looking at a project for a woman who took a bunch of kids who were born here but their parents were undocumented. They got caught when a meatpacking plant was raided by the INS, and they were deported."

"That happens?" Nick frowned with concern. "Kids separated from their parents?"

"All kinds of stuff happens when people are caught between a rock and a hard place," Ella said with a shrug. "I don't know the details yet, but this woman has a three-bedroom house and she's taken in eight kids. It could be an interesting story. We have a legal team checking out the particulars and the ramifications of the particulars. Part of my job is to make sure we don't walk into any minefields."

"Sounds like a dangerous job," Dillon said. "Like scouting for Custer."

"Yep. Clowns to the left, jokers to the right, me watching every step."

A voice from behind said, "I know the feeling."

Ella turned to find Lauren smiling, first woman-to-woman and then hostess to table. She carried her daughter on one hip as she delivered a basket of hot fry bread with her free hand. "Can I get anyone anything else?"

No requests came amid the pithy compliments around the table. Ella had almost forgotten the drill. She could hear the women laughing and chatting in the kitchen, riding herd on the children, rattling dishes in the sink, and she remembered being thirteen and making every effort to avoid that scene. When she grew up, no way would she hide out in the kitchen while the men sat around the table and called for refills. She would keep to herself and do her own thing. Something interesting and important.

Movement next to her elbow caught her attention. Was Dillon a mind reader?

"Sit down here, Mrs. Red Shield," he said as he bussed his place, glanced at Ella for permission to take her plate and chucked the baby's chin. Three seconds, three females charmed. "Trade tales of fame and glamour with Ella while I hold my goddaughter. Hey, little Nicole. Little *kola*." He grabbed glasses and spoons, took the stack to the kitchen, and returned to take the baby from her mother before Ella had fully formed a timely baby compliment.

She followed Dillon's lead on the chin chucking. "You

must've been named for your daddy, because you look so much like him."

"What're you, crazy?" Dillon jiggled his armful of drooling, Clara Bow-mouthed kid. He didn't seem to mind her gnawing on his thumb. "This is one beautiful little girl we've got here. She looks a little bit like her aunties, a little bit like her mom and a little bit like a spring filly with big brown eyes and long, skinny legs. Ouch! And sharp teeth. You definitely got *those* from your daddy."

"Daddy," the little girl said as she leaned toward Nick, arms outstretched. He stood up from his chair, grinning, offering his big hands as a come-on.

"Go, then. Break my heart," Dillon said.

Lauren offered coffee and suggested the three of them escape to the lower-level family room, which boasted a gorgeous rock fireplace surrounded by a view of the South Dakota buttes and a plentiful dose of quiet.

"How did you get into television production, Ella?" Lauren asked after noting that the house was little more than a year old, still a lot to do, excuse the mess—nothing Ella hadn't heard every time she walked into someone's home once they found out what she did for a living and to which Ella generally replied, *What mess?* "It must be exciting, getting to make a TV show."

Ella nodded, surprised to find herself grateful for Lauren's interest. "I started out in Minneapolis, like Dillon's... Like Monica. You've probably seen the show. Or *her* show, anyway. I studied filmmaking and got a job at a local TV station. There was still a good deal of local programming then, but now, with more cable..." She glanced at Dillon, whose gaze skittered away as he took a sip from his cup. "Do you know Monica?" she asked Lauren.

"I haven't met her, but I got to know Emily last summer, and I know she's very proud of her mother's work. Which I haven't seen, since we don't have satellite. We just don't have much time for TV."

"A voice from the real world. We don't like to hear that. We like to think we're the center of everyone's world. All eyes on the box." Ella shrugged. "Monica's show is local. Mine's national. But if you're not into home improvement or home decorating or reality…"

"This is my reality." Lauren's blue eyes twinkled as she gave an expansive gesture. "I've tried the bling-seeker's life where the world is some kind of oyster and you think it's all yours. It's not. And, really, who wants to live in an oyster?"

"Lauren is one of the best jockeys who ever straddled a racehorse," Dillon explained.

"*Was,*" said Lauren. "Not that I couldn't still beat the breeches off most of them if I really wanted to."

"Daddy!"

Three heads turned as Emily came bounding down the steps like a thundering steam engine. "Daddy, why didn't you tell me about Jimmy Taylor?"

The leather chair squeaked as Dillon straightened. "I haven't had much of a chance."

"But you knew," she said, standing over him.

"Just barely, and I thought it would keep until—"

"Danny and I are going up to see him."

"They won't let you in, Pinky." He reached for her hand. "I called."

"Did you talk to him? Is he okay?"

"I talked to his mother, and he's doin' good. He's lucky they—"

"Lucky? Daddy!" Eyes wide, Emily stepped back, and

Dillon stood as her hand slid away from his. "I can't believe that boy would try to kill himself, I just can't. Danny says his girlfriend ditched him. I don't even believe he had a girlfriend."

"No matter what you believe, the kid's layin' up there in the psych ward." Dillon laid a hand on his daughter's shoulder, quietly adding, "Shit happens, Em. I don't care who you are or where you live."

"He can't be more than sixteen," Emily said softly. "D.J.'s age."

"I know." He slid his arm around her shoulder and turned to include the women. "We've all been sixteen. Who wants to be sixteen again? Let's see a show of hands."

"Stop it, Daddy. You're not fooling anybody. This is why we needed that grant. Why we need—"

"We'll do it just like we did last year. No, better." Dillon squeezed Emily's shoulders once, twice, as though he were inflating a balloon with a hand pump. "We'll do a three-day ride at the end, after everybody's all bonded with their horses, and we'll have—"

"Without a dorm, we need daily transportation," she reminded her father as she separated herself from his embrace and, presumably, his fantasy. "And we need insurance, no matter what."

"I can get the church…" He jammed his hands into the back pockets of his jeans. "Hell, I've been screwin' around with different plans long enough. I need to settle on one and just get 'er done. It won't take me more than—"

"Even with a dorm, we'd have to pass all kinds of inspections, Daddy. *We need help.*"

"Nick's offer still stands," Lauren said gently.

Dillon ignored her. "That was a damn good proposal. I

was sure it would get funded." He shook his head. "Guess I fell asleep at the wheel."

"Nick wants to help, Dillon," Lauren was more insistent this time. "He really wants—"

"Yeah, I know. Super Nick. He thrives on saving the day," Dillon said, but then he shook off the attitude, beseeching his daughter with his hand out like a supplicant. "Look, we've got people here. We've got family and neighbors, even Hollywood's come calling." With no taker on the hand, he buried it in his pocket again. "We'll keep tabs on Jimmy, Em. I'll call again tonight. Right now, the one thing I need help with is pitchin' the pants off your uncle Nick in the horseshoe pit. I could use a partner."

Emily begged off. Ella accepted the role of second choice. She thought better of asking any questions or making any offers herself, especially in front of witnesses. But she knew more than she cared to about Indians and suicide statistics. The numbers were bad. Turning a number into a name made it worse. Jimmy Taylor, suicide attempted.

Thelma Bear Dancer, found dead in the woods. Suicide accomplished.

Chapter Nine

Dillon was surprised to find the little white rental car parked beside the trailer when he got back from Nick's. She'd said she was going back to the hotel, and he was sure he'd seen the last of her. He was sorry about that, but he would get over it. She was pretty much Monica's emissary, anyway. People were always passing through Indian country. And sometimes those people were Indians.

Dillon himself had left Indian country once, thinking he could take his heritage with him. All he'd needed was a decent job—one that could hold a candle to his wife's profession—and he would be able to build a house, turn it into a home and take care of his family.

He'd followed Nick to the western oil fields and taken to roughnecking like a duck to water—or an Indian cowboy to anything that bucked. But an oil-rig explosion was more than a kicker. It was like a plane crash. It had taken the life of Nick's younger brother and most of the skin off Nick's body, leaving him with wounds that would have killed most men. Nobody got out unscathed. Soon afterward, Dillon and Monica had lost their second baby. That was enough sojourning in the wilderness for Dillon. To her credit, his wife had given him a few more years and another child, but his home had never suited her. She'd started telling him so, straight out. He'd refused to believe her until she was gone.

No matter what you believe, shit happens.

She'd done well.

No matter what you believe, you gotta know Monica's gonna do well. And that's no shit. That's Monica.

She was the mother of his kids, and she'd done well by them. Through it all—with a little help from a man who had been to hell and back—Dillon had learned to hold his head up and give his family what they were willing to accept from him. They never talked about the bad times. He was lucky to get more than a few words at a time out of his son, but his daughter still seemed to think he'd hung the moon. And Monica?

She tolerated him. He wondered what she thought he'd taken from her, besides the years. They'd given each other two children, and she'd had her say over them until Emmie decided for herself where she was going to college and what she was going to study. That hadn't gone over too good at first, but now…

Now what was she up to?

In the dark, Dillon patted the two dogs as he mounted the steps to the trailer door.

What was Monica's friend's rented car doing in his driveway way the hell out in what Monica liked to call God's country? What in the name of all that was holy was this damn TV thing *really* about?

She looked up from whatever she was doing with the papers spread all over the kitchen table and smiled. "Hi."

"Hi, yourself." He closed the door behind him and swept

off his cowboy hat. He felt as though he was the guest. Probably just out of habit. He generally was.

"You don't lock your doors."

"I've got discriminating dogs." He set his hat on the shelf above the coat hooks beside the door. "They only keep the bad people out. Much better than locks." He gave a quizzical look. "Did you forget something?"

"No. Is Emily…?" She glanced past him expectantly.

"I thought she might've left with you, but Lauren found her asleep in the baby's room." He'd stood there between the crib that held Nick's sleeping daughter and the twin bed where his own daughter slept and entertained the kind of where-does-the-time-go thoughts a guy's heart could only stand for about thirty seconds. "Surprised she lasted as long as she did."

"What about the boy?" she asked, and again his question was in his look. "The one who tried to commit suicide. She was pretty upset. Have you heard any more?"

"We'll try to see him tomorrow." He eased himself into the chair across the table from her. "She's right. I sure didn't see that one comin'. I know I sounded hard-assed, sayin' stuff like nobody wants to be sixteen. Thank God my sixteen-year-old wasn't there to hear it. Thank God he's got…" he gestured, open- and empty-handed "…so much goin' for him."

"As opposed to this other boy?"

"As opposed to what he might have had. As opposed to…" Dillon turned his palms to the table and stared at the backs of his brown, rough, unadorned hands. "I've always liked kids. Always wanted a houseful. Last summer we had ten, fifteen at a time here, and, man, we had some good times. Not that it wasn't work, but the kids worked, too. Jimmy—the boy we were just talkin' about—Jimmy was scared to try, at first, and he didn't say much, kinda hung back and watched. I kept thinkin', *we won't be seein' this kid around tomorrow.* But he kept on coming back." He shook his head. "But now, Christ, he almost left us for good."

"He's back," Ella said quietly. "He gets to be sixteen until he turns seventeen."

"Instead of forever." And that was the long and short of it. Shit happened sometimes, but not always. Close calls happened. Wake-up calls. Second chances. If you could turn a kid around at sixteen, help him find a good way... "What would we have to do for this TV show?"

"If we were to choose this project, you'd basically have to sign a few weeks of your life away. You'd agree to let us completely rebuild your place, film the project and televise it, and you'd agree to participate in certain aspects of the production. That's all. When the film crew leaves, it's all yours."

"No strings?"

She shrugged. "You actually get warranties on tons of stuff, which is protection for the production company, as well as for you. We treat you better than most construction contractors would. We can't afford not to. We're a feel-good show, and we don't want anyone feeling bad and calling a press conference over it."

"A few weeks," he echoed. "What's a few?"

"Usually no more than two. Production time is the most expensive part of the deal, so we employ a lot of highly-trained people to get the actual job done. There's some pre-production, and we also do a little follow-up segment about six weeks later, give or take, so that people can see how well things are going."

He continued to stare at his hands. "Emily's pretty excited about the idea, but to me..."

"I wanted to show you some of the possibilities I've come up with, but I was hoping Emily would be with you," she said as she slid one paper behind another. "I need an ally."

"If it's an ally you want, you've got me. I'm a full-blooded ally." He looked up, smiled a little. "That's what Lakota means. So you're never really friendless."

"What about Dakota? That would be me."

"And you would be one letter off." His smile broadened. He liked the new topic. "Different dialect is all. But you guys missed out on all the fun by hangin' back East while we went west and found the horses."

"Don't you mean, stole the horses?"

"Okay, sometimes they had to be liberated. And that's what allies do for their friends, they set them free. And then if they follow you home, well…" He lifted one shoulder. "*Sunka wakan* is what we called our friend the horse—holy dog—and they blessed us with a mystical alliance that made us who we are. Have you ever read *Mystic Warriors of the Plains?*"

She shook her head, and he went to the living room, then came back with the hefty book. He plunked it down on the table, ignoring the papers she'd arranged like a checkerboard. Drawings. He figured she would get to those. But this was his territory—the surroundings *and* the subject. He flipped through the pages for her benefit. The book was full of drawings. Warriors in all their ancient glory—gear, garb, wisdom and ways. He loved the artwork. He knew the text. He believed in the title.

"We had a good thing goin' there for a while." This he believed with his whole heart and soul.

"The casino is called Prairie Knights. The lords of the Plains?"

"That's not it. Stewards of the Plains, maybe. Wasn't no Dust Bowl when we were in charge." He drummed the book with all four right-hand fingertips. "It's important for our kids to see these pictures and put them together with who we are. This is in our blood. Horses changed our ancestors' lives, and they can change our kids' lives, too."

"*Your* kids. My mother's people hung back in the East and missed all the fun, remember?"

"You had a few horses. And you ended up with better casino sites," he reminded her. He liked her smile. Damn, he really liked her smile.

"More power to us, huh?"

"More *maza ska*. Money is power in the world we're livin' in now."

"Yeah, but *Casino Power* would make a crappy bumper sticker. Remember *Red Power?*" She tapped his arm, that smile sparkling in her eyes. "Remember *Fry Bread Power?*"

"You were just a kid," he said.

"I watched a lot of demonstrations as a kid. My mother was an urban Indian, just like most of the rabble-rousers back in the day. She had her standing list of demands, but as far as I know, tribal gaming wasn't among them. All that came along after she died, and by that time I had my own interests and issues. And dreams."

"Movies?"

"Television, the way it can be and ought to be. It reaches virtually everyone and there's so much you can do with it. There's no reason why we have to do twenty-nine versions of the same show." She leaned in, dark eyes flashing with enthusiasm. "I love documentaries. What you've got here could be the basis for a wonderful prime-time documentary. What you said. Put these pictures together with who we…who you are. Not the same old poorest-county-in-the-country exposé of one of our reservations. But you have to put the two together, and it has to be…" She flattened her palms over her checkerboard. "Can I show you some sketches?"

"This is for a documentary?"

"I'm not there yet. You can't do those until you've racked up a lot of credits. I need to hook up with somebody like Ken Burns, or…" She chose a page from the middle row and turned it toward him. "No, this is where I am, and this is what I do. And these are just some ideas for your youth camp. This would be like a little village. Nothing hokey like a movie set."

"Why not?" He was looking at circles and cones.

"Because you wouldn't go for it."

He looked up and gave a single-shoulder shrug. "Some of the best-known Indian activists went Hollywood."

"You're not an Indian activist. You're an Indian cowboy, and this is a ranch," Ella reminded him. "The Wolf Trail Ranch. This is about the past meeting the present in a community of…stewards of the Plains. A horse culture. A place where young people…commune with horses. And caring adults like you." She turned another page toward him. "I love the old church, and I think it should be the centerpiece."

"Why?" She'd drawn a floor plan, and filled it up with boxes and labels. He didn't want to look too closely, get too serious. "Do you know about its history?"

"No, but giving new life to old buildings is one of our specialties."

"How 'bout some coffee?" He pushed his chair back from the table. "Or tea, if you wanna try Black Bear's custom blend."

"Black Bear?"

"My grandfather. My father went and shortened it. The name, not the recipe." On the three-stride way to the kitchen, he tossed back, "You like herbal tea, you might like this. The prairie provides all the ingredients."

"I never knew any of my grandparents," she said offhandedly as she trailed him around the counter separating kitchen from dinette. "So maybe that's why I don't feel...connected."

He questioned her with a look as he handed her two mugs.

She glanced away. "Anyway, I see the church as a gathering place. Kitchen, dining hall, meeting place."

"Makes sense." He checked the contents of the tin box, making sure he could deliver on his promise. The mint smelled almost fresh.

"I haven't really got the lay of the land, but obviously acreage is no object." She inhaled the scent when he offered the tin, and spared a smile and a quick nod. So far, he was so not impressed. "I was thinking two bunkhouses or several smaller cabins," she went on. "At summer camp you always have your cabin mates."

"Did you go to summer camp?" he asked as he filled a saucepan with bottled water.

"No, but I always loved those camp movies."

He turned from the stove. "Did you go to boarding school?"

"No. Did you?"

"Sure did. Used to be, two kinds of kids knew about boarding schools—the rich kind and the Indian kind." He scooped dry leaves into a mesh strainer. "Not so much anymore. They closed most of them."

"That's a good thing, isn't it?"

"Yeah, that's mostly a good thing."

"Emily thinks we should do real tipis, but how could we make those into more permanent structures?"

"You can't. That's the beauty of tipis."

"But then I remembered an episode of Extreme Homes—"

"You talkin' a game or a sport?"

"It's a show about offbeat houses. This hippie couple in Montana, Idaho, bumfuck Canada, someplace in the Rocky Mountains, they lived year-round in this huge tipi they'd built. They used regular furniture, propane powered kitchen, all the comforts."

"You wanna get me laughed into the next county?"

"That's why they call it 'extreme,'" she said, watching his every move. "But maybe some version—"

"Thought you said you didn't wanna do more of the same."

"But right now I'm in reality television, and the reality is that if we didn't use cookie cutters, how would we get our products to fit into the boxes?"

"Whatever that means." Strainer in place, lid on the pan, he folded his arms to await the steeped product. "How about log houses?"

"I said cabins, but that's not Indian."

"It's not *urban* Indian." He chuckled. "Our people have been living in cabins here for more than a hundred years."

"And living in cities for at least half that long," she reminded him. "As long as I can see a growing interest, I won't take offense."

"As long as I keep hearing my daughter's name, I'll act interested."

"So much for the mystic warrior." She set the mugs aside, leaned back against the counter and mirrored his stance. "A good warrior doesn't expose his vulnerable side."

"A Lakota warrior does. He wants you to keep comin' at him. We're not lookin' for a kill. We're counting coups." Holding her gaze with his, he lifted his hand and reached across the scant divide. She stood her ground. "All I want is a touch," he said, and she lifted her chin as he traced the line of her jaw with the backs of his fingers. Slowly, lightly, from her studded earlobe to that small, square chin.

"Dillon…"

"Ella," he answered, as he stepped close, took her face in his hands and touched lips to lips, taking quick sips, one, two, three, four, saying hello. *Hello, hello. Who are you? What is this?*

Hello, yourself, said her lips, giving his pause on a fifth connection.

But then she smiled and whispered, "Who's coming at whom?"

"Depends on how you look at it," he said as he closed his mouth over hers and counted coups on her tongue. He stepped back, smiling. "Coffee, tea or me?"

"Let's keep it simple for now," she said. "Just the tea."

He agreed. "For now."

"And for later, will you consider letting me pitch *your* program for…" she gave a little shrug "…for *my* program?"

"Plugging our programs together." He sucked air through his teeth as though he almost relished the thought. "Sounds hot. I see sparks and spin-offs flyin' in all four directions."

"Six," she quipped, and he gave her a second glance. "You're forgetting sky and earth."

"Four," he insisted, but her glance gave no ground. "Four is the way I've always heard it. It's sacred, you know. Four."

"But you kissed me four little times and two big ones."

She moved the mugs closer to the stove. "I've heard four, but I've also heard six."

"Now you're making it sound like a superstition." He eyed her as he lifted the strainer from the pan. "Don't get the directions confused with rolling dice."

"Counting coups, you said. So I counted."

He laughed.

She poured. "What do you say? Permission granted? I'm talking about giving you a whole lot more than…" She handed him the first mug. "You're a difficult man."

"Hard to get, too." He raised his tea in toast. "Makes me irresistible."

"To nutcrackers and ball breakers, maybe. But I'm not that sporting."

He laughed again. "I love a woman who has an answer for everything."

"Let's see," she began as she ambled toward the table, cradling her mug in both hands. "When a man loves a woman. What's a good comeback?" She picked up one of her drawings, studied it for a moment, shook her head. "Side out."

"Out?"

"My side. Out. I fold." With a soft-handed gesture she drew the vertical half of a cross. "Taking the tipi down—" and then the horizontal "—and going home."

"Is this a Dakota cut and run?"

She tasted her tea, pressed her lips together and smiled. "This is good. You should package it up and sell it."

"Where? In the casino gift…" She was looking at that drawing again, her smile turning wistful. "Is that all there is to it? A church and some tipis? The guy in Oklahoma rated considerably more than that." He leaned closer. "You were supposed to make me drool. I ain't even salivated yet."

"Did, too. You tasted like coffee and cigarettes."

"One drag," he protested, counting on his index finger. "I'm hangin' with the program. Now, what are you *dyin'* to show me this time?"

She slid the edge of the paper slowly between thumb and forefinger, her eyes gleaming. "I asked Emily for ideas, and I told her to dream big."

"Now I'm listening."

She presented the drawing as though she'd written her whole name for the first time. It was an indoor arena—floor plan and elevated views.

"The ultimate training facility." She moved to his side and peered over his arm. "Because that's what these kids will be doing, right? Gentling and training wild Indian ponies? This would be the best part, Dillon." She grabbed another paper from the table and thrust it under his nose. "Here's the updated barn. Corrals, a round pen—Emily said you'd like that—and two arenas. Just some ideas."

"Where's the pool?" he asked, deadpan. He got the look he wanted from her. *Huh?* "Like you see in the movies. They use water therapy whenever they're whisperin' on a crazy horse."

"A pool seems a little excessive, but—"

Excessive? He didn't want to get in the way of all this delicious dreaming, but he couldn't help laughing so hard, he had to sit down.

She pulled a chair up next to him. "Seriously, I think a laundry and shower facility is more important."

"And all Hollywood gets out of this is one TV show?"

"An Emmy would be nice."

"And you've got her believing in all this," he said with

mock sadness. "You're not a very nice woman, Ella Champion."

"What?"

He laid the drawing aside. "Outsiders bring their big ideas out here, they get us all going on something, pretty soon we're fighting among ourselves. See, we're all about consensus. We'll talk a thing over until we give it wings with some kind of agreement or chisel in enough threads that we can finally screw it into the ground.

"You people don't have the patience for any of that. You outsiders can't wait for consensus, so you throw up your hands and tell the world you tried, but those damn Indians are their own worst enemies. And sometimes you've got a point."

"I'm an outsider? Totally?"

"Totally?" he aped, and then he squeezed her shoulder. *Just kidding.* "You don't look like one. I'll give you that." He jiggled her shoulder. "Hey, you said yourself, you're television people. You've got it made, Ella. I'm sure you worked real hard and paid some heavy dues. I say, good for you. *Good* for you. Who wouldn't wanna be a Hollywood insider?"

"I'm not an insider. I'm marginal everywhere I go." She claimed her prized drawing of the indoor arena and looked at it hard. "I believe in this show, Dillon. We've done some wonderful projects, and I know this could be one of those." She turned to him, eyes all chocolaty sweet and sincere. "I'm not bringing this before your local council. I'm offering it to one person. Two, really. These are the bones of something you and Emily would flesh out together."

He glanced at the damn sketches—the one in her hand, the others on the table. "I went to the Tribe lookin' for a little help with expenses. I could handle that. I'm a member, we're a community, it takes a village and all like that. But this…"

"You're salivating," she said.

He swallowed.

"It's a perfectly natural glandular function. Every human being does it. Even Lakota warriors." She patted his knee. "I lied about the cigarette taste. Coffee with something else. Vanilla, maybe."

He had to laugh, but, man, she was spooky. He wasn't sure whether she'd fallen off a spaceship or emerged from the fires of hell. Pure-D Hollywood, either way.

Except the part where she could see right through his skin.

Chapter Ten

The good news was that Emily was coming back today, and she was bringing her brother with her.

The bad news was, she was also bringing her mother.

Monica had reserved one of the two suites at the casino hotel, which meant there was a fifty-fifty chance she would be staying in the room where Dillon had nearly scored with Ella. Could've made it if he'd wanted to, but their association had taken a funny turn. She was working him, hoping to get some kind of mileage out of him, kind of toying with his wires, and damn if he wasn't getting a charge out of it. It tickled him, knowing he had the final say. Even if she backed off, he could live without anything she was offering, so it was all good. No pressure, no desperation. He had nothing to prove.

Now he knew why women got off on foreplay.

Damn. What had Ella's room number been? He glanced at the clock as he strode toward the lobby, wondering how stupid he would look asking whoever was on duty at the desk to make sure Monica got the other suite.

Too late. They were here.

D.J. saw him first. The beautiful boy of the slight build, slightly curly hair, slightly perched on a chair in the vicinity of Registration but slightly distant from his mother and sister. Dillon's son saw him coming, but he didn't move until the desk clerk clued the women in.

There was a hug from Emmie, a handshake from D.J. and an air kiss from Monica. Dillon managed to get an arm around her before she backed away, and it occurred to him that the one arm—which wasn't particularly long—would've gone around her twice. Ordinarily he would have had a joke on the tip of his tongue, but he'd never seen her this thin, and it shook him. You always heard about people's weight being a big deal in Hollywood. He was glad Ella had an off-camera job.

Which had nothing to do with Monica being too skinny. Somebody oughta tell her to forget about the cigarettes and try some food.

But that somebody would not be him.

"It's good to see you." Easy to say. So far, so good.

She finger combed her three shades of blond hair away from her face. "Are you surprised?"

"Not a bit." More like *not entirely.* He'd been warned about the appearance she planned to make, but not about *her* appearance. He covered with a smile. "I gave you ten years of expecting the unexpected, and you've spent nearly ten years givin' it right back."

"I hadn't thought of it that way. Didn't know you were paying much attention to what I was doing."

"I try. Helps me keep up with these two." His attempt to hook an arm around both kids' shoulders fell short on one side. "I see you brought your fiddle, son," he said to the boy, who'd stepped out of reach.

"How else would I practice?" D.J. glanced at his mother. "They'll let me practice here, won't they?"

"When they hear how you can play, they'll wanna put you on the program," Dillon said.

The boy ran his thumb under the shoulder strap of the violin case he was carrying. "I hope they have Internet access."

"For you, twenty-four seven." With his rejected hand, Dillon gave a thumbs-up. "You mention my name, they'll hook you up."

"Wireless comes with the suite, Dylan. I checked." Monica turned from Dylan to Dillon. "He can't be away from his e-mail. It's an addiction."

"In that case, you get all the credit for hookin' him up." Luggage. Dillon started for the handle of a leather two-wheeler. "Is this all your stuff?"

"That's just my office. There's more in the car." She handed him a ring of keys with one extended. "It's the blue Beamer, out that door."

"The what?"

"It's the only car out there, Daddy," Emily said. "If it hasn't been towed."

"Nobody gets towed here." Monica gave him a sweet smile. "But maybe Daddy wouldn't mind parking it for us? It's brand-new, so please—"

"Us?" Emily pocketed her own keys. "I parked mine in the lot. I'm back for the summer."

"Good." Dillon bounced the keys in his hand. "Daddy is honored by this display of trust."

"I didn't mean…" As he walked away he heard her assure someone, "He knows I didn't mean it that way."

Concerning himself with what she did or didn't mean would have rivaled the foolishness of any number of thoughts he'd wasted brain energy on lately. Like Monica staying in Ella's room. Turned out she wasn't, but he felt stupid for even thinking about it. He'd been thinking about Ella a lot in the last couple of weeks. A lot of the time and in a lot of ways.

"Are you free for dinner?"

Dillon turned from the third-floor window facing a world of spring-green pasture and clear blue sky. "I traded shifts so I could be. Thought I'd do the cooking." The three looked up from their separate settling-in chores—Emily scanning the eight-page newspaper, D.J. getting online, Monica unpacking one of the bags Dillon had hauled up two flights of steps in preference to sharing the elevator with a trio of drunken rednecks. He glanced from face to face to face and lifted one shoulder. "You'll have to come out to the place sooner or later."

"Sooner," Monica said cheerfully as she zipped one suitcase closed and opened another one. "I'm so excited about this project."

"Yeah, that's what I hear." Ever since he'd told Ella she could put him on her list of prospective charity cases, he'd heard all kinds of stuff. He'd discounted most of it. The whole thing was way too Disney for the world he lived in, and he'd given up trying to figure Monica's angle. He laughed. "Expect the unexpected."

"Emily said you almost turned it down. But you came to your senses, and that's all that matters. Was it because you didn't want to work with me?"

"Work with you?"

"I'll be your decorator. Didn't Ella tell you?"

Indignant, he put his hands on his hips. "I just found

out she got the 'conditional go-ahead,' whatever the hell that means."

"It just means that Ella pitched a program they like, but there are always conditions to be met, mostly legal technicalities, but some that have to do with the storyline. Even though they call it reality TV and it's not supposed to be scripted, they're counting on a certain dynamic. I'm not sure exactly how she pitched it." She faced him, smiling. "But I know I'm part of the package."

He frowned. "Now, that is just wrong."

"That sounds like Emily. *That is just wrong.* Have you been getting your father up to speed on the latest catchphrases? It'll be better if you stick with your own voice, Dillon. We want western. We want cowboy cool, Indian cool. Don't try to—"

Dillon turned to Emily, giving an open-handed gesture. "Who is this woman?"

"Daddy, this is *the* Monica Wilson-Black. She's very good at what she does, and she's bringing it to you live from studio three."

"Well, take it on home, honey," he told Monica. "I am not your trick pony."

"That's what I'm talking about. That's Dillon Black. They'll be offering you your own show before this is over." She folded her arms—one case closed, on to the next. "What do you think of Ella? You like her, don't you?"

A smile tugged at one side of this mouth. "She da bomb."

"Hmm. Meaning what? Never mind. We'll discuss that later."

"No, we won't." He took a step toward Monica. "I thought this was mostly Emmie's idea. I knew you were in on it, but nobody said anything about you being *in on it.* The last time I tried to live in a house that had your thumbprints all over it—"

"You burned it down. I heard all about it. Your children, however, had been spared that knowledge—until now."

"I knew about it," Emily said quietly.

"Not from me," Monica insisted, but she toned down, doling out patience in measured phrases. "Let's not do this. I don't have time for it." On second thought, she added, "We don't have time for it. Dillon, part of what makes this project so appealing is the human-interest aspect. People who watch the show know me. I'm a celebrity. Okay, on the scale of celebrity, I'm like a two—a very minor goddess—but it's something I've achieved, something we can cash in on." She stared hard at him. "Don't say it."

He didn't have to. She knew damn well that the ideas of her celebrity and him "cashing in" didn't mix.

"Let's start with the one thing we can all agree on," Monica instructed. "The horse program is a wonderful idea. What the two of you started last summer should continue. I listened to you both talk about it at Christmas, and I was…impressed. I was *impressed*, Dillon."

Sarcasm made his tongue itch. He glanced at Emily, who was all ears, then D.J., who only had eyes for the laptop, and he held back.

"Let me be part of it," Monica said quietly. He recognized the old pregoddess Monica in her tentative smile. "I promise not to leave any thumbprints. I'll wear rubber gloves."

It was the first time they'd been together in his home in ten years. Different house, but it was where he lived, and he was feeling some attachment to the ol' tin box. The steaks he'd thought to please them with had succeeded with two out of four. D.J. had stopped eating red meat "a long time ago," and Monica, it seemed, had stopped eating much of anything. Dillon beefed up the salad with hard-boiled eggs, canned chicken and a packet of sunflower seeds—which he taste-tested, because he couldn't remember how they'd come to be in his cabinet. D.J. tried to be subtle about eating around the chicken, and Monica toyed with the lettuce while she offered high praise for whatever he'd used to spice up the two bites of steak she'd choked down.

Dillon wanted to take it all back and start over. He could have done better. Learning his way around a kitchen had been one of the benefits of living with Monica. For a while there she'd taken on country living like any other challenge. Get the most for your money, waste nothing, use your imagination and watch the details. He remembered how she used to take time—both hers and his—picking over the produce at the grocery store, and he wondered how many of her former high-school home-economics students still joked about their "field trips" to Super Valu to choose their fruits and vegetables right off the weekly delivery truck. A few, probably. Once in a while someone would ask him how she was doing and whether it was true she was on TV. Monica had been a good teacher, they said.

Dillon had no doubt that Monica Wilson-Black was good at what she did, but from the looks of her, there wasn't much cooking involved. Her half of splitting the sheets hadn't been much more than that—one sheet and a pillow case—but at least she'd had some meat on her bones. His first chance to feed her in ten years, and he was sorry he hadn't made a meal more to her liking.

She was already throwing in the napkin. "Delicious, but I'm stuffed. Generally, I don't eat much on a long drive, but we did sit down for a meal when we stopped for gas on the way out here."

"This morning," Emily clarified. "I don't know what you're trying to prove, Mother, but you're getting too thin again. You need to eat more."

"I just wanted to lose a few extra pounds so I'd have some cushion."

"I think you got it—"

"—backwards," Emily said in unison with her father. "At your age, Mother, you don't want to be too thin."

Dillon smiled, anticipating anything but a fragile glance, small voice and wounded tone. "My age?"

But she recovered quickly, stuck out her chin, rolled the eyelids down and turned the volume up. "I thought we'd agreed: I'm ageless. My producer says so."

"And the man knows his onions," Dillon said, relieved by her quick turnaround. "Right, D.J.?"

"Her producer is a woman."

"Even better. They're harder on each other than we could ever be. Your mom doesn't look a day older than…" Dillon snapped his fingers. "Help me out, Emmie. What's the magic number?"

"How old is Ella?" Emily asked.

"Midthirties." Dillon shrugged, gave a diffident smile. "I'm guessin'."

"That's the magic number."

"There is no magic number for someone who's ageless," said Monica, her sails now fully refilled. "Age is nothing except a means to experience. Experience and education lead to accomplishment and—"

"—accomplishment is everything," the children recited with her. She lifted a prim shoulder. "All right, it might not be the most profound philosophy you've ever heard, but it's something."

"If accomplishment is everything, I guess it's all a guy should bother himself over," Dillon said. "What about somebody who's not ageless? If he hasn't accomplished anything, is there a magic number where he can just say fuck it?" He looked to Monica for the answer, and she rolled her eyes. "I didn't think so." He turned to his son. "But don't worry, grasshopper. There are more things in heaven and earth than are dreamt of in your mother's philosophy."

"That's Shakespeare, Dad. You just quoted Shake-speare," Emily enthused, as though he'd just sounded out his first printed word.

"Expect the unexpected." Dillon caught a flash of the old Monica's smile—spontaneous, unguarded, and, yes, age-less. "Did I see you slip that fiddle case in the backseat of your mother's car before we left the hotel?" he asked D.J.

"She told me to."

"Dylan," Monica challenged as she reached for his half-full and Emily's mostly empty plates. "It was really your idea."

"I could play something for you," the boy offered ten-tatively. "But I wish you'd stop calling it a fiddle."

"That's what my father called it." Dead for twenty-five years and rarely mentioned, his ol' man had had three ob-sessions: boozing, brawling and making music. "He was pretty good."

"My grandfather played the violin?"

"He tried to get me to take it up, but I was too damn lazy. They say real talent skips a generation." Dillon glanced at Monica. "Don't they?"

"They say a lot of things, but you've never said much about your father."

"One of those things we never took the time for, I guess." He pointed toward the ceiling and sketched a circle. "He's around here somewhere. You play for him, he'll hear you."

And play he did. Dillon could quote a little Shakespeare, but since he didn't know a sonata from a symphony, he had no requests. D.J. played two numbers—a sixth and a second, apparently—and then Monica suggested a waltz, whose swirling, soaring notes promised to pop the tin off the trailer roof. Dillon thrilled to the beauty filling his ears, not only because it poured from his son's hands but because it came to life where Dillon lived, breathed the air he breathed.

And crammed his throat with saltwater.

He sat very still until the strings' last lovely vibrations had drifted well beyond ears' reach before giving gravelly voice to the Lakota expression for that which is warm and life-giving and fills the heart. *"Sha."* Red.

It was only after he had bathed his throat with half a bottle of water that Dillon had full breath, if not full control. "I've gotta run out to the barn real quick," he said as he bolted to his feet. He raised a hand to D.J., who was putting his violin in its case, and to Monica, the proud mom. "Don't go anywhere. I've got a mare out there with a wire cut."

"You stay, Daddy." Emily touched his arm, pushing off for the back door. "I'll have a look."

"She's pretty skittish." He wanted to go, needed to collect himself around the echo of his son's music and hold fast.

But Emily was a step ahead. "I think I can… Oh!" She pointed to her brother. "D.J., come with me, and bring your violin. I want to try something."

After the whomp of the door, clomp-clomp on the wooden steps and trail-away voices, the silence that was left began to thicken. With the neatly squared-off white-white tip of an index fingernail, Monica traced a crease in the blue-and-white checked oilcloth table cover she'd found in the cupboard where he kept the salad bowls and the good glasses—the ones made of real glass. Everything she had in common with him had just walked out the door. Every reason he had left for being in the same room with her was headed for the barn.

Man, these were some close quarters.

"She's always comin' up with something she wants to try," Dillon said, crashing the silence. "That program she's in at her school, it's all horses all the time."

"You love seeing that, don't you?"

"I do. I didn't push it, though. You know I didn't."

"Please. It's in her blood. As are you." She lifted her shoulder as she rounded up a small herd of bread crumbs with the edge of her hand. "It wasn't what I had in mind for her, but I think you'll find…as we go forward now, I think you'll find that I've mellowed a bit."

"We're going forward now," he reflected, trying to imagine what version of *we* she was thinking of shifting into some kind of forward gear. How long had it been since the two of them had pulled together in any direction?

But incredibly she said, "I hope so."

No use biting his tongue.

"What does that mean, exactly?"

"With the…project."

He nodded, considering. The project. Pure-D fairy tale was what that was, and every sane man knew that fairy tales were all about women. Outnumbered by those he cared about, Dillon had taken the first step on the old familiar *What the hell?* path. It had been years since he'd trusted a decision hastily made, but what the hell? They really wanted this thing, and what could it hurt to go along? It would never happen.

He nodded toward the door. "The boy doesn't wanna be here."

"He desperately needs to get out more. He's so smart, so talented, but he keeps to himself too much."

"Can't imagine where he gets that."

"He is who he is, Dillon. So…your father played the violin. Was he shy, too? Your son's shy. You can't attribute everything to one side or the other. I mean…he's a private person."

"Like his uncle Nick," Dillon said.

"Nick isn't his uncle. You and Nick may have grown up like brothers, but you're cousins. You…" She tipped her head in assent. "All right, yes, a little bit like his uncle Nick."

"Man, you're so agreeable tonight. What was that stuff I put on the steak?"

"I told you, I'm mellowing. And I understand your need to make these connections, because the kids… I took them away from here, but roots are roots, as you well know. In some ways that scares me, but they grow up, don't they? They go their own ways. Lord knows I don't have much family for them to…and you define family relations a little differently. The Indian way, which I admire, for the most part. I think it's great that a kid can have ten grandmothers. I wish I had even one."

"You could've claimed mine." He opened his hand on the table, palm up. "You won't take my money, maybe you'll accept my grandmothers."

"What money?"

"Checks I sent for the kids. You never cashed them."

"Oh, that." She avoided his eyes. "At first I just stuck them in a drawer. Then I thought, why not let him help out? Because it was tough at first. But after a couple of them bounced, I thought I'd spare us both the bank fees. I never said anything, and neither did you, so…" She studied him until he shifted uncomfortably in the vinyl-covered chair. "You didn't even notice, did you? About the bouncing checks."

"I've lost track a few times," he confessed. "Gave up on banking altogether for a while there, but I'm better at it now." He drew his hand back, tucking it underneath the table, on his lap. "Sorry."

"We're good financially, Dillon. We have been for some time. When I left, I knew what I wanted, and I was motivated. No apologies necessary, either way." She leaned across the table to confide, "All I meant about Dylan being private like Nick was that Nick went through a terrible ordeal. You both went through—"

"What about you?"

"I wasn't much help to any of you, was I? I was selfish."

"You… We lost a baby. It all happened at once. No, you weren't selfish. You were just trying to keep it together." He pushed back from the table. "We had some bad times. Experience, huh? Nick has his scars, we have ours."

"I don't—"

"Okay, you don't. You're ageless, scarless and motivated." He stood, thinking kitchen, coffee, water—*anything*—and he started in that direction, but he stopped, keeping his back to her. *Don't ask questions. Don't ask, don't…*

"Why did you come, Monica?"

"Which time?"

He turned. Stared. Caught the spark in her eyes, tried to shake it off, but gave up and smiled. And together they laughed.

"Oh, Dillon," she said, leaving the table and moving indirectly in his direction, giving him cause to stand pat when he wanted to step back. "You never ask the right questions, but you have a way of coming up with the hard ones. You're the only thing I've ever done without having a good reason or a sensible plan. I didn't think it through. I just…" Her hand landed on his arm like a windblown bird trying to cross his territory, and she gave a quick squeeze, an apologetic chuckle. "I just kept on coming."

"Well…" He lent a steady hand. "I'd say we've got half an hour, tops."

She laughed again, then ended up coughing, which sent him after the water he'd started for. He unscrewed the cap and gave her the first bottle.

The drink settled her, and she leaned back against the counter, gesturing with the bottle. "I'm looking for a little more than that, timewise. For the kids. For Dylan, especially."

"He's like you," Dillon said as he opened another bottle. "He doesn't like it here. Unlike you, he doesn't mind saying so." And that wasn't the only thing she minded saying, he thought, but that was fine with him, unless it had to do with the kids. Her stuff was her stuff.

"Unlike me," she echoed, strangely melancholy, "your son has real roots here, and he needs to be comfortable with them. At least get a feel for them, so that down the road, when he's trying to get a handle on all the pieces of himself, he'll remember how to find this one."

"What the hell are you talkin' about, Monica? He

doesn't have to go lookin' for me. Haven't I been the one truckin' down that road in your direction?"

"I know I haven't always made it easy for you."

"I never asked you to. You never had it easy with me. But after all's said and done, I'm still their father. And this is still my home, where my people live. Emmie got old enough, she started coming out here more, so she knows me better than D.J. does."

"And you know her. You don't know him."

"I'm not gonna shove anything down his throat. Maybe he doesn't like… Hell, maybe he's embarrassed about me. He never brings any friends around when I'm there."

"He doesn't have much social life, Dillon. He's studious. He's serious about his music. He's…private."

"That's all good," he insisted. "Nick was always pretty private and serious. Not everybody needs a big social life. And Nick… Wait'll you see him with his wife and kids. It just makes you wanna sing and dance circles around them. Except that he's still a private man. A private man with a big neon happy sign hangin' over him. But don't say anything." She shook her head and promised. "So it's okay for—"

Music. Dillon shut his mouth and alerted every nerve in his head. The sound rose in the distance, soft as a dream, but crisp and clear, drawn from fine strings by sure hands. His gaze met Monica's, and he hoped she could see how he marveled, how words failed. He couldn't imagine the hands of the violinist being related to the hands of a laborer without making the connection through his fiddling father, a man who'd made looking out for number one his life's work. There was that about him, but there was also this. And now that the man was gone, he was only what Dillon chose to remember.

He shook his head at the wonder of it all.

Monica's birdlike hand landed on his arm again, and she smiled as though she understood. He believed she did.

"Let's go outside and listen," she whispered. "I really need a cigarette."

He frowned. "Haven't you quit yet?"

"Working on it. Again." She threaded her arm through the crook of his elbow. "You?"

"Pretty much. Can't afford it. Had to choose between cigarettes and gas."

"So you've learned something about budgeting," she concluded as they headed for the door.

"A few new things and some I already knew." He grinned. "Like it's much harder to mooch gas."

They laughed. And then they went outside and stood together under a blanket of stars and listened to their son make marvelous music to comfort a wounded horse.

Chapter Eleven

The effect on the horse was better than the cases Emily had read about, but the music was live, and her brother was the musician. She'd heard him play for years, trying not to listen during the first few, but when he was about ten, she had made a deal with her mother that she would supervise his after-school practice if she could finally quit taking piano lessons. It was a relief for all parties. Mother had achieved her promise—made primarily to herself—to see to it that both children played an instrument. But only one of them reached a level of performance that anyone but family could enjoy. The tranquil mustang was living proof. Emily had dressed a nasty wire cut without dodging a flying hoof.

"You could tame a grizzly bear the way you play, D.J." She grinned at him across the spotted back of the mare she'd cross tied in the barn. She was halterbroke, but with a month-old colt curled up in the open stall a few feet away, the mare's willingness to allow Emily to brush her after messing with her wound was a testament to the effect of the music. "Davy Crockett's got nothing on my brother."

"That was awesome, watching her kind of unwind, one muscle at a time," D.J. said, keeping his distance, but, like the wary animal, he looked considerably more comfortable than either of them had when Emily had introduced them.

"You were watching? You looked like you were in another world." And from the dreamy look in his eyes, he hadn't quite come back. He reminded her of Mary Poppins, drifting down from the clouds clutching the handle of a violin case instead of an umbrella. "Why don't you go riding with me tomorrow?"

"Negative." He took a single step toward the horse. "This is as close as I get, and as close as she wants me to be."

"You used to ride when you were little. Daddy had you up on a horse before you could walk."

"Before I could say no."

"Put your hand near her nostril, give her a whiff, and then scratch the side of her neck a little bit." She could tell he wanted to. "Your first word was *dada*. I know that for a fact. *No* came soon after."

"The two words most kids start with. I read that somewhere." He extended his free hand slowly the way she'd instructed, speaking quietly. "And you can stop pushing this bonding thing at me right now. We've got nothing to say to each other. Nothing of any consequence."

"You scare him, D.J."

"*Me* scare *him?* That's rich." He moved from the first offering of a sniff to tentative scratching as he spoke. "He's a manly man. He puts on his cowboy boots and his cowboy hat and heads for the monster truck show. *Fiddle players* don't scare guys like him. He doesn't have to do anything particularly well, or be particularly aware of anything other than the size and location of his balls."

"Sick." Emily peered over the horse's back, grimacing. "D.J., that is totally sick."

"But true." He inched closer to his new friend.

"Horseback riding won't damage yours, by the way, if that's what you're worried about."

"I'm not worried." He glanced toward the mare's head, the big brown eye matching the one on Emily's side. "Right, girl? It's not going to be an issue for either of us." He sighed. "How long is she going to make me stay here?"

"I didn't know she was going to do this, D.J. I thought she'd fly out to film the show and go back as soon as she was finished." A moment passed. Should she say it? "I'm worried about her, frankly."

"Why? You think she's—"

She brushed the mare's belly. "I don't think she looks good."

"Because of what *he* said?"

"Because…something's going on with her. She went to the doctor twice last week and again just before we left. She said it was routine stuff, but I don't know."

"Did you ask?"

"Did *you?*" Emily unhooked the cross-ties. "You're around her all the time, and you see exactly the same thing I see."

"In certain areas I'm content to operate on a need-to-know basis, and the kind of routine stuff women see doctors about would be one of those areas. If she says she's okay, I'm good with that."

"Yeah, I know. I asked but didn't press," she admitted as she turned the mare into the big box stall with her baby. "Same when she had her surgery. A week before midterms and she says don't come home, so I don't. She says it's not serious, and I take her at her word."

"Works for me. But I do wish she'd stop smoking. It's unhealthy and irritating, even if she does keep it out of the house."

Emily bent to pick up the grooming box. "I hope her coming out here means they're going to get started on the show soon."

"I hope she's got another doctor's appointment soon so we have to go home."

"Be careful what you wish for, D.J." She stored the box on a shelf and hung the lead on a hook. "What if something happens to her?"

"Like what? She's only fifty-two. Old, but not *that* old."

"Women in the entertainment business worry about age," she said as she claimed a seat on a hay bale. "Age, looks, weight. No matter what she says, she's very much aware of all three. But the greatest of these, so the Bible says, is age. That's the one you can't change." She patted the space beside her on the hay bale. He accepted the invitation for his violin.

She shrugged. "But she'll get some mileage out of this show. It's win-win—for her *and* for Dad." A protruding piece of hay poked her in the thigh. She plucked it from the bale and examined it. "As for me. I've revised my independent study plan from the modest grant proposal version to the making of a dream version, and my advisor went for it. We agreed that, when the stakes are this high and the opportunity for doing good is within your grasp, a person shouldn't shrink from working her connections." She glanced up. "You agree?" He was leaning over the stall door, watching the colt nurse. "D.J.?"

Intent on the feeding, he wondered, "Is it true that in the wild, only one male breeds a whole bunch of mares?"

"Yep."

"What do the rest of them do if there aren't any humans around to make geldings out of them? They just go around acting like they never think about sex?"

"They form bachelor bands." She toyed with the piece of hay. "They hang out a safe distance from the herd, talk trash, play Fantasy Hoofball and Capture the Filly."

"And jack off?"

"Naturally." She laughed. "When they're not working out. Eventually somebody takes on the breeding stallion and wins his position."

He came to sit beside her, elevating the violin to his lap.

"Do you ever imagine what people might say about you at your funeral?" He turned toward her. "Say you died right now. You ever sort of play it out in your mind, people giving their little speeches over your casket, saying how good you were and how sorry they are?"

"Doesn't everybody?" She tapped his cleft chin with the hay. "Let me guess. You've scored your funeral scenario. Mother gets 'Swan Lake,' and I'm backed up by…what?"

"Me." He looked dead serious. "You're the only one brave enough to play a recording of the real me. You don't break down or leave out the best parts, and there's not a dry eye in the place except for yours."

"Are you kidding? I'd be a mess."

"That's because you know I'm coming back to haunt you for going off to college in the boonies and leaving me to deal with the queen." He stared at his hands, resting atop the violin case. "She's gonna turn me into one."

No comment. No pretense. She knew his mind, and he trusted hers. Fears, frustrations, bright ideas and dark desires, were safe in each other's care. *Let come what comes.*

He smiled. "Did you know that you're more likely to die of a heart attack if you sleep on your left side?" She shook her head, and he nodded. "Remember that kid, Stuart Scully? Used to live down the street until he died of a heart attack? He was, like, twelve. Didn't accomplish anything except dying young."

"He had a heart murmur, D.J. It wasn't like…" Generally she tried to keep it light when her brother went all philosophic or morose on her—too often lately it was both—but she had her ghosts, too. "One of our kids from last summer tried to kill himself."

"Yeah? How?"

She slid him a warning glance. "Tried to hang himself, probably while he was thinking about what people were going to say at his funeral. Some girl in particular, who probably hardly knew he existed, quiet as he is. His sister found him in time."

"Good thing she was there for him, huh?"

Emily answered with a look that said she wasn't biting.

"I think Mom's trying to lose weight again." Hay crackled, punctuating his conversational shift. "You should tell her she looks good."

"She doesn't."

"Tell her she does. She really misses you, Em. I think that's what this makeover thing is all about. She's doing it for you. I mean, she sure wouldn't be doing it for him."

"It's not like she doesn't recognize a great idea when she sees one. It's about the show, first and foremost." It was a claim that put Mother back in the driver's seat. Emily shouldn't have mentioned her niggling concern, which was just the kind of notion D.J. would take too seriously.

She put her arm around her brother's shoulders. "Two

more years and you'll be headed for college, too. You'll be able to go as far away as you want."

His glance betrayed a child's fear and nudged her toward playing Sister Superior. But she was beyond that. "Or stay in Minnesota. Whatever." She gave him a squeeze. "All doors will be open for you."

"Locker rooms, too? I was thinking maybe Jock U." He gave a sweet brotherly smile. "You know, I could've skipped first grade, but she says I was small for my age anyway, and she was afraid skipping a grade would keep me off the football team. If it weren't for football, I could be looking at one more year."

"Don't rush it. It's too good a time in your life for you to go cannonballing through."

"For you, maybe." He drifted away for a moment. "He isn't very tall, is he?"

"Daddy?" she asked, and he nodded. "He's tall enough. Get him on a horse, he's like—"

"Not what I expect. Every time I see him, I think, geez, I remember you being taller. Is it his fault I'm short, or was it her?"

"You're not short, D.J. You're average height. And what difference does it make when you're brilliant? Cut yourself half a break once in a while." She cuffed him playfully on the chin. "Not only brilliant, but beautiful. Bordering on hot, but you're my brother. Every time I see you lately, I think, geez, what did you do with my ugly little brother?"

He squared his shoulders and launched a television voice. "And for stubborn teenage acne, you can spend a fortune on a dermatologist, orrrr…" He stirred up an imaginary potion for an imaginary camera and poured on Mother's voice, which he imitated better than Emily did. "Try using a simple solution of household bleach and lighter fluid. We were able to cure my son's case of the uglies in one treatment. His own sister hardly recognizes him."

"You look more like Daddy—"

"Give it up, Em." He playfully cuffed her, a tap on the chin. "I'm here. Let that be enough."

Chapter Twelve

Monica loved driving in the country at night. It had been ten years, but not much had changed, and she'd driven the road back to the casino alone how many hundreds of times? Alone on the road at night in this part of the world was not really a bad thing, unless you blew a tire or ran into bad weather. And she'd done both and lived to tell about it.

A lanky white cowboy had stopped to help her change the tire. *You're not from around here, are you?* It wasn't just that she was white. It was as though she had a "Hello" tag on her dress—or maybe it was just the dress itself— and she never claimed otherwise. Assuming she'd gotten lost in the dark, the cowboy had warned her to stay in the car and keep the doors locked if it ever happened again west of the river, especially at night. *Indians,* he'd said. *Harmless when they're sober, crazy when they're drinking.*

She'd said nothing, told herself she needed the man to finish changing her tire. Even now, she felt guilty just thinking about it.

Emily had somehow talked Dylan into staying with their father after Monica announced that she was going back to the hotel. Just like old times. Emily the adventuress, introducing her shy brother to territory she'd already scoped out. And Dylan the genius, following not for any interest in new surroundings but because he cherished his sister's invitation. She was the only person in the world he trusted completely. A good thing.

Complete trust was a burden Monica didn't covet. She was dependable, but she understood, finally, that no part of her was completely available to anyone else. Anyone who chose to believe otherwise hadn't been paying attention. She needed space to breathe and room to maneuver.

It was a relief to leave them all there together and put them behind her for a few hours. It was like walking out on a classroom and closing the door, just for a few minutes. Let them talk about her if that was what it would take to pull them together and make something of them. Something she could work with. She was no artist—a crafter, certainly, which was not the same—but she was good at reshaping things. The world was full of all kinds of things that periodically just needed reshaping.

The desk clerk looked familiar. A former student. Monica was tired, but she seldom passed up an opportunity to be recognized by people she'd known before she'd been "discovered." It was like mainlining vitamin B, especially if their memory was as romantic as hers and they'd since seen her on TV. But the full fix wasn't there for her tonight. She was remembered—*I still make my own quick biscuit mix the way you taught us*—but her celebrity had gone unnoticed. The girl—*woman*—recalled the marriage that had shocked the school board, the split that had surprised no one, and the cute kids. Monica let her know that the kids were doing well but offered no further details. She was still tired.

There was no bar in the room, so Monica took a detour

through the casino for a gin-and-tonic to take upstairs with her. Slot machines played their five-note mating calls. She remembered the dawn of reservation casinos and her own surprise when gambling made its way to Standing Rock. She'd predicted failure—too isolated, she'd said—but she'd pushed Dillon to apply for a job when the place opened. He could get some training and become a manager, she'd insisted. He'd never taken to being pushed, but he'd gone to work there sometime after she'd left. Whatever training he'd gotten out of it hadn't led to management, but he seemed content.

It was quiet on the third floor. Hotel solitude. Nothing quite like it. There was an e-mail from Ella with a fat attachment, which had to be a sign of progress on the project. Bad news came in skinny envelopes or phone calls.

This is Doctor Lavin's nurse calling for Monica Wilson-Black. Please call the office as soon as possible to schedule a consultation with the doctor regarding the results of your recent lab tests.

She had specifically asked that no messages regarding anything to do with lab tests or lungs or Lavin be left on her home phone. Nurse No-name was lucky Monica had been first to see the blinking light, first to listen and erase. Medical information was considered privileged for a reason. The owner of the body being treated had the right to divulge the information on her own terms. Or not. For Monica, the less divulging the better. *Not at all* would have been ideal. *Not at all* would have meant it could all go away.

Monica lit a cigarette and opened the e-mail attachment. There was a tentative shooting schedule and a complete delineation of Monica's role in each aspect of the project, including sketches, lists of names, sources, preferences, a few choices she could make if she got back with them quickly.

Oh, she would have her say, all right. She would give them their show if they would give her her say. The ideas were good, and the sketches were getting there. But it wasn't big enough yet. She'd done some research. There were all kinds of equine facilities out there, and Hollywood people owned some of the best. Her project—her legacy, her gift—hadn't quite reached the magnitude she had in mind. But it was getting there.

She reached for the remote and pressed buttons until she found something real, or at least something taped live. A raunchy comedy special on HBO. Perfect. A fat fortysome-thing female regaled a Vegas crowd with painfully funny, excruciatingly explicit stories about the sex life in her head and the one in her bed. No shame, Dillon would say. He was always a good storyteller, but the story to be avoided was the "telling on yourself" kind. Who knew how much of this woman's routine was true, other than the fat, forty and female parts? Tomorrow, though, she would be laughing all the way to the bank, and more power to her for making her mark in the process of making her way. Women were born knowing how to play to their strengths.

The phone startled her.

"Hey, it's Dillon James."

When had she last called him by both names? She re-membered when she'd started it—soon after she'd coaxed him to tell her his middle name—and thereafter she'd used it only in the best and the worst of times. Why was he drag-ging it out now?

"Is everyone all right?"

His voice faded slightly as he said over his shoulder,

"Your mom wants to know if her kids are all right. Any complaints you guys want me to relay?" Hearing none, he was back in her ear. "They're reading up on their history. We're goin' over to Nick's in the morning for breakfast. Thought you might wanna come."

"What time?"

"Indian time. We're goin' over on horseback. You know, breakfast time."

Breakfast was Dillon's most—and Monica's least—favorite meal. "I just got some new schematics from Ella. Did she send them your way, too? E-mail or—"

He laughed.

"You're not in touch with her?"

"Sure I am. We use the phone."

"How about the U.S. Postal Service? Do you open your mail these days?"

"Oh, yeah, she's back," he said with a sigh.

"All right, I'll take a do-over. She should be sending you some of the same stuff she's sending me, and I just thought we could go over it together as long as I'm here."

"I probably won't make it to the post office tomorrow, but—"

"Not a problem. If I can hook up to a printer here, I'll make a hard copy."

"None of this has to be hard. You can meet us at Nick's place, which is—"

"Dillon, you know, this isn't one of those big surprise shows. This is about taking a good idea and turning it into a great reality. Your idea has been kicked up to the money-is-no-object level. Everyone's dream. But it really is supposed to be based on your idea."

"Great. You comin', or not?"

"Where's Nick's place?"

"On the other side of the highway," he said. "You shouldn't have any trouble finding it. Same place ours used to be."

Why would they do that? she wondered. With all the land they had available to them, why would Nick and his instant family build their house on a pile of ashes? Any reminder of fire should have been anathema to a man who'd suffered as he had. But maybe Dillon's big, tough cousin had a little phoenix envy.

Monica seldom thought about the time they'd lived in Montana. The jobs and the change of scene had sounded promising, and she'd packed up her fledgling household, small child and the seeds of a home-decorating sideline that would eventually change her professional life. But not in eastern Montana, where they'd moved sight—at least for Monica's part—unseen. She'd expected Rocky Mountains. She'd gotten still more Great Basin. Dillon's response to her disappointment: *Maybe Tunkasila stored the oil where the land had nothing else going for it. Figured it for a place where His children wouldn't be gettin' into stuff. It's flammable.*

But life had been good for a while. Good jobs, good housing in a bigger town than the one they'd left, new friends and new activities. Dillon had all but given up his dream of filling his permit as an amateur bronc rider and becoming a professional rodeo cowboy. *Thank God, Tunkasila, Saint Jude or whoever.* Monica had not married the man thinking she would change him—between exchanging names and exchanging vows there hadn't been a whole lot of thinking ahead, actually—but she'd hoped that pregnancy and marriage, in that order, would inspire change.

Would *require* change. Hadn't he sworn he couldn't live without her? And so, on with the taming of the Sioux.

The first pregnancy had taken Monica by surprise, but allowing a second baby to take up residence in her body before the first one had taken a step was just plain stupid. She was nursing the first child and sleeping with the sexiest man alive, but there were no excuses for fool-me-twice. Monica had lived with illness and anger for what had seemed an eternity, and it had all been for nothing. For guilt. And for grief, which was already thriving in the Black household at that point over that awful oil-rig fire. Nick Red Shield had been burned within an inch of his life, and his brother had been killed. Horrible, yes, but Dillon had dodged a bullet that night. Nick had taken his place on the ill-fated rig, sending Dillon home to his wife. With the possible exception of the hapless younger brother—considered by everyone but Nick to be too immature for such a hazardous job—it was nobody's fault.

Dillon used to tell her she would make a better door than a window, and she'd agreed. *Come in, go out, but don't even try to look through me.* Like most women, she could be used, but she would be the one to set the terms, and she would make a better coach than a crutch. Nick didn't want people watching him suffer, and John was dead. What should Dillon do?

Wasn't it obvious? Close the door on the bad stuff, turn away from the window, fill in the grave and move on.

The fire hadn't killed their relationship, but it had hastened its demise. The miscarriage followed quickly as they'd passed another year in Montana, where neither of them wanted to be. With Dillon quitting job after job, the Dakotas started looking pretty good to her again. She'd been a good teacher looking to get away from the city when she'd first gone out there. She'd been young and eager to make a difference, and she'd been doing just that when she'd met Dillon Black. No reason she couldn't pick up her career where she'd left off.

No reason other than Dillon's desire to move "out to the country." From Monica's perspective, everything west of the Twin Cities was out in the country, but Dillon wanted horses. And not just any horses. He wanted wild horses from a particular bunch that some people believed to be the descendants of nineteenth-century Indian ponies.

Monica decided that if wild horses could drag her husband out of his funk, so be it. The first time she'd seen him on a horse, she'd fallen for him as hard and fast as the setting sun. Maybe horses would do it for him again, and then for her, and finally for them. She'd agreed to take up residence in a sad little house out in the middle of nowhere and drive fifty miles each way to work. The house had become her first project.

But the isolation did her in. That and a third hard pregnancy, a second child and a husband who couldn't figure out what he wanted to be if and when he grew up. She wanted to travel to other countries. He wanted to visit relatives in the next county. She wanted more education. He wanted more kids. She wanted to entertain in her home. He wanted to party on a one-block Main Street. He thought she would stay, truly wanted her to stay, but, as a matter of cold hard fact, she'd almost stayed too long.

When she left, they'd both known she wasn't coming back. She'd felt terrible. She'd felt liberated. She'd felt younger than her years, which, oddly, was the way she had felt when she'd first met Dillon Black. But her "country period" was over. Done and done.

Until now.

It would be Monica's job to furnish and decorate the project. She was known for making dramatic interior changes with paint, and performing miracles with inexpensive fabric. As much as she enjoyed the hunt, she'd recently trained an assistant to scour secondhand outlets for furniture with good bones. Viewers responded well to her reupholstering segments. They liked to think they would do it themselves someday. Some might try, start on it themselves and then end up taking it to a pro or tossing it out, but it was mostly a fantasy segment for would-be do-it-yourselfers, who comprised the majority of her viewers.

The crafters would love the denim projects she had planned, and the garage-salers and eBayers would soon be looking for television cowboy collectibles and bits of antique horse tack. The architectural salvage outlets would see a run on church remnants. And while the mail would run three to one against her use of antlers, leather, hides and feathers, the instructions for projects featuring those items would rank near the top for Web site downloads.

Monica drained her drink, lit a cigarette, grabbed the phone and called Ella.

"I'm glad you called," said the familiar voice. "You got my e-mail?"

"I'm looking at it now. I like. There's room for additions and corrections, of course."

"If you can keep the cost down on your end, we can beef up the horse facilities."

"My end interests the viewers," Monica said. "Especially when I keep the cost down and show them how they can, too. But just between you and me, I've already spent more on my end than they put in the budget."

"Before you even looked at—"

"But don't skimp on the horse stuff. I'll cover things myself if I have to. Just do what you can for me, okay?"

"Monica…"

"El-la," Monica sang. "Oh, Ella, Stephanie found an old church organ. Parts of one, anyway, exactly the parts I need, and the woodwork is amazing."

"Do you think that's necessary? Or appropriate? I don't know that we want to play up the mission thing on an Indian reservation. There's a real downside to all that."

"You'll find that Dillon has a unique perspective." Monica drew a quick puff of smoke. She was over her daily limit. "Or maybe you already have. I can't help noticing the way he tunes in whenever your name comes up."

"Where are you calling from?"

"The Dakotas. I'm staying at the casino. The kids are staying with their father. *Both* of them. Isn't that something?"

"If you say so. Did you notice the house we added to the plan?"

"House?" Monica pulled the laptop closer and scrolled down. "I thought we were going to remodel the trailer?"

"We might, but for a different purpose. I found a local prefab log house company that I want to use on the project, but I want it to be a surprise, so don't say anything to anyone."

"You don't do surprise houses."

"We are this time. But here's the deal: I want to do this sooner rather than later."

"What are you talking about?"

"The bottom fell out of the project I had slotted before this one. That little town in Texas that was trying to save Main Street? They sold out to developers in the eleventh hour. For a forty-acre outlet mall, they sent the mule to the glue factory."

"How much sooner are we talking?"

"ASAP," said Ella. "It sounds like you've already got a good handle on your end, and you know the more pressure they put on us time-wise, the more slack they'll cut us on budget. I like June, don't you?"

"It can be pretty here, with a little rain." Monica coughed wisps of smoke.

"How are you feeling, Monica?"

"I'm fine, thanks. You really don't have to worry about me, Ella. Especially out loud."

"Whose ears are we protecting?"

"We're protecting my rather late-blooming career, for starters. In our business, any sign of weakness and the jackals start sneaking into your camera shots."

"I tend to mind my own business, Monica. You know that."

"And I know you're not asking about my health for business reasons. I really do appreciate your concern, so let's just say, treat it like privileged information. Like you're my shrink or my confessor or something. I don't have many friends, and…" She caught herself. Since when was she allowed to wax pathetic? "Well, who has time, right? Friends take time."

"Right. And time is money in our business. How does your schedule look?"

"Tight." Like her chest. She stubbed the cigarette out in a clean ashtray.

"We'll work around you. You don't mind racking up the frequent flyers miles, do you?"

"I'll expect major slack. *Unlimited* slack."

"Duly noted," Ella said. "When you see Dillon, would you tell him to call my cell? I've tried him a couple of times today."

"He's home. I just spoke with him."

"Did you?"

"I'll let him know when I see him tomorrow morning. You haven't forgotten about the time difference, have you?"

"You talking L.A. time versus Indian time?"

"I'm talking time is money versus 'Who needs watches and wallets?'" Monica laughed. "Oh, my friend, this is going to be an interesting episode of *Who's Our Neighbor?*"

Chapter Thirteen

Dillon woke to early morning half-light feeling vaguely guilty. He was sleeping on the sofa, and he had no memory of what he'd done to get himself there. Blinking didn't hurt. Turning his head went okay. But his back was killing him, and Monica loomed large in his foggy brain. The kids...Pinky and D.J. were around somewhere, and they were all...

Grown.

A cleansing chill washed through him as he dragged himself off the sofa, pressed the kinks out of his back and headed straight for the phone.

"Hey." Happy sound. Then warm, rich, deep and singularly sincere. All good. All Ella. "I'm glad you called."

"Hey. Glad who called?"

"My phone says it's Dillon Black. I've been trying to call you. They've got this new gadget out now that you can put on your phone for people to leave messages."

"I don't want any messages." The long phone cord gave him leave to start the morning coffee. "I prefer live voices, and it's good to hear yours. Been trying to call you, too."

"I haven't...did you leave any messages?"

"There's no message. There's only you and me talking. You doin' okay?"

"Everything's lining up just fine. Better than fine, really, if you'd be interested in us getting our show on the road very soon—sooner than we projected."

"What did we project?" Keep her going, he thought. He didn't care what she talked about this morning, as long as she was talking to him.

"Last part of July, but now we're thinking early June, which would give you more time to use the camp this summer."

"It's June now, isn't it?"

"Almost. You'd be surprised how quickly we can switch gears in this business. I'd like to get together with you ASAP. When can you make time?"

"What day is ASAP?"

"I can be there as early as four."

"Today?"

"Unless that doesn't work for you. I want to meet with the Tribal Council, set up some merchant accounts, figure out where to put the trucks and trailers. And I'll need to interview prospective friends."

"Are you gonna get me some friends, too?" He laughed. "Man, I've hit the jackpot with this deal."

"We can use lots of community extras, but we'll pick a few to feature with special assignments. Nick and Lauren, of course."

"I've tried to keep the lid on this thing, but the word must be out on the moccasin telegraph, 'cause people are starting to offer all kinds of services. But good luck gettin' Nick in front of a camera." *Today. As early as four.* "You want me to meet you at the airport?"

"I'll need my own car, but thank you. I just sprang the schedule change on Monica, too, so—"

"She's here."

"I know. We spoke last night. I wasn't planning on bringing her on-site just yet, but I guess it'll be okay. You're not going to be butting heads with her over the interior decoration, are you?"

Was she kidding? "That's always been her department. I'm working tonight, so I'll look in on you. Say around—"

"The three of us could get together for dinner."

"How 'bout the two of us? On me this time."

"I'll be working with both of you," Ella reminded him. "Cooperation is key, and the family dynamic could make or break the whole production. Relatives count, too. And be thinking about those friends, okay?"

Friends, family, Indian countrymen. They all counted. Dillon wasn't counting on some pie-in-the-sky project down the road, but today counted in a big way. Today he would see friends, and he would have his family. He would spend this day with his children, who had returned to Indian country, if only briefly.

Emily had lived the life long enough that horses were in her blood, and Monica had found a stable close enough to their place in the Cities that Emily could take riding lessons. Monica was a great one for kids and lessons. By the time he'd started school, D.J. was already into music. But he'd never developed the fever for four-leggeds, gave even the dogs wide berth.

D.J. had tagged along out to the barn after Dillon had run the horses in at sunrise. Emily had her brother's mount all picked out. He said he liked the way the sorrel gelding looked without a saddle, but Emily had that all picked out for him, too, and the sheer weight of her attention seemed to carry him along. Dillon hung back and let her take charge. The boy drifted a distance from him, enclosed in a transparent bubble that Dillon didn't dare disturb. He kept stealing glances at the long, slight fingers and remembering the music. Anyone who could do what D.J. did with the strings of such a simple-looking instrument had power, and that kind of power wanted protection. *We can take the pickup,* Dillon had said before the saddles were all in place, but Emily had given him the *don't even* look, and D.J. had carefully climbed into the saddle.

Dillon rode a big buckskin gelding, and Emily chose a young Paint mare she'd worked with the previous summer. They started out slowly, following the trail worn over the years by horses and cattle coming and going from pens and people to grass and water. It took them over a hill and into a long, winding draw, where young calves had tucked into the sagebrush thickets while a single cow stood watch over them. The rest of the herd dotted the grassy slope. Dillon counted silently, while Emily automatically took a backup count. D.J. seemed to be enjoying the scenery, and that counted, too.

Emily looked the way Dillon felt on horseback—an extension of the motion more than the mount. Unlike her father, she moved the same way on the ground. Self-assured, like her mother. Dillon felt good about that. Monica had done well for herself, and her example would serve the kids in a world she understood better than he did. Emily had maybe gotten the best of both sets of genes. With D.J., it was hard to tell. He wasn't out to grab anything by the tail, but when he picked up that fiddle, he grabbed everything, heart and soul. The quiet man whose deep and private passion went on display in ways that proved the old saying: Actions speak louder than words. Like Nick Red Shield? Dillon had no doubt.

Near the Grand River Bridge they crossed the highway and rode the ridge above the river bottom, until they could see the shelter belt flanking the Red Shields' new house. A full-grown north-side shelter belt was worth almost as much as a house, and Dillon felt good every time he saw those trees guarding Nick's home against the winds from the white direction. The memory of his own despair had been transformed.

He'd done a stupid thing, but he'd been rolling in stupidity in those days. Like a trail of gunpowder, one fire had led to another. He'd fallen hard for a woman who had her act together when he was just learning the lines. Fallen in step, in synch, into bed and kept on rolling. Damn, she was hot. Older, smarter, situated better inside her skin, Monica's only weakness in those days had been her crazy attraction to him. He'd taken it for what it was worth and then some. And he'd tried to do right by her.

It was hard at first, but Nick had helped him get a job in the oil fields. He missed the rush he'd always gotten riding roughstock, but working as a roughneck, he'd brought home the best paychecks of his life. Emily was getting out of diapers and into everything, and Monica was miserable with her second pregnancy, barely able to sub occasionally at the local high school. It was the only time in their marriage when he could actually call himself the breadwinner.

But the fire on the number six rig had changed all that. Nick had been bound and determined to make a man of his younger brother, but manhood was not to be John's fate. He would never erase the memory of Nick bearing John's blackened corpse from the inferno that had been the rig

Dillon had been working. He had left early, leaving Nick to finish his shift and take the heat in a way that nobody could have foreseen.

Hindsight was a horrible companion to the image of what the flames had done to the two men he loved like brothers. It was the end of Dillon's roughneck days and the beginning of some rough-edged ways. He'd lost his grip that night, like losing his seat on a trusted horse, but it had taken him a while to finally land flat on his belly, pull his face up from the mud and find himself looking up at another fire—this time of his own making—and realize that what they always said was true. A guy either had to get himself back in the saddle or turn the horse loose and spend the rest of his sorry life dragging his own ass around. Pitiful thing, a cowboy on foot.

Beautiful thing, a man like Nick Red Shield astride the horse he'd chosen to sire Wolf Trail Paints. Riding out to meet them, Nick showed his trust in the majestic black-and-white racehorse by carrying his adopted son, four-year-old "Little Joe," on the saddle in front of him.

"We used to do that." Dillon squinted into the morning sun as he grinned at his own son. "You and me. Remember?"

"I don't remember much about living out here. I remember getting in trouble for leaving my tricycle in the driveway because somebody ran over it, and I remember starting school. Is Mr. Hanson still around?"

"The music teacher? Last I heard, he moved to Bismarck. Maybe he's in the phone book." Dillon adjusted his hat against the sun. "Who was that kid you used to take lessons with? Maybe he's still around."

"I don't need to connect, Dad. We were five, six years old." D.J. shrugged. "Brian Kessler."

"Oh, yeah, Kessler. Come to think of it, they moved away. His mom was a teacher, too."

"Isn't that where we used to live?"

"Same spot, brand-new house. You remember the old one?"

"Kinda."

"Uncle Nick pretty much built that house. Right, Daddy?" Pinky chimed in.

"Can't swing a hammer worth a damn, but see the horse Uncle Nick's riding? You won't find a prettier sawhorse than True Colors."

"I don't know what kinda bullshit your ol' man's trying to feed you, D.J., but around here, we don't go by appearances. True Colors is too pretty to be a racehorse, and Little Joe here is way too good-lookin' to be my son. Like they say, the Lord works in mysterious ways." Nick shook hands with D.J. "Welcome back. It's been too long."

"We were just talking about the kids he remembers, the teachers, how he started taking violin lessons right here on the rez. Wait till you hear him play, Nick. You'll think you just tuned in to Prairie Public Radio."

"He's been on Minnesota Public Radio," Emily said. "But last night he played for Sugar and her colt while I dressed a wire cut. The music really helped her settle down."

"I've heard of using music with milk cows."

"D.J. let her check him out, then the violin. Apparently they both smelled okay." Emily glanced her brother's way and wrinkled her nose. "To a horse."

"You be sure and tell Lauren all about it over breakfast. She'll want a demonstration."

"Auntie Lauren is a professional jockey," Emily said with pride.

"She rides in horse races?" D.J. asked.

"Not anymore. She's talking like she's gonna ride the filly she's been training, but she can talk all she wants."

"Like you could stop her. Any woman with that kind of skill—" Emily objected.

"She's like your mom."

"Like a woman with skills is such a rarity," she chided.

"Like the blisters on my ass are such a rarity," D.J. grumbled. "Can we stop bouncing?"

"Try standing in the stirrups," Emily suggested, and she demonstrated.

"It's hard to stand when your legs have turned into jelly."

"You need to start working out."

"You need to practice your piano."

"I don't play—"

"Smile, kids," Dillon said. "Here comes your mother."

The blueberry pancakes were delicious. Monica ate the better part of a short stack and was impressed, which was to say that if she weren't predisposed to weigh the merits of every piece of food she put into her mouth, she would have enjoyed eating Lauren's pancakes. She was impressed with the house, too. Lauren had excellent taste in furniture and an eye for color, and she seemed happy to put both to use in her little abode on the prairie, where almost no one would ever see the results.

"I love the fireplace," Monica said, admiring the stonework surrounded by windows, which would later turn the sunset into part of the décor. "It's classic. It'll never look dated. And gas is so much easier than wood."

"We have a woodstove in the rec room for backup heating, but we did the fireplace this way for the view," Lauren said of buttes squaring off under the cerulean sky. "It just doesn't get any prettier than that."

"Or any more desolate."

"It was Dillon's idea," Lauren said quietly.

"The windows over the fireplace?"

"Trading home sites." She said it sympathetically, as though she owed Monica some kind of justification or apology. "Building our house here. I guess Nick always admired this spot, and according to Dillon, Indian tradition holds that when you really want to honor somebody, you give them something of yours that they admire." She touched Monica's arm. "I know this is where your house was."

Monica resisted a strong urge to step away from the smaller woman's touch. "Does Dillon talk about it?"

"Only to say that he burned it down."

Her jaw tightened. "Does he say it like it was a joke?"

"No."

Monica drew a deep breath. As she released it, the tension drained from her shoulders. Softly she asked, "Does he say why?"

"Only that he went a little crazy. So, no, he really doesn't talk about it much."

"How about me?" She avoided Lauren's eyes. "Does he talk about me?"

"Not really."

"I'm sorry. I have no business… You hardly know me, and I'm grilling you about my ex-husband, who's part of your family now and not…" She gave a wistful smile. "I put a lot of myself into that house, small as it was. I think I left some of it behind, and I don't know whether that's good or bad."

"I think it's exciting, what you're doing. Dillon has

told us a little about the plans. Nick is a bit skeptical, but that's Nick."

Monica was glad to change the subject. "I just got the plans myself, and I have some changes to offer."

"He did say that Ella's plans were tentative. But whatever you can do to help them keep that camp going…" Lauren had a pretty smile. "I think it's exciting. Emily is ecstatic. She's very proud of all your success."

"So am I. Of hers, I mean. I never dreamed she'd go to school in Montana, of all places, or get into veterinary science, but she's doing very well." She turned as the men descended the steps, each carrying two cups. The scent said coffee. "Isn't she, Dillon? Ella's been trying to call you, by the way."

"Since when?" He handed her a cup. "I talked with her first thing this morning."

"She told you she wants to start sooner?"

"What she said was she's coming back out to see me. She called it groundwork. Said groundwork is key." He smiled. "I couldn't agree more. Big proponent of groundwork, me." Hesitating before taking a drink from his cup, he turned to Nick. "Hey, the plans Ella drew up include a roundpen. We can really use that. And to think she says she doesn't know anything about training horses." Cup on its way to his lips, he mused, "Groundwork."

"Ella knows her business, Dillon," Lauren said. "She's a very successful woman."

Dillon glanced from one woman to the other. "Hell, I'm surrounded by successful women. They don't scare me."

"We can tell, D," Nick said. "Lauren was goin' for the word to the wise, giving you the benefit of the doubt. But it looks to me like you're rushing in."

"And you didn't?"

"Never claimed it didn't scare me," Nick said as he slipped his arm around his wife. And the look he gave his partner said, *Back at'cha*.

"Never claimed to be all that wise." Dillon smiled. "But seems like she's the one rushin' back to see me."

Chapter Fourteen

Alone at last.

Ella knew she was in deep trouble when she realized how much attention she'd devoted to ditching Monica. So be it. The ex-wife and kids had finally gone elsewhere, and here was Dillon on the couch in her hotel suite with a whole hour to spare. And how did she propose they spend it?

Watching a CD.

Hey, business was business.

They had spent the day rounding up potential crafters and seamstresses, roof-beam raisers and fence-post setters. Sandwiches, coffee and a few phone calls were all it took to spread the word to enough people to fill every chair in each of two of Dillon's sisters' homes thirty miles apart. Little attention had been paid to Emily's video camera as Monica renewed acquaintances, Dillon introduced Ella around and Ella talked up her project. It was all about getting a feel for the community.

And Dillon was loving it. Friends and family were curious to find out what was what and who might be part of it. They came and went and took part in the conversation, the chitchat, the clowning. It was all on the CD, which had Dillon wearing an outdated pair of glasses—apparently he was slightly near-sighted, which Ella hadn't noticed before—and glued to the set. Same set, same suite, same show under discussion as the first time they'd done this together. Different Dillon. This Dillon was invested, and he was bouncing between celebrating and fretting over the nature of his investment, which had nothing to do with money.

"That's a ready-made comedy cast right there," he said. "I don't see how you're gonna pick a few and leave the rest out."

"They weren't trying out," Ella claimed. "Well, okay, they were, but we'll use everyone in one way or another. We shoot a ton of film over the course of an erection."

He feigned shock and then laughed. "Use me on another play, coach, I'm not touchin' that one."

"Hollywood humor. Not quite as dry as the Indian variety."

"Dry?" He shook his head, chuckling. "Tempting, but I'm still gonna pass. Keep my dignity intact." He glanced from one corner of the ceiling to the other. "For all I know, you've got a camera rollin' right now."

"And that, my friend, is Lesson One. The hidden camera. Beware." She hiked her eyebrows. "Be *very* aware."

"Hiding a camera to get the kind of stuff you're talkin' about sounds like entrapment to me. Are you some kind of detective?"

"That's already being done on another network. *Caught In the Act.* People actually apply to be on the show hoping—*hoping*—to catch their spouse cheating."

"Real people?" His wonderment was refreshing. "And they use real private—" He broke off and laughed.

"Yes, real, but obviously there's nothing private about it, which might be why they prefer to be called professional investigators these days."

"Real dicks are sensitive," he said, nodding in sympathy.

"Damn. It must be hard out there for a spouse these days. What does a guy get for going on *that* show?"

"Justice or just deserts, I guess, depending. Not exactly television's finest hour, as far as I'm concerned, but I'm not a critic." She glanced at the TV screen as the camera shifted from two windblown women clipping colorful quilts to a clothesline to four men clustered around a kitchen counter where they were filling their plates with sandwich fixings. "This is really going to be an interesting mix."

"You say you feed twice a day?" asked the young man on TV. His long braids were bound so tightly in strips of red cloth that they lay against his shoulders in stiff curves, like a pair of parentheses.

"Two hot, sit-down meals, but there's always food available," Ella said off-camera.

"West Coast style, or real food?"

"It's all catered, and we arrange as much as we can locally. And I'm really fussy about craft services, which is your snack wagon, as opposed to catering, which is your serious chuck wagon. Craft services puts out food all day long, and I insist on substance, because we're not sitting around. We're working. We'll keep you well fed."

"See how Bobby perks right up?" Dillon asked with a chuckle.

"But not for you, Big Eagle," said Dillon's recorded voice, also off-camera. "Hollywood's lookin' for that lean and hungry look."

"Like you get when we cue up 'Doggie In the Window'?" Bobby Big Eagle of the parenthetical braids had a daily show on rez radio. Ella had already been tapped for a guest interview.

She glanced at Dillon and caught him grinning at the TV screen. "He got me good, huh?"

She gave a tight-lipped nod for the joke, which would be misconstrued outside Indian country. Puppy soup had once been a traditional delicacy, but no one still indulged these days.

"The dog-eating Sioux jokes will probably end up on the cutting-room floor," she said. "We'd be flooded with mail."

"Better add that to my notes. Erection: in." He air-sketched a check mark, followed by an *X*. "Puppy soup: out."

"But don't tell Bobby. We don't want to throw a wet blanket over anything."

Another air *X*. "No back-to-the-blanket jokes."

"I was just trying to let you in on things." Impulsively, she grabbed his arm. "Because I'm counting on you to work with me here."

"I thought Emily was your chosen ally?" He nodded toward the video, but what she noticed was the warmth of his hand, now covering hers. "How about this? This is funny."

"...for the heavy lifting," Vincent Many Wounds was saying, as he turned chin to shoulder in profile and flexed his right bicep. "You're lookin' at a man of iron."

"Better knock the rust off before you try movin' any rocks, man," said an off-camera voice.

Another chimed in. "Looks like the ol' lady left her man of iron out in the rain."

"Locked out again, Vince?"

"We can also edit stuff in," Ella told Dillon. "Ordinarily our owners and guests wouldn't see any of this preliminary stuff, but I wanted to get your perspective on..." She looked up at him. "Dillon, this show is going to be different. We did one other project using a crew member's hometown, but it was about old school friends. This is going to be about a deeper, denser kind of circle, or system of circles, or…" He was smiling, as though it was cute, this excitement of hers. He still didn't get it. "I really think we can take this to the next level."

His thumb stirred slightly against the back of her hand. "No doubt."

"Which would be great for me, but along with the obvious benefits to you, it would mean a lot to Monica."

"All three of us? Sounds like a crowd."

"Our needs and our interests are totally different, but it's like the perfect storm," she rushed on. "The confluence of the right components at the right moment creating an irresistible opportunity."

"Just what is the next level? I mean, yeah, I'm enjoying this little show a lot more than the last one you got me up here for, but I was thinkin' more like…" He cupped her chin in his palm and lowered his head for a soft, sweet kiss. "What level would you call this?"

"Basic," she said, hushed.

"Let's try again." He peeled off his glasses and set them aside, turned, took her in his arms, took more time and gave more care, caress, cosseting. "Hmm?"

"Kicks it up a notch," she said when she recovered her breath.

"But not to a whole new level?" He touched his forehead to hers. "Which is okay. You don't wanna force the drama part, especially if you're goin' for a triangle. Gotta build the tension by…" Another sweet, soft kiss. "…slow degrees."

She was pretty sure he knew she was talking about

taking this episode of the show to the next level, but she wasn't going to ask. The basics need not be rushed.

Dillon knew the crew was due to arrive while he was at work, but he wasn't expecting to find a whole damn circus when he got home. An array of trucks, trailers, campers, cars and strange people had turned his quiet country place into what could pass for redneck heaven—a trailer park/truck stop island in a sea of grass. Unable to mount a convincing defense, the dogs had given up their barking and retreated to the doghouse, where Mama rested her muzzle on her paws and watched through the doorway. On his way to the barn, Dillon stopped to reassure her, but she offered no more than an upward roll of those big, sad eyes, which was her way of telling him she'd tried to hold them off, but she was outnumbered.

"It's okay, Mama."

The mongrel shepherd turned her face from him and gave a disgusted sigh. She knew the truth. He'd authorized an invasion.

He checked on the horses he'd kept in overnight and found only the brood mare and her colt. No saddle horses. Somebody—three somebodies—had gone for a ride. If it turned out that Emily wasn't one of them, he would start worrying. He made a mental note to start laying down the law, regardless. The Wolf Trail was no dude ranch. Riders were to follow his rules.

He checked the water in the tank and filled the hay rack, all the while mentally girding himself to walk into the little piece of Hollywood that was camped on his doorstep. He half expected them to notice his presence and send out an emissary, and he knew damn well he was summoning a layer of cool to cover for the unexpected combination of butterflies and knots in his gut.

Wing knots?

Dillon smiled. He'd been a fun-lover and a thrill-seeker in his time, a time when he would easily have said, *Bring it on.* What could hold more diversionary promise than a freakin' carnie camp?

But they weren't sitting next to some stock-car track or parked at the powwow grounds. They had circled their trailers on top of his roots. Crisp prairie grass crunched beneath his boots as he headed for a truck emblazoned with "Who's Our Neighbor?" and a logo of what looked like a community barn-raising. As he rounded the corner of the church, he heard his name called.

Ella looked sweet in jeans and a straw hat that was cowboy in style, if not the real thing. She smiled and waved him over to where she stood with some spiky-haired guy in the long, late afternoon shade from the church building. The guy wore a pale blue t-shirt that fit him as though he'd had it custom made. You could count the cans in his abs. And they both had on sunglasses. Dillon could use a pair himself.

He greeted Ella with a grin. "Is this what they mean when they say, 'It takes a village'?"

"Who's *they?*" she asked him, returning his smile. Which was a good sign.

"Not us," said Wears His Six Pack. "We say, 'It takes money.' That's our mantra. It takes money to make money. He's got what it takes, and what it takes is money. Villages are like scripts—a dime a dozen. All this stuff…" His sweeping gesture took in sundry mobile units. "Just stuff. Money and star power." Hands on hips, the man nodded. "You must be our home owner."

"Dillon Black." He offered a handshake. "I'm sorry, I didn't catch your name."

The man looked confused as he turned to Ella. Either he didn't remember his own name, or it was somebody else's job to announce it.

"Tate Fox is our carpenter."

"This one's got plans for you, man." Fox indicated Ella as he pumped Dillon's hand. "Hope you brought your posse."

"I'm more the Lone Ranger type."

Oddly, Fox laughed like a fox—a high-pitched sound that started no deeper than the back of his tongue. It didn't fit the abs nearly as well as the smile did. The smile had fizz. "Have I got a part for you," Fox said jovially.

"If it calls for a tomahawk, forget it, but I can swing a hammer as good as the next guy."

"Would I suggest a role that wasn't perfectly PC?" Fox raised his right hand, then quickly clapped it over his sculpted chest. "Not me, I swear on my SAG card. But just so you know, Ella doesn't plan for me. She *suggests*. I have final say." He slid Ella a wink. "Just so happens my final say pretty much coincides with her ideas most of the time."

"Don't worry," Ella told Dillon. "We've got professionals drawing up the final plans, and Tate has a crew, a personal assistant and a hairstylist."

"That's called star treatment," Fox explained.

"We also have a designer, who's officially responsible for the overall plan."

Fox cast a glance toward the highway. "Where is Zooey, anyway?"

"She's coming in tomorrow," Ella said.

"You mean, I could've taken another day?"

"We're going to get some interior stuff in the church with you and Monica."

Dillon was getting confused. "I thought Monica was the designer."

"She's the decorator," Ella said.

"Nice thing about Monica, she's not out to steal the show. Regular team player. She's really into decorating, and she's good at it." Fox turned his blackout shades toward Dillon. "I take it you've met her."

"I used to be married to her."

Ella touched Fox's shoulder. "That's part of the storyline, Tate."

"Seriously?" Fox cocked his head, considering. "Dillon Black. Monica Wilson-Black. Interesting angle." His gaze swept the hills. "She actually lived out here?"

"It's been a while," Dillon acknowledged.

"And you're divorced?"

Dillon gave a curt nod.

"But still on speaking terms? Man, that's cool. I thought this Indian reservation thing was about Ella." Fox turned to her briefly. "Not *about* Ella. The Ella *connection*. I thought you might have an on-camera moment, you know, stepping out of the woodwork…" He tapped her on the back. "Woodwork? Yeah?"

"I get it, Tate, but I'm not connected. And I like being invisible."

"Like you could ever be invisible, love." The shoulder pat turned into a friendly, two-second rub. Two seconds too long, from where Dillon stood. "But, no, the interior decorator and her cowboy ex could be a good hook. Could be fun to see what happens. A little soap-opera thing, maybe. Horse opera."

"You want a singin' cowboy, you gotta to go back to Hollywood," Dillon said.

"I think we've finally buried the last of that breed. But you've got the Native-American mystique going for you." Fox looked Dillon down and up. "This is one handsome buck, huh? Good find, Ella. Any luck yet in the disabled war vet department? Guy with a pregnant wife, two or three kids on the ground?" He punched himself in the chest. "Hits you right where you live. I see us setting them up with an in-home day-care facility."

Dillon gave Ella a *what's-up-with-this-guy?* look.

She smiled. "What if the disabled soldier's a woman, Tate?"

"That could work. Especially if you can find a pregnant one. So I'm thinking tomorrow…" Fox's continual scanning hit pay dirt in the distance past Dillon's shoulder. "We've got incoming."

Dillon turned toward the sound of hoofbeats. "Where's she been?"

"All my life, huh?" Tate asked. "That's one pretty picture. Hope somebody has a camera focused in her dir—"

"That's my daughter."

It was as though he'd said *watch your mouth*. The three stood in silence watching the Paint horse and its pretty rider gallop toward them. When she pulled up, Dillon half expected her to shout, "Take cover!"

"What's up, Em?" He stepped closer as she swung down from the saddle. The Paint pranced in place, while Dillon lent a calming hand, taking over the reins.

"We went out for a ride, and Mother must have pulled something in her leg."

"Where is she?"

"On the river bluff, almost due north. That big old cottonwood?"

Dillon nodded.

"D.J.'s with her. She thought it was a cramp, but I don't know. We had to get her off the horse because we were afraid she'd—"

"We'll take the pickup." Dillon turned to Ella. "Can you take care of the horse?"

"You mean…"

Suddenly, there Ella stood, holding reins that were attached to a very large, sweaty, wide-eyed animal. She looked up at the horse, back at the withdrawing horsemen, up at the horse again.

Wide-eyed? More like *wild*.

"Just pull the saddle and turn her loose in the corral," Dillon called out as he opened the pickup door.

"Sh-sure."

Ella turned to Tate. "You know anything about horses?"

"I know I'd look good on one." He was watching Emily get into the truck. "But maybe not as good as she does."

"I don't think you wanna go there, Tate. Now, help me get this—"

"Why not?"

"Because you really don't want to get hit where you live. They actually cut off balls here," she said as she reached for his hand and filled it with the two leather straps. "I've actually seen them do it."

Chapter Fifteen

The pain had struck so suddenly and so intensely that Monica had lost it. It being her Monica-ness, and the loss, of course, being temporary.

She turned to her son, who stood by her quietly, as always, awaiting his cue. She was sitting in hard grass on hard ground, hurting and feeling stupid—two conditions she tolerated poorly—and he stood nearby, unhappy with his mother for getting him into all this, and with his sister for leaving him holding all the reins. At a glance Monica read Dylan's mind—anxiety warring with antipathy—but she wouldn't hear of it. Not if she set the proper tone, regardless of ground and grass and untimely pain.

"Wow." She made a project of flexing each joint in her left leg, starting easily at the ankle. "Talk about blindsided. But it seems to be letting up, thank God." Testing, she slowly drew her knee to her chest, renewing the shooting pain, but with less bite. The first hit had been a royal bitch. She drew a deep breath. "I'll be back in the saddle before anyone else sees me like this."

"You're getting back up there?" Dylan slid his gaze up the grazing sorrel's neck, as though she'd asked him to haul her ass up to the top of Pike's Peak.

"In a minute. I don't want to spaz out again."

He squatted, bracing one knee on the ground. "You think it's just some kind of spasm?"

"Absolutely. Reality spasms. My body's saying, whoa, when was the last time you rode a bicycle, never mind a horse? Escalator, that's my speed."

"This was all your idea," he reminded her. He didn't know what else to do. She could hear it in his voice. He hated it that Emily was the rider, the one who'd had a good excuse to leave the scene.

"I know. Admittedly, I was trying to show off for you and Emily before I tried showing off for everyone else. Which I will. You know me."

"Thought I did." He looked at the ends of the four long leather reins he held in his gifted hands. He might have been holding worms. Harmless, but strange. "I don't know what we're doing here, Mom. I don't know what this is all about."

"Yes, you do. Or you will. You're like me. Our intuition rarely fails us. We don't have to talk these things to death." She patted his knee, a gesture he tolerated. He wasn't much for physical affection. But then, neither was she. "We know each other."

"Right." He meant *wrong*, but they both knew better than to say so. "You said this was for Emily, but my unfailing intuition tells me there's more to it. I'm probably in for a reality spasm, too."

"My beautiful, beautiful boy." Another knee pat. This time he moved just enough to break the contact, all but a pinky fingertip. "I'm so proud of you. I can't say that often enough."

His smile was oddly forgiving. "'The lady protests too much, methinks.'"

"Don't even go there. You know the difference between

praise and protest." She scanned the far hills. "This is for all of us. I haven't given your father his due in recent years."

"And what is he due?"

"Time with his children. Before they're gone, replaced by adults whose time is less and less their own."

"We could've gone to Disneyland."

She laughed a little. Enough to make herself feel better, anyway. "We're going Disneyland one better. We'll have more than a bunch of pictures to show for this trip."

"Here they come." He stood to get a better look at the red pickup bouncing over the wild ground. "I think you should see your doctor about this."

"He'll tell me to stay off of horses."

Both pickup doors swung open, but Dillon got to her first. When Dillon was good, he was very, very good, and it was good to see him coming for her, looking sure and strong, good to know he'd brought his good hands and his easy ways.

"Lose your seat?"

"Not lost. Vacated it voluntarily. Thanks to Charley." She rubbed her left leg with the heel of her hand.

"His name is Sha." He nodded in the direction of the sorrel gelding. "Lakota for *red*."

"I'm more concerned about a horse called Charley. Slang for pain."

"You realize what this means," Dillon glanced at their son. "Ma fought the Sha, and the Sha won."

Emily groaned, but Dylan gave in to his father's charm, his tentative laugh lifting Monica's spirits. His father could never make up for lost time, but he would win his son's affection as surely as he had Emily's. And Monica would probably begrudge Dillon his gain, but he *was* due. Overdue, to be honest, and she couldn't afford to be anything less.

"Need a hand?" He reached down, but rather than try to pull her up, he drew her hand around the back of his neck, slipped his arm around her back and lifted her. "Okay?" he asked when he had her standing mostly on her right leg. She nodded. The pain was withdrawing by slow degrees.

"D.J. and I can take the horses back," Emily said as Dillon led Monica slowly toward the truck.

A few moments later he turned the pickup around and headed for the highway.

"How're you doin'?"

"Better, thanks. No fuss when we get back, okay?"

He gave half a smile. "I wouldn't know how."

"Just a crazy muscle spasm." She dug her fingers into her thigh, kneading the mound of dough she pictured inside her jeans. "It's always something. After forty, it's patch, patch, patch. Have you noticed?"

"Not yet."

"Of course not. You're still just a kid at heart. I've had trouble with RLS lately. Maybe this is related." She looked up from her kneading and caught his quizzical eyebrow. "Restless Leg Syndrome."

"Sounds like a theme for Hank Williams."

"No, it's real."

"So's terminal lonesome."

She dropped her head back against the headrest and sighed. "God, you're cute when you do that."

"Do what?"

"Sing 'I'm just a country boy.' I still get weak in the knees."

"Rub 'em real hard. It's just Charley again."

She wanted to laugh but didn't quite have it in her.

"Surprised you decided to go out riding. You should've waited for me."

"Surprising you was part of the plan. Obviously we're going to want to feature horses in the show, and I thought I'd be part of that. I used to ride."

"Sure you did."

"I did," she insisted. "Before we had Dylan. And then there were two." There had been a time when she would have said three. Two little ones and a big one, with only one of her and little time left for remembering that. But that time was over. Almost over. "I was doing fine today until I got that cramp. But I'll get back in the groove. From what Emily says, your horse program is all-inclusive. Novice riders, troubled teenagers, kids lacking confidence, seeking identity, all that."

"And you fit into which category?"

"Seeking identity. Looking for my inner cowboy."

"Hell, honey, where do you think the restless legs come from? I planted more than just…" They exchanged glances as he made the turn through an open gate and into safer discourse. "Do I have to teach my old farm dogs new tricks? Or will these new TV neighbors be satisfied with the same old Indian dog and pony show?"

"We can get by with being ourselves, Dillon. Our clever, charming selves."

"You didn't tell me they were bringing a small army."

"How else would you build a horse camp from the ground up in less than two weeks?"

"Guess I'm gonna find out." Approaching the television show's signature truck, he slowed the pickup. "How do you wanna handle this? Can you walk okay?"

She nodded. Among the setup crew she noticed one of her favorite faces engrossed in the contents of a tool locker, before he glanced up, recognized her and brightened. She wasn't ready. "Could you take me over to your house and grab my purse out of the car on the way?"

Too late. He waved, and she returned it.

Dillon nodded toward the man. "You know this guy?"

"That's Mike Murphy, the lead carpenter. The *real* carpenter. *Reality* is a relative term. Stop." She leaned out the window, anticipating a cheek-to-cheek moment with the man whose salt-and-pepper hair, natural tan and slight Australian accent distinguished him from the rest of the cast and crew. "How was your trip?" she asked. .

"I rode in on the truck, so it was a little long. Just completing my check-in. I don't know about the crew, but tools and materials are present and accounted for." Mike tipped his head to one side for an eye-to-eye with Dillon. "You've got some beautiful country here."

Dillon nodded as she introduced them. These two would get on well, she thought. Television "reality" couldn't touch them. They were genuine.

"Tate and Ella are here," she told her friend, "and Zooey's on her way. I'm sure demolition can start anytime."

"Demolition?"

"Oh, Dillon, you'll be amazed at how fast it goes. It's really fun to watch." She turned from the doubt in her former husband's eyes to the warmth in the eyes of the other man. "What do you think, Mike?"

"It looks like a great project. Now that I see all this..." He glanced across the hood of the pickup toward the distant, sky-buttressing buttes. "This country reminds me of where I grew up."

"I knew you'd be jazzed about it, Mike. I can't wait for you to meet my kids. They're out riding."

"I heard they'd gotten you on a horse."

"I overdid it a little, but don't tell anyone." She patted the callused hand he'd rested on the door. "Save me a place for supper."

"Third star from the left and three tables down," he quipped as he pushed back, acknowledged Dillon with a nod and stood aside while they moved on.

"That's a pain-free smile." Dillon raised his brow, daring denial as he shut off the pickup.

She smiled bigger and opened the door. "I like Mike."

"And when Monica likes someone, it shows. Need any help?"

"Just my purse and some water, if you wouldn't mind."

Dillon watched her out of the corner of his eye while he greeted the dogs and detoured to her car for what looked more like a fancy shopping bag than a purse. She strode with barely a hitch until she reached the steps, and then she relied heavily on the railing. She was still hurting. Whatever the problem, he for sure didn't know the half of it. With Monica, keeping up appearances was an art form.

He followed her inside, where she'd already claimed a seat on the sofa. He delivered the big black leather bag with a glass of water and watched her sort through several pill bottles before she opened one.

"For the restless legs?"

She tossed back pills and water, swallowed and smiled. "Medicating the inner cowboy."

"He's probably lookin' for a shot of whiskey. Sorry I can't accommodate him."

"These don't mix well with whiskey."

She was missing the point—one he realized he had little cause to make with his former wife.

He sat down beside her. "With Murphy and Fox, your

carpentry department seems long on chiefs. I hope you've got a few Indians for them to boss around."

"Mike's a professional carpenter. Journeyman? Whatever, he's top of the line. Tate Fox is one of the stars. You met him?" Dillon nodded. "Did he say something stupid?"

"Matter of opinion, and I'm keepin' all mine to myself. What's this about demolition?"

"That's what we call the first stage of any project. Clearing out whatever goes, prepping what stays, doing the groundwork. Lots of heavy equipment, which doesn't make the best TV. They'll grab a few shots that they'll edit in when—"

"From building a house to training a horse, it's all in the groundwork."

"Good line." She touched his arm. "Be sure to say it again when the camera's rolling."

"I thought we had a deal, Monica. No script."

"It's your line. I'm only trying to—"

"I don't need you to tell me what to say. Okay?" Her turn to nod. "The plan is to add to what's here. There's not gonna be any big teardown, right?"

"You're talking about—"

"Demolition."

"We're not planning major demolition, so keep the matches in your pocket."

"I don't carry matches anymore." He looked down at his hands, braced on his knees. "Don't need to."

"I'm sorry. That was…"

He waited, mildly curious to hear what she thought it was.

"I've been trying to quit, too," she said softly. "What's your secret?"

He looked her in the eye. "I've got no secrets."

"Maybe that's it," she said cheerfully. "No secrets."

"Monica, you…" He drew a deep breath and blew it out wearily. "You being here, it kinda feels like the past is breathing down my neck again."

"What does that mean?"

"I don't know," he claimed. "I don't know why I let you…" He shook his head. "Shit."

"What?"

"I didn't let anybody talk me into this. I talked myself into it. I looked at those plans, and I heard some big announcer's voice in my head saying, 'All this could be yours.' And I said, 'Hell, yeah, bring it on.'"

"What's wrong with that?"

"I don't know yet. I've been building my life up piece by piece, and it's taken years. Now this two-week transformation comes along, and it's supposed to leave me with…" He rolled his eyes, gave another sigh. "It's that word *demolition*. Makes me a little nervous."

"If you don't trust me, trust Ella."

"I hardly know Ella."

"But you want to." She pulled a pack of a cigarettes and a lighter from the big purse, then glanced up, smiling. "When Dillon wants to get to know someone better, it shows."

She was about to light up, and he wasn't smiling. "You'll have to take that outside," he said.

"Oh."

Surprised, Monica?

"You don't allow smoking in *your* house," he pointed out.

"No, but—"

"But this isn't much of a house, right? It's a POS trailer. Maybe you didn't notice, but it doesn't smell like smoke."

"—but I do it anyway. In my house. Occasionally. More

all the time." The proof lay awkwardly in her hands. And her pale, thin face was fast turning pink. "I'm a smoker, Dillon. I'm a good cook who can't taste much, and I don't notice the presence or absence of the smell of smoke." She dropped the cigarettes back into her purse. "I don't need this."

"Yeah? Well, neither do I."

"I meant the cigarette. You're right." She tossed the lighter into the bag. It clattered against something, maybe a pill bottle. "You're absolutely right, and I'm sorry. Your home is not a piece of shit." Her forefinger signaled the beginning of an enumeration. "No smoking inside, no telling you what to say, no trying to have the last word or claiming to speak on your behalf or, or… What else?"

He only counted three fingers. Wasn't she on four?

"We're not married anymore," he reminded her. "We're two separate people."

"Two *very different* people."

"That's always been true." He spoke patiently, when he could have added *no rewording what I say and trying to pass it off as your point.* "But when we were married, we tried to be together. Now we're two *separate* people."

"And it's been good for both of us." She gave a tight smile. "I'm sure anyone who knew us together thought, *whew!* I mean, your friends probably wondered, why didn't he leave sooner? She's such a tight-ass. And mine probably said…" She gave her head a quick shake and stared off across the room.

"I didn't leave you," he said quietly.

"I didn't have any friends."

"Bullshit. You've got friends all over the country. You've got friends here. Out there." He pointed toward the window. "What about Mike, the carpenter?" he insisted, and she shrugged and smiled like a girl with a secret crush. "Ah, that's different."

"Same difference?"

"You being a woman, yeah, that's more difference than most guys know what to do with. We're good at putting the parts together, but beyond that, we're all thumbs."

"Which can be quite effective." She laughed, groaned, drew a breath and sighed. "It's that inner cowboy. I'd better take another pill."

"If your legs are feeling restless, maybe we should go for a little—" He frowned and cocked his head at the sound of more noise outside. Another invasion? A convoy of tanks? "What now?"

"Heavy equipment," Monica said. "Do you mind if I lie down for a while? I promise not to smoke in the house."

Dillon peered out the window. "It's Pete Two Horse's outfit. Bulldozer, backhoe, cement truck. Looks like they actually hired an Indian contractor."

"That's Ella's doing."

"Cool." He grinned. "I gotta hand it to her...."

Monica closed her eyes. "You go do that."

Chapter Sixteen

Shortly before noon the next day, the caterers served the first full meal under a huge tent that reminded Dillon of a big summertime church meeting he'd attended with his grandfather. He wasn't sure how old he'd been, but he remembered a big white tent pitched in the middle of a sundried field, with cars lined up on one side and more people milling about than he'd ever seen at church. He remembered how electrifying his expectations had been, and how disappointing his discovery of a tent full of folding chairs. No performing elephants, no clowns, no girls on big swings and not much air.

Moving from sun to shade and breathing air scented with barbequed beef and fresh-baked bread took him back, but when he saw Vincent Many Wounds and Bobby Big Eagle edging along the buffet table, filling their plates and jawing with the cooks, Dillon decided that this time there *would* be clowns. He claimed a table at the back of the tent, where he felt a cross breeze, and waved his friends over. They gave him full credit for a good spread and persuaded him to join them when they returned to the buffet for refills. By that time somebody up front was fiddling with knobs, testing a microphone, trying to get enough sound out of the portable speaker so that a show could go on. Introductions were on the agenda, but making them heard over the roar of the bulldozer and the rumble of the backhoe threatened to be a challenge.

There were more titles than you could find in the library. The director of photography—an upbeat black guy named Darius Bird—got to run the meeting and maybe the whole show. At least part of his title was "director," and Dillon hoped that meant somebody was actually in charge of all these people. The camera handlers and sound recorders barely rated a mention, probably because they worked behind the scenes. It seemed as though there were people in charge of real work, like painting and carpentry, and people with titles like set dresser and technical supervisor, who were in charge of fantasy. As Bird repeatedly pointed out, "We're building two things simultaneously—a fabulous facility for Mr. Black's wonderful Mystic Warrior Horse Camp, and a fabulous TV show for Mr. and Mrs. America."

There was no mistaking the stars of the show. Monica Wilson-Black, the decorator, was given credit for bringing *Who's Our Neighbor?* to the South Dakota prairie and, more specifically, the reservation. But Dillon was relieved to see that she wasn't vying for the spotlight, which was too small for the two bodies already contending for it. The biggest cheers and applause had been saved for "hot carpenter" Tate Fox and "designer hottie" Zooey Farmer. To Dillon they looked like brother and sister—streaky blond hair, blue eyes, teeth, skin and shape all picture perfect. Fox was bouncy. Farmer was cool. "Our shining stars," Bird called them.

Dillon leaned toward Vince. "Remember, it's hot for a man and hottie if it's a woman."

Vince cocked a thumb.

Up front, the microphone changed hands. Both stars went for it, but Fox had the longer reach.

"And now I have the privilege of introducing our very special neighbor, Dillon Black," he said. "Speaking of hot, Dillon, we've gotta get you some trees out here. That sun is relentless."

"Keepin' the natives brown," Dillon quipped as he touched the brim of his cowboy hat in response to scattered applause.

Fox laughed. "Zooey's spray tan pales in comparison."

Zooey leaned toward the mike. "Have you found a two-forty outlet for your tanning bed yet, Tate?"

"We'll be putting one in the new utility facility." He grinned. "You guys like that? That's what we're calling the building housing laundry, showers and toilets. Utility facility. Catchy, no?" He tossed the mike from right hand to left, distancing it from his fellow star. "Which brings me to our next order of business. Once the loaders and dozers get out of the way, we'll divide into three teams. We're looking at three areas, or three main—"

"This site actually becomes a quadrangle," Zooey shouted as she reached for Fox's mike hand. "Quadrangle," she repeated into the mike. "The church is a historic building, so we're repurposing it. We've already started. Behind that, we're turning the barn and those pens next to it into an equestrian center. And over that way will be camp housing." She gestured with one hand while she kept the mike—still nominally under Fox's control—within shouting distance with the other. She flashed him a loaded glance. "With its *utility facility*."

"And the fourth part of the quad is, appropriately, home base, which will be—"

"Which is Mr. Black's house. But our focus for right

now is the church remodel, equestrian expansion, and two new buildings."

"Two *round* buildings," Fox said. "I'll be using lodgepole pine from right here in South Dakota throughout the project."

"Not exclusively," Zooey shot back.

"Exclusively lodgepole or exclusively from South Dakota?" Without turning over the coveted microphone, he turned to the nearest table. "Ella, what did we end up with? You said—"

"When the trucks get here, I'll go over the manifests with you, Tate." Ella's voice came out of the crowd. "Mike has the specs."

"And the blueprints," Mike contributed from the far corner.

"We'll get your story straight before you tell it in front of a camera," Ella added, "but you're safe in saying that lodgepole pine will be the dominant feature, and that it comes from the Black Hills of South Dakota."

Vince leaned toward Dillon's ear. "You brought in that Two Horse from Cheyenne River?"

"*They* did. Ella must have done her research. He does good road work—I know that much."

"It's good they got an Indian to do the job," Bobby said, toning his radio voice down to a stage whisper.

"Even if he ain't exactly from here," Vince allowed. "What's he getting paid?"

Dillon lifted a shoulder. "I keep hearing them talk about paying scale. Whatever the hell that means."

"Fish?" Vince had a twinkle in his eye.

"Two Horse got screwed, then," Dillon whispered. "He could've had trinkets and beads."

"It's scale wages, man," Bobby said. "You get on the scale, you get paid by what you weigh."

Vince tapped Bobby's gut with the back of his hand. "Bobby's pickin' up my check, then."

"You're gettin' free food and any fame that comes of stickin' your face in front of a camera," said Dillon.

"I'm good with that." Vince turned his head to the side, posing. "Nice, huh?"

"Good luck stealing any face time from our shining stars," Dillon muttered as he turned for a better look at an approaching car. He'd lost track of what was being said up front, but keeping track of the comings and goings on the mile-long approach to the house was a routine part of country living.

"Two Horse ain't gettin' paid with no face time," Vince said. "He's too ugly."

"They contracted…" With a quick smile Dillon left his seat. "My kids are back."

"My brother has a Bobcat they could've…" Vincent turned his attention to Emily's car, checking out the passengers. Two of them turned out to be his own kids. "Danny and Donna. I wondered where those two got to this morning," he said as they watched five young people emerge through two doors.

"We recruited some more hands, Daddy," Emily announced as Dillon approached the group. She reached for one in particular, who stepped forward with a handshake for Dillon.

"How's it goin', Jimmy T? You're looking a whole lot better." A relief to Dillon, who had visited the boy in the hospital after the suicide attempt.

"It's goin'," Jimmy said softly. "I don't wanna be on TV or anything, but you said I could come out and ride."

"You sure can." Dillon turned to Emily. "They haven't

called for any of our hands yet, so you can either hang around and watch, or run a couple more horses in and get these guys to help you check cows. Better do it now. The way they're tearin' everything up here, pretty soon we won't have a place to bring the horses into."

"Temporarily, Daddy. It'll be over in two weeks."

"I'll believe that when—"

"Come with us," Emily urged.

"I'm takin' the dogs over to Nick's. All this commotion is driving them crazy. I'm hoping your uncle Nick will…" He turned to Vincent, who was still chewing on a piece of buttered bread as he joined the group. "They're gonna saddle up some horses after they get something to eat. Ella says they'll have something for us to do somewhere in all this mess before the day's over, but everyone eats whether there's work or not."

Vincent led the new arrivals over to the buffet, while Dillon headed for his pickup, which was parked near the trailer. He whistled for the dogs, lowered the tailgate, and they leaped into the bed of the truck. Behind the wheel, Dillon shifted gears, glanced into the mirror at two happy dog faces and started to roll.

"Dad! Wait!" D.J. jerked open the passenger door and hopped in. "I want to go with you."

Surprised, Dillon turned his mouth down with a nod, then up in a smile. He said nothing as they barreled down the sparsely graveled road toward the highway. *Don't ask why. It's a gift, pure and simple.* The boy's words rang in his ears, and he wanted to hang on to them. He slowed down to cross the highway, and took it easy on the approach to Nick's, keeping his eyes on the recently graded dirt road. Nick kept it up better than Dillon had when it had led to the house he'd shared with Monica and their children, but it was the same path. He could see the trees, but not the house. He half expected to glance to his right and see a black-haired, black-eyed little boy looking up at him expectantly. *What next, Dad?*

"What do you remember?"

"Not much," D.J. said quietly. He turned to the side window. "Catching salamanders and frogs by the creek. I don't know why. I always had to let them go before we went home."

"You were supposed to let them go, but you usually managed to sneak one back with you. Remember when that frog got loose in the washing machine?" Dillon chuckled. "Your mom 'bout had a heart attack."

"Let's go down there," D.J. suggested, pointing to a copse of cottonwood trees that sheltered a creek, invisible from the high ground. "It's that way, isn't it?"

Dillon arced the steering wheel in deference to his son's welcome impulse. They left the pickup and followed their memories down a path overgrown by time and scrub brush to a break in the stand of juneberry bushes that Dillon had visited with his small sisters and years later with his small children. It was a kid's paradise, with lush grass and shade for comfort, driftwood and mud for construction and plenty of other irresistible attractions. In early spring the water was deep, the current treacherous, but by late summer it was as tame as the trickle from a garden hose. But no matter what the season, his wife had issued the same warning he'd heard from his mother. *If you go near that creek, don't let those kids out of your sight.*

The dogs were content to follow until a jackrabbit baited them into giving chase. D.J. laughed at their confusion when the rabbit seemed to vanish in the brush. He picked up a stick and threw it for them, but the smell of rabbit had them pacing and whining pathetically.

Dillon hooked his thumbs in the front pockets of his jeans and listened to flowing water, a singing bird, rattling cottonwood leaves, romping dogs and laughing boy. Peaceful sounds. Timeless summer sounds. The Mystic Warrior Horse Camp would be home to more of the same.

"What kind of a bird is that?" D.J. asked.

"Meadowlark." Dillon smiled. His favorite.

"Awesome." D.J. paused, his whole body seemingly attune to the tweedling call. "Light, joyful, like he's celebrating." Another bird joined in, and they sang rounds. "Each note full and crisp. With such a broad stage and this towering sky, the clarity almost startles you, doesn't it?"

Dillon turned his insides out on a smile. The boy who loved fine music knew a gift when he heard it. He squatted on his heels, plucked a piece of grass and listened with new appreciation for an old familiar song. Only after one bird had taken flight to follow the other did he say, "Doesn't matter how often you hear that call. It's like a mouthful of mint. Fresh and surprising."

"Exactly!" D.J. snapped his fingers. "Exactly. People who wonder how you can play the same music over and over, they don't hear the notes coming together through the strings the way I do."

"I can't read music, and I don't know how you make it happen, but what it does to me listening to you…" Dillon lifted his head, smiling, one eye closed against the sun. "It opens me up."

"Totally?"

"Totally." He gave a dry chuckle. "It's almost scary."

"Not to you. You don't scare easily. You're always…" D.J. shrugged. "You always seem…"

Dillon waited, but the rest didn't come. He wouldn't push for it. He would have given his right arm for any one of a hundred words it was probably too late to hope for, but he wouldn't push. It felt like something good was coming, but he would have to wait.

They found Nick hosing out his handsome eight-horse trailer in the shade of his new barn. Nick had worked hard. They were partners in the horse-breeding business and they owned cattle together, but Nick had built his successful horse-hauling business on his own. Dillon had looked up to Nick all his life, but in recent years he'd truly taken Nick's example to heart. And the man had helped him find a new path.

"The TV people have built a small city in my front yard," Dillon said.

"We noticed." Nick pointed to the faucet on the side of the barn. "You wanna shut that off?"

"Yeah, it's quite a sight from the road."

"Backin' up traffic like mangled cars and fresh blood on the highway."

"Not *that* damn bad," Dillon protested, turning the faucet handle until it squealed. "The dogs're goin' nuts with the racket over there. Can you keep them here for a few days?"

"If they'll stay. I couldn't tear that bitch away from her house when we moved over here." Nick eyed the two faces peeking at him from the pickup bed. "You had enough television, Mama? If you want, we can keep all four of you here." Nick winked a D.J. "Play a little Red Rover, huh? Who should we send over?"

"Who've you got?" D.J. asked with a conspirator's smile. "They need camera fodder."

Nick laughed. "My kids love cameras."

"And they love tearin' into stuff, which is what they're doing over there," Dillon said.

"You knew that was part of the package. I didn't realize you were so hot for bringing this Hollywood crew around."

"Not all of it."

Nick looked at D.J. "Do we know which part he's hot for?"

"You mean, Ella Champion?"

"Hey, I'll admit it." Dillon raised his palms in surrender. "What single, red-blooded male wouldn't be hot for Ella?" He shrugged. "I'll admit havin' the white hots for that indoor arena, too. And a nice round pen like that? Somebody just comes along and offers to build that stuff for you? Pretty hard to turn down."

"So why should you?"

"Yeah," D.J. said. "It's like winning the lottery. If you turned that down, we'd be checking you in for a head examination."

"You and what army?" Dillon gave his son a playful shoulder punch, and then he turned to Nick. "I know you'd'a turned it down."

"My wife says I have an appointment next Thursday. Something to do with my head." Nick chuckled. "Oh, yeah, dentist. Could be a trick, huh?"

"Marriage has done wonders for your sense of humor, partner. How 'bout bringing it on over to my place, give us a little moral support?"

Nick glanced at D.J. "You want moral support, too?"

"I wanna go home," the boy said. "But since that won't

be happening for a couple of weeks, sure. Bring on the moral support."

"I'm not goin' on TV, but I guess I'm as curious as the next guy."

"Just stay away from the cameras," Dillon said.

"I gotta say, partner, what with what's mine being yours and yours being mine, an indoor arena sure will be nice come winter. C'mon, Mama." Nick whistled for the dog he'd left to keep his partner company. "Your old friend Buzz is around here somewhere."

Dillon forgot all about cameras when he got back home and saw people crawling all over his church. Over, under, in and out, they were like ants on a hill. Only it wasn't their hill. He knew every inch of every two-by-four the crew had hauled out and piled unceremoniously in the yard. He'd bought each one and nailed it into place according to his plan. Then he'd rethought, redesigned, ripped it out and nailed it into a different place. Finding them tossed aside like kindling was like walking up to a pile of old friends that had come out on the losing end of a bar fight.

"We'll put it to use, some of it," said a voice behind him. He turned to find Mike Murphy coming out of the church, leaving the doors open to the tapping and pounding that was going on inside. "It's good lumber."

"Handpicked," Dillon said ruefully.

"I can see that. We've got it coming in by the truckload, but we handpick our suppliers. That's part of my job."

"Good to know," Dillon said as he stepped past the carpenter and entered the building through the heavy doors. The place was crawling with workers who had taken the inside walls down to the studs, thrown up scaffolding and were now turning their prying attention to the old windows. "Hey! You can't take those out. Those are the original—" Dillon felt ready to shake down some scaffolding. "Hey, don't fuck with those windows!"

"We'll be able to use most of the windows, but we have to refit the—"

Dillon shrugged Mike's hand off his shoulder. "Shit, they're ripping out the floor!"

"Only in a few places. Most of it is—"

"What places?" Dillon squatted on his boot heels and reached between his knees to touch wood planed smooth by years of foot traffic. "This was an Indian mission. My ancestors walked here."

"I doubt their feet caused the damage to the few boards we're taking out," Mike said calmly. "Time takes a toll, usually with the help of weather and pest infestation. But the good news is that you'll have plenty of original floor left, and you'll be hard-pressed to tell the old from the new when we're finished."

"You said you'd protect the—"

"The integrity of the building, yes. We rarely take on this kind of renovation, because it usually involves too much time and money, but this one is manageable, and it's the kind of makeover we get asked about all the time."

"Mike knows what he's doing," said a familiar voice. Dillon looked up to find Ella standing over him. He imagined being at the bottom of a bowl waiting for her to drop fish flakes on him. Instead, she dropped the words, "Trust me."

"Trust you?" Suddenly short of air, he braced his hands on his knees and pushed himself upright. "You're not the one with the crowbar. I wanted to save it, Ella, not—"

"Is there a problem?" Tate Fox asked, swooping in as though he had a role to play.

"You tell me," Dillon said. "I had an agreement. I saw a plan. I met the lead carpenter and the shining star carpenter, and now I'm lookin' at…" Ella. He wanted to trust her, but the variables were multiplying way too quickly. "Who's really doing the work?"

"I am," Mike said. "Tate gets it done on camera. I get it done right."

"I make it entertaining," Fox said. "We stage a piss-off like this periodically. Helps me keep in shape for when the big dogs come around."

"You seem like a guy who might have some skill with a saw," Mike told Dillon. "If I were you, man, I wouldn't trust any of us. I'd be doing just what you're doing. And I'd get involved."

Dillon glanced up at the windows, down at the damaged floor, finally at Mike. "Show me exactly what has to come out."

"Sure thing," Mike said as he laid a hand on Dillon's shoulder. "And you tell me more about those ancestors."

Chapter Seventeen

Talk about his ancestors? Dillon had to think about that. Talk about history, talk about customs, talk about where his Wolf Trail Paints came from? Easy. But talk about him dragging that old building home and defending it as though he were the delusional veteran of some lost cause? Not so easy. Good bones, they said. Good windows, good wood, good size. Good luck fixing it up. Hey, what do you plan to use it for?

Something sacred. It was a church, wasn't it? He'd said, yeah, I'll take it, and he'd thought, *Damn, these people, they'll throw anything away*. Even a church. And not just *any* church. Whether they knew or cared, it was a fact that this one was special. It was a bridge.

Dillon couldn't remember the last time he'd attended a church service, unless he counted funerals. Which he didn't. He went, but he didn't count. He'd started practicing more Lakota traditions after his wife had left and taken the main reasons he'd had for occasionally going to church. He remembered his grandfather being pretty traditional—attending ceremonies and talking about practices that scared the bejesus out of a six-year-old—things like feeding the spirits and burning a dead person's personal possessions to keep the *gigi* from "bothering around." But Lala Black Bear had also been a church deacon, and Dillon's parents were in and out of the churchgoing habit, as was Monica.

For Dillon, the connection to church had always been once-removed, through someone else, and once that some-one else was removed, so was the connection. With his church building, the connectedness seemed to work on him a little differently. The people were long dead, but their stories were not. He didn't want any *gigi* hanging around, but a church wasn't personal property. It had been part of a community that, like Dillon's family, boasted both Indian and white members.

When he'd acquired the old building for little more than the cost of moving it, he'd had nothing to his name but a piece of land across the highway and a partnership with a man who was willing to pool their bet without making a show of stacking their chips side by side. He'd had no il-lusions about the old building adding to his worth and no better blueprint for its use than he'd had for his life. But saving it felt like an accomplishment, a step toward find-ing his way home. He'd always been interested in stories from his people's past, and the fact that the church had been built early in the twentieth century by a missionary who had been a friend and rare white supporter of Sitting Bull's—rarer still, a woman—meant that it necessarily had some interesting stories to tell. So he'd borrowed the money—more than he'd dreamed such a thing would cost—to move the building.

He figured that Mike, the carpenter—the *real* carpenter—was just being polite, asking about the ances-tors. But after Dillon had inspected the boards that had been removed from the floor and agreed that water and critter damage had rendered them unsafe, and after he and Mike had supervised the removal of windows and Mike had spread the schematics for the remodel on a table at the snack shack, and after Dillon had rereassured himself that his whole world was in capable hands, Mike asked again.

And he seemed to be genuinely interested.

"So this missionary," Dillon said, "Mary Collins, she worked around here from the 1880s into the early 1900s, and she built the first YMCA in South Dakota right here on the reservation. She didn't like what the government was doing, making the people dependent on handouts, and she spoke up. She even went to Washington to complain about it. Her father was some kind of representative, so she thought she could get somebody to listen. But there were no ears in D.C. back then, either.

"She spoke up again after Sitting Bull was assassinated. She was gone when it happened, and she didn't believe he was making trouble, inciting an uprising, resisting arrest, that whole spin they managed to put on it. She went to Washington and demanded an investigation. Again, no ears. But at least she tried."

"Good woman," Mike said.

"This was one of her last projects, this church. Started out with mostly Indians, but after she was gone, the white people eventually took over. The farmers moved in, bought Indian land for little or nothing, leased it for even less. The white towns started popping up, and this church ended up in the middle of one. The town fathers knew it was an old building, but I don't think they knew a lot about Mary Collins. They decided it would cost too much to keep it up."

Dillon eyed the drawings. "Guess I haven't done such a hot job. But I thought it should be used for something."

"It's in good shape." Mike toyed with the tab on his pop can. "Easily worth saving."

"The floor was a good call," Dillon admitted with a smile. "What else do we have to do to save it?"

"You did a nice job on the foundation. I want to do some reinforcement on the south side, where the kitchen's going in, and add insulation."

"How? I couldn't see any way short of—" A woman's hand landed lightly on Dillon's shoulder. He followed the arm up to Ella's face and smiled. "Hey."

"We'd like to get you up on the bulldozer, Dillon. Monica says you've operated one before."

"That was on a bet," he said. "There was this big sign on the highway that needed taking down, so a buddy and me, we rustled a 'dozer." He glanced askance at Mike. "Is that part of the entertainment? Monica and me, we're gonna be tellin' on each other?"

"She didn't say anything about rustling," Ella said. "Just that you know how to run a bulldozer." She, too, glanced at Mike, who shrugged. She turned a second-thought look on Dillon. "What kind of a highway sign?"

"The billboard kind. Big, bad Indian cartoon advertising the Tee Pee Motel. Spelled with double *e*'s. The damn bug-eyed character with the fat lips, big *pahsu*—" he cupped his hand in front of his nose "—and that pitiful feather stickin' up in back. Figured the artist got his start drawing mascots in college. But there was something about those double *e*'s."

"My mother would have loved you. She once pulled down an offensive sign with a rope," Ella said. "And a little help from her friends."

"Sounds like the hard way. Did they get caught?"

Ella shrugged. "When you call the local TV station first, you get caught. And you get arrested."

"We wouldn't have gotten caught if my buddy hadn't lost his…" He frowned. "Hell, that was another lifetime, and I was no Thelma Bear Dancer. She was one Indian who knew how to make her point. I made the inside back page of the newspaper under 'police calls.'"

"You don't want to give it a try?" Ella challenged him. "You'd have to be able to hit the broad side of a barn. Probably not, huh?"

"You're tearing the barn down? I thought you were taking off the lean-to and just adding on."

"Better come see." She held out her hand.

He took it, allowing her to reel him in because the bait tasted so damn good he almost didn't care how sharp the hook was. She was sweet. He could see the big yellow cabless Cat crouching next to the corral, rails chewed ragged over the years by cribbing horses. He could hear the purring diesel and practically feel its power surging through his limbs.

They headed toward the barn, where Monica was having an animated discussion with a young woman cradling a camera.

Ella gave Dillon's hand a quick squeeze. "You told on yourself, cowboy. We just want to show you having some fun with this."

And he did. Almost as much as he'd had the night he'd operated his first bulldozer. Hell, he'd been a legal driver, and he'd had a Class One license back then. And a classic case of adrenaline addiction, which he thought he'd beaten into civilized submission by now. But knocking down the corrals and the "broad side of a barn" slated for replacement gave him such a rush that he caught himself caressing the 'dozer blade's joystick and looking for more targets.

Bad sign, he thought. Blowing off steam he didn't know he'd bottled up. But it sure felt good. He swung down from the big yellow bull with the swagger of a guy who'd scored high enough to win the go-round. And he had a female audience, which pleased him. Emily had joined the group sometime during his performance. Turning the heavy equipment back over to its regular operator, he surveyed the rubble he'd created. Ella had a word with the woman behind the camera, who then moved on.

"That was great," Ella told Dillon. "Your enthusiasm plays well."

"Once you've operated a 'dozer, it's like riding a bike," he claimed, elbowing embarrassment out of the picture. Hell, he'd whooped it up a little, bellowed "the wall came tumblin' down" a few times, but surely the Cat had drowned him out. And he was entitled.

"What do you know about riding a bike?" Monica challenged.

"I rode one once. Figure I could do it again if I had to." He shrugged. "If I couldn't find a horse."

"See, Mother, that's what we're about." Emily injected a little tattling of her own. "Mother's trying to get me to upholster furniture and make stuff for the walls, but I think I should be working on the equestrian center."

Dillon took a quick look around. People were talking about this facility and that center, but all he could see was a backhoe punching a hole in the ground and a bulldozer pushing the remnants of his latest improvements on the barn into another pile of sticks and stones. Handy for breaking good bones. And all he could hear were diesel engines and demanding women. Great for breaking perfectly good balls.

Get a grip, Black Bear.

He draped an arm around his daughter's shoulders. "How old are you now, Pinky?"

"Old enough, but it's like *her party.*"

"You know the score. If your Mama don't dance, then your Daddy won't—"

"I know, I know. Work it out, baby." They'd had this exchange before. Dillon was in no position to run interference for her, even if he wanted to. "But D.J. would love to work on wall stuff. She's doing things with old organ parts."

"That's my specialty," Monica said, her pride showing.

"Traditional Indian decorations, huh?" Dillon teased. "Buffalo bladders and finger necklaces? Nice touch."

"I think she's doing the musical kind of organ parts," Ella shouted over the noise of the backhoe. The four began to move as one away from the machines.

"You can also make dance rattles out of testicle sacs," Dillon suggested.

Monica's eyes narrowed. "I could make a sandwich out of your tongue."

He lifted one shoulder. "So much for secret recipes."

Monica laughed. "I have the traditional art covered with…" she gave a sweeping gesture "…traditional art. But don't think yours are the only balls I've ever busted, Dillon James. I refused to hang a single bit of taxidermy in the lodge-theme guesthouse we did for a VA hospital."

"I saw the salvaged organ parts," Ella said. "They're great. Having D.J. on that part of the project would be a nice segue into doing something special with his music. I have some ideas. Is he camera-shy?"

"When he's making music, he's not shy about anything." Emily linked arms with Ella. "Let's go run your ideas by him. He'll play hard to get, but he's not that good at it. His buttons are just *so* out there."

"We'll leave you two to reminisce," Ella said over her shoulder.

Dillon watched them walk away, trading words between women, giggling like girls. "Is that what we're doing?" he asked absently, wishing he could follow along without looking like a panting puppy. "Reminiscing?"

"Kind of." Monica had that superior smile of hers ready for him when he glanced her way. "You know what I think?"

"My buttons are out there, but be careful which one you pick." She shrugged off the invitation, leaving him to button up or back down. He glanced away. "What do you think?"

"You might be trying too hard." She laughed as she touched his arm. "You're a bad boy, Dillon, but being yourself—"

"You think so?" He eyed her for truth. "Still?"

"Don't worry." She gave him a patronizing pat. "Good women are attracted to your kind like silk-winged moths glomming onto a porch light."

"I ain't like that no more," he recited. "Not the bad boy part. Can't quarrel with the attractive part."

"Of course not."

"What's wrong with that? A blessing is something you just accept. When it comes to women, there's no tellin' why. A guy gets a good response, he tries to figure out what he did right, so he can do it again."

"When he feels like it," she said.

"We always feel like it. Whenever we try, it looks too hard. That's the way we're made."

"And we just can't believe anyone could be that simple."

"Hell, you've got your curses, we've got ours." He slid his arm around his former wife's shoulders as easily as he had done with his daughter. "But keep it under your hat, okay? I shouldn't be tellin' on us. It's better you go on thinkin' there's more to it." He gave a quick squeeze. "Makes you guys try harder."

"Not this old girl. My trying days are over."

He turned his head, peered toward the church, squinting against the sun for dramatic effect. And for lack of glasses. "Looks like Mike's taking some serious instruction over there from your designer."

"Where?"

"Right there, old girl. Front of the…" He lifted his hand from her shoulder and pointed, deadpan. Then he smiled, and finally he looked her in the eye. "What's wrong?"

"Nothing."

"A little whiplash?"

"That's right." She stole another glance at the brawny carpenter and the willowy California girl, who was probably young enough to be his daughter. "You got me."

"Hey." He gave her a buck-up shoulder squeeze before stepping back. "I don't mind helping you upholster chairs. I've done it before. Remember?"

"This will be a little more complicated than fake leather over foam rubber," she said, shifting eagerly into her comfort zone. "We found some boxy, retro-style chairs— firm cushions, wood trim—very good bones. We're going to reupholster them with real cowhides, mostly spotted. What breed would that be?"

"Dairy cows."

"They're gorgeous. They'll give the church—the main building—a nice Western feel without going all—"

"What's Western about dairy cows?"

"I'll show you." She reached for him, and once again he found himself being led by the hand and a woman's invitation to come and see. "In my business, if it looks like a cow and acts like a chair, it's Western décor. I'm going for durability and easy care. You're going to like it. The kids are going to *love* it, Dillon."

"Right or wrong, I'm countin' on it, Monica."

"You really are, aren't you?" She looked up at him, making sure she had him on course before she released his hand. "I mean, you believe in the camp as much as Emily does."

"I believe in what we did last summer. And this place…" He had to look past the trucks and the tents, look to the hills and the horizon that anchored *this place*. "When we traded home sites, Nick was all set to turn everything on this side over to me free and clear. Trade me straight up. It wasn't that much, he said. But for a guy who's spent the last few years of his life crawlin' out of a hole he dug for himself…"

He pulled up short, digging his boot heels into the gravel as he imitated a chin-up. "Hell, here I am pulling myself up to ground level, lookin' out over the prairie, and for the first time in years I can see the horizon. And what do I do? I climb up on that Cat and start knockin' stuff down, thinking somehow I'm gonna get a better view."

"It's what you want, isn't it? The horse camp?"

He nodded absently. "I've been working on it, too, but I just leveled the corral and 'dozed half the barn away."

"We're here to help. We're going to build something better."

He nodded again, dazed by what felt like spin. He was standing still, but he knew spin. It was the kind of ride every bull rider wanted, the kind that earned the most points if you could stick the bull until you heard the whistle. He'd never said it aloud, but it was the reason he'd chosen broncs over bulls. It wasn't the relative size or strength of the animal that rattled him. It was the necessity for something he knew he couldn't control. Spin.

"I'm paying for it."

She looked quizzical. "For…?"

"For what's here. What *was* here. Whether it's here or not, I'm still gonna make those payments."

"Knowing Nick, he'd be just as happy with an even trade and you putting the place to good use."

Dillon smiled. "These days he's pretty happy with everything. Took to the role of family man like—"

"Do you mind living alone?"

"Hell, no. It's a good thing Lauren came along and split us up." They fell into step again, going her way. He chuckled. "There's something creepy about two straight men growing old together under the same roof."

She stiffened and scowled. "Why straight men?"

He lifted one shoulder. "Because there's nothing wrong with two *winktes* living together." He used the Lakota word for *homosexual.*

"Nothing creepy about it?"

"Couldn't say. Guess it depends on the *winktes.* But that would be their business."

"And there's nothing wrong with being a *winkte?*"

"Guess it depends—"

"—on the *winkte,*" she presumed, which irritated him.

"'Nothing's good or bad but thinking makes it so.'"

"According to who?" Obviously somebody who could finish his own sentences his own way. He was going to say that it probably depended on where the *winkte* lived, but if he lived in her world, he wouldn't be a *winkte,* and he'd be dealing with *good* and *bad* on different terms.

"Shakespeare, I think. It's interesting that you—" She suddenly stumbled, grabbing his arm for balance.

"You okay?" Her hand was quivering against his bare arm.

"I'm fine. Turned my ankle." But she was kneading her hip and thigh. "No more expensive cowboy boots for me. I'm going back to good ol' hundred-dollar sneakers." She straightened, squared up, Monica-in-charge once more. "Frankly, I'm a little stiff from getting on that horse. Can a charley horse leave a bruise?"

"On your ego, maybe." He eyed her speculatively. She seemed steady enough now. Maybe she needed something to eat. She'd let herself get too damn skinny lately. "You had something to show me?"

"My 'Decorator's Den.'" She pointed to a trailer with a green-and-white awning shading the full length of one side. "And my lovely spotted hides."

He sighted down her finger and nodded. "We're stopping at the snack shack along the way, and then you can show me what you want done with your dairy cow skins."

Chapter Eighteen

"**Y**ou two are quite a team," Zooey observed for the benefit of a rolling camera.

Ella stood behind cameraman Charlie Verick and watched the progress of an upholstering project. They were filming under the huge canvas awning dubbed the Decorator's Den, and Zooey, who was busy reloading a staple gun, was supposed to encourage conversation. Covering the foam cushions on four midcentury easy chairs with black-and-white cowhide was the subject of the shoot, but Monica and Dillon were the focus. Monica sat in one of the ubiquitous directors' chairs stenciled with the name of an advertiser, and he sat at her feet on the canvas-covered ground. Monica was fitting a hide over a thick cushion, while Dillon was stapling it in place. With Zooey standing at Monica's shoulder, it was a perfectly balanced tableau.

"We were just like everyone else when we were first married," Monica said. She was obviously working hard at getting something going here. Too hard. Too obvious. "You have to get creative when the money runs out before the month does. We had the usual early marriage décor." She smiled at her former husband. "We made our share of newlywed projects, didn't we?"

"Oh, yeah."

Wait for it, Ella told herself. His yes and no answers had prompted them to try turning his back to the camera to get him going. *Oh, yeah* was an improvement.

And then he added, "Talk about creative, man, Monica's always been a pro. She taught me a lot. Hell, creating was something we did together—" Monica rolled her eyes and shook her head "—a lot. Sorry. What did I say? Hell?"

"Don't worry about it, Dillon. Editors can do wonders." Zooey laughed. "You're too cute. Isn't he, Ella?"

"Too cute. Let's relax and keep it going."

On the set, they called it "whistle while you work," and Ella would be setting up similar sequences throughout the two weeks of the shoot. Hours of film would be edited with an eye to telling a human-interest story, which was what gave the show its special appeal. From her preproduction work—applications, interviews, research on location—she always had a clear idea of the kind of story that might unfold. But the show's best episodes were the ones that blew her expectations out of the water.

As were the rare disasters.

"You're quite a team and quite a story," Zooey said. "The perfect…"

"The perfect divorce? As close as it gets, wouldn't you say, Dillon? Be sure to keep that taut." Monica smoothed the hide, pushing the slack into Dillon's territory. "It's never easy, but there was no War of the Blacks. We're still good friends. Don't you agree, Dillon?"

"Sure, darlin'. It's your show." He shot a staple perilously close to her invasive fingers and returned her smile. "Taut enough, teach?"

"Too cute," Monica said. "He always has been."

"Ain't no has-been, honey. Plenty of projects left in my possibles bag."

"Tell Zooey what a possibles bag is," she suggested, but she cut his reply off at the pass. "He really should have been the teacher in the family. He knows all about Lakota history and traditions. I could never—"

"A possibles bag was something white trappers and mountain men carried," Dillon supplied. "It was a man purse."

"He doesn't carry a purse," Monica told the camera.

"But I've always carried a possibles bag. Hung onto it even when there wasn't much left inside." He shot another staple into the chair. "Nope, you don't wanna give up your possibles."

"Mountain man trappings," Monica said smiling. "Who knew?"

"Who asked?" he muttered. Glancing up, he lifted one shoulder and tried again. "Hey, it's like Sitting Bull said, take what's good and walk away from the rest. Now, these chairs are good. *Waste yelo*. That means *good* in—"

"Wait a minute," Monica said, scowling. "*Who asked?* What happened to *watch and learn?*" she asked. "Hmm? Isn't that your motto? And you need to keep the staples close together in a nice, straight line."

"Fair enough." He filled the space she'd pointed to. "You got me there. Watch and learn. My grandfather's motto, actually. Less talk, more—" he directed two fingers at his own eyes "—eyes and ears. The Lakota way. The man was—"

"Not that there's anything wrong with a man purse, but it's just not Dillon," Monica said to the camera. "All kinds of possibilities and never any shortage of projects. He's very handy when he wants to be. Dillon built us quite a nice

TV cabinet in the early days, and his only power tool was a skill saw." She gave him her smile of approval. "An amazing piece of work."

"The man was what?" Ella put in quietly. She didn't want to lose that thread. "What did you learn from your grandfather, Dillon?"

"Horse sense. He was a hell of a horseman. Stories, games. He wanted us to settle down, he'd tell a story."

"In Lakota?" Monica asked, taking Ella's cue.

"Mostly, but with enough English mixed in so we'd understand. He's the reason I understand as much Lakota as I do. Between BIA boarding schools and mission-school nuns, the language was pretty well scrubbed off my parents' generation's tongues." He looked up at Ella. "How 'bout your mother?"

"She spoke the language," Ella said, adding sadly, "but I don't."

"I've been trying to work on it. You want some lessons? I don't know how many words I have, but I'll trade them all for the indoor arena in that picture you showed me."

"Careful, Ella, he's a wily trader. It's worth at least a thousand words."

"And I can't just write 'em down and hand 'em over. Between us Indians, we gotta do this the Indian way."

"Oral tradition," Monica said. "Could take a good long time."

"Really good long time." He grinned.

"What are you offering for the other buildings?" Ella asked.

"Grammar. Without the nails, you can't do much with the boards."

"What did I tell you?" Monica said. "Winsome but wily."

"I'm getting a little confused here, Ella," Zooey put in, meaning she was feeling left out.

"Sorry, Zooey," Ella said. "Jump in on Dillon's grandfather, and we'll dice and splice."

"What the…?" Dillon's attention drifted.

Ella followed his lead and groaned inwardly at the sight of Tate doing his signature fox trot around Emily. Emerging from the church, where camera two was supposed to be taping him roughing out the new kitchen, Tate was instead regaling Emily in his famous animated fashion— big gestures, bold moves, clownish facial expressions. He was quite the entertainer.

"Daddy, check this out," Emily announced as they neared the Den. "Killer idea. You're gonna love this. I want to put together a team of college kids to work on the equestrian center for a couple of days. I know at least ten kids I can get to come out for the chance to be on the program."

"From your school?" Dillon glanced at Ella. *Whose killer idea?*

"Dress them up in school color shirts with the name…" Tate made a cross-chest gesture. "What college is it? Montana State?"

"Montana Western," Emily said.

Tate beamed. "I've got Montana connections myself."

"What, you go skiing there?" said Zooey, gesturing with the staple gun.

"Every year," Tate said. "Emily will be the team captain, and I'll play coach. This project runs two segments, right?"

Ella nodded. "Two-part program. Definitely justified."

Zooey shook her head. "We've got enough—"

"I like it," Ella said. "But you'll have to get it organized."

Tate hooked his arm around Emily. "Leave the driving to us."

"What driving?" Dillon demanded.

"Just a figure of speech," Tate said. "Although that's an idea. We can go rounding up our co-eds. Honk the horn, sweet blonde comes running out of the house with her duffel bag, jumps in a van. We'll have the new bunkhouse up and running, and those kids will be our first campers."

"What about the people around here?" Dillon asked. "*My* neighbors? I've got plenty of kids ready to sign on as soon as—"

"The locals are with us from day one. And we're doing the overnight trail ride," Tate said, butt bouncing in an imaginary saddle. "So we've already got the horse campers covered. This way, we're bringing in the face of the college volunteer, Emily's connections making local connections. Hey, we're all about making connections. Giddyup, giddyup, giddyup, whoa!" He pulled on a set of air reins and grinned. "Right, Em? When do I get to ride a real horse?"

Emily was too enchanted to answer with anything but a giggle.

"I really do like it," Ella said. "If you promise to give me at least ten minutes of good interplay. Stuff I can use."

Emily's giggle fell away. "Ten minutes?"

"At least."

"What, he can't go ten minutes?" Dillon said.

Zooey hooted.

"It's only an hour show, two episodes, that's an hour and thirty minutes that we fill. And Tate's a big draw." Ella gave a mock bow in his direction. "For obvious reasons."

"Thank you." Tate gave an imperious nod. "You're too

kind, but thank you. We'll be moseyin' on now, heading for that watering hole over yonder. Had a real beauty of an idea and just couldn't wait to share." One hand poised on the "reins," the other set to slap his own flank, he challenged Emily with a nod. "Let's ride."

And off they pranced.

"Oh, *please*, Ella," Zooey grumbled.

"I'm sorry, Zooey, but it pays to encourage him. And this is the kind of thing he does well. College crew, bullhorn, big-stud-on-campus stuff."

"Watch out for your daughter," Zooey warned.

"Him?" Dillon took another look, paused, shook his head. "Nah. He's all form and no function, that guy. Not her type."

"I'm just saying, a word to the wise."

"That would be her mother." Dillon glanced at Monica as he switched staplers with Zooey. "You heard the word?"

"I heard. Tate's harmless. Strictly for show." She adjusted her chair. "What do you call a gelding who doesn't know what he's missing?"

"Cut proud."

"That's it," Monica said. "So descriptive. Thank you."

"Just doin' my job." Dillon tested the stapler. "Fillin' in the blanks."

"What you need to be doing is filling in *these* blanks." Monica ran her fingertips over his work. "This is too much space between staples, Dillon. These are the ones I put in. Look how much neater this—"

"Whoa." Dillon lifted his free hand. "Lost my head there for a minute. Monica wants it done right, there's only one way. She does it herself." He handed her the stapler. "Here's your tool."

"Oh, for pity's sake, Dillon, *get over* yourself."

"If it's gonna be your way or the highway, I'm takin' the highway, honey. Like I said, it's your show."

"It's not that—"

"Yeah, it is. It's exactly that." He got to his feet. "Anybody want anything to drink? I'm headed for the snack shack. Call it lack of male pride, but when a guy's outnumbered in the Decorator's Den, running looks a helluva lot better than gettin' cut."

He walked away, commanding the full, wordless attention of three women. Ella's laughter broke their silence, and Zooey joined in. Monica opened fire on the chair with the staple gun.

"You two are scheduled to film with the quilters this evening," Ella said. "We'll pick the chairs up again on the finish end."

"I'll be in my trailer when you're ready," Zooey said. "I have some calls to make about appliances."

Monica was fuming, but she waited to make her softspoken demand until Zooey was out of earshot and the cameraman had been assigned elsewhere.

"I want you to talk to him, Ella."

"About what?"

Ella wanted to kick herself. She'd meant to say *no way*. No way was she getting in the middle. No way was she taking sides. No way…

Ella sighed. No way would she let two exes drop-kick her show to Texas.

"You know how this works. We get what we can from the home owners, hoping for fabulous, expecting ordinary, and doing everything in our power to avert major meltdown. We're okay with minor meltdown, but not so it screws with the schedule." She laid a hand on Monica's shoulder. "That wasn't like you, Monica. Zooey's supposed to be the temperamental one on camera."

"I wasn't being temperamental."

"Bossy, then. Fussy, hard to please. That's Zooey's persona. You're the patient teacher, and people love you for that." Ella drew a deep breath. "Try to think of Dillon as just another neighbor."

"You're right. Neighbor." Monica shot another staple. "Very distant neighbor. We haven't lived together in years. *Years.* It doesn't matter if I have to go back and fix a few of his—"

"Like you always do."

"Not anymore," Monica averred, needlessly throwing her shoulder into the stapling.

"With anyone *else.* You make the home owner look good on camera, but you're always fixing things later. Or you quietly assign it to one of the assistants. That's what they're for."

Monica drew back with a tight smile. She rested the stapler on her knee and shook her head. "Ten years, and it still bugs me when he does that."

"What?"

"He agrees to the plan—doesn't object to it, anyway—and then he ignores the directions. Purposely. Then when I call it to his attention, try to get him to do it right, he gets to walk away. I'm *nagging* him." She frowned and glanced up at Ella. "Is it just me?"

"Is *what* just you?"

"Some people simply aren't cut out for marriage, right?"

"Dillon?"

"Me," she said, and "Me, me, me," she sang, ending on a self-deprecating laugh. "I won't go there again, that's for sure. Oh, but he was deliciously sexy and *totally* male. Absolutely irresistible."

Ella said nothing. Too close to home.

"It isn't for you, either, is it?" Monica said, and Ella did a double take. "Marriage."

"If you're going to have children, I think marriage is the way to go."

"Otherwise no?"

"I didn't say that."

"Well, either way, you haven't done it, so I take it—"

"No, you don't. You can't take something I'm not offering."

Monica looked surprised.

Ella shrugged. "You speak from experience, Monica. I have none. There's nothing for you to take."

"Why so touchy?"

"If you weren't being temperamental, then I'm not being touchy." She touched Monica's shoulder again. "And if denial isn't an option, then let's try this. I'm not a therapist. I'm not a counselor. I'll wear a lot of hats for this job, but that's where I draw the line."

Monica's gaze drifted toward the snack shack. "He'll be less testy when the outbuildings start taking shape. The kind of stuff I do is window dressing, which means nothing to him."

And I'm not interested, Ella told herself. What meant much or little to Monica's ex-husband was important to her only for the sake of the project. How much or how little it had to do with Monica was more information than she cared to get into. Ella had known a few divorced couples who claimed that they were "still friends," and she'd taken them at their word. It sounded a lot better than "*just* friends," which might make a person wonder just who was kidding whom. If a person were inclined to take someone else's word and add a bunch of her own.

"You'll get Zooey to the community center tomorrow?" Ella asked.

"I have some things to do in Bismarck tomorrow morning, so I'm taking my own car. The crew can follow me. I've checked the schedule. You really don't need me tomorrow." Monica's gaze skittered away. "It's important."

"Are you okay?"

"Strictly between us—and I do mean strictly—I'm seeing a doctor here. My doctor at home made the arrangements. It's just part of the medical drill. I had it planned so it wouldn't interfere, and then we rescheduled the project." She brushed off the possibility of concern with a wave of her hand. "But it's all good. Fortunately, doctors network across state lines."

"Do the kids know what's going on?"

"They know I go to the clinic so often I practically qualify for reserved parking." Monica smoothed the cow hide as though she expected the chair to moo. "That's enough. They don't ask, and I don't tell. Especially not now." She looked up. "And Dillon is out of the loop entirely. I don't want to get into any discussions, any details. I don't want to think about it any more than I have to right now."

Monica smiled appreciatively. "That's one of the many things I love about you, Ella. You listen, but you don't press. You respect people's privacy, and that's so rare these days. I trust you completely."

"Okay, okay. Point taken," Ella said. "But if your private matter threatens the project or the production schedule…"

"I know you're sticking your neck out for this project, and I won't let you down."

"Not intentionally. I've always known you to be utterly dependable. You've only cancelled out on one assignment, and that was because you were flat on your back in a hospital. But, Monica, if you had to back out of this one—"

"I won't."

"—it would change the whole dynamic."

"I know," Monica said with a sigh. "No more nit-picking. I know the kind of exchanges we want between Dillon and me, and I'll make sure they happen. We really are friends again. *Again?*" She smiled on a second thought. "Maybe for the first time."

"That's the way you sold it to us," Ella reminded her.

Ella had thought it was simply good human interest back when she'd made the buy. Hardly more personal than her token interest in the familiar faces that came and went through a front door not far from her own. She equated doors with fences. Good doors made good neighbors. But friends? What about doors and friends?

"Darius is in love with the prairie," Ella said, looking to the quiet hills for fresh fodder. "He wants to shoot D.J. playing his violin in magic-hour silhouette, morning and evening both."

"I don't want to miss that, so… Well, look who's here."

Ella looked. Nick Red Shield was just arriving on the scene with his towheaded toddler son in tow, Dillon and Vincent serving as welcoming committee. Dillon's ear-to-ear grin gave her pause. No telling what was being said, but the free and easy laughter was telling. It said *friends*.

"I'll tell Darius to let you know when he schedules it," Ella said absently as she watched the three men greet each other like teammates taking the floor. Dillon punched Nick's arm in response to something he said. Nick backhanded

Vincent's paunch in response to something *he* said. Cowboy hats bobbing, boots shifting, shoulders flexing, all but running in place as they loosened up to take on the visitors. Ella smiled. "Tomorrow morning we've got post-hole digging. I hope it's warm enough to take a few shirts off."

Monica laughed. "Two out of three ain't bad, huh?"

Dillon felt better about the whole damn TV business now that Nick had given his blessing by showing up. He couldn't believe it when he saw the dust wake and recognized the source as the familiar blue pickup. Nick had shed some of his shell since Lauren had come into his world, but not so much that he would be looking for his fifteen minutes of fame, so it felt like a blessing.

"You shoulda been here," Vince told Nick as the three of them ambled down the driveway, viewing disassembly here, the promise of something new over there. Little Joey had the best view from Nick's shoulders. "Dillon took after that barn like it was a big birthday cake and he had a 'dozer for dentures."

Two of the big Cats were idling, while their operators smoked and chatted in the shade of an oversize tire. The distant roar of a third machine came from the field where the arena and the training pen would be built. There was lots of hammering going on at the church. Near the trailer house, another hammer ensemble sounded where foundation forms were being prepared for the bunkhouse and the utility facility.

"Looks like they mean business," Nick said. "I see an Indian contractor. That's cool. Two Horse did some of the work on my place. Did they bring the rest of these guys in with them?"

"*Some*body brought 'em in," Dillon said. "I got nobody working for me."

"Lotta people," Nick observed skeptically. "Hope it's not like some government program where they let the contractors name their price and then run out of money. They could back out and leave you with half a barn."

"I'm not dealin' with the BIA on this, partner. These Hollywood people, they don't have time for 'Bossin' Indians Around.' They put it all down in writing, and then they start the cameras rollin'. All I have to do is smile."

"Where have we heard that before?" Vince put in.

"That's what they told the ancestors," Dillon agreed. "Make your X on the treaty and watch the birdie. So they stood there thinking, *That damn box is stealing my soul, but that Gatling gun was killing my kids.* They didn't get what was really being stolen, though. I'm not worried about my soul, and they can't touch our land anymore." He scowled. "Can they?"

"I don't know what you signed," Nick said. "How much small print was there that you didn't read?"

"None," Dillon was proud to say. This time he'd done his due diligence, and he had an ace in the hole that was diligence in a dress. Two, if he could count Ella, who would look great in a dress. He grinned. "So let's have some fun with it, bro."

"That's why I'm here. Little Joe wants to go to the circus, and this is the closest one. Right, son?" Nick tipped his head to the side and winked at the happy camper riding tall. "Plus, I've met the birdie you're watchin', and I want a ringside seat for that little sideshow."

"With friends like this one…" Dillon glanced at Vince as he jerked his chin toward Nick, who laughed heartily.

"Yeah, you go easy on the humor, ol' man, or you'll be havin' a stroke." He peered closely at Nick's face. "Damn, you're putting cracks in the stone."

"Hey, we're all pullin' for you, D. I wanted to see her jump out of your birthday cake." Vincent drew an hourglass figure in the air with both hands. "Wearing some very skimpy underwear."

"I don't know about any birdie, but this is a family show, and we're all family men," Dillon said as they approached the barn.

"A guy can dream," Vince said.

"You're dreamin', all right. How many Indian women you know order out of Victoria's Secret?" Dillon grilled Vince.

"Or jump out of cakes?" Nick added.

"Doesn't mean it won't happen," Vince said. "Women get around in the world, they change, and you don't know what they'll do next. That's why those Arab guys make their women wear the whole damn tent. A woman could be belly dancin' up a sandstorm under there and nobody suspects she's anything but a tent pole."

"You're the one lookin' for the woman in skimpy underwear," Dillon teased.

"Not my woman." Vince backhanded Dillon's arm. "Yours."

"Yeah, well, if I ever get one, consider yourself crossed off my visitors list. From that day on my tipi's closed to you."

"You're right, D, some things are private." Vincent looked at him, straight-faced. They pulled up in front of what was left of the barn. "Like your pole doin' the belly dance."

"You better watch it, man." Dillon glanced up at the basketball rim he'd hung over the barn door. No net, just rim. "There's a hidden camera around here somewhere."

"No shit?"

Dillon laughed. "*Shit* gets bleeped, but they're totally cool with *skimpy underwear*."

"Aren't we all?" Nick lowered Little Joe to the ground. "Hey, star of the show, come upgrade this conversation to first class."

Emily and her new sidekick had caught Nick's eye.

"Don't let Zooey hear you say that." Dressed in a black T-shirt emblazoned with the show's WON logo, slim jeans, steel-toed work boots and a fully-loaded tool belt buckled low on his hips, Tate was looking his part. "We're supposed to be costars."

"Talkin' about Emily," Nick said. Talking *to* Emily, as well. "Your dad says this was your idea. Now it's really happening. Hard to believe, huh?"

"It is. I'm already planning this summer's Mystic Warrior Horse Camp. I'm thinking two-week sessions. You can't do much in a week. Right, Tate?"

"Not without a lot of help. I'm looking for manpower on the bunkhouse as soon as the foundation's cured."

"We'll get you all you need," Vince promised. "Say when."

Dillon slid his friend a grateful smile.

"Once the cement work is done, it's gonna be full speed ahead. Now, when I say *manpower,* I mean folks prepared to pitch in. Remember, we've got a construction project *and* a TV show." He put his hands on his hips, anchored by the tool belt. "Did anybody tell you to batten down the hatches in the trailer, Dillon? We'll be moving it at some point."

"What for?"

"We're pouring a basement. We don't want a tornado to come along and whisk the director of the Indian Warrior Summer Camp off to Oz."

"Mystic Warrior Horse Camp," Emily quietly amended.

Dillon felt oddly threatened by the thought of anyone displacing the trailer. He'd been a bird without a nest for so long, until… "That trailer's been sitting there for probably twenty years with no—"

"I'll let you know when it's gonna happen. I've never seen a tornado, but I've weathered some squalls on my boat. I live by the same motto on water as I do on land. What's our motto, Emily?"

With his finger pointed, Tate directed their recitation in unison, "Safety first." He beamed. "That's right, safety first, in all venues."

"I'm with you," Vince said. "Like I told my wife. She thinks she wants to go on one o' them cruise ships they advertise on TV, but you hear stories about fires and stuff. You think they're safe?"

"I've never been on one," Tate said. "When you've sailed your own boat, you have no interest in cruising."

"You got a yacht?" Vince was prepared to be impressed.

"Sailboat," said Tate. "Sixty-six-foot ketch, wood hull, hundred-and-sixty-horse Volvo engine, and she's the love of my life." He turned to Dillon. "I was just telling Emily to check her school calendar, let me know when she's off for spring break, and we'll go sailing. You'll have a hard time keeping her down on the farm after she's seen the sea."

"What farm?" Beneath pinched eyebrows, Dillon's eyes shifted left and right. *Ranch. This was a ranch.*

"You know that old song. It's from…I don't know, some movie, I guess. Point is, I can promise her a great time."

Dillon elbowed Nick. "You think it's true that when you've ridden your own bull, you're less inclined to throw it?"

"You're the bull rider, D."

"Never quite made it to the whistle on a bull. Plenty of broncs, but no bull." Dillon gave a slit-eyed smile. "How 'bout we round up a couple bulls, I'll take you on, Fox. See who sticks the longest."

Tate turned the corners of his mouth down and nodded once. "What do I get when I win?"

"Cured."

Nick leaned toward Emily. "Who're you bettin' on?"

"Are they riding or throwing?"

"A little of both," Dillon said with a laugh. "I've never been on a sailboat, but I can imagine buckin' those waves, catchin' the wind, watchin' the stars."

"It's probably a lot like riding a horse across this amazing sea of grass you have here," Tate said.

"Whenever you're up for it."

"Depends on the shooting schedule. If we make the day while there's still light, maybe you guys wouldn't mind hooking me up with a tame horse for starters."

"Give us some work to do, man," Dillon said. From what he'd seen so far, it took a lot of people to make a TV show. A lot of people spending most of their time hanging around. "We'll leave you with plenty of light to spare."

"The construction schedule is more…" Tate made a pretense of scanning the premises. "Where's Mike? He likes to get things kinda squared up at each step before we bring the neighbors in." He started walking backward. "I'll find him and tell him the natives are getting restless. The *neighbors*." Still backpedaling, but with a Colgate smile. "The neighbors want to get involved."

"They're filming around the church now," Emily explained as Tate headed in that direction. She held her hand out. "Do you want to see how they make a TV show, Joey?"

"TV shows aren't real," the little boy said as he grabbed Emily's hand. "It's all pretend. Right, Daddy? Except the news."

"Are you kidding?" Vincent laughed. "These days, the news is the least real of all."

"This TV show is different," Nick explained. "It's about real people fixing things up. So that's what they're doing while the TV cameras make a movie of the whole thing."

"Just real people?" Joey was disappointed. "No cartoons?"

"Well, now, that's a good question," Dillon said. "They're filming everything we say and do. I guess they could end up making us out to be just about anything."

"It's called editing," Emily put in. "Tate says we're so interesting, they're going to have a hard time deciding what to leave out. And of course, he and Zooey have to be in almost everything. It's in their contracts."

"So the trick is to stay away from those two when there's a camera around," Nick decided.

"Or have a little fun one-upping them." Dillon lifted one shoulder. "You know anything like that won't make the cut."

"Do us all a favor and watch out for your dad," Nick said to Emily. "We don't want him causing any trouble."

"*Tuale,* not that damn bad." Dillon shoved his hands into the front pockets of his jeans. "Hell, I've got a contract, too. Iron horse. Can't be edited."

"You mean, iron-clad?"

"I mean what I said. They get their TV show. We get the Mystic Warrior Horse Camp." He glanced at his daughter. "And that damn well better be the reality."

Chapter Nineteen

The craft center at Sitting Bull College was abuzz with activity. The company that produced *Who's Our Neighbor?* had donated half a dozen new sewing machines and a dozen quilt frames to the college, and they were all set up, many of them already in use. Monica recognized some of the fabrics she'd chosen—blues, reds, purples, solids and patterns—splashes of color throughout an otherwise colorless workroom. It was a generous space made up of white walls, beige linoleum floor, flickering fluorescent bulbs and few windows. Once cameraman Charlie Verick finished changing the bad lightbulbs himself—clearly somebody hadn't gotten the word—the bland craft center would be the perfect background for colorful quilts and the women who made them.

Among the crafters were two of Dillon's sisters, Josie and Jocelyn, and Nick's sisters, the gregarious Bernadette and soft-spoken Louise, along with several of Monica's former students, whose younger faces lived in a memory that wanted a little jogging for names. Three of the women presented their children, who were expected—be they three years old or ten—to offer a handshake. She'd forgotten to ask the women to leave the children home. So be it, she decided. This was a reality show, after all, and the reality in Indian country was that children were never excluded.

Monica introduced Zooey to the whole room at once, and while Charlie was setting up for the shoot, Monica took a turn around the room getting acquainted and reacquainted, admiring the work in progress, the ways the colors were combined and noticing the many variations on the theme of the traditional Lakota star blanket. There would be sixteen small quilts for the bunkhouse and three larger ones for the bedrooms of the main house, along with several quilted wall hangings.

Emily popped in with Vincent Many Wounds' daughter, Donna, a pretty young teen who was eager to be part of the project and part of the circle. A college girl and a teenager. Perfect. Two for show. Monica was a firm believer in a circle's power to provide safe passage through the rocky shoals of adolescence.

In theory, anyway. In practice, she was finally facing the fact that one person did not a circle make. And no matter what the extent of her talents, she was only one person.

The college coffee shop was handling craft services for the quilters, and Bernadette of the smiling black eyes and crisp red blouse had appointed herself craft service liaison. The smell of coffee preceded her announcement of a fresh pot. When a serving cart was wheeled in, she checked the contents and announced, "Pie. Looks like apple, blueberry…" she lifted a covered plate to eye level for closer scrutiny "…and some peach. And it's still warm, so we should eat it now. What kind do you want, Louise?"

There was no answer, but Bernadette delivered a plate to her sister anyway. "Keep up your strength," she said, as she deposited the plate on a TV tray near Louise's quilt frame.

She took her own plate back to the table where she had been turning fat quarters of fabric into small squares and addressed the room. "Louise could be as famous as Monica if she talked herself up a little more. Her quilts are works of art. You see a whole line of quilts hanging there at a giveaway, you can tell right away if Louise made any of them."

Monica looked around for affirmation, but it came only in silent nods, which would not do.

"The young people naturally look to master quilters like Louise for direction," Monica said to the camera. It sounded good, and she hoped it was true. To the group she said, "And this center, which is all new since I lived here, is a wonderful place for crafters to gather. Do you come here often?" She laughed. "That sounded like a bad pickup line."

Responses came from all over the room.

"It's nice not to have a quilt frame taking up half the living room."

"And the kids can't get into it here."

"I keep mine at home. I like to work at night sometimes."

"Louise always has one going at home, but she keeps one here, too," Bernadette said. "You should do a show about her, Monica. She teaches a class right here at the college."

"That's wonderful," Monica enthused. "You know, that's a great idea, Bernie. We'd have to do it in Minneapolis, though. My show is a very small production compared to this one." Monica led Charlie to Louise's quilting frame, where he focused on her quick hand poking the needle over and under for eight tiny, perfectly even and equal stitches. Pierce eight times, pull once. "Would you be interested?"

"Just me?" Louise asked softly.

"You'd be the feature segment. It would just be the two

of us talking about quilting, giving some background on Indian star quilts and showing some of your work." Monica glanced at Bernadette, who was eating her second piece of pie. "What a great idea, Bernie."

"I don't ever get to Minneapolis," Louise said.

"We'd pay for your travel and lodging. Or you could stay with me."

"I don't think so. This is bad enough."

"Think *positive,* Louise. You could be famous," Bernie insisted. "We'd have to double the price for your quilts. Maybe more than double."

"We?"

"You need to hire me to manage the business part. And the promotion. Listen to you. Your mouth is saying 'I don't think so,' just out of habit. You could be making quilts for the rich and famous."

"The rich and famous have nothing to do with me," Louise said, her soft voice a counterpoint for Bernadette's effervescence. "I make quilts for family and friends."

"But they don't pay."

"Some do. Depends on what it's for."

"I really would love to get you on my show, Louise. Many of my guests feel shy at first, but we're very good at—"

"Is it better than teaching?" Bespectacled Josie bobbed up from a sewing machine. "Being on TV, I mean."

"It pays better," Monica allowed. "It shouldn't, but it does."

"They tell you what to say, or do you make it up yourself?"

"For a show like mine, they—generally the production assistant—anyway, somebody gives me the background on a guest, and depending on the complexity, we set things up and talk about it before the taping. Then we usually wing it while we work."

Strolling from one quilting station to another, Zooey broke into song. "Wing it while we work. Dum dee dum dum dum dum dummm."

"I could do that," Bernadette said. "Just sit and talk to people. You have to stay skinny? Or are you diabetic?"

"No, I'm not…" Monica glanced at her hand as she reached for a pile of Bernadette's cotton squares. Her favorite lapis and turquoise ring rode her finger like a hula hoop. It was a good thing she had knobby knuckles. "Ordinarily, I have to watch it, but lately…"

Josie's wire-rimmed glasses rose above her machine. "Jeez, you guys, just because she looks like that doesn't mean she's sick."

"Yeah, Bernie, you've gotta get off the rez more often," said Carla Looking Back, one of Monica's former students. "What they do is, they go on these diets."

"Well, I wanna know what she eats," Bernadette said. "They say if I don't lose fifty pounds *at least,* I might have to go on medication. I try, but I look in the refrigerator, and I hear voices. Like, 'Hey! It's me, Cheese. Put me in bed with Mac right now, or else I'm just gonna go bad on you.'"

"A little mac and cheese won't hurt," Monica said, jumping at the chance to give a lesson. "The trick is to limit your portions and not to keep leftovers around."

Bernadette grinned. "What do you mean, *leftovers?*"

"It's all about portion and cupboard control. Don't give the chips and donuts any shelf space."

"What shelf space?" Carla challenged. "I have to eat 'em on the way home from the store or I don't get any. I've got kids."

"Don't buy them," Monica said easily. It seemed like

such an obvious solution. *Don't buy crap.* "I know we talked about this in class many times. It's a habit. Most of us buy the same things every time we shop. Make a list, stick to the list, and after a couple of months of being really strict about it, you'll be amazed how much…" She glanced at her leather tote bag, where her next cigarette waited. "Of course, some habits are more stubborn than others. It depends on the person."

"I always like that Rice-a-Rookie we made in your class," Carla said.

Emily laughed. "What in the world is Rice-a-Rookie, Mother?"

"Oh, it's really good," said Carla. "You make balls out of rice and hamburger, and then you use these special noodles and make them look like basketball nets, and then you add—"

"And what about those Slam Dunkers?" Josie put in. "That's the only way I can get carrots and broccoli into my kids. Rabbit food, my husband calls it, but he'll eat it that way. He goes heavy on the slam, though. Is that low-calorie?"

"It depends on how you make it. I'd have to look it up in my files. It's been a long time since I've looked at those recipes. But I never throw anything like that away. You never know when…" she glanced at Zooey "…you might be teaching again."

"Maybe after you retire from TV," Louise said.

"TV stars don't retire," Bernadette contributed. "They do commercials when they get old."

"Oh my, no rest for the weary. So, Bernie, we need to get Louise over her camera shyness before I get put out to pasture in commercial country." Monica pulled a chair up next to Louise's quilt frame. "How do you like it so far? It really isn't so hard, is it?"

"It wasn't, but then you started talkin' about it. Now I can't think about— Ouch!" Louise peered at her hand. "Stuck the needle in my thumb. See? I never do that."

"It's not bad karma or anything, is it?" Zooey rushed into the camera shot. "Bad luck?"

"It could mean death," Emily warned, eyes twinkling. "Unless you have the power to change it to a long sleep. But don't forget to send in a prince."

"Bad luck." Louise sucked the ball of her thumb, tsked, finally nodded at Zooey. "Too much TV, this woman."

On the way to Bismarck that night, Monica treated herself to a chain of cigarettes. Call it one smoke, she told herself, the only one for today. No leftovers to get into later. The trick was to keep the flame alive, keep the fire going. *Breaking the chain brings bad luck.*

Too full of tricks, this woman.

Monica was the master of tricks, the *trompe l'œil* expert in a world where appearance was everything and deception simply a tool. No-sew drapery, flourless cake, false fronts and cardboard backs. But smokeless tobacco? Such a thing existed, but it was a disgusting alternative. And the crutches for quitting were no better. Why would anyone want to get her nicotine from a patch stuck to her arm? What was she supposed to do with her hands? Great tricks abounded for every purpose but the kind that really mattered.

And what difference did it make now, anyway? As Dillon used to say, you have to die of something. Not that she'd heard him say it lately. Not that she wanted to. She didn't want to die or *say* die or hear *him* say die. She wanted to be able to count on him for once, the way everyone else had always been able to count on her. Could continue, *would* continue, to count on her, if she had anything to say about it. She wasn't quite as certain as she wanted to be, but that was for her to know and for no one else to find out.

This setback was not supposed to be happening. She'd had the disease removed from her body, and that should have been the end of it. But when she'd learned otherwise, she'd worked the next round of treatment back into her schedule. She would beat this thing yet, and she would do it, as the current catchphrase would have it, on so many levels. She had good doctors, great drugs and the best wig-maker in Fantasyland on her side. She was good for the foreseeable future.

Beyond that, she hoped she could finally count on the erstwhile unaccountable Dillon Black.

Dillon was mesmerized. He took flight on D.J.'s music the way he rode a horse, by giving himself over to the lift and the glide. His heart and mind were one with the sound, and he was fascinated by the image of his son standing alone on a prairie rise, tall grass ebbing and flowing about his feet as though his strings had concert with the wind. Against the glory of a sky made bruised and bloody by the sinking sun stood the soft, slender silhouette of a boy plying bow and fingering strings.

It was a moment out of time, and Dillon had half a mind to snatch the rolling camera from its operator's hands lest it truly was a thief of souls. It was the half of his mind that was programmed to protect and defend. But the other half would not be distracted from storing a singular moment in a father's memory. Dillon understood the meaning of *once in a lifetime.* He'd learned the hard way.

"How can he do that so perfect?"

Dillon turned to the boy standing beside him. Jimmy Taylor's eyes were brimming with tears.

"So beautiful," the boy whispered. The music had stopped, and D.J. was conferring with Darius.

"He practices all the time," Dillon said.

"He seems like a regular kid."

"He's a special kid. But, then…" Dillon laid his hand on the back of the boy's neck, which would soon be covered by the hair he was growing out. In the twilight, Dillon couldn't see the remnant of rope burn, but he knew it was there. "…so are you."

"Yeah," Jimmy said skeptically. "D.J. hasn't ridden much. I showed him how to stand in the stirrups on a horse with a choppy trot. You know, like you taught us last summer."

"I showed D.J., too, but…"

"But he wasn't doin' it until I got him to try. Aren't you worried about him maybe fallin' off and hurting his hands?"

"All the time," Dillon admitted. He smiled. "What do you think about boxing gloves?"

Laughter coming from Jimmy's throat was a rare but welcome sound.

"Hey, I'm glad you're here, Jim. D.J.'s mom made him come out here for this deal, and I think he was kinda miserable until you showed up."

"I beat him at Counter-Strike. It's a computer game. He beat me twice, but it's his game, and I never played it. He says you don't even have dial-up at your place. You should ask the TV people to hook you up."

"I don't have time for the…" Dillon's face drew down in a frown. "What do you mean, ask the TV people? You think this is Christmas in June?"

Jimmy grinned. "More like *Who Wants To Be a Millionaire?*"

"Well, it ain't me, babe," he said as Ella withdrew from the clutch of TV people who had been watching and came over to join them. "Some people think I've hit the jackpot here. My partner thinks I've joined the circus. And it's all because of this lady right here." He lifted his free arm, unsure whether he'd be left hanging.

Bad word. You find yourself twistin' in the wind, Black Bear, you got it comin'.

But he didn't.

Ella tucked herself under his wing, and he told himself to quit looking over his shoulder for some *gigi* to snatch the rug out from under him.

He smiled. "What do you think, Jim? Can we trust her?"

"My counselor says nothing hurts worse than misplaced trust comin' back to bite you in the ass."

"Ouch! Did he tell you how to figure that out before you misplace it?"

"Not really. And my counselor's a she."

"Figures."

"But it's too late for you to start thinkin' about trust. They've already torn your place up."

"Nothin' I haven't done myself a time or two." He gave Ella a quick squeeze. "But this one has some nice plans in the works for us, Jim. We'll have our camp. I'm gonna need help. You interested?"

"Sure. You mean, like…?"

"I probably can't pay much besides room and board this

summer, but now that I know how to put together these grant proposals, I'm thinkin' next summer—"

"You don't have to pay me. You let me stay, I'll work for free."

"We'll ask your mom and your counselor. Put together a proposal for them."

Jimmy glanced up at the hill, where the cameraman was showing D.J. the scene he'd just taped. "Is D.J. staying?"

"He's itchin' to go back to the Cities. He takes music lessons every week. I knew he was good, but I see now…" Dillon chased a mosquito off the back of his neck. "His music is his life, and I can sure see why."

"I hope he'll stay a while longer. Darius wants more of the same," Ella said. "Well, not exactly the same, but variations on a theme. He's in love with this place. He says he seldom has a chance to work with this kind of light."

"Where does my son's music fit into a remodeling show?"

"Sense of place. The buildings we make are designed to be part of a landscape. The people here are part of a community, which is also part of a landscape. Part of this land."

"Always has been. But my boy…"

"It's about bringing the viewer on board, body and soul," Ella explained. "Our directors find ways to do that, and sight and sound are the senses they have to work with." She slipped her arm around his waist. "Your boy is beautiful both ways."

"I don't want to see him pushed any more than he has been already. He doesn't want to be here."

"Does it look like he's getting pushed?" She nodded toward the boy, the man and the camera, which was replaying the video. "If you think he's uncomfortable with anything we ask him to do, if he says anything to you…"

"What do I know? Seriously." He chuckled. "You think this is fun, Jim? Being on TV?"

"Kinda. It doesn't feel like being on TV. It just feels like we're doin' stuff and somebody's taking pictures."

D.J. noticed them and called out, "Hey, Jimmy, come see this!"

Jimmy came to attention and fairly flew up the hill at the invitation.

"Emily called." Ella took a swipe at a mosquito buzzing around her face. "They're wrapping up with the sewing circle for today—the taping, anyway. She says those women are glued to those quilt frames. Probably won't leave as long as there's food and water there for them."

"Are they coming back here tonight?" Dillon asked. "Emmie and Monica, I mean."

"Monica went to Bismarck for…" She caught herself. "Well, she had a list of things."

"Thought you had a team of prairie dogs for that. Go-fers." Dillon chuckled. "Monica went to Bismarck for…" His open-handed gesture invited her to complete the sentence.

"She said she had an early morning appointment, among other things."

He nodded. That was all she was going to say, and he had no right to ask for more. Not about Monica.

He should be asking Monica herself.

He didn't want to ask Monica.

"When are you gonna invite me over to your trailer for supper?" he asked instead. "You haven't been eating with the rest of us. Hell, cookin' for two is as easy as cookin' for one."

"That's my downtime," she claimed, but quickly added, "Whenever you're free."

"I'm free now."

"Did you miss the second meal?" she asked.

"I had pork chops. I don't know whether that was first or second. All I know is, whenever I look up, there's a camera in my face." He swallowed, lowered his voice. "Invite me, Ella. You don't have to cook anything."

"You're invited. Give me an hour to wrap up for the day."

"Dad!"

Dillon stepped back, trying to remember the last time his kid had barged in on a key move.

D.J. slowed from a run to a long-legged walk. "Where's Emily? She's supposed to give Jimmy a ride home."

"Your sister's on her way, but I guess your mom went to Bismarck and probably won't be back until tomorrow."

"Her doctor's appointment isn't until tomorrow. Why did she go today?"

"She had a lot to do," Dillon said, slipping Ella a questioning glance. "You guys can take the pickup if you want to."

"Awesome," D.J. said. Then he turned to Jimmy. "You'll have to drive."

"If it's okay that I don't have a license," Jimmy said. He caught the look Dillon shot him and hung his head. "I shouldn't've said anything."

"I wasn't thinking." He was too busy trying to be the cool dad. "Jimmy, why don't you give your mom a call and see if you can stay overnight?"

"If you'll talk to her. She's all, like, *what's going on?* every time I leave the house ever since…you know."

"Get her on the phone and I'll talk to her. Maybe you guys could grain those horses we kept in to use tomorrow."

"I just took a shower and changed clothes before we did that shoot," D.J. said.

"So?"

"So I don't want to get around horses. Danny and his sister…we were going to hang out."

"Perfect." Dillon put a hand on each boy's back. "Women love the smell of horse on a man."

Chapter Twenty

Ella turned on a lone light in her trailer.

It was the one over the little banquette and table that would illuminate the south window like a beacon. She knew she was asking for trouble, but how long had it been since she'd had any?

Any *trouble*. Serious, pulse-pounding trouble. Mind-messing trouble. The toe-curling kind of trouble she so studiously avoided that she wasn't sure she knew how to keep it contained when it came knocking. If it came knocking.

It didn't knock. It walked right in, closed the door and shut off the light.

"Trouble?" She might have laughed had he not been so close she could feel the heat.

"Your window's like a drive-in movie, and I don't wanna be tonight's feature." He took her in his arms. "No cameras," he whispered. "No show."

"Just us."

She put her arms around his neck, and he backed her up to the sliver of a counter next to the stovetop. He covered her mouth with his and lifted her in the same instant, sitting her on the counter, sliding his hands to her waist and kissing her lips hard, softly, hard again, hands pressing along her thighs, over her shorts to her knees, callused palms at once warm and chill against her bare skin. His tongue found hers, touched its tip, drew back and made another foray, filling her mouth with the salt-sweet taste of his as he moved her legs apart and stepped between them.

He kissed her neck, the hollow at the base of her throat, slid his way into her tank top with his chin and lightly kissed the swell of her breast. The jersey cotton trapped his warm breath, and her nipples pinched up tight.

Touch them, she willed. *Kiss them and suck them.*

"Something's missing." His nose traced a line from the well between her breasts to the ridge of her collarbone. He kissed her shoulder and her neck and whispered, "You always wear one."

"I showered and…" His smooth cheek brushed hers, his fingers threading through her damp hair, spreading it over his face, and he inhaled deeply close to her ear while he slipped a spaghetti strap off her shoulder with a deft thumb. She drew a shallow breath. "I didn't know whether…"

"Yes, you did." He pushed the second strap down. "You told me to come to you." Sweet lips on her shoulder. "Said the magic words."

Her top clung to her like a bit of cloth caught on a hillside. He used it to tantalize, abrading her nipples with his thumbs before his mouth took over, his thumbs heading for lower territory. Her knit shorts gave his hands easy access through their wide legs. Her skin tingled at his touch, his fingers trailing over her inner thighs, under her panties and into deep, dark, tight, wet secrets— Oh! The attack on two tender fronts at once took her breath away. She opened her legs farther, and he teased and tortured more, suckled and played, and she extracted sounds of helplessness and hunger from a throat she didn't know, a body she no longer owned. She shuddered uncontrollably and soared unthinkably. He dispensed with her shorts and his jeans, and she hung in the balance, forearms braced on his shoulders, touching forehead to forehead, mingling breath with breath.

The tip of his penis touched and teased, and he whispered, "Invite me, Ella."

Legs wrapped around his waist, she lifted, centered herself over him, made her claim, sucked him inside her and swallowed, swallowed, held, swallowed, held tight and slowly, slowly retreated, determined to draw him, *all of him,* into the deepest part of herself.

He gave guttural, wordless voice to his pleasure and deep, probing reply to her body's slightest signal. She was on the up and up and up, and she wanted it all, *his* all. She reached back with one hand, found the counter and used it to lift and steady herself, to control her side and drain his. But he caught her hips and made her hold steady while he rocked inside her, touched off charge after charge as he whispered her name. He took her down with him to the floor, where she straddled him, and he suckled her, and they rocked and rolled.

And one on one made one.

Ella enjoyed the way Dillon's fingers played over her skin—unhurried and unabashed, but careful, too, like a child given his first liberty with something he'd never been allowed to touch before. From masterful to mesmerized, his wonders were working. She was charmed, which was probably dangerous. She couldn't let him stay, but she would hate to see him go, and she blessed the small bed for keeping them close. Ambivalence, perhaps, kept them quiet. Taken together, pleasure, proximity and peace would have been plenty for one night, at least if she could get him out the door before morning and be done with the risk of him.

It will be, and you can. Simply say nothing more.

She would have let him sleep some. She would have held him a little while, covered him against the night's chill, stroked his hair and awakened him when the time came to send him on his way. But he didn't sleep. And her brain filled itself up with clever things to say. Easy, breezy things that would cancel any impressions—false impressions— she might have given or he might have gotten.

Talking between the sheets is like reading between the lines. Who needs it?

Good question. But even if the mother inside her head didn't, maybe Ella did.

"What's your M.O., Mr. Black?" she asked, keeping it soft and light. "Do you hang around and cuddle, or jump into your jeans and skedaddle?"

"What's *M.O.*?" He leaned back. Moonlight brightened his face. "Man Overboard? Because that's what I feel like right now."

"Take a clue from the captain. Sailing your own boat is probably safer than cruising the trailer court."

"I'm not a sailor or a cruiser, and I'll take my clues from the horse's mouth." He traced her bottom lip with the rough pad of his forefinger. "A small hint. Would an M.O. be a Missed Opportunity?"

She drew his finger into her mouth, drew back on it slowly, sucked the callused tip and smiled. "More like Major Orgasm."

He chuckled. "Whose M.O. are we talking about? We had two of those goin'."

"At least." She propped her head on her hand. "I don't know why I asked. I guess I'm trying to stay a step ahead."

"That's a game for the world you live in. You won't need it here."

"I'm no good at games anyway." She lifted one bare shoulder. "Trying to sound like I know something about men and the way they operate, but the truth is, I haven't made much of a study."

"We're easy, no matter where you're from. Take Fox…"

"No thanks."

"You don't think he's after my daughter, do you?"

"She might have a crush on him. They usually do."

"Who's *they*?"

"His demographic. Girls her age." She lay back and stared at the close ceiling. "Don't worry. Zooey put that little bug in your ear for her own amusement. Tate's not as dumb as he acts."

"I'm not worried. I know how smart she is. Smart as they come, that girl. He can act as dumb as the market'll bear, but if he tries anything stupid…" His turn to brace himself up on his elbow and look down at her. "Somebody might wanna warn him, his boat ain't gonna get him out of Indian country if he sails it up shit creek."

"I suppose warning him would probably be my job." She laughed. "What an image. I can just see poor Tate. Clogged propeller. No paddle."

"Any way the wind blows, he's got his hands full." He demonstrated, one hand pinching his nose, the other chasing imaginary flies. "Let me know when the time comes for that part of your job and I'll be your AP. I don't wanna miss it."

"My AP?"

"Assistant producer, right?" He tapped his temple with a forefinger. "Listen and learn."

"You have a copy of the schedule. It's pretty full. Not much time for…"

"Me?"

"Plenty of time for you. It's all about you," she said. "*Mainly* about you. It's about the Mystic Warrior Horse Camp, and you're the mystic horseman."

"Let's make this about you and me," he amended softly.

"We made this time. We shouldn't have, but we did, and we probably will again, given the way…" She turned her face toward him. "But it doesn't make much sense. You and me."

"Never does. When you think about two separate people desperately looking for ways to crawl inside each other, *sense* isn't the first word that comes to mind."

"I'm not desperate."

"There's all kinds of desperate. Take it from a guy who knows."

"Scary."

"Only when it really means something, when you've got something on the line that matters. Otherwise it's just a thrill ride. When it's over, you get off and walk away." He smoothed her hair away from her face and tucked it behind her ear. "Or turn everything off and go to bed."

"Safe and sound."

"You're right, Hollywood. It doesn't make much sense." He kissed her close to her ear. "And that's also coming from a guy who knows."

Dillon was torn between investigating the lights on in the barn or those in his trailer. In defense of his good mood he opted for the trailer, where he was betting the light in

the kitchen had nothing to do with a camera. He found his
son eating an apple and paging through *Mystic Warriors
Of the Plains* at the kitchen table, a sight that kicked his
mood up to the next level. Especially when D.J. looked up
from the book and they connected.

"Are you packin' it in for the night or waitin' on the pack?"

"I've done my howling for the night," D.J. said. He sank
his teeth into the apple, slurping as he snapped off a mouthful. "You?"

"Oh, yeah." Dillon pulled a chair away from the table,
spun it around on one back leg and straddled the seat.
"Had about all the Hollywood I can handle until, say, early
tomorrow." He stacked his fists on the chair back and
planted his chin in the curl of his thumb and forefinger.
"How'd it go?"

"What?"

"Your run with the pack."

D.J. turned a page. Dillon had an upside-down view of
drawings he knew well—a horse outfitted with travois and
pack and several diagrams of Lakota bridles and saddles.
D.J. turned another page. And another.

Finally he looked up. "Do you realize what time it is,
Dad? I can't believe how late the sun sets here, and how—"

"We're on the edge of the time zone."

"Yeah, well, these TV people don't seem to quit, and
Emily thinks she's one of the directors or something. She
had us cleaning up the saddles and stuff, while Darius
taped them talking about how great the camp was last year
and how great you are, and how Indian kids have so many
problems, probably because Indian adults have so many
problems, but, hey, they're all about the horses, and you
most of all. Emily's going to school to devote her life to

horses and Indians because her father has inspired her. It was all very heartwarming."

It was the longest speech Dillon had ever heard his son make.

"Tell you what I thought was heartwarming, and that was your music bringing the sun down."

D.J. turned two more pages.

"Darius says they'll record me a couple more times," he said without looking up. "Maybe even in a studio, and they're going to record the night sounds around here, and they'll do some mixing. Plus, he was talking to Jimmy about some traditional Indian singers. He says this might be the best one of these shows he's ever worked on."

"Really."

"Yeah. Darius is pretty excited about it." He glanced up tentatively. "Have you seen all the equipment they brought for filming?" Dillon shook his head, and D.J. plunged on. "They have to be able to look at what they're getting every day. They've got a whole truck full of stuff. It's interesting."

"You can study this stuff in college. That's what Ella did." Dillon gave a little smile. "Along with your music. You could probably do both."

"I could probably even take classes in a few different departments. You think?"

Dillon frowned. "Sometimes I do, yeah." Where had the sarcasm come from all of a sudden?

D.J. turned another page of the book he obviously had little interest in. "I'm actually thinking about becoming a policeman."

"A policeman?"

The boy bristled. "Why not?"

"I don't know. You tell me."

"You don't think I'd make a good policeman?"

"I don't think you wouldn't."

"Yeah, you do. You don't think I'm tough enough. You think I'm a *winyan*."

"A girl?" Dillon stiffened. "Where'd you get that idea? Who said that?"

"What difference does it make?" D.J. challenged him with a hard, cold look. "Somebody around here said it. Somebody thinks Dillon Black's son is a wimp. A *winkte*."

Which meant female everywhere except between the legs. A chill shimmied down Dillon's spine. His shirt-sleeves hid goose bumps. The book would have told the boy that while such a person might well be a mystic, he would probably not be a warrior. No one would fault him. No one would deny him a place in Lakota society: healer, artisan, holy one, contrary, caretaker—important roles all. He would be protected, honored, permitted to live according to his nature. There was no Lakota word for *hormones*, but a woman with a *ce*, or penis, was a *winkte*. Dillon was pretty sure the *winkte* of old had it better than the modern gay man. After all, there was also no Lakota word for *sinner*.

"Can I go home now?" D.J. asked after a weighted silence.

"If that's what you want to do," Dillon said quietly. "I'd like it better if you stayed a while, but I'll back you either way."

"What if it's true?" D.J. looked up, quickly adding, "Don't ask what. You know what. It's not like you haven't thought about it."

"I've thought about a million things regarding my kids. Big things, little things. Wonderings, worries, wishes, all kinds of things."

"You know what I'm talking about. Why can't you just say it?"

God. Tunkasila. Help me out here.

"I don't know what to say, son."

"Are you scared?"

"Of what? I'm surprised somebody around here would be calling you names like that, but scared?" He couldn't actually say no, but he shook his head. "I'll stand with you, however you want to handle it."

"I said, *what if it's—*"

The door flew open, and Emily burst in.

"Daddy, wait till you hear…" She stopped, squared up, looked from father's face to brother's—both turned to her, startled and tight-lipped. "What's going on?"

"What's this about…?" *What's this about somebody pickin' on your little brother?* Dillon glanced at D.J., bit his tongue—almost literally—and missed no more than half a beat. "…them moving my trailer? Have you heard anything about when?"

Emily shifted her glance between the two of them—once suspicious, twice perplexed. "What have you heard about it?"

"That they're pouring a basement. Why would anybody put a basement under a trailer?"

"I think it's Mother's idea," she said, guardedly approaching the table, as well as the subject. "You'll have to ask her. They always redo everything for this show, so you'll probably end up with a laundry room or something."

"They're putting in a whole damn laundry building," he protested, pleased with the turn he'd engineered. "And how would you get down there? Are they putting a hole in the floor?"

"I don't know the details, Daddy. I'm guessing. But

don't say anything to Mother. Let her surprise you. It's probably part of the show." Emily laid her hand on Dillon's shoulder. "They know what they're doing."

He glanced across the table at D.J. "First she says ask Mother. Then don't say anything to Mother." He turned his head to look up at his daughter. "Which is it?"

"I'm gonna say play it by ear." She glanced at D.J. "Did I interrupt something?"

"Well, yeah, we were talking." He bit into the apple with renewed gusto.

"Everybody wondered where you went. I told them you were allergic to saddle soap. Soap of any kind." She grinned. "The thought of cleaning anything but your spoiled rotten self makes you break out in— Ouch!" she said as she took a flying apple core to the chest.

"Cut it out now." Dillon winked at his son, then turned to Emily. "Give your brother a chance to get to know people a little bit before you start that stuff. You've had a head start."

"Just kidding. I didn't tell anyone it was past his bedtime." She ducked, but D.J. had nothing left to throw. "Seriously, everybody's hitting it off nicely, I think."

D.J.'s turn. "Especially you and Tate Fox."

"He's hot," she acknowledged as she bent to pick up the apple core. "But I'm not, so don't even go there."

Dillon fielded D.J.'s tattletale glance. "Don't listen to her," the boy said. "She's wicked starstruck, and what does the guy really do? He doesn't act, doesn't sing, doesn't even do much carpentry."

"I'm not..." Emily cocked her arm, but changed her mind about her target, lobbing the apple core toward the kitchen sink for a surprise score. "Daddy, I am *not* starstruck. But Tate's so much fun to be around. This whole thing is incredibly—"

"He's a star in his own galaxy far, far away, maybe," D.J. said.

"You two do this all the time?"

"Only when she's home, which is hardly ever."

"He misses me," Emily teased, singsong.

"Right." D.J. closed the book on that idea. "I don't want you making a fool of yourself. Not even out here in the desert. Word spreads fast and far."

Dillon nodded, fighting off a smile. "The wind generally blows west to east."

"Carry on where you left off." Emily gave her father's shoulder a parting pat. "I'm going to bed."

"Can I ask you about something first?" Dillon grabbed her hand. "Since it's just the three of us. And, hey, if it's something you don't wanna talk about, that's fine. But I feel like I'm missin' something I should maybe be in on." He glanced across the table at one beautiful face and then up and sideways toward the other. "Something about your mom."

"Mom?" D.J. looked more relieved than anything else, but he sounded surprised.

"She's got a doctor's appointment *out here in the desert.*" He slid D.J. a crooked smile. "Is she okay?"

His kids exchanged allied-sibling looks.

"She gave me some bullshit about restless legs the other day," Dillon explained, hoping to help them out.

"She does have that," Emily said.

"Yeah, restless leg syndrome," D.J. put in. "They advertise it all the time on TV."

"What did she do? Call the eight-hundred number and order up?"

Brother and sister laughed uneasily.

"Only nineteen-ninety-five a pair," Dillon said.

"No, she really has the symptoms they show on TV," D.J. insisted, smile dissolving. "Like the skin on her legs is too tight, and she's, like, pulling and stretching."

"And complaining," Emily said. "Even though she's lost so much weight you wonder how anything can be tight on her."

"Without even using all those exercise machines she's accumulated." D.J. lifted one shoulder. "She actually does have an itchy trigger finger when it comes to those eight-hundred numbers."

"Last time I was out to your place, I saw one of those bikes that goes nowhere in the rec room, but that was the only—"

"The rest is in the third garage," Emily said. "Treadmill retirement home. Also known as Last Gasp."

"Thighmaster graveyard." D.J. held his hand parallel to the table. "Little hand weights for headstones."

"Okay, let's not…" Dillon called time-out on their little comedy with a wave of his hand. "So that's all it is, this restless-leg thing?"

"If you want to worry about something, worry about the way she's started coughing again," D.J. said in earnest. "She thinks she's hiding it, but I know she hasn't quit smoking. Not even close."

"Easier said than done," Dillon admitted.

"You'd think she'd learn after all she's—"

"She's doing fine." Emily glared at her brother. Dillon looked up, surprised, and she relaxed. "She has great doctors. Minnesota is the medical Mecca. The doctors tell her what to do, and she does it. They set something up for her here because this project got pushed up. And she's signed up for some sort of quit-smoking program later this summer. All kinds of special attention." She gave each man at the table a perfunctory smile. "So it's all good."

"Does she rate all this special attention for having a big TV show or a big bank account?" Dillon asked.

"It's for having the right doctors. She's had a few problems, and they're being taken care of. So." Her confident, end-of-story gesture reminded him of her mother.

"As far as money in the bank goes, you're probably about even," D.J. reported quietly.

Dillon started to laugh but held off when no one joined in. "Either you're kidding or you're overestimating your ol' man's progress in the finances department. But I can honestly say that having money in the bank is right up there on the do-before-I-die list."

"He's not kidding." Emily pulled out a chair and sat down. "Mother spends like she has all the money in the world. As far as we know, she doesn't. And we're pretty sure she knows she doesn't."

"You guys are livin' in a pretty nice place for no money in the bank, which is what you'd have if you were even with me. I'm what we call horse poor."

Emily gave him a warm smile. "You're rich in horses."

"That's *love,* Pinky. Rich in love of horses. That only translates to money in the bank if you sell colts and *deposit* the cash, which is what Nick does. But any money comes to me, I have a tendency to buy more horses."

"You've bought cattle, too."

"Like I told your mom, I'm getting better. And I'm sure she has plenty of assets, too."

"Which only translate to money in the bank if you sell them," D.J. said. "Do you know what it cost to put that pool in the backyard? In Minnesota, for God's sake. It's a liability more than anything. I don't know what she's going to do with it once we leave home."

"She never swims," Emily said. "It's all for show."

We don't need a showplace, Monica. Who's gonna see all this?

All this had been a pretty amazing paint job in their tiny living room—she'd made it look like adobe—and some curtains and slipcovers he'd refused to believe she'd made from thrift store bedsheets.

"Monica knows what she's doing," he said. "The place is probably worth a lot more than what she paid. Besides, she works hard. She oughta be able to spend some of that money fixing up her house if it makes her happy."

"What really makes her happy is making cool stuff happen on a shoestring," Emily said, her pride in her mother beginning to show. "Her show is called *It Only Looks Expensive* for a reason. Mother is at her best when she's pinching pennies."

D.J. jumped on board. "She doesn't clip coupons anymore, but remember when she used to brag about how much she saved at the store with her coupons?"

"This was on sale, *plus* I had a coupon, *plus* it was double coupon day, so it was practically free," Emily recited, imitating her mother with the fidelity only a daughter could achieve. "I counted a veritable canned soup coup."

Dillon laughed. "She said that? She counted coup?"

Emily nodded, eyes sparkling with affection. "And when they went to doubling no more than five coupons at a time, she was undaunted. She'd go through the line as many times as she had coupons divided by five."

D.J. added, "I don't think she's mentioned that on her show."

"Thank God," Emily said.

"So why all the spending?"

"I suspect demons," said Emily.

"Jekyll and Hyde," was D.J.'s guess.

"That would be a new wrinkle, wouldn't it? I was the one with all the wrinkles," Dillon recalled. "She was always neatly pressed. Maybe hard-pressed, thanks to me. Steamed and pressed toward the end."

"You're too hard on yourself, Daddy."

"She was way ahead of me before I knew we were in a race. I just couldn't catch up. Didn't really try, didn't think..." Didn't think she would leave and take everything he cared about with her, which was the kind of thing that happened when a guy stopped thinking and started running. And then he'd found himself running wild.

"You wanna call yourself a man—" he turned his attention from his son to his daughter "—a woman, either side of the coin, you have to think about your family. Whoever depends on you, and you depend on them, that's your family, and you have to think." He touched his temple with a blunt fingertip. "Every step of the way. You can't run like some kid, just to be runnin'. You get to be a kid until you have kids yourself, and then..." Palms up, he slid his right hand beneath the left. "Man or woman, mother or father, you do what's right for them."

"Did you?" D.J. asked.

"Not every step, no. Like I said, I didn't always try. That's why, the Lakota way, kids get backup parents. Your mother's sisters are your mothers, and your father's brothers are also your fathers. And you get lots of grandparents that way, too." He nested his hands again. "Kids can't raise themselves. And I've gotta say, your mother is an amazing woman. What was right for her turned out to be good for you. Just look at you two."

"Well, you both have your wrinkles," Emily said.

"And you'll get 'em, too, believe it or not." Dillon laughed. "Yeah, the wrinkles come and go. We're all human." He smiled. "Even Monica Wilson-Black."

Chapter Twenty-One

Dillon had done some building and boasted some degree of skill in many manly trades, but he had never seen anything like what was going on in his own front yard. It was like watching a time lapse sequence in a builder's television ad. Each day began with separate meetings on construction and production. All activity, down to the smallest finishing or furnishing detail, was scheduled though Ella, who was the central coordinator for the entire project. She decided where to put the cameras and who would be in front of, as well as behind them.

Conceived by an unlikely team of dreamers, the Mystic Warrior Horse Camp took shape from the ground up, layer on layer, changing and growing day by day. Since time was money and labor was relatively cheap—or so the TV people said—construction was given over to what seemed like a cast of thousands, who took after the project like a colony of ants.

They worked in teams. Once the concrete work was complete, the bunkhouse and the utility facility went up quickly. Most of the materials arrived on trucks from a company that sold log homes in packages, custom designed and ready for assembly. With a specialized sub-contractor and experienced crew working under Mike Murphy's supervision, the subfloors went down, outside walls went up and roofs went on within three days. Dillon had worked construction on prefab housing years ago, and he was prepared to point out shoddy workmanship and declare the TV project an unacceptable rush job. He also expected to be told that you get what you pay for. But neither conversation came to pass.

So far, so good.

It was late in the day, and Dillon was skipping second meal in favor of spending quality time with the trim on the church when he noticed a new visitor on the scene. Terry Yellow Horn drove past the line of local vehicles parked along the driveway like mourners at a wake and cozied his pickup up to Dillon's—parked near the trailer house—like he was a particular friend. Dillon dipped his brush in brown paint, spared the man a glance and a nod and went right on painting. If Terry required anything more from him, he would have to come and ask. Nicely.

"Hell of a production," Terry announced when he reached the foot of Dillon's ladder. Tall and otherwise slim, Terry looked like a basketball player who'd swallowed the ball. He sported a cap with the casino logo and a crisply ironed Western shirt, perfect production material.

"Yep." Long, rhythmic brush strokes. "They're serving supper in the big tent. Go help yourself."

"Man, this is gonna be nice." Terry wrapped a hand around the off-side ladder support and turned his face up to watch Dillon's progress. "Looks like your divorce is workin' out pretty good for you."

"Not so I'd wish it on a friend." Dillon loaded his paintbrush. "Wouldn't even wish it on you, Terry."

"Hell, I just meant…"

"Yeah, me, too." Dillon applied more paint.

"We've had movie people come around before, but I never paid it no mind. Here today, gone tomorrow."

"These are TV people. Reality show, they call it." Long on paint and short on bare wood, Dillon slowed his stroke. "Since they started, first thing I do every morning is look outside to see if they're still here."

"What do you have to do for them?"

"When it's all done, they get to go in peace. They have my word."

Terry laughed. Dillon had to laugh, too. And he had to get down and move the ladder or risk looking like a cat who couldn't figure out how to get out of the damn tree.

"This is good." Terry made a sweeping gesture— expanded barn, improved church, two partly-constructed log buildings and stacks of materials ready to be applied— and ended with a proffered handshake. "*Waste yelo.*"

Dillon accepted. "We made a good start last year, but we can do better. With this setup, we can do a lot more."

"Who's *we?*"

"So far it's my daughter and me, but the gate's open."

Terry turned his attention to the square-topped buttes at the edge of their world. "I had the same idea as you, getting a horse program started for our young people."

"I heard." Dillon granted the point with tight lips and a nod. "What do they say about great minds?"

"But I wanted to run it out of the college. Better location."

"Not anymore. Not after this gets built." Dillon wasn't expected to look the man in the eye. It would have been rude, not to mention damned undignified, considering Dillon was shorter.

Smarter, better-looking, in a helluvalot better shape, but just not quite as tall.

"Listen Terry, I'll be looking for support from the Tribal Council and the college, churches, parents, teachers, anybody interested in kids or horses or both. Committee members." He arched an eyebrow. "Your sister-in-law."

"I can't speak for Janice."

"Would you ask her not to speak against me?"

"She doesn't take advice from me. Hell, her sister doesn't take advice from me half the time even though she's married to me." Terry gave a lopsided smile and half a shrug. "It shoulda been more central. That's all I'm sayin'."

"The South Dakota side's always gettin' the short end of the stick. It's been that way for a hundred years, and you guys up on the north side, you know that." Dillon pointed toward the new foundations. "We're getting a bunkhouse here. Showers, laundry, a big kitchen. Location doesn't matter." He pulled down a paint rag he'd looped over a brace on the ladder and rubbed off a brown spot that nearly blended with his skin. "'Course if I don't get some help, I hope everybody likes macaroni and commodity cheese."

"You really lucked out with this. It's like you hit the big one at the casino."

"Better." Dillon grinned. The admission hadn't hurt a bit. *So let's up the ante.* "These guys handle the money, the labor, the ex-wife, everything. Plus they put on a twenty-four-seven feed."

"Well, hell." Terry offered another handshake. "I hope they come through for you."

"Thanks." Dillon embraced the gesture with a smile. "I see it as something for *us*. When outsiders come along with some big idea, what's in it for them turns out to be the biggest part. I don't know for sure what they're getting out of this, but Hollywood's usually pretty harmless these days. They don't dress us up like tourist souvenirs anymore and make us sound like retards." He glanced over his shoulder. Ella would be taking off points. "I mean, like we're *mentally challenged.* Damn."

"You know, they've got rehab for that kind of problem now. Your Hollywood friends can probably give you a referral."

Dillon raised his brow. "You think Indian Health would cover it?"

"Tell you what would cover it. You make sure you save a spot for my niece in one of your first camp sessions."

Dillon nodded, feeling the sting, seeing the face of Terry's niece in his mind. Down syndrome. "I wasn't thinking. One more question I'll need help finding answers for."

"You said the gate was open."

"Gates are a pain in the ass. Gotta have 'em for livestock, but people?" He shook his head. "Where my kids live, some of the rich people have gates on their neighborhoods. And no livestock."

"Gotta protect your assets," Terry said. He glanced around again. "Is all this gonna belong to you?"

"That's what they say."

"You could turn it into a nice business. Charge people to send their kids here. Advertise. They say the bigger the price tag, the more people are willing to pay."

"Like I said, gates are a pain in the ass." Dillon flipped the rag over an aluminum ladder rung. "I'll need help making this work, Terry. My partner's a good businessman. My kids' mother, she's got brains, talents, connections I never imagined. And my kids... Well, who knows where

the road leads for them? For myself, I've got these horses."
He stuck his hands in his back pockets and took a look
around. "Now all this kinda falls in my lap. Put it together
with what we learned from last summer, with ideas from
guys like you, with support from…" He turned to Terry.
"From within. Neighbors. Friends and family."

"Yeah. Sounds good." Terry jerked his chin toward the
framework beginning to take shape beyond the barn.
"What are they building over there?"

"That's gonna be an indoor arena. The barn's finishing
out to almost twice what it was. And we're getting a round
pen." He shook his head in amazement. "That's what they
say, anyway."

"Sounds real good. Expensive proposition, though."
Terry clipped Dillon's shoulder with a friendly fist. "Hope
they come through for you, man."

For him?

A good idea had swelled overnight like yeast dough into
a grand scheme. It was hard to remember what part of it
had started with him or might be *for* him. Except for the
round pen. That would be sweet.

Otherwise, Dillon wanted to see something materialize
for them. For Emily, for Ella and Monica, for Jimmy and
Danny and countless more. He loved a big idea as much
as the next guy, but the closer this one came to becoming
more than an idea, the clearer Dillon's vision of making it
work became. Because over the long haul, he would have
to come through for them. Big-time.

"Does it ever scare you?"

D.J.'s question startled him. The boy had been quiet
since he'd spotted Dillon heading for his pickup and

jumped in with him. Again. Dillon's lame protest that he was only going out to the north pasture to check livestock hadn't discouraged him.

Discouraged him?

Look out. Big head, narrow door. What are the odds on ol' Black Bear coming through?

The pickup topped the windswept ridge. Normally Dillon would take a count of the animals grazing on the grassy flat below, make a few notes and move on. But on this fine morning he drew a deep breath, shut off the engine and turned to his son.

"Ever? That's a pretty scary thought right there."

"I mean, like at night or in the winter or when you're maybe way out here alone on a horse or something. Doesn't this place scare you?"

Dillon scanned the layers of vastness beyond the dusty windshield. Cattle and horses dotted the immediate lowland, but beyond a winding ribbon of water flowing out of the hills and beyond the hills themselves, beyond the tall buttes there was only sky. Ever sky. *For*ever sky. The biggest, bluest sky he'd found anywhere. Not that he'd looked for bigger or bluer. Why bother? Everything Dillon wanted or needed would fit under this sky in this place.

Physically, anyway. Mentally might be another story, especially for somebody like D.J.

"Yeah." Dillon smiled. "Not the dark so much, although it did when I was a kid. Weather, you just live with it. It changes. All this space? I'm a big space man. But, yeah, being alone scares the livin' shit outta me sometimes."

"I don't think I could live here," D.J. said quietly.

"You don't have to."

He'd said it too easily. Not enough regret, and for that

he didn't much like himself at the moment. Being alone wasn't so bad. Facing up to something inside himself that was none too pretty gave him a real scare. Because this boy—this son of his—was looking to him for answers. Fathers were supposed to have no fear, and they were supposed to come up with answers.

Hell.

Dillon laid a hand on D.J.'s slender shoulder. "But if you could come and visit sometimes, it would sure help me out."

"I doubt if I'd be much help." His words aside, something in D.J.'s eyes said that his father was on the right track. "I gotta tell you," the boy continued easily, "I think your horses are beautiful animals, but the whole time I'm riding, I'm thinking, 'One false move...'"

Dillon chuckled. "Me, too." *Right now.*

"No way. I can't believe you're scared of anything. Being alone? That's nothing. That's easy."

"One man's demon," Dillon said. "You respect mine, I'll return the favor. A horse is a powerful animal. If it's you against him just pound for pound, he's way ahead of you."

"Obviously."

"Right." Dillon nodded, opened the door and then pointed to the glove box. "Could you grab the pad and pencil from there?"

He was closing up his notes—dates, numbers, location—when D.J. joined him in front of the pickup. Dillon tucked the little notepad and stubby pencil in his back pocket, folded his arms and leaned against the hood. D.J. followed suit. Almost like old times, except for the years and the gear. Pint-size D.J. had insisted on his own little cowboy boots and a half-gallon hat.

"I need to get out here on horseback." Dillon adjusted

the brim of his hat against the sun. D.J. was wearing sun-glasses. "Missin' two calves, but they're probably hidden in the brush."

"There's one." D.J. pointed to a black white-face tucked into a clump of silver-green sage.

"Got that one." He pointed out five more that were barely visible. "See any others, besides out in the open?" D.J. shook his head. Dillon took his glasses out of his shirt pocket. "Okay, let's get serious."

"Why don't you just wear them?"

"Don't hardly need to."

"Right."

They looked at each other. And looked. And laughed.

"You know you don't have to ride, D.J. I mean...you never get on another horse, that's..."

"You'll still love me?"

They looked at each other, each waiting for the other to react. Joke? No joke?

D.J. gave in first, but the laughter was tentative. On both sides.

"If you're doing it for me, I'm grateful. I'm impressed. I'm..." Dillon squeezed his son's shoulder again. "Don't do it anymore. Make music with those hands."

D.J. turned his palms up and stared at them as though there might be something there he hadn't seen before. He reached for his father's hand, turned it palm up, and put them side by side. Dillon's was bigger, brawnier, browner, rougher. He had to steel himself against pulling away before D.J. gave him leave, and he told himself it was not a fair comparison and surely not a declaration of any kind of connection or aspiration. Different as night and day, they were.

Different as...

"Male and female." D.J. looked up at him. "I mean, they could be, if you were just looking at the hands."

"You're not even sixteen yet, son. I've been workin' with my hands for twenty, thirty years." Dillon closed his fingers over his coarse palm. "I hope your hands never look like this."

"I'm almost sixteen, and I've never had a girlfriend. Isn't that just a little bit unusual?" He released Dillon's wrist, but the challenging gaze held, even through the brown tint of the sunglasses.

Dillon wanted to swallow, but he had no spit.

Damn.

"I don't know if I'd really had a girlfriend, seriously, by the time I was sixteen."

"Did you want one?"

"I wanted just about every girl I saw, and I didn't know what to do about it. And it showed, which is probably why I didn't have a girlfriend." He raised his brow. "Seriously."

A breeze ruffled the boy's dark, almost silky hair. "But you wanted one."

"Sure."

"I don't think I do. I mean...I don't *feel* like I do. I'd rather hang with guys."

"That's...that's normal. You wanna hang out, you hang out with the guys."

Silence.

Dillon took his glasses off and tucked them into his pocket, buying a few seconds. If he'd paid cash, it would have been money wasted. He felt stupid. *Normal?* What the hell was that?

"I don't know what to say, son."

"Nothing."

Dillon nodded.

"I'm not like you."

"I know. You're better. You're smarter. You've got so much—"

"Emily says I scare you."

"She does?" *Shit. Worse than stupid.* "She's probably right. She's usually right."

"You're scared that I'm not like you."

"Why don't we stop circling around each other here and just—" Dillon gestured one-on-one "—talk man to man."

"What does that mean?"

"Okay, how about father to son?"

"Sure." The boy braced his elbows behind him on the pickup hood and stared at the pasture below the ridge. "And what does that mean?"

"I'm sorry, D.J. You drew an ace for a mom and a deuce for a dad." Dillon shrugged. "So what do you do? Do you let me deal you another card, or do you leave the table?"

"I don't know what you're talking about," D.J. said with a sigh. "And you don't want to know anything about—"

"*Son to father.* That's what I should have said. That's what I'm sayin' now. Give me one more try."

"I think I might be gay," D.J. said quietly, still staring at the flat where eighteen cows and five horses grazed. "I don't know what to do about it."

Cards on the table. The bet was to the house, and the dealer's hands were shaking.

"Any suggestions?" D.J. turned his head. "Or you still don't know what to say?"

Dillon drew a deep breath. *Hit me, Tunkasila. Supercharge me. Stupid to smart in no time flat.*

"I've thought about having this talk with you someday," he began. "What to say and how to say it. Told myself, let him do most of the talking and you stick to one or two main points, like how to avoid getting pregnant." He put his hand on his son's shoulder again, squeezed, patted, imagined his hand as a prayer. "So I just need a minute to rethink my main points."

On his return to ground zero, Dillon shrugged off Ella's silent scolding and Monica's vocal one. Yeah, he knew they were finishing up the corrals, and he was supposed to be taping with a group of kids and dreaming out loud about the camp. They still had tomorrow. And the next day. And the trail ride. There would be plenty of opportunities to get everybody's lifelong dreams and undying gratitude on film. He did his penance for going AWOL by helping Tate affix a horse weathervane to the roof of the barn in front of a camera dangling from a jib crane.

But he was rewarded later in Ella's bed. He was in love again, sure as hell, and it would be hell when she left. But, man, it was heaven to feel love again, to make it and take it. He hadn't said the word. He knew better. But he held her in his arms and thought the word while he talked to her about anything and everything else he had on his mind.

"Do you know any gays?" Easy and casual, a manly man lying beside a woman temporarily his, her breast in his hand. "I mean, like, friends or family. People you're close to."

"Why would you ask me that?" was the rejoinder in the darkness. "Do you?"

"One or two. I never thought about it much. Which means I've probably made a few remarks, like, uh…"

Don't say *acting like retards*. She'll think you're a bigot. Or maybe socially challenged.

"Jokes?"

"Huh?"

"You said you made remarks, and you laughed. You must have been thinking about a joke."

"Not really. Not unless it counts when it's on me."

"If the joke's on you, and you're laughing out loud, then you ought to let me in on it. Otherwise you and yourself are just being rude," she scolded, adding in a passable De Niro, "'Cause I'm the only one here."

"Why do they call themselves 'gays,' anyway? I wouldn't wanna call myself *gay*. Gay is like all giggly and skipping around. But they say that's what they want to be called."

She shifted in his arms. "How do you feel about being called an Indian? You're not from India."

"Some dumb shit thought I was."

"And you think gay men giggle and skip around."

"No, I don't. I don't think about them at all. Much."

"Do you mind being called an Indian?"

"It's better than the *R* word, huh? Redskin? Better than *prairie nigger*. That's a real beaut. It's even better than Native American. What does that mean? We were born here? Yeah, I'm an American, and, yeah, I was born here. You talk about American Indian, people get it, so I don't mind. I'd rather be called Lakota. We should work that into the conversation at every opportunity. Dakota for you, Lakota for me."

"Let's call the whole thing off," she sang.

"No way. It's just one letter. Okay, it's more than that, but our ancestors settled most of their differences when they looked around and realized there weren't enough of them left to put up a decent fight." On second thought, "*Mostly* settled most of their differences." The Yanktonais on the North Dakota side were still making out like bandits all the time, he thought, and laughed.

"Another private joke?"

"Some things are best kept that way." *Like your pole doin' the belly dance.* He tried to erase the image from the air with a wave of his hand, but that only made him laugh harder. "Sorry. Guess it's a guy thing."

"At least you're not skipping around."

"Oh, yeah." But his belly was shaking now. "Oh, yeah, that. Okay, stop makin' me laugh now. I asked you a serious question. Aren't there a lot of gays in Hollywood? People you know?"

"Sure." She paused. "They're everywhere, Dillon. You know them, too."

"What do you mean?"

"I mean, everybody does. The sooner we go Native on the subject, the better off we'll all be." She gave him a moment. "You know what I'm talking about. With your considerable knowledge of our culture…"

"Oh, yeah. The *winkte.*"

"Perfectly acceptable in Lakota society."

"I don't know about *perfectly.* It was better for a man to be a warrior."

"And there were no gay warriors? If there are gay soldiers, gay football players…gay *cowboys*…" He winced at the last. Tried not to, but in broad daylight it would have showed. "…then there had to be gay warriors, as well as the *winkte* who took a more traditionally feminine role."

"So there was never any stigma to it," he decided.

"I'm gonna guess the 'never say never' rule applies to human beings no matter when or where they dwell."

"But it probably wasn't as bad as it is here and now," he insisted.

"From what I've read, from what I've heard, I think our ancestors were more sensible, more spiritual and probably more socially advanced on so many levels than this country is now. *But…*" Her hand rode up and over his chest, fingers splayed, spreading more warmth than skin-to-skin could account for. "I'm feeling very romantic these days, which might explain my thinking." She kissed close to his nipple. "On so many levels."

He drew a slow, deep breath, taking in cool night and warm lemon and musk. Crickets made music, and the moon lifted soft white edges from the darkness. He soaked it in. *Enjoy this now.*

"It's gotta be tough, huh? Being gay?"

"Probably," she said.

"It's probably tough being an Indian in Hollywood." He trailed a loving hand from her shoulder to her elbow and back again. "Not sayin' you're a *Hollywood Indian*. But an Indian in Hollywood…"

"It's tough being a woman in Hollywood. It's tough being an actor in Hollywood." She lifted her head, looked him in the eye. "You know what?"

"Livin' ain't easy?" he ventured with a smile. "And loving's twice as hard."

"Not if you keep it hidden. If you can hide it, there's less risk. You know, like hiding who you are. Either way, you feel like you can't really be rejected."

"Maybe you're not sure yet. You play your hand close to the chest until all the cards are dealt."

"You sound like my mother, always strategizing." She rested her chin on the back of her hand. "Everything was a contest, a battle of wit and will."

"Thelma Bear Dancer had plenty of both."

"So it seemed."

"Don't be trying to bust my bubbles, woman. Your mother is like Joan of Arc in Indian country. Seriously." He chuckled. "Okay, maybe that's pushing it. Not too many shrines around here. And I know mothers and daughters have this complicated identity thing, so for you she was probably—"

"I hardly remember what it feels like to be a daughter. If there's a complicated identity thing, it's *sub* subconscious." She laid her head back against his shoulder, and side by side they studied the dark. "My mother had wit to spare, but her will gave out on her. The movement lost its steam. It didn't die completely, but times changed, and you know what happened to the leadership."

"You still hear from them once in a while," he said. "Some of them even went Hollywood."

"They either grew up and got out of the rabble-rousing business, or they're still at it but nobody's listening anymore, because, well, the seventies are over. Or they disappeared, which is what happened to Thelma Bear Dancer."

"Disappeared?" He shook his head. "You didn't hear a lot from her, but she was always there until…"

"Until she wasn't. She retreated to the north woods. Talk about a complicated identity thing, Thelma lived for the American Indian Movement. That's who she was. She had the wit to keep on going, thought she still had arguments to make, but she didn't have the will to beat a dead horse."

"Or the heart," Dillon supposed.

"No heart for beating anything, including what ailed her,

which had everything to do with what kept her heart beating. So she decided to pack it in."

"Decided? I thought it was—"

"Exposure. She'd told me many times that she would not become an old, sick, useless woman." Ella ticked off the myths, exploding them one by one. "She was not disoriented. She hadn't been starving herself. She didn't overdose. She wasn't drinking." A respectful silence passed. Then, quietly, "She went the way she said the old ones before her went. On her own terms."

"Must have been hard."

"I tried, Dillon. I bought a place in the Cities and tried to get her to move back there. It wasn't in her old neighborhood, which wasn't safe, but it wasn't physically that far away. She said it wasn't home."

He listened hard—words and spaces, breath and voice—and took her to heart, where he heard even more: that she seldom spoke of her mother, that she seldom spoke of herself, her life, her losses. That he was privileged.

"What about you?" He turned his head in her direction and pressed his lips to her temple. "Where's home?"

"I kept the condo I bought for her. We spent time there together, so…you know, it feels good."

"Not Hollywood?"

"I have an apartment there. Small. Efficient. I sleep there when I'm not at the studio or on the road. I love my job."

"She lives for the movement," he recited.

"Not that way. It's not my whole identity. But this show makes a difference. You'll see."

He gave a dry chuckle. "I keep hearing, 'It's like you won the lottery,' or 'You hit the jackpot,' and it makes me feel uncomfortable. Kinda prickly, like they're really thinking, 'You sneaky bastard, you played an ace out of an old deck.' I don't know whether to laugh it up or punch 'em in the mouth."

"If they're jealous, that's their problem."

Right.

"What if you chose the wrong man for all this? I've been cruisin' along here, thinking I've got a good thing going. But maybe I'm not up to sailin' my own boat." He sighed. "I don't wanna screw this up."

"Then don't."

"And this." He turned to take her fully into his arms. "I really don't wanna screw this up."

"We won't."

Chapter Twenty-Two

Dillon felt like a raft in a lake full of kids. They were hanging on to him, bouncing off, squealing around him and playing verbal tag with each other while the camera rolled. If they got the row of windows trimmed on the new addition to the barn, it would be a bonus. A minor miracle. The distant rattle of spray guns reminded him that most of the serious painting was getting done off camera.

The kids were happy to let the viewers in on their love of Dillon, Emily, horses, summer and Indian tacos. They talked up the Mystic Warrior Horse Camp, recalling the horse that stole Danny Many Wounds' can of snuff and the time Jimmy Taylor had torn out the seat of his jeans. At the mention of a new season they tried to talk Dillon into "first dibs" on mounts, chore assignments, upper and lower bunks, team captains and toothbrush colors.

"I can't wait for that trail ride," Donna Many Wounds announced. Dillon turned to find her sitting on the fence—again—and he signaled her back to work with a jerk of his head. From new corral fence to new barn wall she dragged her heels over the newly scraped hardpan. "Do we have to dress like cowboys? My mom's old shit-kickers fit me, but they're kinda *uhnsh*. They're from back when we lived in the country and Lala Two Shield used to have a bunch of horses, back when I was a baby."

Dillon turned his fist into an imaginary microphone. "Translation for our city neighbors," he said, using a golf announcer's tone. "Donna is using an expression derived from the Lakota word *unsica*, which means poor, or pitiful. Lala means grandfather, and the term *shit kickers*, which will be bleeped by the censors, refers to footwear worn by the native children in the traditional game of horse hockey, in which the poor, pitiful puck is actually made from natural horse bleep."

D.J. leaned close enough to talk to the hand. "And if you believe that load of Dillon Black bleep…"

"Do we have to wear these caps?" Danny flicked thumb and forefinger against the hunter orange bill of a cap that advertised the show on one side and a brand of power tools on the other.

"What's wrong with the cap?" Tate gestured with his ever-present plastic water bottle. "We sell a ton of those on the Web site. And yours are personally autographed."

"That's why I wanna keep mine nice," Donna said.

"I'll get you another one. Have your cap and wear it, too."

"I feel like a duck," Danny grumbled.

"I think we should get to wear cowboy hats on the trail ride," Donna said. "Danny, what did you do with yours? You used to have one."

"Nobody wears cowboy hats. Not since that *Brokeback Mountain* movie." Danny bent to load his paintbrush. "Did you see that movie, Dillon?"

"Missed it," Dillon said. "Been meaning to catch it on video. Tell you what, styles come and go, but I ain't givin' up my hat till they pry it out of my cold, dead hands."

"Did you see it, D.J.?" Danny asked.

"I don't see too many movies, and I don't wear hats."

"Which explains the paint." Dillon leaned over and picked through his son's hair like a daddy chimp. "Okay, *now* you've got paint in your hair." And he tousled it, laughing as Darius Bird appeared in the open doorway.

"May I borrow your son for about an hour?"

Dillon lost that smilin' feelin'. "What for?"

"Monica wants to get him involved in a decorative project over at the church." Darius stepped from shadow to sunlight and turned to D.J. "Remember the traditional Lakota instruments we talked about? The radio guy— Bobby Big Eagle—he's going to hook us up with a drummer. And he brought me a sacred flute."

Dillon winced. "What sacred flute?" Sounded like pure Bobby bleep.

"Don't worry, Dillon," Darius hastened to assure him. "It's safe in my care."

"Helluva relief."

"Bobby got us permission to use it from the Flute Carrier."

"The carrier of the sacred flute." Dillon nodded, lips tightly pressed together.

"Bobby explained that the identity of the carrier isn't widely known. Believe me, I'm not trying to overstep, but ever since we filmed this young man alone with his music and the sky, the grass, I've had this vision. And it's miraculous, really, an audio vision. So I thought Bobby would have some ideas about how to bring in traditional music, since he's our radio guy."

"Yep," Dillon said solemnly. "Bobby's our guy."

"I showed him the magic-hour sequence, shared my vision, and he got it." Darius pointed to his temple. "From my head to his. I mean, he completely got it, and he brought in the flute, knows the right drummer…" He put his hand on D.J.'s shoulder. "It's all coming together through this enormously talented son of yours. The church, the hills, the sky, the ways of your people—and this young man."

"Sounds great." Dillon turned to his son. "Are you cool with all this?"

"I'm totally down with it."

"So we'll shoot this project with your mother," Darius went on. "She's making wall décor from pieces of an old pipe organ, which is ingenious."

"Goes with the cow chairs," Dillon said.

"On so many levels," Darius agreed, and then he laughed. "I'm over the moon on this one myself."

"This one?"

"This project, everything about it." He turned to D.J., who was wiping his hands on a rag. "Just like before, forget I'm there with the camera and let yourself get into the moment."

Great, Dillon thought. So many levels, so few moments.

"This time it's a mother-and-son moment, but think about the preservation of an old organ and an old church, and speak those thoughts. It's important to think out loud for us. I'm not trying to put thoughts in your head, but the music…"

Dillon watched them walk away. His son who thought he might be gay, and some Hollywood *haspa*—black man—who probably was. Possibly was. Did it matter if he was? Maybe he should just ask the guy straight out. *Straight* out.

Maybe he should just mind his own business.

His son was his business.

Business he hadn't been too good at minding.

Damn his sun-baked hide. *On so many levels.*

What the hell did that mean, anyway?

* * *

Monica was pleased with the results of her day's work. Dylan had helped her mount the old church organ keyboard for hanging, and they'd worked on a piece of intricately carved organ facade that would become part of a huge wall grouping in the corner that had once housed a much smaller organ and a choir. Dillon would be surprised when she hung a blowup of an old photograph her assistant had dug up in the State Library. The picture of the church interior had probably been taken after its Indian mission period, but she would pair it with a shot taken of an Indian congregation on the outside steps years earlier. The building had since been separated from its steps, but the doors and windows were the same.

Too tired to face the drive to the hotel, she knocked on the door to Ella's trailer. If it weren't for the new medication, she would have chalked her fatigue up to a long day, because it had been that, and a good one. But she was back to worrying about any little pain, every sign of weakness. Was this the one that would never go away?

"Soup's on," she chirped when the door opened, pulling up some animation from her reserves. Ella looked surprised. "They're serving supper, and I was just wondering if I could…"

Monica glanced past Ella. Dillon was sitting on the banquette.

"Oh." No surprise. *Wipe that big O off your face, Monica.* "I didn't mean to interrupt."

"You're not. Come on in." Ella stepped back with a sweeping gesture for the array of fruit and cold cuts on the little table. "Help yourself. We brought it over from craft services. I didn't feel like a heavy meal."

"I know what you mean. I was looking for a place to crash for an hour, but I don't want to—"

"We were just talking over some of the ideas people have come up with on-site, trying to figure out how much we can handle." Ella folded her arms and leaned against the counter. "How are your projects coming?"

"Great," Monica said too eagerly. "I won't be adding anything to the schedule. I have everything covered on my end." She slid into the banquette beside Dillon. "What did I tell you about those log kits, huh? They're coming together quickly."

"When are they gonna put my house back together?"

"Soon," Monica and Ella said in unison.

Ella straightened. "I think I *will* head over to supper. You're welcome to—"

"I really didn't mean to interrupt. I just need to put my head down and feet up for a few minutes."

"I'll be right behind you," Dillon told Ella. And then, when she had closed the door, he quickly said, "I need your advice, Monica. I don't want to blow this."

"With Ella? I don't think—"

"With D.J." He drew a deep breath. "Is he gay?"

"What gave you that idea? Did somebody—"

"He did."

Monica scowled. Had she been a mother hen, her neck feathers would have been standing on end. "You have a problem with the way he acts? Looks? Talks? What?"

"None of the above. He's brought it up twice now, and I don't know exactly what I should say. How I should—"

Her jaw felt slack. "He *told* you he's gay?"

"So…he is."

"He hasn't discussed it with me."

"He hasn't?" Dillon glanced away. "Damn."

"What did he say?"

"He said he's never had a girlfriend."

"He doesn't have time for girls," she protested. What did this man know? He knew nothing. "He's an excellent student. He's completely absorbed in his music. He's very reserved, very…" She craned her neck. "What else? Did someone…? Some girl probably rejected him somehow."

"I don't think that's it. He says he only wants to be around guys. I told him, hey, no problem. It's a lot easier to be around guys at his age than it is being around girls."

"What did he say?"

"He asked me how I'd felt about being around girls. I told him they made me feel crazy. Stupid, studly, silly, scared."

"And what did he say to that?"

"Not much." Dillon stared at the paper plate in front of him—half a sandwich on white bread, a couple of purple grapes remaining on a stem. "What are his friends like?"

"He has two close friends. Very nice boys. And there's a girl in the school orchestra that he's been friends with for years. He misses Emily, of course. She doesn't realize how much he worships her." On second thought… "Has she said anything to you about…whether *she* thinks he might be…?"

He shook his head. "He never brings his friends around much when I go out to your place to visit. I thought maybe he was embarrassed about me." He tipped his head back, searched the ceiling. "God, he's so smart. So talented. Emily told him she thought I was scared of him. If I am, that's why. He's incredible. Em and me, we've got the same…" He touched the right side of his chest. "We're horse people."

"And you're *people* people." Their eyes met. "Dylan

and I work with people—musicians, students, teachers, professionals—but it's different. We're artists. Not that what I do is anything like what he's able to do, but we don't…" Her turn to look away. "We don't need a lot of…closeness."

"Closeness?"

"We are what we do."

"You might be, but do you really think you can speak for him? You ask me, he's not too sure who he is right now."

"He's just about to turn sixteen. Nobody knows who they are at sixteen."

He gave a humorless chuckle. "They know who they want to have sex with."

"Did he tell you who he wanted to have sex with?"

"Not straight out. Maybe he wasn't ready. Or maybe he could tell that I wasn't ready."

"Maybe he doesn't want to have sex with anybody right now. How about that? Maybe he's not there yet. Maybe, maybe, maybe." She clenched her fists at the edge of the table, sighed and relaxed. "You're right. The possibility *has* occurred to me." She nodded. "That's why I made him come. He wanted to stay in the Cities, but it's important for him to get to know you."

"Don't put that on me, Monica. That's not something I can…"

"Deal with?"

"Do anything about." He pulled a grape from the gnarled stem. "I think I can deal with it. Hell, I've got an uncle I'm pretty sure is gay. And a cousin." He glanced at her, hopeful. "Anybody on your side?"

"What side? I hardly knew my father. My mother's dead, and we were never very close. I don't have much family."

He hiked his brow. "You sound like Ella."

"Ella's mother cast a long shadow. Mine barely made a footprint."

"You're strong women, both of you."

"Can you deal with that?"

He chuckled, avoiding her eyes. "I'm learning."

"Why did he bring it up with you and not me?" She knew the answer. Dillon was easy to talk to. He always had been.

He knew the answer, but he wouldn't say it. No matter what he said or did, there was a kindness about him. *Always had been.*

"Should I bring it up with him?"

"You know him much better than I do, Monica. Play it by ear, go by your instincts, which have served you well. That's not gonna change." His gaze met hers. "You'll probably let it ride for now, huh? Let D.J. call the shots."

"Yes." She nodded, grateful. "We've got a lot going on right now. Actually, he's gotten with the program more than I expected him to. I'm really glad he talked to you. It's exactly what I was hoping for." She lifted one shoulder. "Almost exactly what I was hoping for."

"It's been different, being here with him instead of at your place. I'm a visitor there. He doesn't look to me for anything. Here, I'm not scared of him being gifted or smarter than me, because it all balances out. But I'm scared of this." He folded his arms. "Because I don't get it. I can't think about my son having sex with a man."

"Do you want to think about your daughter having sex with a man?"

"No." He gave a diffident smile. "Good point."

"They don't want to think of us having sex, either."

He laughed. "Remember that Christmas Eve they thought they heard Santa Claus coming, and it was us?"

"Under the tree." She could see it now. She was looking up through the fake tree branches laden with her hand-crocheted snowflakes, origami cranes, pipe cleaner teddy bears, everything in white, including a thousand tiny lights. "I was sure they were asleep."

"Probably scarred them for life."

"Probably. That and a lot of other things." She slid her hand over the back of his. "There was a time when I had pretty much given up on you, Dillon James."

"You and me both."

"I didn't make it easy for you to get back in their lives. But you kept trying." She squeezed his hand. "Mystic Warrior Horse Camp. It's a perfect fit."

"This is Indian country, darlin'. We work a flaw into every pattern." He turned his warm palm toward hers. "There's no life that isn't scarred, and no such thing as perfect."

Chapter Twenty-Three

"Do you think he'll be surprised, Monica?"

Tate leaned against the doorjamb of the newly erected shell of the log and timber house that stood on the foundation fictitiously poured by the reality-show crew for Dillon's humble trailer. The shot through the doorway took in the church, which was finished, and the rolling hills in the background. Tate wore his tool belt like a gunslinger. It was a pretty shot.

Especially when Tate flashed his perfect teeth behind his eager-to-please smile. "You know Dillon Black as well as anyone. Do you think he has any idea what we've been up to?"

The camera pulled back from the single shot of Tate to a two-shot with Monica, standing with her back to the camera in the middle of a plywood subfloor and surrounded everywhere by pine—walls, ceiling, posts, beams—and holes waiting for window glass.

"He sure didn't mind driving the van to Montana, did he?" Tate continued. "You know, when Emily and I came up with the idea, we figured we'd change the plan a few times, send him off at the last minute because suddenly—" Tate waggled his eyebrow and sketched finger quotes "—I couldn't make the drive." He pushed off from the door frame and sauntered across the rough floor while Charlie panned the shot. "Keeping our neighbor in the dark about my secret project is always the trickiest part of the show. We're working round the clock while Dillon and Emily round up a crew of college kids to finish off the equestrian center. Do you think he has any idea what we're up to?"

"I don't, Tate. I think he's going to be totally surprised."

"And this three-bedroom log house with a full basement is the best surprise I think we've ever come up with. Certainly the biggest. I have a feeling your Mr. Black is going to enjoy being 'Outfoxed By Fox.'"

"When you do a special surprise for the home owner it's always a highlight for me, Tate, but this time it's personal. Dillon and I are no longer married, but we're good friends. I believe so strongly in what he's trying to do here. The kids…our kids, too, and the crew that will come and the one that's here…young people pitching in to build something together, it's…"

Tate draped his arm around Monica's shoulders and gave a neighborly squeeze. "It's a privilege for *Who's Our Neighbor?* to be allowed to contribute, Monica. You've been part of our family on how many episodes? Quite a few. And now I feel like a brother to your former husband. It's real people with real dreams who make this show what it is. I can't wait to see what kind of furnishings you and Zooey have in store."

"Most of them are stored in that truck, Tate, so hurry up and give us a place to put them."

"Yes, ma'am." Tate saluted, then leaned through a window opening, where another camera caught his two-fingered whistle. "Window-and-door team, you're up!"

Eyes bright with unshed tears, Monica turned to camera one and confided to countless strangers, "Sometimes dreams really do come true."

The ruse had gained an added benefit when Dylan decided to ride along with his father and sister to gather up the college crowd. He wasn't in on the secret, and with the two of them growing closer, the surprise would pack a double punch. One of Monica's visions of late—one of the hazards of being creative—had given her a look at her world without her in it. Having a will in place was one thing, but *being* a will in place seemed altogether appropriate for someone with her gifts, not to mention her connections. Not that she was really going to die anytime soon, but just in case.

She was glad father and son were talking. Envious? All right, that, too. But Dylan knew he could tell her anything he wanted to anytime he was ready. That he had chosen to talk with his father rankled in theory, but in practice it was a relief. It was Dillon's turn. He would do fine.

And then there was Ella. They were obviously sleeping together. This was a good thing. Dillon loved being in love, especially the early stages. And Ella? Still waters, that woman, but clear, open and steady. There was nothing wrong with getting good people together with good ideas and bright possibilities. All Ella was doing was adding a few options. She was entitled.

Charlie followed Monica to the bunkhouse, where Mike Murphy met them for a final "handoff" between carpenter and decorator. Monica was shown making up the last bunk. Mike was a master craftsman and a low-key foil for Tate, who was basically an actor. Mike's few chat scenes were always practical and focused on the details of his craft.

And they were Monica's favorite spots.

"These bunks seem to be an integral part of the structure," she said as she shook the pillow down into its bright blue case.

"They are." Mike demonstrated their strength by hoisting himself onto the upper bunk and sitting and bouncing without squeaks or sags. "Kids will be kids, and when three or more are gathered together, I think it's best to nail the furniture down as much as possible. Less worry for the camp director. But they can be removed if you know the secret."

"And I've designated a file drawer in the camp director's office specifically for owner's manuals. How do you like the textiles we've used?" Monica walked across the industrial grade flooring, ran her hand over the bedding on the far side and affected a grand gesture toward the window. "The traditional star quilts, café curtains, the wall hanging?"

"The colors are dramatic. And I love the stained glass in that window."

"We did the other room in purples and reds, but we made no attempt to use color to designate one for boys and one for girls. Dillon doesn't know whether he's going to try to run them at the same time. He's thinking he could use the two rooms to separate the kids by age, as well. So we kept the colors bold and stayed away from themes other than horses and traditional geometric motifs and…" Pain snaked into her hip and slithered down her leg. She paused for it to pass while she drew a breath. "Shall we take a look at the other room?"

"Something wrong?"

She forced a smile. "Just a cramp."

"Turn it off," Mike told the cameraman as he shoved off

the upper bunk and landed boots on the floor. "Sometimes it helps to walk." He offered a hand, but she was using both of hers, seeking a place to perch. "Or sit. Monica?"

"I'm okay." She located one of her finds—a midcentury blue fiberglass stacking chair, one of eight she'd practically stolen at auction. *Nothing like recalling a great gavel-down moment when you needed to get a grip.* "I have something in my…purse. In the car."

"Charlie, would you get her purse?" Mike asked. Clearly grateful to be excused, Charlie was already half-way out the door. Mike called a change of plans. "No, get the car. I'm taking her—"

"No, Mike, I'll be fine. Just the purse, Charlie." She nodded, and the cameraman immediately took her word as final. She gave Mike a tight smile. "A pill, half a cigarette and I'll be fine. *Damn.*"

"Radiation, chemo or both?" Mike shoved a matching chair close to hers, took a seat and answered the question in her eyes. "Been there, love. That's not your hair. It's real, and it looks good, but it's not yours."

The pain ebbed, and her smile warmed. That Australian twang of his was both sexy and soothing. "What do you mean, *been there?*"

"I'm a cancer survivor. Four years ago. Damnedest thing."

"No…shit."

"How did you know?" He reached for her hand. "I wasn't going to get into specifics, but, yes, it played hell with that particular function."

"And now?" She squeezed his hand. "How are you do-ing with it?"

"Specifically?"

It hurt to laugh, but she did anyway. A little. "Generally."

"Very well, thank you. I've learned that you can live without the cigarettes."

"This project means a lot to me. Once we wrap, I'll get my health back and then some." She squeezed his hand again. Assurance. Gratitude. "My doctor at home hooked me up here, so I'm following the plan. Due diligence."

"If I can help…" Her big black purse was suddenly thrust between them. Mike reached for it with both hands, while Monica tightened hers, hanging on to the feel of his vitality. "Ah, here we go. And a bottle of Perrier. Perfect."

Charlie nodded toward the tripod and camera. "I'll set up in the other bunk room."

"The utility facility next." Mike uncapped the bottle Monica had fished out of her purse.

"I feel fine now, but just to be sure…" Monica took her pill. Nobody spoke until Charlie and his equipment were gone. "You won't mention this to anyone, will you, Mike? I'll deal with all that once we wrap."

"I'm not interested in intruding."

"I know." She gave a tight smile, separating herself from a wish that would soon pass. "That wouldn't be you."

"I'm interested in *you*."

"Thank you for that. And for all you've done, all you're doing."

"Like you, I'm good at what I do, and that's my pleasure. It's the pleasure I've dared to permit myself." He reached for the wall and ran his fingertips over the stacked logs. "I have complete control over the wood."

"This will be an accomplishment for us, don't you think? A beautiful facility, and it could make a difference with Dillon's… If he'll only do what he's so very capable of doing."

Mike smiled. "For us, it ends with the beautiful facility. That's what the show is about. After we wrap, it's up to them."

"My problem is that my dreams extend past the part that I can control."

"Why is that a problem?"

She shrugged. "I keep scrapbooks. Pictures of everything I've done on these projects."

"So do I," he said, blue eyes brightening.

"And it's not, you know, just to record that this was my idea. They're like school yearbooks from my teaching days. They're like my children. I imagine them doing well, being appreciated, taking a little piece of me with them."

"I don't have any children." He looked down at his hands, laced his fingers together. "Just the bits of wood I've put my hands to over the years. Who was the puppet maker in Pinocchio? That would be me." He looked up, smiling. "Except that I don't want anything I built to start talking back to me. Let it be beautiful and useful. That's all I ask."

"That's good. I like that. Let our neighbors use it as they see fit." She drew a deep, cleansing breath as the pain retreated. "And enjoy it."

"If they do, good on 'em. If they don't, so be it. I look at the pictures and think happy thoughts, but it's up to them. The pressure on us is over when we wrap."

"I *like* that."

"Stress is hard on wood, ever harder on people." He took her hand again. "Our bodies have enough to deal with, love. Let's not have our imaginations adding worries we don't need."

"Pressure is unavoidable," she said.

"Some, yes. But you can avoid creating more for yourself. What Dillon does with all this is up to him."

"But what if—"

"What if, what if? What if I used quarter sawn oak or granite or glass? Good thinking. But what if I build it and nobody comes? Or what if they come and nobody steps up to bat? Or what if they step up and run out?" He shook his head. "That way lies madness, darlin'. Unless you have some way of making sure he does what he's so very capable of doing."

"Beyond madness."

"Are you willing to do it yourself?"

"Oh, no." She lifted her free hand. "I've done my time in the country. If I only have one life to live, let me live it in a house with a paved driveway." She scanned the room. Color, comfort, convenience. Two furnished rooms and a loft for expansion. "And let them use this and enjoy it. Or not."

"That's the spirit."

"After the follow-up shoot, which is supposed to be the first camp session. Whether it's real or not, we'll see then. If he doesn't get it together, we can always make it look real."

"*Tsk tsk tsk!*" He laughed. "It's elusive, that spirit. Grab it and hang on."

"For dear life," she said.

Charlie appeared in the doorway. "You guys ready? We show off Mike's utility facility linen-storage feature, and then I'm due at the new house."

"Mike." Monica leaned close to him. "Would you mind driving me back to the hotel tonight?"

"Not at all."

Ella missed Dillon. She was acting like a teenager in love, counting the hours and watching the highway, even though it was too soon and a sighting would screw up her precious schedule. Since when had she measured time by anything but the shooting schedule?

Since Dillon Black had first come knocking.

Thanks to clear skies and efficient crews, the construction schedule was keeping pace with the plan, and Ella was pleased. The show would be a good one, maybe the best in the series. The project was exemplary. Taking the old church building from a do-it-yourselfer's frustration to a fully repurposed structure with much of its charm intact was almost enough. But *Who's Our Neighbor?* never stopped at *almost*. The barn was almost finished, the skeleton for the indoor arena had taken shape, and the three log structures were icing on the cake. Ella had done *never say almost* one better. She had brought it home. Her mother's home, anyway. Indian country.

Now all she had to do was keep the peace between Zooey and Tate until Dillon returned with the college crew, which would create a new team for Tate. He was driving Zooey crazy trying to change her designs in the house, although his idea for a decorative saddle rack as a partition instead of a half wall was a good one, and she said as much now.

"There you go." He pounded the sketch he'd laid on the kitchen island that was waiting to be moved into position. "Ella's on my side."

"Big whoop," Zooey shouted over the rapping and tapping that was going on all around them. There were stonemasons, electricians, plumbers and carpenters, all laying claim to a piece of the action. "Ella's always on your side."

"I'll roll over for you next time, Zo. Promise. Our neighbor is a man, and this is a man thing."

Zooey folded her golden-tanned arms under her perfect breasts, achieving a nice hint of cleavage. "Yeah, you know your men."

Tate bristled. "What's that supposed to mean?"

"Children," Monica called, popping up from her huddle with the lighting installer.

Charlie turned the camera off.

"It means you keep trying to build more of a role for yourself," Zooey shouted, "acting like you really know something about building a house."

"I do."

"Acting like carpenter, architect, landscaper, boss of all bosses and stud of all studs. You're just an actor!" Zooey turned to Ella. "I'm a designer. I really did those designs. I'm not just a—"

"Hottie?" Tate challenged.

"I have substance!"

"Yes, you do, Zo." Tate reached for Zooey's shoulder, but she knocked his hand away. "The endorsements will come."

"Tate got another endorsement deal," Monica explained to Ella as she left one huddle for another.

"The point is, I don't want him fucking with my designs." Zooey turned on Ella. "Or I will go over your head. You think I don't know why we're doing this project?"

"We've done cast family projects before, Zooey," Monica said. "It's no secret that I approached Ella—"

"You're not the only one who has an interest, Monica. Our neighbor's no actor. He's the real stud around here." Zooey's chin jutted defiantly. "What's the budget on this one, Ella? We like to throw in a surprise, but a whole house on top of all the rest?"

"I, for one, applaud you, Ella," said Tate. "We got a

lot of product placement on this project. This is the best thing we've—"

"Cut the crap, Tate. It's all out on the table now." Zooey waved her hands in surrender. "Let's just finish it."

"If I get another offer, I'll put in a word for you, Zo." He tried again and failed to get a hand on her. "I'm over-extending myself a little, what with all my professions."

"Time to put *will sell anything* on your business card and add prostitute to your resume."

"Forgive me for trespassing on your turf." Tate grinned, then turned to the photographer. "This is good. You should be rolling, Charlie."

Mike stuck his head in the back door. "We're bringing in the cabinets."

"The voice of reason," Monica gleefully proclaimed. "A sound for sore ears."

"The real carpenter," Zooey added.

"And the *real* lady." Tate's gestured theatrically to-ward Monica.

Zooey raised her middle finger just as Tate thrust out his tongue.

"Tongue beats finger. I win."

Chapter Twenty-Four

"They're almost here!" Monica climbed onto the spring seat of the old horse-drawn wagon that had become a landscaping centerpiece. "Look! Tail feathers!" She pointed to the van flying down the road, churning up a dust wake.

When she'd lived in the house across the highway, where a doorbell would have made as much sense as oars on a prairie schooner, the sight of "tail feathers" had been a big deal. Big excitement, big expectation. But never this big. Never had an approaching vehicle jacked her pulse rate into such a dizzyingly high gear. Her summer dress billowed. Hair whipped her face. She grabbed the backrest to steady herself against the relentless wind and tore her attention from the road for a quick visual check-in with her fellow miracle workers.

Tate and Zooey stood together on the covered porch. *Together*, arm in arm, with no camera pointed at them. Rez Radio host, Bobby Big Eagle, had stationed himself next to the new split rail fence at the edge of the yard, where he was talking into a microphone. Heavy equipment contractor, Pete Two Horse, who had worked through the night loading in tons of landscaping rock, sat with Vincent Many

Wounds on his pickup tailgate. Darius was filming from a cherry-picker brought in by the rural electric co-op.

Monica turned to discover that Ella had joined her on the wagon, her face the picture of what Monica felt. The day, the hour, the moment. *Coming, coming, coming.*

Five gregarious strangers piled out of the van behind two reticent Blacks and one who could barely restrain herself. But Emily was mindful of her guests, while Monica climbed down from her lookout post and slid between dumbfounded father and poker-faced son. She put an arm around each slim waist, gazed at the house as though she'd led them to the front gate of Oz, and said, "Welcome home."

"Where?" Dillon glanced at Monica and then Ella, the cherry-picker, the gravel and flagstone path to the front porch. "I mean, I don't see… Where's the trailer?"

"It's being refurbished for a new owner. I'll tell you about that later. What do you think of the house?"

"House?" Dillon gave her an incredulous look. "Is it real?"

"Put your glasses on, Dad."

"We're on TV. You go around back, it's like a billboard." Dillon glanced at the house, then back to Monica. "Right? Turn your mike off for a second and tell me what's goin' on."

"This is the headquarters for the Mystic Warrior Horse Camp."

"Okay."

"And the director's—"

"Daddy, tell us what you think of your new house," Emily enthused. She grabbed his free arm and wrapped it around her shoulders like a shawl.

Monica glanced around. Her family was standing side by side like pickets in a cottage fence. *Once in a lifetime, Monica. Frame this one.*

"I'm not even sure where I am, Pinky. Did you see a sign where we turned off the road? I thought it said 'Wolf Trail Ranch.'"

"This is it, Daddy." Emily tugged on him. "Come on. I don't know about you, but I'm dying to look inside."

"How in hell did you do this so fast?" he asked Monica as they broke ranks, kids giving parents the lead in the parade up the path. Neighbors had been instructed to respond, give support, attend to the director and honor the camera.

"Dillon Black, you've been 'Outfoxed'!" Tate announced as they mounted the porch steps. He slapped Dillon on the back. "I try to come up with a neighborly good deed or two on every project, and this house is yours."

Dillon looked up at the porch roof, touched a pillar and shook his head. "A good deed is jumping somebody's battery or givin' him a ride into town."

"Absolutely!" Tate got his gestures going full throttle. "Your battery goes dead out here, the guy coming along with the jumper cables must look like Saint Jude. But since we're always trying to outdo ourselves, you never know what we'll come up with on *Who's Our Neighbor?*" He let his hand rest on Dillon's shoulder. "So let's go in and take a look."

Zooey opened the door and led the way past the saddle rack that Tate had suggested for the entry and into a reverse-angle camera shot. "We still have some details to attend to, but one of the great things about a log home is that you don't have to worry about painting," she said. "Hillcraft Log Homes did an amazing job putting together the packages for this project for us. They worked with us, as they do with all their clients, customizing the plans to fit our specifications. Your house was trucked here, every log numbered, all the components ready for our amazing team to assemble."

Dillon stopped to examine the three vintage saddles displayed on the rack. Monica smiled to herself. He wouldn't recognize them. She'd picked them up on eBay. Ella was the only other person who would ever know how many of the decorating elements she had paid for privately. And that was only because Ella knew every detail of her budget. As far as anyone else involved with the production was concerned, Monica's budget was just a category. Stretching a dollar was her stock-in-trade.

"He's speechless," Tate said. "Don't worry, Dillon, we've seen this reaction before."

Monica had been sparing with the furniture. A gently used leather sofa and chair on one side of the great room, a rustic table with two chairs and two long benches on the other. The kitchen was open to the great room and there was a private office off the kitchen. Two and a half bathrooms and three modest bedrooms completed the house.

"This has to be my room." Emily took a turn around the bedroom Monica had dressed predominantly in white, accented with her daughter's favorite shades of blue. "I chose this broken star quilt. Look, Daddy, we have an extra bathroom."

The bathrooms hadn't been finished, but they would be edited in later. Emily had been apprised of the drill, but Dillon's surprise was genuine. Wide-eyed and wordless, he looked like someone getting a tour of an alien spaceship. An *ooh* or an *aah* would have been nice, Monica thought. Maybe Ella could get them out of him later. Those could be edited in, as well.

While Tate talked up the major sponsors responsible

for the kitchen appliances, wood flooring, ceiling fans, energy-efficient windows, fireplace in the great room and wood stove in the master bedroom, Zooey did the Vanna White role with her usual aplomb, all her fingers gracefully in play. The tour ended on the deck, where Nick, Lauren and the Wolf Trail partners' sisters, together with the caterers, had cooked up a feast on the new barbeque. Surrounded by family, old and new friends, and new construction in a place where every face of every hill was etched in ancestral memory, Dillon recovered his wits, his humor and the easy manner even a cold camera had to love.

Tate and Emily had taken the college crew to the bunkhouse, where Ella had scheduled another taping session. The finishing crew was back at work inside the house and a power post-hole digger droned in the distance. The sun had set. It was Dillon's favorite time of day, when there was plenty of light left but it was soft, the air calm, birds and bugs making music in the grass. Nick and Lauren, Vincent and his kids, Bobby and the Red Shield and Black girls had all gone home, leaving Dillon to ponder what had happened to his. Half afraid to turn around, he braced his arms on the new deck railing and grounded himself in the sounds of evening and the sight of the shadowed hills. At his back an unfamiliar door opened and closed in an unfamiliar way, but he recognized his former wife's measured approach.

"Your room's ready, sir," she said cheerfully. "They'll knock off work in a couple of hours, but I left some earplugs by the bed. The way we work, by the time you get back from the trail ride, you'll be amazed."

"I'm amazed now." Still, he couldn't turn around. But

he was able to turn his head when she joined him at the railing. "What did you do with my house?"

"It's being completely redone for Nick's sister, Louise. Another surprise, which we'll shoot with her later. She'll no longer be renting. She's done such a beautiful job for us with the quilting." She gave him a soft smile, but she looked tired. "You don't mind, do you?"

"How could I mind? It was Nick's trailer, and it's getting all made over for his sister. I'm cool with that part. If she wanted it before, she could have said something."

"It's a *surprise,* Dillon. Just like this house was for you. It's part of the show."

"I *was* payin' him for it."

"Dillon, this is what the show's all about. You heard who the sponsors are. I know what you're thinking, but it's not charity. It's advertising."

"You don't know what I'm thinking, Monica. You just *think* you do. I signed on for the horse camp, not for a new house."

"As a matter of fact, you did. You agreed to let the show pretty much have its way with your property. But you read the agreement about as carefully as you do any contract, and you said you didn't feel the need for legal representation *and* you signed several waivers."

"I signed on for the horse camp," he insisted.

"You don't like the house?"

"What's not to like? It's great. It's…it's unbelievable."

"It fits with the other buildings. It's part of the design, part of the horse camp." She turned around, folded her arms and leaned against the railing. "We would have told you, but the big surprise is part of the show."

"So I've heard. The kids knew?"

"Emily did. I'm proud of her for not spilling the beans. Which apparently she didn't."

"We talked about a lot of things, but not this. It's too much, Monica. It's nice, but I feel…" He glanced at her. She had a strange look in her eyes, like she was almost out of gas and suddenly realizing she might have taken the wrong road. He shrugged. "Hell, it's gonna take some getting used to."

"You've adjusted to changes before."

"Yeah." He glanced away. "I don't like being pushed. You know that."

"The camp was your idea, and nominating the project for the show was Emily's, so don't look at me. I'm just one of Santa's elves." She touched his arm, her voice shifting into serious gear. "Now, tell me about the trip. How did the three of you get along? What did you talk about?"

Dillon said nothing. It had been that kind of a day. He didn't much like being speechless, but there it was. Words failed for a reason. In twenty years, he'd learned that much.

Monica waited. No pushing. No pulling, no prodding, no prying. She wasn't doing any of that, was she? She was only asking. Everything seemed to be working out so well, but how would she know exactly how well, unless someone let her in on the particulars? She hadn't been there to guide them along, but she'd trained two of them pretty well. She wasn't looking for any particular particulars. Just promising particulars. Was that too much? *Dillon?*

All she could do was ask nicely. And grab a cigarette, try to be cool, let him take his damn sweet time. Either the three of them hadn't gotten along at all, or they'd made the connection she'd been denying them for years. They had probably agreed on at least one thing—that she was to blame—and then proceeded to discuss her in excruciating detail.

She sucked in several shallow puffs, coughed a little, happily handed over the cigarette when he reached for it and watched him savor a drag. It seemed like a good sign.

"Did Dylan say any more about…?"

"They're worried about you, Monica." Smoke trailed from his lips as softly as his words. He handed the cigarette back to her.

She moved away.

"I'm sure he's confided in Emily. And now you. It was a long drive, the three of you together."

"Yeah, but look how many of your purposes it served."

"*My* purposes?" she spat bitterly. She closed her eyes and drew as deep a breath as she dared impose on her abused lung. "All right, yes, my purposes. I bought some time to finagle a surprise to meet the demands of the show, time for my children to spend with their father, time to build your house."

"How much did you buy, and what did you have to give for it?" He took the cigarette from her again, and she realized that her hand was shaking. He puffed again, then offered it back even as the look in his eyes warned against it—for both of them.

She shook her head. "What did they tell you?"

"Not much." He stubbed out the ash on the side of his boot heel. "You had part of a lung taken out a couple of years ago, and there was cancer in it, but that's gone now."

"All true except the last, and it's being treated."

"I guess they don't know about that part." He flicked the butt into the backyard. It landed between two newly planted five-year-old pines. "Why the big secret?"

"It's not a big secret. It's a private matter." She wrapped her arms around her slim torso. "It's mine to deal with, and I can do that quite well on my own. Keep your thoughts and prayers, folks. I'm the same person I was before, and I don't want to be treated differently by anyone but my doctor."

"Different how?"

"Like I might be dead next week." She flashed a mock fiendish smile. "Like if they get too close, they might be next."

He laughed.

"You think it's funny, do you?" Her smile softened. "And you thought I'd suck up all the attention I could get."

"I've got news for you, honey, it's been years since I lost any sleep over what you were doing to get attention." But he put his arm around her. "Hell, Monica Wilson-Black might live to fight another fifty years."

"Or not. In which case I get to die while there are still people around who care."

"You think so," he said.

"I do. And I think you're one of them."

He made a sweeping gesture toward the house and beyond. "That's not what all this is about, is it?"

"Of course not," she said too quickly, then sighed, shook her head. "I don't know. This is what I do, and I thought, why not do it here? You know? If I can. If they'll let me. There's a need. There's a good man who's ready and able to fill it. If I can bring something to the table, maybe... maybe I'll be remembered kindly."

"Shit, Monica, is this really you? Remembered *kindly?*" He took hold of her shoulders and turned her to face him, belying his flippant tone with eyes full of wonder or worry or something equally un-Dillon. "How many days do we have left on this thing? I've got a friend works for a funeral home. I'll get us a deal on a monument, inscribe your name, nice dedication. My surprise for you on the last day. Big monument erection."

Laughing, she wagged her finger. "Now you're getting the idea. It's about pathos, but not pity."

"What I'm getting is that last word, and we'll have none of this 'maybe I'll be remembered kindly.' Cancer's the bitch that took your lung, but no way do you get cancer of the ego. Not you."

Warmth surged through her. Had to be the words or the drugs, but it felt like an intravenous blast of bourbon. She smiled. "You do like the house, don't you?"

"Yeah, sure, I like the house. It's not mobile, but it has its good points." He stepped up to the patio door, put his face up to the glass and made blinders with his hands. "Always wanted a log house. Used to be a lot of them around here, but nothing like this."

"It's your door, Dillon. Go ahead and—"

He shoved his hands in his pockets as he turned to her. "You could have found another man, easy."

"I didn't look. Who needs the aggravation?" She reached for her purse. "Who needs for somebody to come along now, when the future is so iffy?"

"If you looked up the word *future* in the Lakota dictionary—if we had a word for *future* and if we wrote ourselves a dictionary—the definition would be *iffy.*" He slid the door open and stepped aside for her. "So you meet the right somebody, you wear that confidence like a great new pair of boots and you walk tall while the walking's good."

"When did you get to be so smart?"

"When you weren't looking," he said as she came up

beside him. She looked over and found him grinning. "So he came along from where? England or someplace like that?"

"Australia."

"Came all this way for a job Americans don't want to do," he recited, and she backhanded his flat gut. "Is he legal? Because if he's not, we're thinking about starting a guest-worker program here."

"On the reservation?" She took a quick look around, from kitchen through great room. The legs sticking out from under the sink weren't Mike's. Neither was either of the heads bent over a set of blueprints laid out on the dining table.

"This is the Lakota Nation, honey, and we don't believe in *too late*. I like Mike, too. He'd make a good father."

"You're their father."

"You hook up with him, I'll adopt him as a brother. Then they get two for the price of one." Dillon laid a hand on her shoulder. "Like I said, they're worried about you. They don't know what's goin' on, and they don't ask, because they just want it to go away."

"I do, too. I'm working on it. Okay?" She eyed the ceiling beams. "You like the house? Really?"

"I like the damn house. Now, that arena, the way that's going up, that's gonna be amazing. I could live out there."

"And probably will." She tucked her arm through the crook of his elbow. "So, where would we put my monument?"

Chapter Twenty-Five

Dillon watched Monica's taillights until they disappeared in the night, and then his thoughts turned to Ella. He scolded himself as he headed for the equestrian quad—that damn Tate Fox had him thinking of what used to be a few simple fences as the *equestrian quad*—for wanting to look for Ella at every turn, when he had so much else going on. Monica was sick. His kids were worried about their mother. Trusting in their father was a whole new deal—speaking of which, he'd used up a lot of the vacation time he'd been saving for summer camp. He ought to be getting back to work at the casino, where nobody seemed to be missing him, if the lack of phone calls was any indication. Maybe they'd replaced him.

Or maybe he didn't have a phone anymore. He turned for another quick look at the "residential quad," taking a few steps backward. There were two lights on inside. Someone could actually live there, might be living there now. There was a *master* bedroom, for heaven's sake, with a bed in it, all made up and ready for somebody to show it off in pictures or even sleep in it.

He turned and strode toward the arena, where the night crew had a machine digging post holes. He could be digging post holes. He'd dug plenty of them in his time. Hell, he could dig post holes all night long. He stopped well short of the fence line under construction, shoved his hands in the back pockets of his jeans and stood there watching the power takeoff-driven digger, his quick breaths visible in the crisp night air. He could grab a hand tool and get to it right now. Of course, he would have to stop the machine operator and ask him where to dig.

He glanced toward Ella's trailer. No light there. He could go try the door. If she'd left it open, he would make himself at home. God, he felt good about Ella.

He nearly jumped out of his jeans when someone touched his back.

Ella.

"I'm sorry." She sidestepped his outstretched hand. "Deep in thought?"

"Yeah." He peered into the dark behind her. *Am I missing something?* "Finished shooting?"

"We'll get started again early in the morning. Are you ready for tomorrow?"

"Nope. Probably won't be startin' out too early on my end." He touched her hair, but he could feel her resistance. "Nobody's looking."

"Did Monica go back to the hotel?"

"Ah." Monica. The word that explained everything. "Yes, she did."

"I went back to the house to see if you two wanted to get in on making the plans for tomorrow with Emily and crew." A chilly breeze slid past them, and she shivered. "I decided not to interrupt."

"Why?"

"It wasn't my moment."

"Not on any level?" He chuckled. "Seems like it's either *so many levels* or none at all. Is that a Hollywood thing, or is it female? Either way, I'm just guessin'."

"I'm not." She shivered again, and he stepped between her and the breeze. "What I came to say wasn't that important."

Brisk night poured over his collar and down his back. He welcomed the bracing chill. "I didn't know she was sick."

"I know you didn't."

"The house is nice, but the trailer was enough. It was mine. Almost."

"You can have it back. It's being—"

"Fixed up for Louise, which is great. Hell, I can get used to the house." He laughed. "That sounds crazy. Like when you go someplace fancy, and you say, 'I could get used to this,' but it's not like it's ever gonna happen." He laughed again. "Unreal, this reality show of yours."

"We always go overboard." She scrunched her shoulders and shivered. "*That's* a Hollywood thing."

"Can I put my arm around you now?" At his back, the power takeoff shifted into high gear. "Or do you like being cold?"

She slid her arm around his back and tucked herself under his arm. "How does one more night in a trailer sound?"

"Like heaven."

Dillon finished loading his homemade pack saddle, taking care to distribute the weight evenly. He'd given craft services specific orders on food, but they'd doubled it. Jimmy and D.J. were returning the surplus. It was Jimmy who had talked D.J. into going on the overnight trail ride. Emily and her five college friends would stay behind to complete the equestrian center. Tate's bullhorn was all tuned up, and Charlie was behind the camera on the college-team segment. Darius would go along to film the ride.

Dillon had been warned this time. "When you and your posse ride back into town, everything will be red," Tate had promised on camera. "Only not the color. I'm learning Lakota, and red is the best. *Sha*."

From his vantage point just inside the door of the new barn, he could imagine the scene. Beyond the corrals, the wood post and white metal rail fencing would enclose paddocks and an outdoor arena adjacent to the indoor arena, which would be painted to match the brown-and-white barn. The church had a new coat of white paint, but the restored roof and the trim were brown. Inside was a kitchen he couldn't imagine himself cooking in, and he didn't know where he could get the money to hire anyone, but, hell, it wasn't lacking any equipment.

There were four round tables in the main area of the main building, four big "cow" chairs, four "repurposed" church pews, a huge central woodstove, spiral steps leading to a library loft, and decorator touches that included bold stained-glass designs reminiscent of Lakota painter Oscar Howe. It was a blend of antique and contemporary forms, warm feel and full function, and it was a showplace worthy of Monica Wilson-Black. Dillon didn't doubt that missionary Mary Collins would approve of the place or that the memory of his ancestors would find itself at home here, but the enormity of it all scared him half crazy.

A little piece of Hollywood stood behind the building that had long been Dillon Black's folly to everyone except Dillon Black. From where he stood, the gypsy trailer park was the backdrop for rural renewal the likes of which had been unimaginable two weeks ago. He tried to imagine

Little Hollywood vanishing and the rest not. But in his mind's eye everything evaporated, the smoke and mirrors, the curtains and screens—the stuff all shows were made of. Hell, they were always making movies in Indian Country. Not his corner of it so much, and not so often in recent years, but eventually Hollywood always came back. He didn't know who they were trying to kid with this *reality* stuff. It was all about fantasy, which was exactly what he was looking at.

But for now it sure was pretty.

The overnight trail ride, like everything else, was part show and part project. But for Dillon, it was all Mystic Warrior Horse Camp. Horses together with once and future horse people. For the sake of the show, Tate put in a few minutes at the beginning of the ride, went back to the college crew and then showed up in the evening for the sunset shots, pitching camp and fireside chatting. For the sake of the project, all serious decorating, construction and carpentry hands remained on deck, which might have been Tate's metaphor had he not "gone native." *On so many levels.*

"Meanwhile, back at the ranch," he was saying while he unloaded an armful of firewood he was somehow supposed to have collected on the treeless ridge when in reality he'd unloaded it from the pickup that brought him there, "they're finishing up the utility facility, so we'll have a place to wash our dusty jeans after long hours in the saddle. Are you partial to the tipi method or the log cabin for your campfires, Dillon?"

"Tipi, of course." Sounded right. In fact, Dillon was partial to staying away from matches and telling the truth most days, but he was learning that sequences had to be adjusted, and the fact that the laundry building was long past finished in real time had nothing to do with show time.

"I'm a log-cabin man myself. Eagle scout."

"No shit?" Alternate response. "No kidding? That's quite an accomplishment."

"I was always prepared, wicked clean, awesome brave and big-time reverent." Tate arranged a few sticks in the fire pit. "How's this shaping up, dudes?"

"Awesome," Jimmy Taylor observed dutifully.

"What else did you bring in that shiny new pickup?" Bobby Big Eagle wanted to know. "Air mattresses, I hope."

"If ignorance is bliss, Bobby has found heaven on earth." Hank dropped his saddle on the ground near the fire.

"What?" Bobby complained. "He got to drive out here, and he said he came prepared, so I'm thinking, tell us what you got. Like they say, go big or go home."

"*Wahnka!*" Hank said, expressing disbelief. Lauren was here with Nick. This wasn't exactly guys' night out.

"Yeah," said Bobby, his boot heels scraping in the dirt as he dropped his butt on the saddle blanket he'd thrown on the ground. "A *real* man can't be ordering wine in public." He pounded his palm with his fist. "It's gotta be whiskey. Go big or go home. That's what they say."

Hank laughed heartily. "You sure it's not what *she* said, Bobby? Missed the point, as usual."

Dillon chuckled. The circle formed around a growing campfire. Jimmy and D.J. sat next to him. Danny joined his father, Vince, while his sister cozied up to Lauren, who was hanging with her husband. Darius had taken up a camera position behind D.J., who had taken an interest in filming, much to Darius's delight. Dillon figured he had his own bases covered, paternally speaking. He was in perfect position to keep one eye on Tate and the other on Darius, just to take their measure. *Any friend of my kid's...*

It was the magic hour. Perfect light. Coming night.

"What do you think of that new truck of yours?" Vincent asked Tate.

"It's a rental," Tate said as he poked at the fire with a stick, sending up a shower of sparks. "I've never really driven a pickup truck, so I thought I'd try one out."

"How does it handle? I've been having a lot of trouble with mine."

"It's a new century, Dad," Danny said.

"Yeah, Dad," Tate echoed. "Maybe it's time to get a new one. Spend some of that casino money."

"Is that what you call *your* paycheck?" Hank demanded. "TV money?"

"No, I mean, you get a cut of the profits from your casino, right?" Tate took another jab at the burning wood. "Indians are doing pretty well these days, from what I hear. Not that you don't have it coming, after all that your people have been through. The tribe that runs that casino in Connecticut, those people are all millionaires. And the one in Minneapolis, I read they each get a monthly check for twenty thousand or so." He sat back and draped his forearms over upraised knees. "Rich Indians in southern California, too."

"Well, lemme tell you about South Dakota," Vince said. "First of all, they're lucky if they've got a hundred enrolled members in that Connecticut tribe, and we've got more than ten thousand, counting all them troublemakers that went off the reservation."

The laughter didn't come from Tate, who only asked, "Which... Where'd they go?"

"They could be anywhere," Dillon said, deadpan. "Just over the next hill. Maybe even your own backyard."

"Wait." Tate lifted his hands, palms out. "It's okay to go off the reservation, right? You don't have to, like, sign out or anything, right?"

Bobby's laugh outstripped the rest.

"About six thousand of us live here on Standing Rock," Vince said. "The Dakota tribe that owns the Minnesota casino you're talkin' about, they have about two hundred. And look where they're located. So, yeah, they're pullin' down big checks. Around here, each of us got five hundred dollars at Christmas, which was nice, but it doesn't get me a new pickup."

"So the casino doesn't turn a profit?" Tate asked.

"It does," Vince said.

"It's ours now, free and clear, and we've made improvements. We've put money into community development, education, housing," Dillon said. "Tell you what, I've got a good job. We have a thriving business. People from off the reservation are taking Highway 1806 to come here, not just driving through and hoping the car doesn't break down before they get to the other side. They come to the casino for a night out, and guess what? We treat them well."

"Like we have since Day One, Year Fourteen Hundred and Ninety-Two," said Bobby.

"Hey, you picked off a few at the Little Bighorn," Tate reminded them. "What year was that?"

"It's always about Custer," Dillon said with a dramatic sigh. "That was 1876. Our finest hour. You guys owe us for keeping him from becoming president. He wanted to run, and he was out here putting together his press kit."

"Here we go," Nick warned.

"I guaran-damn-tee you, that's one George you'd be embarrassed to claim on President's Day," Dillon said. "You wouldn't catch him freezin' out at Valley Forge. That guy was all for show. Ol' Splash and Dash didn't mind sacrificing good warriors to make a name for himself. A Lakota warrior believes in sacrificing his own skin to make a name for himself, but you got no right to offer up somebody else's."

"Did you see that *Custer's Last Stand* show on the Discovery Channel?" Vince took his turn poking at the fire. "They said it was embarrassing for you guys because the army was essentially defeated by a Stone Age people. But then they said the Indians had better guns. And the old 'thousands of Indians against a few hundred troopers,' story. Like it was us attacking *their* village. They talk about the number of Indians, they're counting babies, children, women, old people."

"Dogs, rats, lice…"

"I don't think they meant…" Tate squirmed. "I mean, nowadays historians try to—"

"*Tuale*," Nick protested with a chuckle. "These people are guests, you guys. They come in peace."

"No, I'm interested in history, too," Tate said. "I know mistakes were made back then, and, yeah, the army attacked villages full of women and children. But there were a lotta braves at the Little Bighorn. I mean, Crazy Horse, Sitting Bull…"

"They sent soldiers into our country," Dillon said. He glanced around the circle. The kids were listening. This was story hour, and he had the kids' eyes and ears. "Our people couldn't figure this out. Who are these men who have no families? Their camps have big walls, but inside it's almost all men. Fighting men."

"You had your war parties," Tate reminded him.

"But the women and children were never far away. That's what it was all about."

"For our people, too," Lauren said. She hooked her small hands around her husband's arm and clutched the sleeve of his denim jacket. "The army was clearing the way for people who were, many of them, leaving bad conditions and trying to feed their families. Whole families. You do what you have to do for your children. And nowadays in the army, we've got women right there on the front lines. It's not just men we're sending over to the Middle East. They leave their children home, of course, but that's hard."

"It's not right, you ask me," Vince said. "Sometimes it's both parents over there."

"You don't think women should have equal rights?" Tate challenged.

"Equal rights, sure. And equal responsibilities. I don't say you can stop them if that's what they wanna do. I'm just sayin' men and women share the responsibility to protect the womb. That's like sacred ground. It *is* sacred ground."

"Yeah, but you can't separate the womb from the woman," said Hank. "They carry their part, and we carry ours. They're not gonna tell us what to do with our tools."

Staring into the fire, Dillon smiled. "The tipi belongs to them. Like Sitting Bull said, they can kick us out, but the tool goes with us."

"Sitting Bull said that?" D.J. asked.

"He might have. He had a hell of a sense of humor. The missionary who ran the church we're fixin' up, she was his friend. She wrote about him, how she tried to convert him, how he loved to trade stories and ideas. She told him Jesus would want him to send one of his two wives away, and he told her to pick one and give her the message." There was chuckling on all sides of the fire. "Sitting Bull and Crazy Horse lived and died trying to take care of their people. They fought to try to feed them. They surrendered to try to feed them. And those horses…"

"The descendants of Sitting Bull's horses," Jimmy recalled.

It was the way stories were to be told—the campfire, crickets, coyotes, and the boy getting in his line.

"The blood of the old ones runs warm in you," Dillon said. "And that's why we need you, Jimmy. You're their living memory."

"This is what the Mystic Warrior Horse Camp…" A silent flash of lightning distracted Tate from finishing his observation. "Wow. Did you see that?"

"The bs is gettin' so deep around here, the ancestors are warmin' up to dance us a gully-washer," said Nick. "Jeez, D, lighten up. How 'bout we break out the marshmallows and sing some campfire songs?"

"Who's got the guitar?"

"I've got the tom-tom." Tate pounded out a four-beat rhythm on the saddle he'd been using as an armrest.

"And I'm an Indian out-laaw," Dillon crooned.

Sawtooth cracks snaked across the night sky a heartbeat ahead of earsplitting thunder.

"Was that applause?" Tate asked.

The thunder crashed again.

"Yep." Dillon glanced over his shoulder at the rope line where the horses were staked out. "Question is, are they your ancestors or mine?"

More thunder.

"It's both," Nick shouted, galvanized by the rising wind.

He squeezed his wife's hand and pointed toward the nearby slope. "Get everybody down to that low spot. I'll cut the horses loose."

D.J. grabbed Dillon's arm. "What's happening?"

"Head for that buffalo wallow down there. Can you see it?" Dillon pointed toward what might have been a giant's bowl stuck in the ground as he kicked dirt over the fire pit. "That's our basement."

"This is great!" Darius pointed the camera toward the sky. "This is reality."

"It doesn't get any more real," Dillon shouted as he grabbed the man by the back of his jacket. "We've got about thirty seconds."

"Until what?"

"The next damn level!"

Chapter Twenty-Si.

Dillon's boots weren't made for walking. The smoot
soles skittered precariously in the slick clay as he le
his hushed little party up the final stretch of cow patl
Having to walk back from camp was a small price to pa
for the saddle horses' safety. He'd spotted them a few hill
back, uneasily hanging together like creatures fresh o
the Ark. The source of the wrath that had struck the cam
was unclear—straight-line winds, tornado or Biblica
disaster—but its power was undeniable. The same ele
ments raging last night on the ridge had, over time, carve
the gash in the ground that had protected the riders fror
harm. Everything they'd left behind, from saddles and bec
rolls to Tate's rented pickup, had been tossed, turned an
scattered like so much cardboard.

With his charges uninjured and his Hollywood guest
"totally pumped," falling on his ass in front of a camer
should have been Dillon's only remaining worry. But h
had a bad feeling about coming home.

Today's schedule called for a final "reveal." He wa
supposed to be riding to the top of the embankment behin
his place. From there he would have a commanding vie
of the equine center fit for the mythical casino-rich prairi

knight. But the plan was already screwed. He'd been re-
duced to trudging up the rise on foot, which was a bad sign
for any horseman. Unhorsed, he was just another man.

He reached the top of the ridge at last and then, mind
blown, he was for an instant unmanned. The view from the
overlook was unspeakable. There was no equestrian center.
Where the barn had stood, there was rubble. Sheets of
metal and a jumble of lumber littered the arena grounds.
His coveted round pen was nothing but a few stubborn
posts. Dillon's heart jammed itself in his throat.

Oh God, where were his women?

At his back, one by one his companions' responses told
him that his less-than-perfect eyes weren't lying.

"*Ho*-ly…"

"…shit."

"Oh…my…"

"God."

"Looks like it's only the—"

The quick warning blast of an emergency siren drew
Dillon's attention toward the road to the ranch. *Ambulance.*
He recognized a tribal police car parked near the barn, and
his legs responded.

The emergency team was already lifting someone onto
a collapsed gurney when Dillon scrabbled over a pile of
shingles and shredded tarpaper and rounded a piece of wall
whose studs had been snapped like toothpicks. He skidded
on his boot heels in the mud as the gurney unfolded and was
lifted by the hand of two men with Indian Health insignias
on their caps. Dillon recognized Emily's pink shirt. Her
favorite color. Tongue, tears, terror clogged his throat. He
grabbed one of the medics by the arm and pulled him away
from the side of the gurney so he could get close himself.

He reached for her hand, and she turned her head toward him. Her dark eyes lit up. "Daddy!"

"Hey, Pinky."

"You're okay." Her hand trembled, but she managed to smile for him. "We were so scared."

He looked to the foot of the gurney for the answer to a question he couldn't voice. Tom Iron Hand said, "She's doin' good."

"I am, Daddy. I'm totally all right except for my leg."

Dillon nodded, sparing another glance for the end of the gurney and his daughter's feet. One shoe off and one shoe on sent some silly song about a dumpling bouncing through his head. She was wearing pants that ended halfway between her knee and an ankle that looked like overgrown zucchini exposed by a vine-shriveling, fruit-blackening September frost.

"And this." Emily brushed her pink sleeve up to her shoulder to show him her purpling forearm. "Which was kinda making me feel sick, but they gave me something for the pain."

Dillon glanced at Tom again. He was a physician's assistant. He knew what he was doing.

"I've got ice!" Mike Murphy appeared and pushed a large plastic bag at Tom. "Dillon, thank God. Is everybody okay?"

Zooey came up behind Mike. "Emily would have been fine if she'd stayed with the group."

"I left the barn door open." Emily gave a girlish giggle. "I know that sounds like a bad joke. 'Your barn door's open. Horse might get out.'"

"Pinky…"

"Sorry, Daddy." She forced a straight face. "That was terrible."

"That was funny. *This* is terrible." He nodded toward her injuries and wondered what they'd given her for the pain, and whether they had anything for heart palpitations. He was pretty sure the pounding in his ears wasn't normal. He glanced at the rubble. "You were in that barn?"

"I was under it, actually, but the way it fell kinda protected me from the flying monkeys and stuff." She struggled to prop herself up on her uninjured side. "Was it a tornado? Did anybody ever—"

"We need to get you to a doctor, Emily." EMT Karen Tall Tree laid her hand on Emily's shoulder.

"No, wait. Where's D.J.?"

"He's fine," Dillon said. "Everybody on the ride is fine."

"She wanted to go out and look for you," Mike said.

"Because I knew where to look." Emily lifted her head to see what was going on at the foot of the gurney where Tom was positioning the bag of ice. "I was the only one. No one else…everybody who knew was out there with you."

"They're supposed to be sending out a helicopter from somewhere to search for you," Mike told him. "It took us a while to get our heads around all this. That rain started coming down in buckets, so we were all running for cover when the wind hit. There was work still going on at the house. Some of us made it to the basement. The kids ran for the bunkhouse, which came through without a scratch. We were lucky, except for…"

Emily wasn't lucky. Emily had been blessed. "Tornado tested, *Tunkasila* approved," Dillon said.

"We couldn't tell whether it was a tornado," Emily said. "Did you see a funnel, Daddy? What did you guys run into out there?"

"Lightning. Wind big enough to roll a pickup. We cut

the horses loose and got down in the draw. Had to walk back." His eyes sought Mike's. "Anyone else hurt?"

"Not from what I've seen, but I don't know who's actually called the roll. Amazing, isn't it, when you look at this mess? Ella's out with one of the policemen looking for you."

"It came on like a bat out of hell. No warning, nothing."

"Yeah, first real quiet, and then, *whoosh,*" said D.J., coming up behind his father.

"Snap, crackle, pow, pow, pow," Jimmy Taylor added from somewhere in the periphery.

"At night," said Zooey. "Who knew?"

"That's the worst time for tornados. If that's what it was," Dillon said.

"Whatever it was had it in for horse people. Took out the equestrian center and the trail ride," said Tate's voice. "But it looks like your church wasn't touched."

"Yeah, what's that about?" D.J. said. "Two big buildings totally crashed, and everything around them looks, like, totally unscratched."

"Weather isn't *about* anything," Dillon said. "It just is."

Sounded reasonable.

He didn't believe it for a moment. At least, not for *this* moment.

The burly ambulance driver emerged from the vehicle. "Hey, the girl's mother wants to know what's going on."

"She's waiting at the clinic," Emily said.

"The police got hold of her at the hotel."

"Let's move," Dillon said. He was still holding his daughter's hand.

"No, Daddy, you stay with D.J. Ella's out looking for you, and they need you here."

"I wanna make sure you're okay."

"You did," she said, as the gurney and her hand slipped away. "I'm tough, like my father. Cowboy *and* Indian. And a woman to boot, which puts me one up on you when it comes to tolerating pain."

"Like your mom," Dillon called after her. "I'll be there soon."

"No, Daddy, I'll be back soon." *Just like her mom, calling the shots.* "We're going to be fine."

A white SUV with the police emblem on the side drove into the yard, and Ella got out. Dillon's spirit rose to greet her in advance of his weary body. The ambulance had just carried his children away. He was glad D.J. had accompanied his sister, but he was sorry for himself. He wanted to be with them. Ella was a most welcome sight.

"Show me your clipboard," he demanded as soon as he could get his arms around her. He probably squeezed her too hard, and she could probably feel the clumsy quiver in his hands, but he tried to sound halfway cool. "I just wanna make sure this wasn't one of the 'surprises' on your shooting schedule."

"We needed a money shot," she said with a big grin in her voice. "I've never been so happy to get word from a cop. 'Riders are back safely. Patient's in stable condition and on her way to the clinic.' Music, music, music."

"On the radio?"

"Police radio." She stepped away but kept a tight hold on his hand. "Thank God," she whispered as she turned her attention toward a trio nearby.

Cameraman and two stars.

"You're never prepared for something like this," Zooey was saying. "And you certainly can't script it. Our post-Katrina projects have been a little different from this one, haven't they, Tate?"

Dillon scowled into the morning sun. Were they really…?

"This isn't Katrina-level damage by any means," Tate said. "But when you experience the storm yourself…I mean, builders, decorators, production crew, neighbors and home owners, we were in this thing together last night. It was terrifying."

"It certainly was, Tate. I don't know about you, but I haven't stopped shaking."

"Or bullshitting," Dillon bellowed as he stepped into the shot. "Give it a rest, will you? You're like a pair of magpies on steroids. It's no wonder you can't stop shaking." His hand became a stop sign for Charlie's camera. "Will you turn that damn thing off?"

"No offense taken, man. I totally understand. You kept it together…" Tate reclaimed his place in the shot. "Dillon was like our priest from *Poseidon Adventure,* our king of the world from *Titanic.* He led the trail riders through what you could call a long night's journey into day."

"Only *you* could call it that, Tate." Zooey jostled for position, edging Dillon aside. "You do remember what happened to those characters, don't you?"

"I go for alternate endings. If they don't offer one, I make one up," Tate told the camera. "Heroes don't die in my movies. And Dillon Black…"

Dillon Black gave up. These were not real people.

Except for Ella. She slipped her arm around his waist and walked him away from the circle. She got it. He didn't, and he had no need to. The Hollywood circus would be leaving soon, and they would take their alien circle and their two-dimensional selves with them.

And Ella. They would steal her again. Like Pocahontas, she would be taken back to their world and presented to their powerful potentates. She didn't die. The friendly aliens got her.

"You must be tired," she said. "How far did you have to walk?"

"Like the man said, night to day." Some kind of camera shot, *night to day*. He'd even learned to speak a little Hollywood. "Aside from a few blisters, everyone's okay. Have I seen the worst of it here?"

"We're still assessing, but the barn and the arena are pretty much—"

"I was thinkin' about my daughter." And he was watching his own circle break up. Nick and Lauren had already headed home and Vincent was loading his kids in the car.

"Injuries, of course, that's the worst." She laid her head against his shoulder as they walked. "Emily's the only one who got hurt. I can say that now that we know you're all safe." She gripped his waist. "It was awful."

"Yeah." He realized that she was walking him toward the house. Strange house. Nice house, but it was new and unfamiliar. Unmarked territory. Guess that job would be up to him. "We'll be okay."

"We're so lucky."

He dared to breathe deeply, smell the rain-washed air and the wet prairie grass and the South Dakota clay.

"Yeah, we are."

Ella had thought long and hard. Well, maybe not so long, but… All, right, maybe it hadn't been so hard. But she'd given her announcement some thought. There was food on the steamer table, and the crew was gathered under the tent, which had crumpled during the storm but sustained no actual damage. She didn't need a microphone, and she didn't have to look to the back table to know that Dillon was sitting there, minus his local posse. She had thought about telling him first and decided against it. Maybe she had more of a taste for drama than she cared to admit. Or less nerve.

"I've been on the phone all morning with our executive producers," she began. "As some of you know, every home owner signs an agreement with *Who's Our Neighbor?* And that agreement spells everything out, all our responsibilities to the home owner. We agree to complete our building project. I know it doesn't look like it, but we actually did that. The barn and the arena that were in the proposal were essentially finished when the storm hit."

"They were short-lived," Mike said.

"But they *did* live." Zooey braced the soles of her designer running shoes on the edge of an empty chair and sipped from a bottle of designer water. "We have the pictures to prove it. Right, Charlie?"

"Right. But they're dead and gone now."

"Won't take much to rebuild," Mike said.

"You're right. It won't." Ella drank from her own water bottle, pressed her lips together and glanced at Zooey. "But it won't be rebuilt on *Who's Our Neighbor?*"

"Why not?" Charlie wanted to know. "The show's got all kinds of insurance."

"And every kind explicitly excludes war and acts of God."

Charlie was indignant. "So what? With all that's gone into this—"

"Did you tell them what kind of story this is?" Darius put in. "The kind of—"

"I did. We were supposed to wrap today. They'll probably send someone out to look at the damages and then turn the matter over to the lawyers, but they won't give production any more time on this phase. The schedule is more important than the budget." Ella gave a dry chuckle. "What am I saying? The schedule is the budget. They want the truck to be in Kentucky by—"

"That's ridiculous," Darius said. "All we need is a reveal, and we've got a hell of a story. I got some amazing storm video."

Ella gave an all's-well-and-good gesture. "Look, I'm flying the students back to Montana, cutting catering and craft services loose, packing up the truck and—"

Mike stood up. "I don't think you gave them a true picture of our situation, Ella. The man had a barn when we got here. We owe him—"

"That storm would have taken the barn out, anyway," Zooey said.

"She's right," Dillon said, rising to his feet. "You don't owe me anything. I know how to build a barn." Absently he adjusted his hat by the brim. "I have a lot more than I did before you came here. Including work to do, so I guess I'll get to it."

"Dillon…"

"*Pilamaya yelo,*" he told Ella across the sea of heads. Then he looked at Mike and Tate, Darius and Charlie, finally swept his gaze over the rest. "Thank you. All of you."

Dillon headed for the pile of rubble that had been his barn. *It's no good looking back,* he told himself. He walked past the church, and gave it a cursory glance and a smile.

Not a single shingle had been disturbed. The ancestors were pleased with the changes. They had decided not to make any of their own.

It wasn't long before Ella joined him amid the tattered sheet metal and the battered boards. He knew she would. She was reliable to a fault, if such a trait could be a fault. He suspected it could be, when push came to shove and one of those agreements she'd talked about had her name on it. She was a hell of a woman, and he felt good about knowing her, which would probably have to be enough.

He tossed two pieces of two-by-four into a pile he'd mentally labeled *firewood,* turned and waved her back with a gloved hand. "Nails stickin' out everywhere," he said. He went to her, pulling off a glove, taking her by the arm and guiding her to safe ground. "I meant what I said," he told her as they stepped gingerly through the debris. "I'm glad you brought your circus to Indian country. It's not your fault the clock ran out and your elephants turned back into mice."

She laughed. "I'm not sure that tortured metaphor really fits. You need to work in a storm somehow."

"And you need to pack up your truck."

She nodded toward the back lot of canvas and cable, temporary quarters and portable privies. "*They* need to pack up their truck."

"Not your job," he concluded.

"I don't know if I have a job." She made a little who cares face. "There have been complaints. No one minds a little backstage hanky-panky, but if I chose this project because I was loving my neighbor twenty-four seven, that doesn't look good on the balance sheet."

"You didn't." He did a double take. "Did you?"

"Of course not." She tried to play-punch him in the gut,

but he sucked it in. "I chose the project long before I started loving this particular neighbor. But it doesn't matter. If they have a problem with this episode for whatever reason, it's their loss. I believe in the concept. I believe in *Who's Our Neighbor?* and this is the best project we've done."

"They're not gonna use it?"

"There's a ton of stuff that gets filmed that never gets aired."

"And you might get fired?" Hollywood was crazier than he'd thought.

"It happens all the time. Not to me so far, so I'm probably due. All I know is that there's supposed to be a barn here and an indoor arena over there." She gestured dramatically, swinging her thick, dark hair from one sweet shoulder to the other. "I'm sending the show on the road, but I'm staying with the project."

"For how long?"

"Until it's finished."

"This?" His turn to gesture. "Or me?" He wagged a finger side to side. "Don't get any ideas about taking over where Monica left off, woman. You'd be wasting your time. And that's money, isn't it?"

"You said *my* time. Which is Indian time, which isn't money."

"Meaning…?"

"Meaning it isn't measured in minutes or dollars. And I'm not taking anything over where *anyone*—" He cut her off with a hard, happy kiss. It left her smiling, but when he opened her eyes, she gave a quick frown. "What's that supposed to mean?"

"What does it feel like?"

"Like the beginning of something."

"Some kind of a project?" he asked, and she shook her head. "A show?"

"Some kind of a life, maybe."

"Ah," he said with a smile. He took off his other stiff rawhide glove and dropped them both on the ground. "Now we're talkin' Indian time."

He came up for air from a serious kiss at the sound of a car, its gravel-crunching tires closing in on his play. He looked up to find his family peering at him through the windows. Monica, Emily, D.J., all giving him the caught-you grin.

"It's not a big deal, Daddy," Emily assured him as her brother helped her line up her crutches for a trial run. "By the time I figure out how to use these things, I won't need them anymore. I'll be ready to ride whenever you're ready to hold the first session of the Mystic Warrior Horse Camp."

"What about this?" He touched the cast on her forearm.

"Everyone has to sign it. Mother already has an idea for making it into a lamp after I get it off."

"Is it…?" He turned toward the highway and the dirt road that connected it to his place. One after another, vehicles were making the turn. Rez runners. Indian pickups. One seriously used black limousine. "What the hell is this?"

"The word's out," Monica said. "The news even beat the ambulance to the clinic. First thing the nurses asked, was it a tornado?"

"Second. First they asked if I could move my fingers." Emily held her hand in front of her father, her new white cast anchored to her thumb, slender fingers dancing as though she might play a song on Dillon's nose.

The little group stood together watching the vehicles file in and park along the drive. Doors slammed, jeans got hitched up, caps and hats were pulled down and ground got covered by hard-soled boots and rubber-soled tennies. At least two dozen pair.

Terry Yellow Horn led the way. "Some of this material can still be used. If we had some blueprints…"

"We have blueprints."

From the Hollywood camp came another crowd. Cameramen, carpenters, sound engineers and decorators. Mike Murphy was the leader of the pack. "I'm staying to fix this. And I'm not the only one. I don't know who you'll get to drive the truck out to Kentucky, Ella." He looked back at his followers. "Any volunteers?"

"I'll drive it," Bobby Big Eagle offered.

"Zooey, maybe?" Tate suggested.

"She'd be my choice," said Ella.

"Mine, too," Bobby said. "Where are we going?"

"Is everybody trying to get fired?" Dillon glanced at Ella. Then Monica. "I can rebuild the damn barn."

"And I can phone in my radio show," Bobby said.

"We've been saying that for years," Vince said.

"Which truck?" Bobby climbed onto a pile of debris for a better view of Visitor Parking. "Is it the one with the TV pictures painted on the sides? That cab's a sleeper, right? I've always wanted to try out one of them sleeper cabs."

Dillon laughed as he draped his arm around Ella's shoulders. "You *do not* wanna let him take your truck to Kentucky."

"It's not my truck."

"This is Bobby Big Eagle comin' to you live from Churchill Downs," Bobby broadcast into his fist. "Wait, I missed the Derby. What else've they got in Kentucky? Besides me and Zooey drivin' around in a flashy eighteen-wheeler."

"What's he doing?" Dillon waved a hand at the ever-

running camera. "The show's been called on account o
weather. You're off the clock, Darius."

"Home movies," Darius called out.

"All right, team, let's remember rule number one." Tat
stepped out of the crowd with his bullhorn. "Safety first
Tip for the day: accessorize with gloves. Stay away from
the nails, 'cause we might not be insured. Keep your eye
on the prize, folks. Coming this summer to a brand-new
barn near you: The Mystic Warrior Horse Camp."

Epilogue

Ella Champion loved the soft gray feel of daybreak. The gentle cooing of the pair of mourning doves that had taken up residence in the row of pine trees beyond the deck was the music she cherished with her morning coffee. Night music often came from D.J.'s violin. It had been a summer filled with all kinds of music—meadowlarks and crickets, kids laughing and complaining, horses snorting and dogs panting, and the voices of family and friends who knew who their neighbors were.

She'd been in and out all summer, of course. Her routine hadn't changed much, but she was frequenting different airports from those she was used to. She had produced a project in Kentucky, and she'd returned to South Dakota for the follow-up sequence for the Mystic Warrior Horse Camp episode. She would be flying to Maine tomorrow to do some scouting for another project—a war veteran's seaside B&B. Tate was over the moon about the idea. He was pretty excited about his new costar, as well. Zooey had moved on after Darius gave his presentation to the executives in L.A.

Ella had not lost her job. Her Indian country episode of *Who's Our Neighbor?* was turning out to be, as Monica had promised, great television and a great project. Ella had helped to make it happen. Dillon wanted to give her more credit than she could accept. She'd done what she knew how to do. She'd given her heart to a man and her being to a circle. She'd gained a real home.

Monica Wilson-Black thanked God for the small favor of being allowed to sleep in her own bed with the window open. She'd spent the last week discovering why so many sick people got sicker from being hospitalized. Hospital windows were kept shut. Monica had suffered a minor setback in her recovery—a brief bout with pneumonia—but she'd been open about it this time, and she'd had a flood of visitors. Her children wouldn't leave her alone. Dillon and Ella had been veritable pests. But she'd persuaded Mike Murphy to stay away until she was back at home. He was flying in tomorrow, and Monica was ready for him. She had tickets for a play at the new Guthrie and plans to rent a boat for a day on Lake Minnetonka.

Monica was learning to live one day at a time. She had temporarily lost her hair, but not her spirit. Her determination to live her life on her own terms would carry her through, night to day.

Dillon Black had a new bed to sleep in and a new woman to share it with. Not every night, but many nights. Red sky nights and blue sky mornings. He loved her when she was with him, loved missing her when she wasn't. It seemed funny to him that he had become home base for his children after all this time, for this woman he loved so much, and for the children who needed to learn what it meant to be the descendants of horse people. It seemed funny, and funny was just fine. He would sleep alone when he had to and with his beloved Ella as often as he could.

But come foaling season next spring, Dillon Black would sleep with the horses.

* * * * *

Turn the page for a look at
RIDE A PAINTED PONY,
Lauren and Nick's story,
available now from
Kathleen Eagle and MIRA Books

Twenty-seven miles of dark road and driving rain were all that stood between Nick and the bed he'd reserved for what was left of the night. He might have pulled over and waited for the downpour to pass, but he was set on having himself some pleasure this night. Real, rock-solid pleasure. He was this close to laying himself down flat, stretching out his whole long, bone-tired body over fresh white sheets and soft pillows. If he had just pulled over, he might have spared himself the one thing he always took care to avoid. Nicholas Red Shield hated surprises.

But more than the surprise of a pair of wild eyes staring back at him in his high beams, he hated making roadkill.

It was a tricky maneuver. His empty horse trailer fishtailed as he shifted into Neutral, kicked the brake and arced the steering wheel to the left. Getting the trailer in line was only half the battle, now that the rubber no longer met the road. Every scrape against the pickup's precious chassis felt like a bloody gouge in Nick's own leathery hide. His beautiful blue two-ton dually—as near to new as any vehicle he'd ever had—mowed down a mile-marker post, jolted, shuddered and went still.

Rain pelted the roof of the cab.

Nick was stuck. He couldn't tell whether the main cause was mud or the mile marker, but his efforts to get loose soon had six tires spinning in all gears.

Nick was not a man to curse his luck. He wasted nothing, including breath. Ever equipped to handle his own problems, he reached under his seat for the flashlight. He exchanged his cowboy hat for a yellow, rubberized poncho and climbed out of the truck. Something behind him snapped. Nick swept the light over the roadside slope until it hit on a clump of bushes and a clutch of bobbing branches. Damn, had he clipped that deer after all? He grabbed his pistol and a loaded clip from the glove box, and then sidled down the steep, wet slope.

The bushes weren't much taller than he was, but they were dense and filled out with new foliage. And they weren't moving on their own. There was definitely something in there.

Nick parted the branches with his gun hand, flashed the light into the tangled thicket and found two more of the night's thousand eyes. They weren't doe eyes, but they were almost as big.

"Don't," a soft voice pleaded as the eyes took refuge from the light behind a small, colorless, quivering palm. "Please don't."

A woman? Nick's heart wedged itself in his throat, and he flashed the light away from her face. "It's okay. I won't…"

"Wh-who are you? Who sent you?"

"No one sent me. Listen, did I…did I hurt you?"

"Who are you?" she demanded.

"Name's Nick Red Shield. How bad are you hurt? Anything broken? Can you move your…"

Move what? The arms she'd knotted around her knees?

He felt like some idiot hunter who'd awkwardly wedged himself into a rabbit's hole. They were nearly nose to nose, but he didn't dare touch her, and she didn't dare move. She couldn't draw back any farther without becoming part of the undergrowth. Her violent quivering made his bones vibrate. "Let me help you. I'll be real careful."

"What kind of name is Red Shield?"

It seemed like a crazy question, under the circumstances. "I'm an Indian." He couldn't help bristling. "Look, I didn't see you until you were right in front of me, and I did everything I could to avoid hitting you. If you want me to try to flag someone else down, I will, but there isn't much traffic tonight, and I don't have any way to call anyone. Do you?"

"C-call who?"

"A cop or an ambulance."

"You…you'd call the police?"

"I would, but I don't have a phone. And if I leave you here and go for help, I'll damn sure get charged with hit and run. So make up your mind. What'll it be?"

"What are my choices?"

"Trust me or don't. Can you walk?"

"I think so."

He put the flashlight in her hand, covered her with his poncho and hauled her up against his side, which left him one hand for grabbing whatever solid ground he could find. And, like a cat, she hung on. He could feel her trembling, feel her fighting for control against chills, pain, fear—probably all three—and he gave her credit for holding back on the noise she could have been making, tears she should have been crying, curses she must have been saving up for a time when the man who'd done this to her wasn't the only help around.

He put her on the backseat of his crew cab, took the we poncho and started backing out the door.

She grabbed his arm. "Can you…please…get me awa from here?" She had him by both arms now, had him wit her eyes and surprisingly strong hands. "Can you, Nick?

He nodded, swallowed hard, tried to ignore the goos bumps crawling over his shoulders and down the back o his neck. He slid into the seat beside her and felt her rela her grip. "Sure. I can do that."

New York Times Bestselling Author

SHERRYL WOODS

Hannah is undeniably tough, but with her grandmother
entering a retirement home, her daughter unexpectedly
pregnant and an old flame suddenly underfoot, Hannah
is facing a few crises. And being back home on Seaview
Key is most definitely adding to the stress.

Luke has some serious issues, as well. While serving
in Iraq he was betrayed by his wife and best friend.
Seaview Key, where he grew up, seems like the perfect
place to hide out until he makes some decisions.
The last thing he expects is to fall in love....

Sometimes the unexpected is what it takes
to start over....

⌘ *Seaview Inn* ⌘

"Flesh-and-blood characters, terrific dialogue and substantial
stakes."—*Publishers Weekly* on *A Slice of Heaven*

Available the first week of March 2008 wherever books are sold!

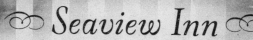

www.MIRABooks.com

MSW2529

An act of desperation divides
a mother and her child

MARCIA PRESTON

Trudy Hulst has no idea if her husband survived
his escape past the Berlin Wall. Now branded
the wife of a defector, she faces a life in prison.
With no real choice, she is forced to follow,
praying she can find a way to claim
their child once she's in West Berlin.

Trudy survives
a harrowing
break for
freedom…only
to learn her
husband is dead.
She wanders the
wall, living for
glimpses of her son,
now out of reach.
Desperate to regain
her child, Trudy
begins an odyssey of
hope to reunite her
shattered family.

Trudy's Promise

"A fascinating, original story."
—*Romantic Times BOOKreviews*
on *The Piano Man*

*Available wherever
books are sold!*

MIRA

New York Times Bestselling Author

JENNIFER BLAKE

They are the pride—and scourge—of New Orleans: a dashing fraternity of master swordsmen whose infamy is matched only by their skill, their allegiance to each other and their passion for the fairer sex....

The New Year begins with alluring widow Ariadne Faucher's request for private lessons from Gavin Blackford, a rakish sword master, in order to challenge her sworn enemy to a duel. Ariadne proves a quick study, her resolve fueled by a vendetta that is all she has left in the world. Their lessons crackle with undeniable electricity...but the secret of her all-consuming vengeance may have rendered her heart impervious, even to such a virtuoso as Gavin.

"Beguiling, sexy heroes...Well done, Ms. Blake!"
—*The Romance Reader's Connection*

GUARDED HEART

Available the first week of February 2008 wherever paperbacks are sold!

MIRA®

www.MIRABooks.com

MJB2454

A riveting novel by acclaimed author

DIANE CHAMBERLAIN

Twenty-eight years ago a North Carolina
governor's young, pregnant wife was
kidnapped. Now her remains have
been found and a man has been
charged with her murder. Only one
person—CeeCee Wilkes—can refute
the charges against him. But CeeCee
disappeared years ago....

Eve Elliot is a successful therapist
to troubled students, a loving wife,
a mother deeply invested in her
family. But her happiness is
built on a lie. Now, forced
to confront her past, she
must decide whether to
reveal to her family that
she is not who she seems,
or allow a man to take the
blame for a crime she
knows he did not commit.

the SECRET LIFE of CeeCee Wilkes

"Diane Chamberlain is
a marvelously gifted author!
Every book she writes is a real gem!"
—*Literary Times*

Available wherever books are sold!

MIR

www.MIRABooks.com

MDC2

REQUEST YOUR FREE BOOKS!

2 FREE NOVELS
FROM THE ROMANCE/SUSPENSE
COLLECTION PLUS 2 FREE GIFTS!

ES! Please send me 2 FREE novels from the Romance/Suspense Collection
nd my 2 FREE gifts (gifts are worth about $10). After receiving them, if I don't wish
receive any more books, I can return the shipping statement marked "cancel." If I
n't cancel, I will receive 4 brand-new novels every month and be billed just $5.49
r book in the U.S. or $5.99 per book in Canada, plus 25¢ shipping and handling
r book plus applicable taxes, if any*. That's a savings of at least 20% off the cover
ice! I understand that accepting the 2 free books and gifts places me under no
ligation to buy anything. I can always return a shipment and cancel at any time.
en if I never buy another book from the Reader Service, the two free books and
ts are mine to keep forever.

185 MDN EF5Y 385 MDN EF6C

me _____ (PLEASE PRINT) _____

dress _____ Apt. # _____

y _____ State/Prov. _____ Zip/Postal Code _____

gnature (if under 18, a parent or guardian must sign)

Mail to **The Reader Service:**
IN U.S.A.: P.O. Box 1867, Buffalo, NY 14240-1867
IN CANADA: P.O. Box 609, Fort Erie, Ontario L2A 5X3

Not valid to current subscribers to the Romance Collection,
the Suspense Collection or the Romance/Suspense Collection.

Want to try two free books from another line?
Call 1-800-873-8635 or visit www.morefreebooks.com.

erms and prices subject to change without notice. N.Y. residents add applicable sales tax.
nadian residents will be charged applicable provináal taxes and GST. This offer is limited to
order per household. All orders subject to approval. Credit or debit balances in a customer's
ount(s) may be offset by any other outstanding balance owed by or to the customer. Please
w 4 to 6 weeks for delivery. Offer available while quantities last.

ur Privacy: Harlequin is committed to protecting your privacy. Our Privacy
icy is available online at www.eHarlequin.com or upon request from the Reader
rvice. From time to time we make our lists of customers available to reputable
d parties who may have a product or service of interest to you. If you
uld prefer we not share your name and address, please check here. ☐

BOB08

HARLEQUIN

More Than Words

"Changing lives
stride by stride—
I did it my way!"

—**Jeanne Greenberg,** real-life heroine

*Jeanne Greenberg is a Harlequin More Than Words
award winner and the founder of **SARI Therapeutic Riding.***

Discover your inner heroine!

SUPPORTING CAUSES OF CONCERN TO WOMEN   **HARLEQUI**
WWW.HARLEQUINMORETHANWORDS.COM

MTW

HARLEQUIN

More Than Words

"Jeanne proves that one woman can change the world, with vision, compassion and hard work."

—**Linda Lael Miller,** author

*Linda wrote "Queen of the Rodeo," inspired by Jeanne Greenberg, founder of **SARI Therapeutic Riding.** Since 1978 Jeanne has devoted her life to enriching the lives of disabled children and their families through innovative and exciting therapies on horseback.*

ook for "*Queen of the Rodeo*" in
More Than Words, Vol. 4,
vailable in April 2008 at eHarlequin.com
r wherever books are sold.

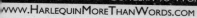

SUPPORTING CAUSES OF CONCERN TO WOMEN   **⚌ HARLEQUIN**
WWW.HARLEQUINMORETHANWORDS.COM

MTW07JG2

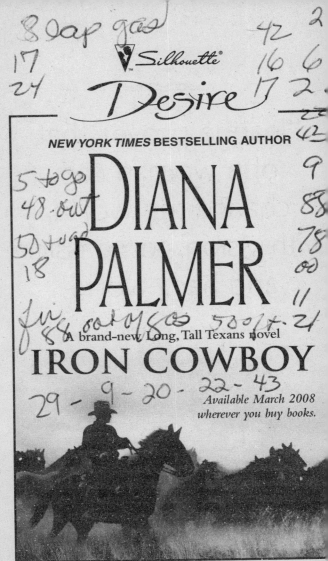

Silhouette® Desire

NEW YORK TIMES BESTSELLING AUTHOR

DIANA PALMER

A brand-new Long, Tall Texans novel

IRON COWBOY

Available March 2008
wherever you buy books.

Visit Silhouette Books at www.eHarlequin.com SD76856